BEYOND ALL WAR

ERIC KELLER

Black Rose Writing | Texas

2019 by Eric Keller
All rights reserved. No part of this book may be reproduced, stored in a retrieval system or transmitted in any form or by any means without the prior written permission of the publishers, except by a reviewer who may quote brief passages in a review to be printed in a newspaper, magazine or journal.

The author grants the final approval for this literary material.

First printing

This is a work of fiction. Names, characters, businesses, places, events, and incidents are either the products of the author's imagination or used in a fictitious manner. Any resemblance to actual persons, living or dead, or actual events is purely coincidental.

ISBN: 978-1-68433-309-7
PUBLISHED BY BLACK ROSE WRITING
www.blackrosewriting.com

Printed in the United States of America
Suggested Retail Price (SRP) $20.95

Beyond All War is printed in Chaparral Pro

Thanks Eunju.

BEYOND ALL WAR

PART ONE

CHAPTER ONE

FEBRUARY 4, 2036
DAY ONE

The lights of civilization disappeared behind them, an escape never felt so constrictive. Instinctively, Morreign relaxed her foot allowing the speeding truck to slow slightly. Only blackness existed beyond the cone of their headlights. The frozen highway slick. Sheets of crystallized snow blowing sideways. They were away. No point risking a crash now.

Paul bent between the seats, trying to entertain the boys in the back who were upset by the impromptu, late night road trip. Checking the rear-view mirror, she saw the lights behind them. Another truck with children traveling through the storm-filled night. The weighty reality of what they were doing pressed down on her even harder.

Not long ago, this plan seemed fanciful. Merely a far-fetched imagined precaution in case the worse happened. Now, fleeing through the darkness, fear filled her as they lived out the ridiculous plan. Unknowns flooded over her. Would they have enough to eat? Would they be able to stay warm? How long would this last? What if someone got sick?

She opened her mouth to explain to Paul that she wanted to turn around, that she was wrong, that she wanted to head back to their apartment, to their home. The orange light of fire suddenly filled the back window followed by the sound of intense, continuous thunder.

Startled, Morreign jolted the wheel. The truck fishtailed. Instincts created by a lifetime of driving on ice took over and, despite a yell escaping from her throat, she calmly let the tires find their own way before carefully inching the truck back straight.

The boys were crying. Their terrier puppy, Rufus, yapped pointlessly from his kennel. Paul tried to calm the kids, but worry tinged his voice as he called over the seat to her, "Leo still back there?"

She checked the mirror, saw the headlights and said, "Yeah, they're there."

"What the hell was that?"

Morreign took a deep breath to keep her voice from wavering and then said, "Bomb. A massive bombing of some sort. Hit the airbase I think."

Paul gave up on placating the kids and turned back in his seat, whispering, "Really?"

"I think so. I mean, what else could it be?"

Paul muttered to himself, "All of this is real. You were right Mo. It's actually happening."

Morreign risked taking her eyes off the road she and glanced over at her husband, "We got away though, we're ok, we'll be ok."

"Son of a ... Jesus Christ. That blast was huge, what can be left? Who can be left? And, Thule, I mean, the whole outpost, that's gotta be targeted next -"

Morreign interrupted, "We can't worry about that now, we need to deal with what we can deal with."

A pause before, out of the darkness and over the crying children, Paul, sounding more composed, said, "You're right. Keep us on the road and we'll figure it out."

As her husband returned his attention to their sons, Morreign returned all of her frayed focus on the black highway.

•   •   •

He felt the gentle shoving but rolled away. She said, "Hale, wake up. Something's happened, I've got to get back to the base right away. Get up. I can drop you off on my way."

He could not remember the woman's name. The bed was soft, he was buried beneath a plush duvet, and the pillow smelled pleasantly of lavender. A throbbing filled his head, his stomach ached. A lifetime of drinking informed him that standing up now would only make these conditions worse. He pulled the blanket tighter around him and said, "No way, it's freezing out there. Nice and warm here, come back to bed."

Anger filled the woman's voice as she said, "Seriously, I'm not kidding around. We need to go right now."

Hale rolled over to look at her. She was hurriedly getting dressed and, even in the dim light, he could tell she felt as hungover as he did. The polite thing would be to get out of the stranger's apartment as requested but the idea of venturing out into the frigid night to return to the miserable one bedroom housing unit he shared with two other men was highly unpalatable.

He raised up on one elbow. "Leave me a key. I'll lock up when I go and slide it under the door."

Distractedly she said, "I'm not leaving you alone in my place, I barely know you."

Fine sleeping with a stranger but leaving that stranger by himself in her apartment was unacceptable. He did not care about the moral or logical merits of her view, a good night's sleep was a rarity for him, so he pushed, "Really? You think I'm going to steal something?"

"No, of course not, it's a privacy thing."

Privacy seemed an odd concern to have at this point, but he knew arguing the issue would not work. He said, "I won't look around, I'm only going to sleep."

She sighed, unable or unwilling to hide her annoyance. She moved out of the room, calling back, "Fine, I don't have time for this. The key's in the drawer by the fridge."

Burying himself back in the freshly laundered linens, Hale reveled in the warmth. His apartment was military housing provided for oil workers which he shared with two truck drivers from Newfoundland who apparently did not need sleep. They worked seven days a week and still partied full throttle all night, every night. Eight hours of quiet, uninterrupted sleep would do Hale a world of good. He gratefully closed his eyes.

•   •   •

The voice coming through the helicopter's headphones carried hardly controlled fear. "The airbase... the airbase, the entire outpost of Thule is..., well, sir, it's all on fire, sir. We'll need to find another LZ."

Colonel Gill turned to Jack Harrison and asked bluntly but with deep worry, "Is there a bunker?"

Harrison wanted to hit the arrogant fool. The Colonel did not even know if there was an emergency bunker at the base he commanded. The helicopter dropped suddenly and then lurched hard to the side in the turbulence of the winter storm as a massive explosion sounded nearby. Looking out the window, Harrison could see flames disappearing in and out of blackness as smoke engulfed them.

He used his professional soldier voice as he responded to his commander, "Sir, there's an alternate entrance three hundred meters northwest of the end of the main runway that will take us to the underground facility. As long as the tunnel is not damaged, we can get access."

The Colonel merely stared out the window at the nothingness, apparently confused about what to do next. For months now, Harrison was certain a disaster such as this was imminent. In the last five years, the world order changed drastically, however, those in charge seemed unable to grasp this fact.

Sea levels began to rise decades ago, but the process occurred gradually allowing richer nations time to react with aggressive engineering projects. Poorer, low-lying areas did not fare so well, but the developed world remained largely unaffected and maintained a general ignorance regarding the scope of the pending crisis. However, when a massive sheet of ice covering half of Greenland sloughed into the ocean, the catastrophe waiting in the wilful blind spot of humanity struck immediately and indiscriminately.

Harrison, with his high school education, did not completely understand the science but reports generally indicated the balance ordering the world's oceans was thrown off, changing the way water and air currents traveled the globe which caused extremes in weather to become more extreme. If a place, such as the Sahara, was normally hot, it became even hotter while if a place, such as Alaska, was normally cold, it became even colder. In Northern Alberta, this meant the normal winter season of five months stretched to over seven and average temperatures plummeted from twenty below to forty below. Crops failed, commodity prices skyrocketed, stock markets collapsed, panicked revolts erupted. The global disarray needed leadership from somewhere.

However, Europe was entangled in nationalistic uprisings, busy fighting against refugees and immigrants while their true enemies mobilized. The United States, the world's last superpower spent decades being ruled by men more familiar with celebrity than governing and their current President spent more energy telling people he was right rather than smartly addressing the calamity. As a result of the chaos, nations withdrew from trade agreements and alliances to become isolated and confrontational. Before long this lack of cooperation and leadership, coupled with the overwhelming suffering and disarray led to a cascading outbreak of escalating conflicts.

Behind the relatively minor skirmishes, the dictatorial powers were able to take action while democracies bickered internally. With no meaningful trade, controlling the planet's resources had become more and more valuable.

The shortage reached a crisis point when, Saudi Arabia, tired of anti-Islam rhetoric coming from the West, decided it would rather turn isolationist and shut down its production rather than provide oil to machines of hatred. Russia easily expanded its borders, taking back over those satellite states with oil which were formerly of the Soviet Union. China acted next and militarized Venezuela. Eventually, these actions compelled the Americans to acquire Mexico as a protectorate before anyone else could take over their offshore oil rights. This lead to insurrection and domestic terrorism as the diplomacy was mishandled by the celebrity Presidency making it seem the action was wholly motivated by racism.

It seemed obvious to Harrison that Western Canada remained the last jewel, the most precious. And, with the US in turmoil, its military stretched by fighting in Mexico and protecting its own territory, its neighbor to the North lost its normal blanket of protection, making it a hittable target. Tonight, someone was taking their shot. Harrison figured it was China opting to destroy the facilities out from under the Americans.

Before the Colonel could make a decision the pilot's shaken voice came through the headphones, "We lost radio contact, we need to find an LZ immediately, or I think-"

An explosion erupted below them, tossing the aircraft. Alarms blared in the cabin as the helicopter began to spin across the sky. Harrison heard the Colonel scream as they plummeted to the earth.

•   •   •

Trying to sound calm, Morreign said, "I think we better get off the highway."

Even in the dim light coming off the dashboard, Morreign could see Paul's eyes had grown wide and wild. "What? Off the highway? We need to get away as fast as possible."

She nodded toward the back seat, silently imploring her husband not to frighten the boys any more than they already were before quietly saying, "The attack is coming quicker and heavier than I predicted. A lot quicker and heavier. I'm worried they might take out the highway."

Paul shook his head and said, "And the US is going to have to retaliate."

She sighed and said, "Right. Probably already are. I think all the diplomacy and strategy is done with, now they'll both only want to destroy everything."

"I guess we should be glad there's no nuclear weapons left."

A treaty entered into in 2024 led to the dismantling of all nuclear armaments. Morreign said, "I suppose, but there's still plenty of missiles and bombers left."

They drove in silence for a heartbeat or two, both contemplating the massive warheads likely screaming down from far over their heads. Morreign reiterated, "We need to get off the highway."

"Ok."

Paul opened the console and pulled out his tablet. A couple of swipes and he said, "Alright, I've got a route. Assuming we're lucky and the roads aren't completely snowed in."

"Better find a couple of extra routes, I don't think our luck is running too strong."

Paul glanced at the rear view mirror as he said, "Our luck is running a lot stronger than all those people back there."

Pushing the gas pedal down, she responded softly, "We can't think about that now. We'll think about it, but we can't think about it now."

•　•　•

Standing naked in a stranger's cramped living room, Hale witnessed Armageddon playing out before him, splayed across the wide window. Rolling waves of flames overtook the buildings as fire seemed to spew out of everything as the steady roar of the explosions pushed in against the thick glass.

For years, wars and disasters filled the news, but it always seemed distant to Hale. He worked, paid his bills, drank beer, worked some more. What happened in Nigeria or Venezuela or Mexico did not concern him. However, ignorant bliss no longer appeared to be an option.

He knew he should be contemplating all the death and destruction, all the pain and suffering being inflicted on the people of Thule right before him but his mind did not work like that. He needed to deal with what he could deal with and ignore all else.

The apartment building he stood in was new, still under construction with only a handful of units occupied, built on the distant outskirts of the outpost to house upper management of the military staff. The bombing seemed to be ignoring it for now, but there was no way of knowing if that would continue. As a residential area, it would not be a priority, but that did not mean the enemy would not flatten it once all the military targets were gone.

Down below, he saw two trucks rush out of the parking garage and tear off into the smoke. Fleeing. Fleeing might be the best option. No vehicle though. The woman surely took hers. He might be able to find one to steal or find someone else in the building to go with.

As he pondered this idea, an especially massive explosion sent a fountain of liquid fire into the night sky. Hale stepped back from the intense heat smashing into the window as a cascade of burning rubble crashed down. He let out a long, soft curse to himself, "Damn..."

Leaving suddenly seemed extremely foolish. Getting through the firestorm outside would be near impossible. Even if he could find a truck and enough drivable road to escape on it would only leave him on a highway in the middle of a freezing night with no idea of the safe direction to go. The decision to stay put was not an easy one to make as it might mean dying buried in the rubble of the apartment building, but he told himself staying remained his best option.

The decision definitively made, his mind immediately began to contemplate things he needed assuming the building remained standing. A lifetime working on oil rigs in far off, inhospitable places taught Hale how to get by when things failed to work, and the chaos of ideas running through his head promptly formed itself into a manageable list. Obtaining a source of drinking water quickly placed itself on the top of the list.

Hale moved to the bathroom and opened the bathtub taps on full. Thankfully the water was still running. Next, he opened the fridge to check his food supply. No welcoming light came on. It took him a moment to appreciate the wrongness of looking into a dark fridge. A bright, orange glow from the numerous fires came through the wide window so he didn't need to turn on lights, but now he realized the power was out.

This realization was followed immediately by another. Cold. The heat also off. Going to be freezing inside before long, forty below kind of freezing.

Frustration at his situation boiled over, and he slammed his hand against the stainless steel of the fridge. A flash of grey crossed his vision and sting of pain lit from his shoulder. Hale spun, moving to defend himself. Crouched on the tile, staring up at him with an arched back, a fat, striped cat. The woman had a cat. Of course, she had a damn cat.

•　　•　　•

Pain filled Harrison's side, but he got the hatch open and climb out of the wreck and into the deep snow, the rigid cold stabbing at him. The pilots managed to regain some control at the last second and soften the crash somewhat. He could hear the Colonel moaning, but Harrison ignored him and struggled to his feet. He half-walked, half-crawled through the drifted snow to the front of the ruined helicopter.

Looking through the busted windshield, Harrison saw both of the pilots strapped in their seats. One slumped over the controls, but the other looked at him with glossy eyes. Harrison said, "Nice landing."

The pilot merely blinked a few times and then, with a slightly slurred voice, asked, "Colonel ok?"

"Heard him whining and moaning, so I guess he's alive," Harrison nodded at the co-pilot, "How's your partner?"

The man took a breath before responding, "We hit nose heavy. Smacked our skulls pretty good. He hasn't moved or said anything, I don't think he made it..."

The stunned pilot began undoing his harness and said, "We should check on the Colonel."

Harrison said, "Stay put. Let your head clear and make sure you don't have any other injuries before moving. I'll go around and check."

As he moved through the heavy snow, Harrison became certain the pain in his side represented cracked ribs. It hurt like hell but considering he climbed out of a crashed helicopter, he counted himself lucky. Then, through the darkness, he heard the rumble of an explosion followed by a chorus of coyote howls, and he recalled the situation. He survived the crash but was now stranded in a frozen wilderness under attack from unseen foes. Lucky may be the wrong word.

Making it around, Harrison took a look at the co-pilot through the window. Hard to tell but Harrison did not think the man's chest was moving and blood covered his neck. Either dead or would soon be dead. He trudged on through the snow to the Colonel.

"Sir, are you alright?"

The elderly officer, face looking especially gaunt, glared at Harrison and growled, "It took you long enough. My leg, my goddamn leg is broken. You need to get me out of here and to a hospital immediately."

Harrison stared back at the clueless man and calmly said, "The pilot has a concussion, the co-pilot is dead or dying."

The comment intended to remind the asshole that his first concern should be the men under his command. The Colonel apparently missed the point as he merely asked, "Do we have radio contact? We need to get out of here."

"I doubt it. I think we need to hunker down for the night, at first light I can hike towards the base and see if there's anything left -"

"I'm wounded. I can't stay out in the freezing woods all goddamn night."

Harrison merely turned away from the Colonel. As he worked his way through the deep snow, back towards the cockpit, he heard the officer yell at his back, "This insubordination will not go unpunished. Get me the hell out of here."

Going to be a long night, the longest night.

•   •   •

Wind shook the truck. Morreign swayed back and forth with her youngest son, Huck, on her lap. He recently turned five and had been trying to fight off sleep, wanting to stay awake to witness all the strangeness of their adventure but sleep finally won out a few minutes ago. His older brother, Jacob, however, remained wide awake.

"Can I help, mommy?"

"Not this time Jake."

The eager seven-year-old asked the predictable question, "Why?"

Outside the windshield, in the brightness of the headlights, Morreign saw Paul fighting with the winch cable in the blowing snow. They got off the highway, but the side roads were heavily drifted making it nearly impossible to see the edge of the road in the darkness. This was the third time they needed to stop to pull one of the trucks out.

"It's really cold out there honey, you stay in here where it's warm with me and Huck, ok?"

The kid climbed up from the backseat like a monkey; they bribed him to behave with candy, and now the sugar was energizing him. Morreign, feeling the powerful strain of the unbelievably stressful night, wished she had a tenth of his energy. Jacob bounced and asked, "Can I at least flip the switch?"

"Ok, but we have to wait until daddy tells us to, ok?"

They watched Paul push through the snow, dragging the winch cable towards his brother's buried truck. When dread over possible attacks first crept into Morreign's consciousness over a year ago, she did not know what to do. She subconsciously started coming up with a plan to get away, at first it came as escapism, something to think about in order to deflect worry. Over time, though, as the dread grew deeper and she became more and more certain attacks were imminent, her plan solidified.

Formally her title was Head Administrative Assistant, 44Canadian Brigade Group, CFB Northern Alberta Outpost 4 (Thule). In practice, she simply organized the support staff which managed the affairs of the forces sent to protect oil production in the area.

The first year Morreign worked at Thule everything seemed relatively standard. Patrols were sent out to make sure no one sabotaged anything while soldiers provided onsite security at the various facilities. Morreign and her staff mainly did the paperwork to make sure the troops had clean socks to wear and enough eggs for breakfast. Things shifted over time though.

More soldiers kept arriving, the increase always explained by a vague need for intensified security. Patrolling increased and they were moving farther and farther afield. Meetings with officials in dark business suits or dress uniforms went from a rarity to commonality. Then came the equipment. Morreign's knowledge of military hardware was sparse but the equipment arriving seemed far more powerful and advanced and aggressive than that needed for a security detail.

Despite this, her concern stemmed from more than the force build up. Wars were breaking out across the globe, and increasing military presence everywhere became a fact of life. The overall alteration of the tone in the office worried her more. The pace increased, from the usually relaxed speed of government work to people continually pressing on matters with all humor replaced by seriousness. Whispers soon replaced office chit-chat, doors were often shut, and "Top-Secret" stamps were dusted off.

As the government began negotiations with the hapless Americans over exclusive access to the oilsands, the urgent, tense aura intensified even further. Media reports of the discussions were mainly positive, couched in terms of the Americans getting a protected oil source in exchange for heightened military support for Canada. However, from inside the base, Morreign sensed far more complexity and confusion than what was being presented to the public. Regardless of the secretive culture, busy officials often overlooked the ever-present admin staff, and she managed to overhear conversations and glimpse documents about the impact the talks were having on the Sino-Russian alliance and their possible reaction.

She continually contemplated telling Paul about her worries and subsequent escape plan but the possibility he would think she was crazy held her in check. Finally, with the help of wine, one-night Morreign told him she suspected Northern Alberta was going to be the first major battlefield in a world war about to erupt between superpowers in disarray. Even though she could not point to any particular piece of concrete evidence and she found putting her vague impressions into words difficult, Paul carefully listened.

When she finished, Paul merely said, "Ok. Should we move back south?"

This simplicity shocked her, and she asked, "Really? You'd be willing to move based on my fuzzy worries?"

"Of course. I can tell you're deeply concerned and I trust your instincts. Remember that time I wanted to invest in that lumber company? You talked me out of it, and it turned out to be a scam. And you convinced your sister not to marry what's his name which was a lifesaver for her."

Looking more serious, Paul continued, "Throughout all our time together, you've been better at big decisions. If you feel it's not going to be safe here, then we should all get the hell out. It's not like Thule is paradise and, listening to you talk, I realized I've noticed a strangeness around here too. Everything is changing, we need to accept that and take the necessary steps."

Her husband normally spoke jovially, and his sudden seriousness worried Morreign even further, made the imagined situation feel harshly real. They opened another bottle of wine, and she explained how she did not think moving to a southern city would be sufficient. The impression she got from her clerical espionage was that global war coming to Alberta meant all of North America, maybe even all of civilization would be at risk. They needed to disappear completely to escape the wide spreading carnage humanity's massive arsenal would inflict. For the first time, she explained her fleeing fantasy.

Again Paul's response was straightforward, "Alright Mo, but if we think all this is best for our family, I need to tell Leo and Ainsley, let them come and bring the girls with us if that's what they want to do. I can't leave them behind."

At first, folding more people into her craziness scared Morreign because of the extra responsibility. But, talking it over at their kitchen table, the idea grew more solid and, if she thought this best for her children, it must also be best for her nieces. Maybe no attack would come. She would merely look foolish for this bizarre suggestion and for wasting their money and time, but she would be happy to look foolish if it meant everyone remained safe. And, if an attack did come, at least this would give them all a chance.

Now, sitting in a truck in the darkness of the snowy night, watching Leo, her brother-in-law help Paul set up the winch, she was intensely glad him and his family agreed to come. Not because she thought it meant more people were safe but because, selfishly, it meant her family was not alone in this frozen, fear-filled blackness.

Paul knocked on the hood of the truck, signaling they were ready to pull Leo's truck from the ditch. Morreign said, "Ok, Jacob, go ahead and flip the switch."

CHAPTER TWO

FEBRUARY 5, 2036
DAY TWO

Forcing himself to ignore the constant roar of the fires punctuated by explosions coming from everywhere about him, Hale spent the night organizing. Most of the innumerable possibilities of what could occur next were bad, but they were all unknown events for which he could not plan. He decided his best hope was the apartment building being ignored by the attack because this new area of Thule did not get included in the attacker's plan, allowing him to shelter there and ride out the worse. Dispiriting to think his best hope was to be left alone in a stranger's freezing apartment with no electricity and no heat but he remained focused on doing what he could in that harsh reality.

The cold immediately pressed itself forward as a dire issue. His absent hostess was much smaller than him, but he found a couple pairs of stretchy workout pants he could put on under his loose jeans. An oversized sweatshirt was only slightly tight across his shoulders. Adding his heavy parka, ski cap and his work boots over this outfit meant he was not overly comfortable but not freezing.

He found extra blankets, sheets, and pillows in a closet. The only room in the apartment without a wall bordering the frigid outside was the bathroom, so Hale set up a nest of bedding in the narrow space between the tub and the vanity. He figured the makeshift campsite would suffice to fend off hypothermia while he tried to sleep.

There was not a lot of food in the apartment beyond popcorn, wine, and yogurt but enough to sustain him for a week or so as long as he ate sparingly.

If he made it that long without being killed by a bomb, he would consider himself lucky and happily worry about finding more to eat at that point.

Thankfully, candles were plentiful even if most were heavily scented. Besides the smelly candles, he found a flashlight with working batteries. It would not be bright, but at least he would not be in complete darkness once the massive fires burning outside the window went out.

Digging through the recycling bin, he managed to collect half-dozen plastic bottles which he filled with water and packed in a duffle bag. He added granola bars, a tin of olives, almond butter and three cans of lima beans. He then put in extra clothes that would fit in a pinch. No toolbox in the apartment but he found a hammer, duct tape, and scissors which he added to his collection along with a number of kitchen utensils he figured might be useful. Sitting the bag by the door, he figured, although it did not contain all he hoped, the makeshift emergency kit could still be helpful if he needed to flee in a hurry.

Unsure what was going on outside, Hale decided he needed to address rudimentary protection. Other than kitchen knives and a brand new, cast iron frying pan, Hale could find nothing to serve as a weapon if anyone were to come to the apartment with malice in mind. However, a few swipes of a knife against a broom handle turned it into a sad looking spear. It would do nothing against anyone with a gun, or even someone with a bigger stick, but, even knowing it was foolish, the pathetic armament made Hale slightly more confident about his position.

All preparations he could think of done, he turned his attention back to the window as the fat cat circled his ankles, purring for attention. Grey sunlight began to penetrate the thick smoke, but sunrise did nothing to improve the view. Total devastation surrounded him. Difficult to see everything with all the smoke but he could tell almost all the buildings once comprising Thule were now burning rubble, the bridge to the north completely gone and the ruin likely spread well beyond what he could see as the distant rumbles of explosions could still be heard. No humans could be seen. He thought he glimpsed a few far-off lights moving across the dawn sky but seeing who was doing this was impossible, the destruction fell invisibly from above.

Letting out a sigh, he decided, the who behind the disaster did not matter to him. He figured he was probably not alone in this realization, thinking people under burning rubble did not care about nationalism or pride or glory but only wanted the bombs to stop. As he watched, a trio of missiles screamed in from the clouds, disappearing for an instant into the smoke to the north before a massive shower of fire and debris shot up.

He picked up the annoying cat and turned away from the window, trying to decide what his next task needed to be.

•　　•　　•

Morreign awoke from her uneasy sleep when Paul gently rubbed her shoulder. Using the quiet tone parents speak in when they don't want to wake children, he said, "We're almost there."

Blinking sleep from her eyes, she saw grey dawn. She said, "Sorry, I fell asleep."

With a tired smile, he said, "I heard the snores. We left the road about ten miles back. A cut line took us right to the river, and we were able to drive pretty fast on the ice."

Looking about she realized the truck was rolling along the frozen river. Up ahead, under a crooked tree extending from the bank, she could see the outline of something protruding from the shore, popping up through the ice. She asked, "Is that the dock?"

"Hard to say for sure but I think so."

They were nearing their new home. Dense masses of pine trees lined the riverbanks as far as Morreign could see in every direction. With a sigh, she said, "We'll definitely be isolated."

"Yeah, but, given all that's going on, isolation sounds pretty good to me."

She put her hand on Paul's leg as she said, "It's only going be us from now on. No one else can help."

He patted her hand. "I know, I know. We'll be ok though, we're smart, you've planned this out, and we'll all work together."

Morreign appreciated the words, but it sounded like Paul was trying to convince himself as much as her. Softly she said, "I'm scared Paul. I'm scared. I brought us, all of us, way out here to nowhere."

"There was no choice. You saw what happened back there, what is happening back there..."

His voice trailed off. He wasn't ready to discuss the tragedy unfolding everywhere, and this was fine with Morreign, she wasn't ready either. Plus, for now, there was far too much to worry about in the future to expend energy thinking of even the most recent past; maybe, if they were lucky, they could grieve for the lost world later.

Now talking to convince herself, Morreign said, "We'll make it work. We always make it work."

They slowed to a stop at the snow-covered remnants of the dock. If there was ever a road up to the lodge, the forest destroyed it long ago. They would need to hike in. She opened the truck door, letting in a gust of bracing winter air. Climbing out she pushed confidence into her voice and said, "Alright, let's go."

•   •   •

Harrison threw a couple more branches onto the flames. The men huddled in the helicopter after building a fire but the night passed in brutal cold regardless. With dawn finally arriving, Harrison stretched slowly, his body ached and his injured ribs screamed in protest, but the pain was tolerable, no serious wounds.

After nearly vomiting, the pilot recovered, however, the co-pilot did not make it, taking his last breath within an hour of crashing. The Colonel's ankle was broken, but he would survive. They gave the Colonel a triple dose of the pain medication in the first aid kit which generally staunched his complaining, but the drug began to wear off as the sun started to rise.

"You need to fashion a sled or a stretcher or something and carry me the Hell out of here."

Harrison shared a look with the pilot. The two men, unable to sleep in the freezing cold, talked through much of the night. The pilot's name was Clarence Chan. Years ago he used to fly tourists around the mountains before air force officers approached him at an airport and conscripted him on the spot as an essential service provider. Since then his valued skills were mainly used to chauffeur generals and politicians from base to base. Harrison and he quickly bonded over their view of the military as a totally inept organization.

Clarence surreptitiously shook his head at the pompous officer's silliness before returning his attention to the radio he had been fiddling with all night to no avail. In the distance, the nearly constant echo of explosions could still be heard. Harrison became certain, if they did make it out of the woods, they would only find smoke, bodies and twisted metal.

"Sir, I may be able to hike out of here, but with the deep snow I think I will need to leave you-."

The old man interrupted, "Unacceptable. I need to get back and survey the situation to prepare for our counter-attack."

An especially aggressive rumble of explosions rolled over them. The man was worse than a fool. The man clearly stupid to the point of insanity.

At sixteen Harrison started driving truck part-time. By the time he turned twenty-two, he owned his own company, a moderate fleet of rigs crisscrossing the country with dispatch centers in Calgary and Winnipeg. He enjoyed the freedom of slamming gears as he sped down a highway, carefully monitoring and controlling all business issues on his phone as he covered the miles.

Then there was the accident. One of his drivers' blew through a stop sign injuring five. The insurance company attempted to refuse coverage on a number of grounds including the driver not having adequate rest or training. All of it was bullshit, but the intense legal battle ate up cash and time. Despite all of his effort, a problem of that magnitude could not be overcome by the fledgling business, and the company collapsed.

With chaos erupting around the globe, unemployment was no longer an allowable option. Within days of his business going bankrupt, Harrison could not provide evidence of necessary employment, and he was conscripted into the army. Despite despising the bloated organization and playing the role of a peon, he rose up the ranks. The idiot officers at the top were not that different than those fools barking out orders at the very bottom but, at least, there were fewer of them which made military life tolerable.

Harrison looked over at the gaunt, elderly man slumped in the helicopter. His eyes were glossed with drugs but were darting with fear. Spittle and white stubble covered his chin. In the firelight, the Colonel formed the very picture of demented leadership. Now, as the metal was hitting the meat, Harrison knew following the fools that got them into this disaster would only get him killed as he tried to endure that very disaster. He needed to stop following, he needed to take control and not let it go.

He growled, "Enough. You're not thinking straight, hell, you're not thinking at all. That sound you hear, that sound you've been hearing all goddamn night, is the sound of the world being destroyed. Pull your dried up, useless bones through the snow so you can yell into a dead radio won't change a goddamn thing so shut the hell up so we can figure out how we all survive."

An overly long life within the military machinery conditioned the Colonel to react to all disobedience, rational or not, in only one way. The confused man turned his attention to Clarence and ordered, "Private, take Captain Harrison's sidearm and place him under arrest for insubordination."

Clarence realized the absurdity of this and responded, "Sir, we're in the middle of nowhere, and under attack, I don't think arresting-."

An explosion erupted closer as the Colonel interrupted, "Place him under arrest immediately and then get me back to base or I'll have you both arrested."

The baffled pilot looked over at Harrison, apparently seeking sane direction. This occurrence was familiar to Harrison. Ever since adolescence, people instinctively looked to him for guidance. Any game on the playground, he became the de facto referee. Any business meeting, he got the last word. Any family dispute, he served as unofficial judge.

The Colonel, not appreciating the mini-mutiny unfolding before him, continued to ramble as the rumble of explosions echoed around them. Harrison calmly drew his sidearm and, in one smooth motion, aimed at the Colonel's head and fired.

In the snow-filled forest, the gunshot only a weak pop against the backdrop of the distant attack. Returning the gun to its holster, Harrison turned to Clarence and calmly said. "We rest up here and then, when we're ready, make the hike to find a place with supplies to shelter in."

Still staring at his former commanding officer's face now covered in blood, the pilot asked, "Then what?"

"Don't know yet."

Clarence turned to look at him, and Harrison held his gaze with confidence. The pilot nodded and said, "Whatever you say."

Moving to pull the body out of the helicopter, Harrison felt a surge of excitement. His days of taking orders were over, and he liked the sensation of being back in control.

• • •

The knock startled him. Hale lay in his nest of blankets in the bathroom, barely noticing the constant bombing barrage going on outside but the simple sound of a knock on the door startled him. Another knock, more urgent.

He moved through the dimly lit apartment that smelled of fake vanilla and looked through the peephole. In the dark hallway, Hale could see the distorted image of a diminutive, balding man buried within a massive, red parka. He could see no weapon and, even in the shadows, the visitor looked more scared than scary. Leaning his ridiculous, pointy stick against the wall, Hale opened the door.

Shocked, the man stepped back and stuttered, "Oh, uh, hello. My name is Asiz, I live downstairs. I'm looking for Rosa?"

Rosa. That was the woman's name. Not sure how to react to this visit, Hale decided truth to be the best option. "I'm her friend. She had to go into work last night. She hasn't been back yet."

The underlying point unsaid but clear: Rosa was likely dead. With no warning, Asiz fell against the door jam and began sobbing. Instinctively, Hale picked him up, led him inside and sat him at the counter. He scooped a cup of icy water out of the bathtub and set it in front of the weeping man. "Have some water. It's been a hard night."

As the visitor picked up the cup, an especially loud explosion echoed in the distance. Water splashed on to the counter, and he muttered, "I'm sorry, so sorry... I'm rattled by this, by all of this. My wife..."

Hale sat next to Asiz as he started sobbing again. An awkward minute passed before his company got under control enough to continue, "She works for food services, the night shift. Normally she'd be home by now, but I've heard nothing. No phones work. No texts. No internet. Nothing. I don't know where she is."

Unsure how to deal with the oddness of this delusional man thinking someone out there in all that destruction would be able to send a text message, Hale dumbly said, "I'm sure it's hard to get around out there, and everything must be down."

He grabbed Hale's arm and said, "I need to go find her, I can't stay here while she's out there in danger."

Insanity. The food services center should not have been a target, but the attack was a carpet bombing, indiscriminate destruction. Even if the center somehow remained and the woman survived, this sobbing man finding her would do neither of them any good.

He opened his mouth to explain this, but Asiz abruptly stood and said, "Sorry, I need to go, I was hoping to borrow Rosa's car. My wife has ours."

"I think Rosa took her car to work." Hale pointed at the window and continued, "Even if you find a vehicle, look out there. The roads are blown to hell or covered in rubble. You won't be able to get two blocks. I haven't seen anything moving anywhere out there."

The visitor stepped to the door saying, "Yeah, you're right I'll have to walk."

Hale got to his feet. "No. No, that's not what I meant. You should stay in the building. They're not bombing this area. We're safe here."

Asiz looked at him with his tear weary eyes and said, "I need to go, need to find her."

Hale said plainly, "That's suicide. Stay here."

He gave Hale a confused look. "I stay here alone with nothing to do but worry and feel guilty, then I'm better off dead."

Asiz left. Hale considered chasing after the man, trying to convince him not to be so foolish. He had seen the man's eyes though. Hale could not understand the craziness, but he knew Asiz would not abandon the idea of searching for his wife. He closed the door and locked the deadbolt.

Back at the window, he looked down at the front door of the building. After a few minutes, he saw a figure in a bright red parka scurry from the entrance. Hale watched Asiz move across the narrow plaza before the red of his coat disappeared into the smoke wondering if he should pity or envy him.

• • • •

The intense cold made the snow squeak beneath Morreign's shoes as she stepped out of the truck on to the solid river. As she walked, she saw Ainsley getting out of the other vehicle. Despite wanting to be, Morreign was not particularly close to her sister-in-law, they were friendly but not exactly friends.

With her blonde hair falling out of her fur-lined hood, Ainsley looked tired but remained pretty as always. Their eyes met. She clearly had been crying, but a harshness remained in her look. Morreign could not tell the reason for the harshness, it could simply be fatigue, but it could be something deeper, perhaps blame directed at her. Morreign nodded and smiled weakly. Ainsley tried to return the gesture, but the smile did not touch her deep blue eyes. They silently stepped over together to join the men.

Paul said, "Looks like we are on foot from here."

Paul's brother, Leo, was heavier set and a few inches taller than Paul who was slight of build. But their matching mops of bushy black hair and mischievous eyes made it obvious they were brothers despite the size difference. Leo stretched his arms above his head and responded, "Yeah, maybe we should leave the kids here and check things out before marching them up there. Might be the wrong place."

Paul tried to joke, "Or it might be inhabited by a family of bears."

Leo played along, "Bears should be sleeping, wolves though…"

Ainsley broke in with a sterner tone, "I'll stay down here and watch the kids. They're finally sleeping. No point in waking 'em up."

Morreign got the impression Leo did not like the idea of leaving his wife and kids alone on the river as he looked about nervously, but he was not one to argue. He leaned over and kissed the exhausted woman on her cheek and said, "Alright, honk the truck horn if you see anything weird, anything at all, and I'll come running."

She smiled weakly and responded, "Might honk regardless to get to see you actually run."

Paul added, "Leo's quicker than he looks, it's a deceptive quickness, but it's there."

With that, the trio began the hike up the river bank. The brothers took the lead, breaking a path through the drifted snow and reaching pine branches. Morreign followed at a distance, preferring to take in the scene on her own. The encompassing silence surprised her, no birds, no squirrels, no anything as if the animals were all frightened away. A trail used to exist but heavy pine branches pressed in, and shrubs filled most of the space. She wondered how many years passed since anyone else ventured though here.

Up ahead, Paul and Leo abruptly stopped walking and talking. Already nervous, Morreign felt an extra strong pang of worry. The two of them were never quiet. She stepped up between them.

The darkness of the trees gave way to a slightly familiar but misshapen vision. She had been here before, as a teenager, and her memory was of a picturesque scene. Camp Malden where she spent a few summers as a child with her family. A wide, sturdy lodge surrounded by pine trees and a dozen cute cottages, all spread out around a groomed clearing.

The scene now before her varied greatly from the childhood vision of Malden in her mind. She saw a squat, unimpressive lodge with a saddle-backed roof and a fallen pine tree crushing one corner. Most of the cottages were collapsed ruins overtaken by forest. The five or six cottages that could be said to still be standing were aged shacks leaning precariously, half buried by drifts. These piles of broken, weathered timber covered in deep snow a hundred miles from anywhere or anyone were their new home.

She brought them, all of them, here, to this. Morreign muttered, "I'm sorry, I didn't know..."

The brothers turned. Leo put a hand on her shoulder as he said, "Don't do that Mo. We knew it wouldn't be easy, but there's no damn missiles falling on our heads. Because of that, you don't apologize for anything, you don't apologize for anything ever."

Paul nodded at her with his boyish grin and then hurried to follow Leo down to the river. "There's a chainsaw in our truck. I think if we drop a few of the lower branches and some shrubs we can drive up here, save us having to haul all the gear and it'll get the vehicles off the river."

Leo answered, "Yeah, we can use the winches if we need to, I ain't carrying all that crap up here."

With that, the two men strode away. Regardless of their confident words, Morreign saw the way they froze when they reached the ruined buildings. She knew they were as afraid as she was, but she appreciated them hiding it, hiding fear would now need to serve as their courage.

CHAPTER THREE

FEBRUARY 11, 2036
DAY FIVE

The intense cold caused Hale's bathtub water supply to solidify. Chipping ice and melting it over the strange campfires he built in the kitchen sink using broken furniture took up a lot of his time. Melting a few cups of ice also took up a shocking amount of fuel, and he was running out of flammable materials. He needed to take a scouting mission.

In reality, he knew he could suck on ice chips all day, and he would be fine, but he also knew he needed to escape the apartment and its perpetual scented candle smell to avoid losing his mind and going to get fuel provided a rational excuse. He grabbed the flashlight, pocketed the hammer and picked up his pointy stick.

Before heading out of the tiny apartment for the first time in five days, he stopped to look once more out the window. The shelling ran nonstop for almost two days, and then it completely ceased. Once the smoke cleared, he could truly survey the scene. The iron skeletons of a handful of half standing buildings remained, all else was scorched rubble. Over the lonely days, Hale spent a great deal of time in front of the window, but he saw no survivors. The once bustling outpost now a destroyed ghost town. Hale turned away from the grisly scene beyond the window, unlocked the door of his refuge and stepped out into the dark hallway.

He did not have much of a plan, but he knew he did not want to be met by someone leveling a rifle at him. He went a few doors down and knocked, saying, "Canadian Arm Forces, we have relief packages."

He watched to see if any shadows moved behind the peephole or under the crack against the floor. Doubtful anyone could see anything much in the dark hall, he figured they would have to open the door if they wanted the nonexistent relief packages. If a door did open, Hale figured he would have to play the situation by ear, relying solely on instinct.

Nothing happened. He waited. Nothing happened. He tried the door. Locked.

Hale went to the next door, and the next and the next until he had covered the whole floor. All knockings had the same result. Concluding he was alone on the third floor, he took out the hafmmer.

$$\cdot \quad \cdot \quad \cdot$$

The chainsaw sputtered briefly and then died. Morreign pulled the starter cord a couple of times even though she knew it was out of gas. Their fuel supply disappearing rapidly. When planning on ZAwhat supplies they needed Morreign grossly underestimated the amount of gas to bring. The shoddy state of the cabins allowed the wind to cut straight through which meant they needed a lot of firewood. It took forever for the out of shape city folk to cut wood by axe and they quickly resorted to the gas-guzzling chainsaw.

Paul picked up a fallen limb so he could drag it through the snow closer to the cabins as he asked, "Out of gas already?"

Morreign moved to help him. "Yeah, it goes fast."

"At some point soon we're going to have to go on a reconnaissance mission, try to find fuel and other supplies."

She always knew resupplying might need to happen at some point if they were going to stay out here long term, but she never suspected the issue would arise after only five days. A trip would be dangerous if the attack still continued. Plus, anyone left alive would be very protective over any useful items. They might be heading into violent chaos all because she failed to bring enough gas.

"Yeah, but not yet. Let's put in some extra effort with the axes before taking that risk."

"Ok, my hands are already nothing but blisters anyway. We can also tear apart some of the other cabins without too much work."

"Good idea. I didn't think enough about heating."

They set the limb down near the woodpile. Paul stumbled through the snow and threw his arms around her. With both of them wrapped in massive parkas and ski pants, it lacked the intimacy of a normal hug, but she appreciated the gesture. Fatigue already pulled at her and each day only got harder.

Morreign set down the useless saw, picked up the lighter axe and turned to waddle back to the trees for more wood when they heard Leo angrily call out, "Stay right there and let me see your hands."

Leo stood on the roof of his family's cabin where he was trying to patch a particularly wide hole. Without looking down at them, he said, "Paul, Mo, we've got company."

Paul cursed and they hurried towards the cabin as Morreign asked nervously, "How many? How far?"

Leo answered, "Can only see one guy with a dog. About a hundred yards out and he's stopped walking for now."

Morreign and Paul instantly scurried to the truck where they kept their two weapons, a thirty aught six hunting rifle and a twelve gauge shotgun. They were a necessity, but having them around curious children made all of them very nervous. In order to alleviate this worry both of the guns had trigger locks with each of the adults wearing a key on a chain around their neck.

Fumbling to dig her key from under her numerous layers of clothing with her freezing hands, she hurriedly said to Paul, "The kids. They're down at the river with Ainsley."

Paul was unlocking the shotgun. "They should be ok. We'll make sure this stranger stays up here, one way or another."

His tone sounded so strange Morreign actually stopped digging for her key and looked over at him. Paul's normally jovial face looked stern, his eyes glaring. The gun. Merely holding the firearm made him aggressive.

For the hundredth time, the ludicrousness of their situation struck at her. Days ago this gentleman worried about playdate schedules and what brand of vitamins to buy, now he clutched a rifle, seemingly eager to do battle. Their life was now overlaid with a constant and powerful sense of the unreal.

Her thoughts were interrupted by Leo yelling at their visitor, but she could not make out what was being said. She looked over at Paul and said, "What if this guy isn't alone? I mean, if there's a group wouldn't it be smart for them to use this guy as a decoy or whatever and send others around to the river so they could come up that way as well?"

Paul nodded. "Right. I'll head down there and make sure they're safe."

He turned and ran awkwardly in his heavy clothes towards the river. Morreign did not actually think more than one person was out there, but the look on Paul's face scared her, made her think he could do something rash.

Best to have him far away. Rushing back to Leo, she made a mental note that the kids getting a hold of the guns might not be the only risk the weapons posed.

"Leo, here's the rifle."

Morreign handed the gun up. Leo called out, "Stay right there. No funny business."

He then bent down and took the rifle, telling Morreign, "He's still standing out there. You want me to tell him to leave?"

She shook his head, "No, if he's dangerous or desperate, he'll only come back at night or something. We need to deal with this now."

Leo blanched at this comment. The idea of using the rifle on a random stranger apparently did not appeal to the fun-loving engineer. His hesitation was a relief. Morreign hastily added, "We'll only talk to him. Talk to him and then decide if he's a threat."

Climbing up onto the low roof, Morreign could see the stranger but could not get much of a sense of the man as the setting sun made deep shadows amongst the trees. Wearing a faded yellow snowmobile suit with a hood and scarf around his face, he could be young or old, massive or small, angry or happy. A rifle hung casually off his shoulder like it lived there and a wooden sled sat behind him. The dog looked to be a German shepherd kind of breed, contently laying on the snow.

Leo, holding the gun low where it was visible but not threatening, whispered over to her, "He says he's a hunter and he wants to know what we're doing here."

"A hunter? Is there any wildlife?"

"Don't know, we've seen nothing. But that's what he said."

"Ok, stay ready."

Morreign moved forward and called down, "You can come closer. We need to talk."

Moving through the deep snow, he worked his way nearer, the dog obediently pulling the sled along. As he moved, he looked from side to side, even glancing behind him once or twice. Morreign realized the visitor was worried there might be others out there with more guns. Maybe he really was only a wayward hunter.

"What's your name?"

The hood tilted up at them, but it was impossible to make out any features. "Sam."

The way he answered sounded slightly like a question, as if he was unsure about his name or, at least, unused to speaking it. "I'm Morreign, and this is Leo. What are you doing out here?"

Sam reached up, lowered the hood and scarf, revealing a head of thick black hair and dark eyes. Maybe mid-twenties. "Hunting. What're you doing here?"

"You don't know what happened?"

This seemed to confuse the young man. "What do you mean?"

Leo glanced over at her, silently expressing how it might be best not to tell this visitor about civilization recently ending. Morreign was unsure what to do, but she hated to lie, so she opted for the truth, "About a week ago, an attack. A massive attack. We fled but assume Thule is destroyed, everything is probably destroyed. War likely rages everywhere."

Sam merely stood and looked up at the stranger who was telling him the earth now burned. After a moment, he bent slightly and scratched the dog's head without lowering his gaze. He said, "Everywhere but here."

"Right, that's why we're here."

He nodded and said calmly, "I sometimes sleep in the lodge, I've got a place about five miles downriver, but sometimes I stay here, in a back room, if I'm out too far to get back before dark."

She leaned over to Leo and asked, "What do you think?"

"Well, now that you've made friends, I sure as hell don't want to shoot the guy."

"Yeah, I hear you," She turned back to Sam, "If you leave the gun on the sled, you can join us for dinner."

He stared up at the two of them, apparently considering his limited options. Finally, without a word, he took the gun off his shoulder and laid it on the sled before untying the dog and trudging through the snow towards them. As they moved to get off the roof, Leo asked her, "Join us for dinner?"

•   •   •

The hammer blow sounded shockingly loud in the frozen, dark hallway as Hale hit the doorknob again, then again. Finally, the cheap metal gave way, breaking off from the door and Hale fiddled the locking mechanism out.

This was the last apartment on the floor for him to check. All the other units he entered were under construction and essentially empty except for scattered building supplies. Rosa had bragged about being one of the first tenants allowed to move in because of her important position, and unfortunately, she had been telling the truth.

Hale took a deep breath as he turned on the flashlight and slowly opened the ruined door. Finally, a completed and inhabited apartment. Furniture had been pushed into an odd pile in the living room. Someone hiding out, having built a fort of sorts to insulate them from the cold. Hale considered leaving, not wanting a confrontation, but curiosity won out, and he moved cautiously inside.

Carefully skirting the mass of furnishings, Hale shone the light along the floor revealing empty food containers among a tangle of blankets. The light fell on a battered, yellow, stuffed elephant. A child? Children were a rarity at Thule but he supposed someone high up in the military could have gotten permission to bring their family.

It took Hale only a couple of minutes to survey the apartment. No one there. They must have fled. Despite not knowing the family, Hale found himself greatly hoping they made it somewhere safe. He also found himself hoping they left behind some useful supplies.

He started in the kitchen where he found a good deal of useable food. He rapidly filled his duffel bag and was looking for another bag to use when he heard a soft thump. Realizing he had let down his guard, Hale grabbed up his pointy stick and shined his flashlight in the direction of the sound. Nothing.

He strained to hear in the dim light, but there was no more noise. Needing to check it out regardless, Hale moved into the bedroom decorated for a child. It was in shambles, the bed pulled apart, clothes covering the floor. Hale moved through the mess, panning the flashlight around the room. When the light hit the closet, he glimpsed movement under the door. His heart began to beat quicker.

Leaving a person hiding in the closet was an option but he worried not addressing this now might make for a bigger problem later. Better to deal with the potential threat immediately.

Deciding that startling them was in his favour, Hale leveled his sad weapon and threw the door aside.

"Please, please, don't hurt me."

The high pitched plea came from a shadow beneath hanging clothes. Shining the light towards the corner, Hale saw a pale face poking out from a heavy blanket. A child. Seven years old or so. Startled by the strange sight, Hale lowered the light and stepped back, saying, "It's ok, it's ok. I won't hurt you."

The kid pleaded again from out of the darkness, "Please don't take all my food, please don't leave me nothing."

The reality of the situation struck at Hale. A kid, apparently all by himself. Could he leave a kid alone in the cold and the dark? Could he take care of some random kid in this disaster?

"Where are your parents?"

"My parents?" The words came tinged with the sound of crying, "I, I, uh, I don't know."

"Ok, come out here."

"You won't hurt me?"

"No, it's alright."

After some rustling, a boy dressed in so many layers of clothes he appeared spherical stumbled out of the closet and into the mess of a room. His greasy hair spilled out of his ski cap in a tangle and his face needed to be washed. He looked up at Hale in the dim light with bright eyes filled with tears, fear, and confusion.

Trying not to sound as awkward as he felt, Hale said, "I'm Hale. What's your name?"

Without looking up, the boy said, "Luke."

"Ok, Luke, are you here by yourself?"

The kid nodded, obviously trying in vain to hold back his sobbing.

"Your folks left you here?"

"I go to school at a friend's house. My friend's mom brought me home, and my dad texted to say they'd be home as soon as possible..."

His voice tapered off, leaving unsaid that his parents never made it home. A part of Hale wanted to turn and walk out of the apartment. It was going to be hard enough to survive this nightmare without having an extra mouth to feed.

He began to leave the room but, without any real thought, Hale called back, "Come on, Luke."

•　　•　　•

Morreign complained about their cramped apartment when they first moved to Thule. Looking back, the condensed, two bedroom unit was a palace. Now five adults huddled over the tiny table in the most liveable cabin, elbowing for enough space to eat while the children sat on the sturdy bed in the corner, balancing plates on their blanket covered laps.

The first day after fleeing they tried to eat dinner in the lodge but immediately discovered heating the drafty dining room to make it comfortable to be too much effort. Since then meals became ad hoc affairs, eaten in either of the two inhabited cabins or grabbed on the go. In the past, meals, at least dinner, was of great import to Morreign, she planned and worried over meals, now meals were necessary inconveniences. Tonight, however, they had a guest and were taking time to sit and consume rice and rehydrated stew like civilized humans.

Sam proved to be a man of few words, but Paul and Leo politely filled the silence with stories of going to school in the frigid winters of Edmonton. Morreign carefully watched the visitor. He ate slowly, deliberately. While youthful, his shoulders were wide and his hairless face appeared sternly weathered with a pale scar running down his forehead before disappearing into an eyebrow.

He mainly kept his eyes lowered, but she caught him glancing at them, not in a menacing way, more like the way a rabbit continually takes in its surroundings. He nodded a couple of times as the brothers talked, but he did not speak. The kids on the bed were more quiet than usual, staring at the stranger. They had met no equivalent for such a person in their short lives making it hard for them to decipher the visitor. Obviously, a hardness emanated from Sam, but Morreign's instincts were not telling her to be afraid, even if his stoic presence made her slightly uneasy as his silence ran contrary to social norms.

Their puppy, Rufus, suddenly yapped and scurried to the door. Sam gracefully stood without a sound. Everyone else stayed in their places, Paul and Leo not even slowing their storytelling until they noticed Sam was no longer sitting.

Sam's dog, which seemed to have no name, was in the lodge because Rufus was too annoying while trying to make friends with the German shepherd. They all sat, listening to the yapping dog as Sam seemed to be straining to hear. Finally, after a few tense heartbeats, their visitor sat back down without a word.

Paul got up to take the yipping puppy outside, and Leo seemed to be about to continue the polite storytelling, but Morreign broke in, "What were you listening for?"

The young man looked over at her, a hint of confusion in his eyes as he seemed to think the answer obvious. He calmly said, "My dog."

"Why?"

"If there was something out there, my dog would bark to let me know."

"Something out there? Like what?"

The confused look again. "A lynx. Wolves. People."

A silence fell over the table. They had worked hard to ignore the seriousness of their situation, pretending they were merely waiting for an awful camping trip to end as this helped keep the overwhelming fear at bay. Morreign now realized this chosen ignorance to be folly and dangerous.

She asked, "Sam, why are you out here?"

He kept his eyes on his stew as he answered, "No job. Got conscripted. Disliked the army, so I left. Came out here, live off the land."

Oddly, the news Sam was AWOL reassured her as it meant he was not a criminal fugitive. Plus, she worried people who liked the army too much also liked the idea of shooting people too much.

She kept prodding, "Is there any game out here?"

Sam looked at a piece of potato on his spoon and nodded. "Last few years it's been too cold for hunters to come up here, so the games come back some. They're thin, but they're around."

"Predators?"

Another nod.

"A lot of predators?"

"They follow the animals. Lots of coyotes, pretty bold, aggressive packs. Been a hard winter already, everything's hungry now. Going to get hungrier."

The idea came instinctively, and without further thought, Morreign said, "Sam, would you like to stay here for a while?"

She heard the slight breath intake from the others around the table but ignored them. Sam did not look up from his bowl, apparently pondering the question. She added, "We could use the help."

He slowly ate a spoonful of thin stew, looked at Morreign and nodded.

CHAPTER FOUR

FEBRUARY 12, 2036
DAY SIX

The awkward situation remained tolerable while moving supplies from Luke's apartment to Rosa's place but, now, with the distracting task done, Hale felt awkward with the orphan. Children never formed part of his world, they were not commonplace on oilfield rigs.

He generally ignored the boy and busied himself sorting and storing the supplies until Luke climbed into the pile of blankets in the bathroom where he could be heard weeping for some time before going silent. Once certain his guest was fast asleep, Hale carefully dug himself a hole in the nest and tried to sleep himself.

Now, with a hint of daylight coming into the bathroom turned bedroom, Hale could hear the sounds of Luke moving around the frozen apartment, talking to the grey cat. He could not ignore the kid forever. A plan. They needed some sort of plan. Things to do.

The fuller cabinets and pile of burnable fuel provided a respite, but the lack of other inhabited apartments was disconcerting as it limited their total store of supplies. Sadly, he knew at least one other apartment existed. Certainly, Asiz never made it back from his doomed attempt to rescue his wife. If there were survivors in the building or nearby, either friendly or unfriendly, it would be wise for Hale to secure Asiz's abandoned supplies before anyone else could. He reluctantly climbed out of the fleeting warmth of the blankets.

Luke stood on the balcony, staring numbly as the sun rose to reveal the devastation through the blowing whiteness of snow. Luke's family's apartment looked out the back of the building, towards the wilderness so this was the first time the kid could survey the burned rubble now comprising the once vibrant outpost. Hard to tell given all the clothes he wore but Hale thought Luke's shoulders were shaking.

Some instinct buried in his psyche indicated that he should move to console the child. At the least put a hand on his shoulder and say something reassuring. Instead, he stepped next to him and asked, "How long have you lived in the building?"

Startled, Luke turned away from the grey destruction. Tears were freezing on his red cheeks. He rubbed at his face as he said, "Huh?"

"How long have you lived here?"

"Maybe a few weeks."

"How many other people in the building?"

"Huh?"

Frustration was already growing inside Hale, patience not a virtue of his. "Do you know if anyone else lives here?"

"I think a couple other apartments have people in them."

Obviously, the kid would not be much help from an intelligence standpoint. Regardless, he needed to get whatever few supplies he could. He began to order Luke to stay in the apartment and work on melting ice for drinking water while he went out scavenging when movement down below caught his attention. At first, they were only shadows on the rocks, the vague idea of a presence seen through blowing snow but, before long, Hale's sharp eye discerned figures, a dozen people.

The group appeared exhausted, meandering and stumbling with no appearance of order. Even though they were carrying military firearms, the black metal clear against their white coats, Hale doubted they were a normal army patrol.

They came near but before they reached the building, the man out front stopped, and all the others came to a staggered halt behind him. For a long moment, the leader stared up at the structure as if appraising it for some purpose. It was impossible to make out any features of the man bundled in winter gear but, when Hale sensed the man's eyes light on the balcony, he instinctively hurried inside, pulling Luke back with him.

Standing in the living room, the orphan staring at him confused, Hale silently pleaded that the group would carry on rather than enter his pathetic sanctuary. He counted to fifty in his head before carefully stepping back to the window. To his relief, the band was wandering off to the East, apparently seeking better looting or sheltering options.

"Who were they? Soldiers?" Luke asked as they watched them disappear.

"I don't think so. Maybe they once were, but now I'd guess they're more like a gang or something."

"They looked freezing and tired. Shouldn't we help them?"

Hale answered, "No."

"Bad guys?"

Turning away from the window, Hale said, "Not sure."

Picking up his pointy stick, the flashlight, the hammer, and the duffel bag, Hale turned back to explain that he was going to look for supplies, deciding he now needed to act quickly. However, the look of worry covering the boy's face made him hesitate. Luke would probably be safer in the apartment but leaving him alone with the vision of evil marauders circling the building seemed cruel.

"I'm going to look for more supplies. Grab a bag, you can come with me, but you have to stay quiet and listen to what I say."

• • • •

"You think this is smart? Having Sam stay here?" Paul asked in a whisper so as not to wake the children.

Morreign had not slept well despite her bone-deep fatigue. She knew her voice would sound annoyed if she answered right away, so she took a drink of weak tea to buy herself some time. They were sitting at the kitchen table, watching out the tiny, dirty window as Sam's unnamed dog, belly deep in snow, crept along the edge of the trees lining the clearing, apparently stalking unseen prey.

After dinner last night, Sam showed them the cozy room he set up around an old wood stove off of the kitchen in the lodge. The tight, insular space could be kept warm with only minimal firewood. The visitor and his dog spent the night there while the others returned to their frigid cabins.

Morreign loved Paul deeply and cherished Leo and Ainsley, they were smart, well educated, kind people with common sense and drive but they were urbanites through and through. The skills and charisma they developed over lifetimes existing amongst others were extremely valuable in the world before, but now those attributes were useless, perhaps worse than useless. Now having knowledge of nature trumped understanding algebra and cold-hearted toughness mattered more than having a proper handshake.

Realizing this truism was one thing, being able to speak of it with her husband of ten years another thing altogether. She put down her cup and decided to hedge. "I don't know, but I think so. He knows things we don't, things we need to know about."

"Sure. I suppose. But he seems, I don't know, dangerous to me."

Morreign wanted to point out that he was right and it was exactly that dangerousness they now needed. While she pondered how to carefully put this into words without hurting Paul's feelings, Sam's dog suddenly exploded forward, spraying snow in every direction. Out of the spray sprinted a startled hare, its feet barely touching the ground as it skittered across the deep snow for a dozen feet before it seemed to be violently thrown sideways. A gunshot echoed across the clearing. Spinning her gaze towards the sound, she saw Sam kneeling in the trees, his rifle smoking.

The kids, scared awake by the bang, were crying from their bed as Rufus yapped. Paul hurried to comfort the boys, saying to her as he went, "I didn't even think there were rabbits around here, least not in the winter."

Morreign continued to look outside, shaking her head in disbelief at the sight she witnessed, and said, "The dog must've found a warren or a lair or whatever. Seems like we'll have some fresh meat at least."

Paul shook his head. "Suppose I should know better than to second guess your instincts by now."

Through the hazy window, she watched as the dog picked up the rabbit corpse and bounded through the snow to Sam, dropping it at his feet. With casual grace, Sam picked up the rabbit by the ears and tossed a piece of dried meat from his pocket which the dog bolted up to catch.

Turning away from the window, Morreign saw Paul holding Huck while explaining to Jacob that Sam was practicing shooting so he should wait a while before taking Rufus outside. The thought filling her mind hurt her to her core because she loved her caring, considerate family dearly, but she now knew that, to survive, the instinctual remnants of animalistic hardness they always suppressed would need to prevail. The days of coddling were over.

•　　•　　•

Sharp pain fought the numbness encompassing in his feet. Harrison appreciated the pain, it meant frostbite had not won out completely. Hard to see anything through the wickedly blowing snow but he figured the squat apartment building standing before him on the outskirts of Thule was recently erected. More space than his group needed and it would make an obvious target to any marauders, but that was not why he turned away from the potential sanctuary to seek out a different shelter. Despite the blinding snow, he glimpsed movement up above, people on a balcony.

Four days ago, he and Clarence managed to hike out of the forest, leaving the crashed helicopter and the corpses to be buried by the falling snow. They eventually reached the destroyed base. Only a couple dozen people, some soldiers, some civilians, remained. They were hiding and huddled in the half-collapsed basement of the maintenance building. A dirty, injured, hungry, frozen mass, clinging to each other in the darkness.

The remaining officers were trying to maintain authority and give the desolate group some order, but Harrison could clearly see that the tenuous situation would not last. Before long, fear, cold and hunger would overrule any historical vestige of the unearned command structure. Regardless, Harrison and Clarence stayed for three days. Partly to heal up and regain some strength before venturing on but also so Harrison could survey the survivors.

When the time came, Clarence hesitated over walking away from the huddled mass in the disgusting basement but Harrison knew the abandonment to be necessary, and the pliable pilot did not argue. He picked the healthiest and strongest and convinced them to leave with him, robbing the miserable remnants of their only hope of survival. As they snuck away in the night as the old and wounded slept in the frigid filth where they would surely die, Harrison told himself that leaving behind the weakest was the only way the others could endure. Many would see this rationalization as cold comfort, but Harrison could accept cold comfort.

All night the chosen marched, following Harrison to Thule, hoping for a useable refuge. The wind chilled at a lethal level while drifted snow made it nearly impossible to walk with any speed. One of their number, a middle-aged mechanic, collapsed and could not be roused and desperation firmly set in, they needed shelter and fire immediately

Regardless, the possibility of people in the residential building worried Harrison. At some point soon he figured the building could become their prime target as it likely held food and other supplies, however, that point could not be now. If his exhausted group entered and were confronted by even a couple of unfriendly, rested people willing to fight from their raised position they could all be wiped out. Better to risk the weather a little longer and find a safe place than risk annihilation. He moved on, hoping the others would continue to follow.

Clarence, his face entirely wrapped in multiple scarves and his eyes hidden behind goggles, caught up to him, "What are you doing? We need to get inside right now, and that's the only place with four walls and a roof we've seen. Hell, there might even be people in there with fires already going."

Harrison knew Clarence would do whatever he said. The pilot apparently realized that without Harrison, they would have died in the woods, the demented Colonel barking out pointless orders all the while. He asked, "Are they following?"

"What?"

"The others, are they coming?"

Clarence glanced back. "Looks like it, I mean they're barely able to move, but I think they're coming."

His hold on these desperate people was even stronger than Harrison thought if they would walk away from the shelter at this point without even saying a word in protest. This was good, a leader with no followers is merely a guy out for a walk.

He looked at Clarence and said, "I think you could be right, there're people in that building. That's the problem."

"What do you mean? We're going freeze to death because we're shy?"

Clarence apparently did not excel at far-ranging thought. Harrison realized the tribal instinct ingrained in people to seek out help when in danger would be the downfall of many in this new world. He also realized that this ingrained flaw could be to his advantage. However, this realization would do him no good if hypothermia killed him before he could put the information to use.

He ignored Clarence's question and forced his frozen legs to move faster through the blinding snow. If the bombing ignored the apartment building, maybe it also left a more suitable structure nearby.

After a few dozen strides, a light post appeared out of the blizzard like a beacon. A handful more steps and fuel tanks became visible. Then the arching hulk of a machine shed nearly buried in snow. Some sort of industrial service station. A place which should be empty of people but full of flammable liquids simply waiting for a match. A perfect port in the storm.

He stopped to let Clarence catch up and then, pointing at the sanctuary, leaned over to him and said, "That's why you don't buy the first house you see."

CHAPTER FIVE

FEBRUARY 23, 2036
DAY FIFTEEN

Holding the gray cat on his lap, Luke jumped his red checker over two of Hale's black ones before calmly declaring, "King me."

With frozen fingers, Hale placed the checker as ordered before pondering is own move. Wanting a conversation, Hale asked, "Do you know why they called this place Thule?"

Luke merely nodded.

"Really?"

"Yeah, it's from Latin. Back in olden days, it meant the place furthest to the North, up past the borders of the known world."

"Right, exactly. How'd you know that?"

As soon as the word left his lips, Hale wanted to pull it back. Luke scratched the cat's neck and said, "My dad told me."

Hale could think of nothing else to say and silently made his own, less impressive move. The boy quickly countered, taking a couple more pieces and easily winning their ten thousandth game. As Hale mechanically moved to reset the board, Luke let out a sigh and asked, "Why can't we go out?"

Expecting the usual question, Hale answered, "You know why."

"It's not windy anymore, not that cold. We could go for a bit, maybe find something useful or fun or something."

"The door's blocked tight."

"We could open it easy enough."

"And if the men come?"

"They won't."

"And if they do?"

"We don't even know they're bad."

Even though he was only six years old, Luke was right. They did not know if they were bad or not. Sixteen days ago, Hale rarely, if ever, thought about the human condition. Since the destruction, he found himself, with too much free time, considering the nature of man often as he tried to predict what might happen next. While his past life involved limited philosophical thought, he knew, mainly from movies, that people figured when society failed, everyone would become solely self-interested in their own survival, but he thought this general idea might be flawed. People needed to help one another wanted to help one another, the child sitting across the table from him served as living proof.

Through his ponderings, Hale decided this altruism likely to be an ingrained characteristic, an evolutionary determination. Humans banded together in tribes and worked together to keep one another alive long before civilization existed, he suspected when civilization collapsed this same instinct, to cooperate, would remain.

However, he also felt this instinctual response would be delayed or heavily diluted by hunger-fuelled fear given the massive uncertainty they all existed in now. But, he hoped, once the survivors became established and the situation became better understood and more predictable, people would remember the rationale of banding together. Based on this basic view of anthropology, he decided it wise to wait before trusting strangers, wait until there was more certainty.

Hale finished resetting the checkers' board, saying, "We have food, shelter, and water. I'm not going to risk that for the joy of taking a freezing walk through rubble to entertain you."

Luke, tears wetting his eyes, dropped the cat, stood from the table and, wrapped in layers of clothing, waddled out onto the balcony. Hale started to follow but decided to give him some space. He took his time slowly packing up the game, truly relieved he did not need to play the boring game again, at least for a while.

For the first days after Hale found him, Luke seemed numb, either because of fear or grief or both. Then the boy started to cry and could not stop. Hale tried to help him, but there was nothing he could present as evidence things would get better. Thankfully, after a few days, the crying stopped on its own, returning occasionally when he was unable to offer the kid any decent distraction.

There had been some interesting work, but it did not last long. They easily completed the looting of the building as only three other apartments, including Asiz's, had once been occupied. After that, with the vision of the men with military rifles passing by their building in mind, they spent a hard day securing their floor from intruders.

Using various construction materials, they ensured the stairwell door could not be opened or forced. Hale would have preferred locking down the main floor so enemies could not establish themselves below but with two main doors and a number of windows on the ground level, closing it down was essentially impossible. Shutting off the stairs created an insular, manageable world but any sense of security came with the heavy taint of constant claustrophobia.

When they finished the task, Luke smartly pointed out that if anyone came up the stairs, they could spend forever working away at their crude barricade system as there would be no way to push them back. Over the lengthy night, Hale laid within the nest of blankets in the bathroom, straining to hear if anyone was scratching away at the door. Through that sleepless fatigue, the unpleasant solution came to him.

In the morning, they chipped and drilled, managing to create a half inch crack in the cement near the floor beside the barricaded stairwell door. They used the dust from their work to camouflage the hole so nothing could be readily detected in the darkness of the hallway. Using the gas scavenged from the parking garage, Hale filled two detergent squirt bottles and placed them next to the hole. Anyone trying to force their way in now would face a fireball. The thought of burning anyone was utterly horrific, but Hale pressed the vision out of his mind under the guise of it being an unlikely possibility, telling himself having the security measure merely allowed him to sleep easier.

With the important work done, melting ice and making sad meals in the frozen kitchen did not provide much in the way of entertainment. Luke spent much of his time on the balcony, silently surveying the destruction which served as his parents' gravesite. With no other ideas, Hale spent much of his time standing silently on the balcony beside the sad boy. Not a very pleasant existence but an existence at least.

Hale closed the lid on the checkers' box as Luke called to him, "Hale, come here. There's something going on."

Normally the morbid view from the balcony remained fixed except for shifting snow and an occasional bird; now a half dozen armed men were walking towards them. The setting sun cast them in shadow, but Hale guessed they were part of the exhausted group that walked by in the storm nine days ago. Now they appeared all too rested.

Despite Hale's first instinct to bolt back inside, a combination of fear and uncertainty held his feet. Instead, he stood next to Luke, clutched his ridiculous pointy stick at his side and looked down at the uninvited visitors. One of the group stepped forward and yelled up at the balcony, "Come down, I want to speak with you."

Sensing Luke looking sideways at him, Hale merely shook his head at the command.

The man called up again, "We want no trouble. We can work together."

Hale felt coldness in those polite words. He did not know what going down there would mean. Perhaps being part of an armed troop would make them safer. Perhaps they would shoot them dead when they stepped out the door. A coin flip, but the coldness in the man's tone caused Hale to choose to stay put.

Hale called down, "No."

"Better you come down than we come up."

A defiant head shake before Hale moved inside, gently pulling Luke back with him.

•   •   •

Harrison would've preferred to wait, let those inside get hungrier and colder before approaching. However, their scrounging efforts elsewhere were not very fruitful, all of Thule essentially ruined and covered in shifting snow. The men were having a hard time ignoring the residential building standing untouched right next door. Harrison could not appear fearful or fragile, his leadership position was strong but was not yet perfectly absolute.

Last night Harrison and Clarence snuck inside and did some reconnaissance. They moved through the unlit hallways finding nothing but half-finished apartments and a few completed units which were emptied of anything useful. Exactly what Harrison did not want to find as it meant whoever was there took all the supplies and moved upstairs where they would be harder to root out.

When he and Clarence moved up to the third floor and tried to open the metal door, it didn't move. Someone barricaded it and barricaded it well. He shared a look with Clarence. The food the men wanted was on the other side, but they did not know what else was waiting for them behind the fortifications.

They only saw one man and a kid out on the balcony, but that did not mean no one else was there. Unlikely anyone living in a residential building would have firearms but military personnel could have taken shelter there during the attack, or someone might have squirreled away a rifle. One person with a gun could do a lot of damage from the fortified position at the top of the stairs. They might incur a great deal of loss trying to get what might only be meager supplies.

Harrison knew the risk of an assault was not warranted, they should hold back and watch the building, waiting for a weakness, another avenue, an opportunity. He also knew his men would see such a delay as weakness on his part, especially while they ate thin rations and drank melted snow. Five days ago, they came across four other survivors, some pathetic maintenance workers. They had put up minor resistance to being robbed, and Harrison immediately killed them which garnered fearful respect from his men, not doing so in this more difficult instance might be seen as cowardice.

As this evening fell, having returned to the building with his group, Harrison needed to act. He told himself he was overly cautious; the chances of anyone up there having a firearm were nominal. He pulled his rifle off his shoulder and marched through the entrance of the building.

• • •

In the dark, frigid hallway, the banging on the barricaded door was overwhelmingly loud. Luke normally kept his distance from Hale, but he now huddled against him as they crouched beside the doorway. The orphan whispered, "Will it hold?"

An especially hard blow shook the metal door, and their homemade barricade moved inward an inch, the gray cat got smart and darted away into the darkness. In the faint glow of the weak flashlight, Hale could barely see Luke's face, but his worry remained clear. Unable to think of what he could say to reassure the child, he merely shrugged while silently wondering if not going downstairs as the man suggested would be his last mistake.

"Aren't you going to use the gas?"

Turning the dying light on the plastic bottles set next to the door, Hale contemplated the bizarreness of his situation. Huddled in a frozen hallway with an abandoned child, considering whether to burn armed men barrelling towards them. He never had an especially great abhorrence of violence but the idea of murder, of actually burning someone to death, remained unthinkable. Another huge bang and the barricade moved in further.

Hale silently handed the flashlight to Luke, picked up one of the bottles and took the lighter from his pocket. When he placed these items here days ago, it seemed like a fantasy, preparing for an emergency that would never come or would only come in some hazy, far off future.

He heard voices from behind the door, men extolling men to smash harder. Hale could picture the scene on the other side, a cluster of them, shoulder to shoulder against the door. He set the nozzle against the hole. Another intense crash. The door was almost free. Hale squeezed the bottle.

The familiar, pervasive smell of gas immediately filled the space. Hale heard curses and shouts from the stairwell. Hopeful the attackers would flee at the idea of being burned to death while trying to get unseen cans of corn, Hale squeezed, again and again, emptying the container as quickly as possible, causing the fuel to spread across the tiled floor.

However, instead of sounds of retreat, a massive collision followed. Panicked by the impending attack and by the idea of lighting a fire in a hallway full of people, Hale blindly grabbed up the second bottle and proceeded to empty it as the men pushed in on the battered door.

With the floor now flammable and no more ammunition at his disposal, Hale dropped the plastic bottle and stepped back. Another crash and the door jamb broke from the cement, their barricade dislodged. A gap of six inches appeared on one side, and powerful illumination came through. A man's face appeared in the wide crack, eerily lit from below and behind like someone telling a ghost story with a flashlight.

Even though Hale only saw him from the balcony, he knew this was the leader with the icy voice who called up at them, the penetrating look the same from a mile as from a foot. For a moment no one said anything, their frosted breath filling the dimly lit space and lingering amongst the petroleum fumes. The face in the gap calmly spoke, "Step aside, we'll take what we need and be on our way."

The offer clear, let them come in unimpeded, and they would merely take everything of value and leave them to starve to death in the frozen darkness. Oppose them and die. No appealing options on the table.

Keeping his eyes on the face, Hale more sensed than saw Luke scurry in behind him. He suddenly knew he could not let them be killed without trying everything to survive. Qualms about committing fiery murder instantly evaporated. Hale flipped the lighter open, slowly shook his head and thumbed the flame to life.

No fear showed on the attacker's face, no anything showed on his face, he merely said, "You can't think your crazy plan will work? All you'll do is make a lot of smoke and piss us off. Open this door, step aside, and you and the kid live to see another day."

Hale lowered his gaze for a second at the pool of gas on the floor where it had spread out. He would only need to toss the lighter a couple of feet, and the vapors would erupt, filling everywhere with fire. He had no idea if fire would spread under a door or if the flames would move fast enough to overtake the attackers. Regardless, the corner he backed himself and Luke into left no choices.

Visions of growing weaker and weaker in the dismal, frigid apartment he inherited from a woman he barely knew with an unknown orphan he inherited from parents he never met, flashed in his mind and he made his decision. Hale calmly replied, "Might as well give it a try. At least we'll be warm for a bit."

Cursing himself for rushing when he knew they should be patient and walking right into such a ridiculous trap, Harrison pondered options. He could hear the men behind him shuffling, obviously unnerved by standing in the gas, but they remained behind him, no one bolting. They were displaying courage if he turned and ordered them to run it would be because of his cowardice, not theirs.

Regardless, the barricade, while damaged, remained in the way. They would all need to push a few more times to get through, and that would give the serious looking man with the lighter more than enough of an opportunity to see if his gas chamber trap actually worked. Harrison's mind spat forth a third option.

"Wait. Wait a moment. We can work something out. We could use someone with ingenuity and courage. Why don't you join in with us?"

The man with the lighter seemed unsure, but at least he did not immediately toss the flame. Harrison continued, "There's a dozen of us, mainly former military, well established, set up in that service station out back. We've got supplies, plenty of heating fuel and are secure. You join us, and we can ride out this mess together. Has to be better than huddling up here waiting for the food to run out."

"The boy?"

"I'll personally vouch for his safety. And we've got lots of chores that'll keep him busy and make him useful to the group."

Harrison hoped he understood the unsaid meaning: the boy would need to work but, doing the jobs adults shirked would serve to protect him.

"You have all the guns, makes agreeing to put away the lighter difficult for me."

Few words from the man but Harrison figured his adversary could clearly take in a difficult situation quickly. This started as a face-saving rouse, but now Harrison wondered if the stranger might actually be a useful resource. "True. Guess you need to take us on trust."

Waving the lighter an inch or two, moving the imposing orange glow, he said, "Not going to happen."

"Ok, one chance. You tell me how you see this working. If I don't like your plan, this discussion is over, and you can stick that lighter up your ass."

No hesitation. "If you want us to join you, then arm me."

Interesting. If Harrison wasn't bluffing about letting them join them, giving him a weapon made sense. While giving up a rifle to a potential enemy made him nervous, years in the military taught Harrison that merely having a gun was a long stretch from being able to use one.

Firearms were a rarity these days. Only those in the army or special positions were allowed to own them. His conversation partner, with his long hair, weathered face and calculating eyes, did not appear to be military. Harrison guessed he was dealing with a construction worker or an oil worker, a man who earned everything he got through hard labor, not from government checks.

Harrison causally lowered his rifle off his shoulder. Holding it by the muzzle, he extended the stock through the gap in the door. Now, he could no longer see his opposition and, as he waited, he caught himself staring at the shadow beneath the door, worried the glimmering, chemical blackness would suddenly explode into a fireball, engulfing his boots and the flesh within.

Finally, the gun was taken from him, and he let out a breath of relief as it was pulled through the gap and this was followed by the sound of the barricade being pulled down as he overheard the man with the lighter strangely saying, "No, you should probably leave the elephant behind."

•   •   •

Huck no longer cried. For hours now he would not wake. Morreign sat on the edge of the bed with the child on her lap, a bowl of water beside her so she could moisten the cloth on his forehead and found herself deeply missing the horrible, sad sobs that had filled the cabin for the last two days.

An earache. They brought medicines, including antibiotics, but no matter what they tried the fever would not break. Simply an ear infection that became a fever and now her youngest child would not wake up. As she rocked him, she silently cursed bringing them here, then she cursed those who forced them to flee, then she cursed all of humanity before returning back to curse herself.

The door opened letting in a blast of intensely cold air. Paul, his arms full of firewood, stumbled inside. "Any change?"

Wiping an errant tear from her cheek with her mitten, Morreign answered, "He's really hot but his breathing, I think, is a little stronger. Maybe."

Dropping the wood next to the stove, Paul began the arduous process of stripping off scarves, gloves, coat, and goggles as he said, "Oh. That's good."

Paul sat next to her on the bed, placing his hand on Huck's blanketed leg and looked at their son as he said, "There's nothing to worry about, but I've got some news you should know about."

"News? What do you mean?"

"A family. Husband and wife with a boy about ten and a teenage girl walked up from the river about an hour ago."

Anger easily pushed through the frustration and fear Morreign felt for the last two days, and it coursed harshly into her voice, "An hour ago, and you're telling me now? They could be dangerous, part of a larger group or something."

Paul, annoyingly patient as ever, put an arm around her shoulder. "It's more important you stay with Huck in case he wakes up. They're no threat. Frostbitten, exhausted, starving and all around battered."

Wetting the cold rag for Huck's forehead for the hundredth time, she tried to quell her irrational anger as she asked, "Where did they come from? How the hell did they find us?"

"They're really distressed. Only the girl is able to say much of anything that makes sense. Her dad is some sort of pilot, and they managed to steal an old bush plane in Fort McMurray. He knew the lodge was up here and thought they could hide out like we are. But the plane crapped out on them, and they crash landed downriver. They've been walking for three days."

For an instant, calculations about the supplies needed to feed strangers ran through her tired mind before eager curiosity over the family surpassed those mundane concerns. Morreign asked, "The woman, the wife, is she a doctor, or a nurse or anything like that?"

Paul shook his head and said, "I asked. She was a chef."

Morreign had to chuckle slightly at the ridiculousness of it all, then, too tired to feel any real sense of disappointment, she merely sat next to her husband, looking at their sick child. Heat poured off of Huck and an odd odor she could only call sickness hung about him. A teardrop fell off her cheek onto her hand. She didn't even notice her crying starting again. The tears merely came now, a symptom of sitting and watching your child slipping away.

In the dim room, lit only by the smoky glow from the stove, the impotent waiting became unbearable, and Morreign began softly talking to fill the silence with something, "Remember, the other night, when we were sitting around the table with Leo and Ainsley? We were saying all the things we missed before we came here."

Paul answered in a near whisper, "Sure. Leo's having a really hard time without internet porn."

A smile touched her lips, but it was only a reflex, vanishing immediately. "Do you remember what you said?"

"Yeah, I think so. Sportscenter. Coffee. Hot showers."

"Do you remember what I said?"

"Of course. Wine. Clothes that don't smell of smoke. Light switches."

"I was wrong, I don't miss any of those things, not really anyway. You know what I actually miss? The things I used to think of as annoying hassles. Running out of milk and having to go to the store. Needing to call the plumber because the washing machine is leaking. Taking a kid with an earache to the doctor. Back then nothing really went wrong, only things sometimes needed to be fixed, now... now things go wrong, now things can't be fixed."

She knew Paul was struggling with what to say. His innate kindness dictated he say something reassuring to try and alleviate her pain, but clearly, nothing could be said here. A powerful part of her wanted to throw herself at him and beat him with her fists, claw at his eyes and stomp on him. Never before had she experienced a true desire for violence but a powerful aggravation filled her because this man, the father of her children, was supposed protect them but he was doing nothing but sitting there, watching Huck die. She forced herself to take a deep breath. The violent instinct passed but she still wanted to be alone.

"Maybe you should check on the newcomers."

Apparently surprised by this, Paul said, "Oh, I'm sure they're all asleep now."

Morreign merely looked at him. He seemed to understand and said, "Leo and Sam were working on some traps, maybe I'll go help them out."

Guilt prodded at Morreign as Paul silently pulled on his winter gear to head back out. She knew this was awful for him as well, but she felt too much pain to care about his feelings. However, she didn't want to fight with him, not with all that was going on, so, as he reached for the door she broke the uneasy tension by asking, "What's their name?"

"Pardon me?"

"The family. If they're going to be our neighbors, I should at least know their name."

He gave her a strained yet quirky grin through his stubbly beard and said, "Hope. The family's name is Hope."

PART TWO

CHAPTER SIX

JUNE 6, 2046

DAY THREE THOUSAND SEVEN HUNDRED AND FIFTY-SIX

A stretch to call it warm, but the bright sun on his face felt great regardless of the actual temperature. Despite having taken a whole box, Hale ate his dry cereal slowly having learned over the last decade to eat slowly and make food last. He could hear others celebrating down below, but he preferred the peace of the building's rooftop. Normally these days, if he disappeared for too long, someone, usually Clarence, would come looking, casually stopping for a visit, making sure he was not up to anything but, with the patrol recently returned with supplies, distractions abounded which allowed him to slip away.

With the harshness of winter disappearing Hale's persistent thoughts of leaving Thule grew stronger; thoughts of finding somewhere less chaotic to live, less harsh, of making a better life. As he aged, the desire to leave increased but so did the paralyzing trepidation. Having seen first-hand that, in this new world, a simple sprained ankle could mean freezing to death in the snow, existing in isolation was a daunting option.

Early on, Luke probably would have come with him but now, approaching him would be risky, likely a mistake. Kinma would obviously come. Milo seemed likely to be on board which meant Taco might come as well. There were a few others he spoke with using vague words and hushed tones, but none seemed wholly committed. Regardless, a handful of people did not create a situation much better than being all alone.

Over the decade, Harrison's original group of chosen survivors grew. Initially, Harrison only wanted healthy, obedient men to join with all others they encountered being chased off or killed except those he deemed to have valuable skills. In that manner, they quickly grew to a stout twenty-five.

Eventually, once they became somewhat established and secure, Harrison became less selective and let some of his favorite men keep the women they found which then led to needing more people to patrol and scavenge so more were allowed to join. They now numbered thirty-eight people.

Seven years ago, when they were still flush with supplies taken from the easy reach of the surrounding area, a band of refugees arrived at Thule and tried to barter for food and gear. The refugees had obviously been wealthy, powerful people in the past and had managed to get as far north as possible to escape the fighting now raging in the south.

The rich fools offered up luxury items with no value in the new world, and they were abruptly and violently dispatched with everything they had taken off their corpses. The men at Thule took great joy in the fact that the wealthy were now coming to them to beg for help. Having lived through the financial crisis of 2022, the men blamed greedy bankers for much of their woes, so the joke started out that they were now the banks, but this bank turned away overfed suits while accepting the rugged poor. The jovial name stuck, and the group eventually began unconsciously referring to itself as the Bank.

No matter how cruel life was with the Bank in the remnants of Thule, living as one of thirty-eight in a fortified building with supplies was safer than surviving with a few others, alone in the woods. Regardless, Hale still had a deep ache to leave. Harrison might hunt them down as deserters, but he might be fine letting them go. If they got away clean they could go to that old farmhouse Hale scavenged years ago, a far distance but that made it a safe distance. A long, unconscious sigh escaped around his mouthful of cereal. These thoughts were far from new, and Hale knew they were worn out, if he truly meant to leave, he would have simply left.

"Best day 'round here in a long damn time and you're hiding on the roof with a box of shredded wheat?"

Harrison's tone was light but, as always, an underlying rigidness existed. Looking over he realized the man's black, coarse beard made his grey eyes even more piercing. Hale made a show of casually leaning back in his chair before answering, "Cornflakes actually."

Harrison flipped over a nearby bucket used to catch rainwater and sat on it. Despite the underlying sense of tension, Hale played it off, tilting the cereal box towards him by way of offering. Harrison took a handful of the stale food. The two men chewed as they stared at their thawing realm in a silence only those who have before spent much time together can endure.

Finally, Harrison asked, "We going to have a problem with winter gone?"

The pointed question did not shock Hale, Harrison always seemed to be able to read his mind. He answered with a shrug, "Nah, only a hint of spring fever."

"Good. I need you to go out again."

This caused Hale to glance over. After the Bombing, Hale actively patrolled the surrounding area with others in the Bank. They attacked those seen as potential threats and looted any supplies they found. Everything being a matter of survival allowed Hale to rationalize the violence becoming a major part of life, a part of life he became shockingly good at. The other Bankers greatly appreciated his skills but, despite Harrison's numerous speeches about existing in a lifeboat and the fittest needing to survive, Hale found it harder and harder to justify battering the weak and desperate as the Bank became more and more established.

Eventually, after an especially bloody patrol, Hale refused to attack innocent people, and this did not sit well with Harrison. The leader subtly threatened him and, by proxy, Kinma. However, everyone respected Hale and all he did to maintain and improve their wellbeing. This respect clearly worried Harrison, so they established an uneasy truce. Hale would not have to kill unless they were attacked and he would ostensibly support Harrison's leadership.

Hale choked down the cereal and said, "Thought that load looked pretty light."

Harrison let out one of his contrived chuckles. "Light's one way of callin' it. Eight men were out for two weeks and came back with enough food for less than a month."

"Me going out to look probably ain't the answer. We need to get better at making our own food."

Another old argument between them. They grew some vegetables in the summer and hunted year round. But planting potatoes and setting squirrel traps still remained a distant second to looting. It took a while, but Hale eventually figured out why Harrison allowed this disparity to continue even after the scavenging became stingy. Men hunched over hoes grew bored and men eating rations of withered carrots all winter grew angry. Bored and angry men became troublesome for their leadership. Getting to go out and rape and pillage was exciting while getting intermittent bounties caused people to forget the lean times.

"You're probably right."

This response did surprise, Hale. Harrison, his voice sounding far off, continued, "Too late now though. We've spent ten years getting good at taking, not enough time left to get good at making. Before we even get a real crop harvested, we'll be starving, hell, we'll be starved out before a crop sprouts. The men are already pissed over the shitty rations and whatever other complaints are going around."

Hale wondered if the reference to "other complaints" was Harrison indicating he knew of his scheming to get people to leave, but he could not know, so he ignored the point. "That can't be right. There's still gotta be stuff out there. Send out a few strong groups to fill the shelves, I'll stay here and get the rest farming like aggressive Amish."

"Might work, but we've got even more immediate problems I need you to deal with. Remember, we're not the only survivors with guns. The patrol took heavy fire and bolted straight for home, that's part of the reason they found so little."

Silence as Hale contemplated this. He softly said, "The Survivalist nuts."

"The goddamn Survivalists. They're getting aggressive. Their supplies are probably thinning like ours, both of us spreading out farther from home."

An all-out war with the Survivalists would be devastating. Hale silently cursed himself, yet again, for not having gotten out of Thule years ago.

•   •   •

Fatigue constantly accompanied Harrison for many days now. Keeping the Bank fed and sheltered was constant work. Keeping the Bank isolated and safe from outside threats was a perpetual struggle. Keeping the Bank from destroying itself from within was a never-ending battle.

Harrison could have relinquished command, early on he was tempted to do so on numerous occasions, but the idea left him wondering what he would do then. His years in the military taught Harrison that living under the rule of others could not be tolerated. He needed to be the one making the decisions. He feared that striking out on his own, or with a couple completely obedient followers like Clarence, would not end well. A stronger group or starvation could end them before long. Staying at Thule, keeping the group separated from outside influence and maintaining dominate control internally was his only viable option. Over the years that option became his life, his calling, he supposed.

Regardless of having this calling, Harrison sensed his control was slipping. More than the minor slippages he easily handled in the past. He knew Hale was actively talking to others either about bolting or revolting, he could not be sure. A splinter group leaving might be manageable, but it would greatly undercut his position, plus, it was not a stretch to go from the idea of some people being able to leave to others getting the idea of trying an outright revolution. This was all made worse because supplies were low and scavenging opportunities were slim which lowered morale.

Harrison now felt true revolt hung in the air. He needed to act and act drastically. Hale was an obvious point of emphasis as his subtle conversations would not stay so subtle for long. The former oil worker they found in the frozen apartment building with the orphan all those years ago proved extremely capable as Harrison predicted but, more importantly now, he was also extremely well-liked. He personified the problem.

Harrison said, "I need you to go. Stop the Survivalists out there before they can come here."

Hale scratched at his reddish-brown beard now streaked slightly with grey as he asked, "You think they're going to attack us? Here? It'd be suicidal."

Hale discovered the Survivalist settlement on a patrol about five years ago and reported back to Harrison. The former oil worker declined to attack those living there, claiming they were too well armed, somehow having rifles even though non-military were not allowed to keep guns, such that he did not think their supplies were worth the risk. Harrison doubted the explanation. Harrison believed Hale, being soft, did not want to attack because of the women and children amongst them.

Hale and he butted heads often over how to treat those weaker than them. Harrison did not like cruelty, he did not seek out hurting others. However, he viewed situations simply and logically. Allowing the weak to overwhelm the strong would only mean devastation for everyone.

Harrison said, "They took shots at the patrol. They're obviously out there looking for shit same as us, digging through the remnants of the remnants. And they know we're here. Won't be long before they make it this far."

"Maybe we can talk with them, see if they want to join up together."

Harrison wanted to laugh at Hale's naïve nature. Two summers ago, another patrol ventured too far and came across the Survivalist camp. In the years since Hale first saw the settlement, the Survivalists grew both in number and strength. The wayward patrol was immediately attacked, two members were killed while the others had no choice but to flee.

The Survivalists were not the talking kind, they would not bend to compromise. Plus, Harrison wanted all of the Survivalists supplies, he did not want more mouths to feed. On top of that, the infant idea was blossoming that naive Hale not returning would remove, not only a mouth he needed to feed but a mouth that was spreading thoughts best left not spread.

"Doubt it. Too much blood spilled, not enough food for everyone. Not worth the risk of trying to deal with them. Need to sneak up on them and attack first and fast."

"I don't do that anymore."

"No choice on this one. You had the chance to properly deal with this years ago and took the coward's way out. That means you need to deal with it now. I'm not sending someone else to fix your damn mistake. And you know you're the best option to pull this type of large-scale ambush off with the fewest casualties possible."

Hale shrugged. "Ok, you're right."

The response came too easily and too fast. Hale was planning something. However, having gotten the answer he came for, Harrison could not protest. He could only stand, deciding to worry about possible problems later.

"Great. Pick fourteen men to go with you. Include Clarence but leave the Vikings so we're not completely unprotected. Don't worry, I'll watch out for Kinma while you're gone."

With the unsaid threat hanging in the air that Hale's *de facto* wife, Kinma, would be at risk if Clarence reported back any strange behavior, Harrison walked away.

·　　·　　·

Morreign's hip hurt, but it hurt much less now that she could see Sam and Paul pulling an obviously heavy sled up the path. They were due back yesterday and fear had clutched at Morreign all night so seeing them allowed her to breathe again. With effort, Morreign got up from her chair and set her knitting down to watch the anticipated scene unfold in the Clearing.

The kids were out first, wearing patched clothes and rubber boots, running across the muddy, slushy lawn. Two boys and one girl, aged four, five and eight. They slipped and laughed with excitement. For an instant, a flash of sorrow struck at Morreign, happy children reminded her of Huck. Her youngest son had been gone now for ten years.

Next came the teenagers. Trying to remain calm and adult but walking briskly to see what the duo brought back. With this group was her son Jacob, now strikingly broad across the shoulders and sporting a patchy beard but still moving with the awkward gait of a young man not completely comfortable in his growing body. Despite his dog, Bear, being gone over five months now, it still seemed odd to see him without the hairy beast loping at his side. Unsurprisingly, Jacob walked next to Louisa, casually holding hands. They were rarely apart when not working.

Sam had brought Louisa back to Malden six years ago, arriving in the middle of the night with the young girl clinging to him on the back of an old snowmobile Leo had found and repaired. The child did not appear to be physically hurt beyond the dehydration, malnourishment and exposure issues one always saw in survivors. However, they could not get her to speak. The story Sam reluctantly told provided reasoning for her muteness.

Sam was hunting when he came across a workers' camp set up on a timber cutline. It appeared long abandoned, but any supplies could be helpful, so he searched the falling down structures. In a trailer he found the girl, hiding in a corner, wrapped in filthy blankets in the cold dark. She cowered from Sam like a skittish rodent. He tried to calm her, but calming people was not one of Sam's talents.

He turned to leave, planning to get food from his snowmobile in hopes a gift would help placate the girl but before he could reach the door to leave she scurried at him, throwing her thin arms around his legs. As he tried to gently escape her fear-soaked clutch, his eyes adjusted to the darkness and he noticed something in the shadows at the far end of the trailer. A man and a woman, their frozen bodies hanging by their necks from the low ceiling.

Sam scooped up the girl and brought her back to Malden.

Jacob, only a child himself back then, came with Morreign when she met Louisa at the Lodge for the first time. She saw it, she saw it, the first time they looked at each other, and the intensity of it scared her. The frightened, damaged girl looked at her son with an amazement which seemed to start to melt all the fear, all the hurt, and all the sadness. Jacob seemed pleasantly surprised, a shy, goofy smile immediately filling his entire face.

After spending many silent days together, Louisa eventually started speaking to Jacob when they were alone, tearfully telling the boy how, with their food running low and the snow getting deeper, her parents gave her a massive bowl of porridge. Before she could finish eating the unexpected treat, sleep overtook her. When she awoke, lying on the floor with vomit freezing on her clothes, she saw her parents hanging from their improvised nooses. Her poisoned porridge didn't work, but their ropes didn't fail.

Now, watching the teenagers, moving across the Clearing, Morreign knew logic dictated she should be glad her son found someone, especially given the new world realities. However, in her heart, she felt nothing but worry. Louisa, while having become a smart, charming and stable member of the Malden community, Morreign thought she saw glimpses of a deeply injured psyche. She worried her son, with limited partner options, became enamored with this girl because of her vulnerability and that such an attraction could not form the basis for a relationship. Regardless, she could not help but grin as she saw them laugh at the excited children tumbling around them.

The constant thwacking of axes coming from the tree line stopped, work put on hold, as the adults now ventured towards the returning pair. Paul, looking tired and dirty but smiling happily beneath the tangle of his own patchy beard and too-long hair, slipped through the crowd which slapped him on the back as he strode towards her. Without a word, they embraced, and he kissed her, first softly, then deeply. As they separated, Morreign fought back the tears which seemed to come more and more easily with each passing year.

With a slightly mocking tone, she said, "Finally. You guys stop at a strip club or something?"

"Yeah, Sam had a coupon for a free lap dance that was about to expire. Couldn't let it go to waste."

She laughed at the idea of silent Sam in a strip club. Waving a hand in front of her face, she said, "You definitely didn't stop to bathe. You must be beat. Let me get you some tea."

He gently eased her back to her chair, taking the weight off her wrecked hip. He said, "I'll get the tea. How're you feeling?"

"Sore but ok. On the plus side, I'm getting pretty good at knitting. More importantly, how'd things go with you guys?"

He hesitated for a heartbeat, the minor thing only married people would notice, before sitting next to her and saying, "Ok, not great, but ok."

"Tell me."

"Not a lot left out there. We didn't find any salt, only a few things with salt, cans of soup and the like but nothing all that significant."

One of the biggest concerns facing Malden in the last few years was finding enough sodium for everyone so they all hoped Sam and Paul would come across processed foods or other salt sources. Not wanting to show her disappointment, she said, "Well there's still that case of pretzels which should last us quite a while as long as we're careful. Anything else?"

Paul went on to explain all about their trip. Morreign leaned back in her chair, letting his natural storytelling ability wash over her, reveling in having her husband and friend back. Finally, he stood up and said, "I guess I better get cleaned up. I hurried to make sure we got back for the big celebration, can't be late now."

She heard the slight marital poke in his voice, and she shook her head at him. "I might claim to be too sore to go."

He called back as he strode into the cabin, "Good luck with that, they'll all just show up here to bask in your importance."

* * *

Noticing the absence of the usual funky, musty smell in the apartment caused Hale to stop in the doorway. Kinma, dressed in her overly large sweater, with her black hair tucked under her yellow toque, bounded out of the bathroom. "Hey. I opened the windows, get some of that smoke and dirty old man smell outta here. Better, right?"

Hale handed her the rest of the cereal and said, "Yeah, much better."

Apparently sensing his unease, she ignored the food, and she asked, "What's wrong? Spring's finally here, and they brought in some new supplies, you should be happy."

He learned over the years that it was pointless to not be straightforward with Kinma. "Harrison wants me to go out on patrol, take care of a problem."

A good head shorter than him, the petite woman tilted her head back to look up at him, "What? I thought you guys had a deal about that?"

Hale had told her of the détente reached with Harrison, explaining why he no longer took turns going on supply patrols. He answered, "We did, but things change, and this is something different."

They walked into the living room and flopped down on the couch. She prodded, "Different how?"

Normally Hale, never keen on discussions, would have shook this question off, but he figured she deserved to know. "The Survivalists. It's the Survivalists."

Concern filled her voice, "Really?"

Over the years, the Survivalists became something of a legend among the Bankers, boogie men in the dark, wolves in the woods. In actuality, Hale knew they were rarely seen, however, stories of them attacking patrols were often told and retold to fend off boredom in a world without TV or internet.

"Yeah."

"Why does it need to be you?"

He sighed, not wanting to have to explain but doubting the woman would leave him be if he didn't. "I had a run in with them few years after the Bombs. Harrison thinks I could've easily shut 'em down back then, so he doesn't want to make someone else go risk their life to fix my mistake. Also, he feels like I'm the best guy to get this done. At least that's the reasoning he's telling me."

Always keen, Kinma caught on and jumped right to the point, "The asshole wants you to get killed."

"Maybe. There's a lot of tension 'round here, even more than usual lately and he probably suspects I could cause problems or am causing problems. It's a no lose for him. If we're successful we come back with a mess of supplies, a great story of victory and everyone celebrates. If we're unsuccessful, he can say nice things about me while extolling the dangers facing the Bank, get everyone to pull in tighter and have a few fewer mouths to feed."

There was a pause as they both contemplated the untenable situation. Finally, seemingly unable to find a solution, she said, "What happened? Back then, with the Survivalists."

It took a great deal of time, but Hale, a mainly silent man, grew somewhat accustomed to Kinma's questionings. This, however, would be difficult to answer. He sighed, "It's kind of a story."

"I got nothing but time. You start talking, I'll make some tea."

Early on after the Bombs, Hale invented a brazier of sorts that could be easily fashioned out of scrap metal. Each of the occupied apartments now contained one of these "Hale Stoves." He watched as she filled the kettle and gently pumped the bellows to get the embers inside the stove hot again. Sensing his gaze, she smiled back at him and said, "Quit stalling."

Knowing there was no getting out of it, Hale decided to tell the story. "A straggler showed up here, a tough white beard trapper guy. In exchange for getting to stay, he told us about a settlement to the West. This was early on, and we still had good gas back then, so five of us got in a truck and took off."

Kinma, taking cups out of the cupboard, asked over her shoulder, "What old trapper? I don't know any trappers?"

"He pissed off Clarence, something to do with when they found Andrea. Clarence got Harrison to step in so the trapper's no longer around."

Familiar with how Harrison dealt with those he deemed troublesome, Kinma merely said, "Oh. Okay, keep going."

"Anyway, the trapper guy's directions were vague, and by the time we found the place we were all tired, starving and irritated, not to mention running low on gas. The settlement looked sort of like, I guess, an old-timey gold mining town or something."

"Gold mining town? What do you mean?"

"You know? Think of a picture of someplace in the Yukon two hundred years ago. Slab board houses built into hills, a low barn, couple of canvas tents. There was even a well with one of those hand pumps."

Kinma poured hot water into cups and asked, "Really? I've never heard of such a place. Why was it built like that?"

Wondering, for the hundredth time, how women always wanted you to tell them about something and then interrupted you as you tried to explain, Hale continued, "I don't know why. At first, I thought it was some sort of government sanctioned enclave for traditional native rights. Giving Indians the opportunity to go back to living on the land if they wanted, or something like that. There were families, and they had hunting rifles, so natives returning to their roots under some government system made sense."

She handed him his weak tea made with a tea bag on about its hundredth use. Taking the warm cup he smiled at her, enjoying the way she tried to give their life at least sliver normality. Sitting next to him she said, "Oh, okay."

He took a sip of the hot water before continuing, "We got lucky, they didn't see us, and we were in good cover, a couple hundred yards away. For hours we watched, trying to get a sense of what we were facing. Clearly, these guys were fine out in the middle of nowhere on their own, doing way better than us. There was a shed full of food, buckets of water were pumped from the well, piles of firewood everywhere. Hell, they even had a herd of these hairy goat things and two mules."

Hale hesitated, using tea drinking as a cover as he thought back, the scene remarkably clear in his mind. Women moved about the space, chatting while they did various chores, apparently taking their time despite the cold. Numerous kids, dressed in bulky coats, chased the goats and played in the snow. Men brought in a sled loaded with firewood, the mules snorting fog. The very vision of peacefulness except for the guns everywhere.

He decided he would feel foolish trying to explain this, even to Kinma. He said, "I'm not going to lie, a pretty tasty looking target. But lots of rifles and the guys looked like they could use them. I was worried we would lose..."

Kinma shifted, looking up at him. He drank some more tea. She knew him too well to buy the story. They spent endless hours together plus stories told about his early victories were common entertainment fodder amongst the Bankers.

He sighed, "Fine. It was the kids, the goddamn kids. There were kids, lots of kids. Families living their lives like families did before the Bombs. I couldn't wreck that. Hell, it was the only good thing I'd witness humans doing in forever."

She rubbed his back lightly and asked, "How'd the guys with you take that decision?"

A slight laugh. "Not well. Got tense fast. Milo was with us, he backed me. And, for once, I was glad for Harrison's rigid rules. They knew what could happen if they disobeyed an order from a patrol leader. Not a happy ride home regardless."

"I can only imagine. Bunch of guys half-starved watching women carrying food around..."

Her voice trailed off as she realized. The men didn't care about the food. They wanted the women. The story showed its violent, true color. She curled up against him, "But they aren't some native band living peacefully?"

"Yeah, a while later we found a map in a government truck, it labels the place Boulder Station. Couple of the guys recognized the name as belonging to a survivalist camp. Guess it's a bunch of nuts that hoped for the apocalypse and got their wish."

They heard yelling coming from somewhere down below followed by the familiar sounds of a fight punctuated by a woman screaming. Neither Hale nor Kinma moved, calmly waiting for the chaos to calm. Finally, the noise subsided, and she asked, "What are you going to do?"

No point in telling her about Harrison's threat, it'd only make her more afraid, cause her unfair guilt. The idea of leaving her here, alone, surrounded by beasts, made his chest ache. Regardless Hale could think of no way to escape Harrison's trap. "I need to go. If I refuse, he'll tell everyone why, get me deemed a coward. Plus, if I am out of here with some of the better men, I can talk with them in safety, come up with a plan for this place."

She seemed to understand the unsaid point that cowards could be executed as she merely asked, "When?"

"Tomorrow."

He could feel her tense up and then she began to shake slightly as the tears came. "Make me a promise."

"Okay."

"If you can get away. If you can get away somewhere safe, you do it. Don't come back here for me."

Hale finished his tea and calmly responded, "No deal."

CHAPTER SEVEN

JUNE 6, 2046
DAY THREE THOUSAND SEVEN HUNDRED AND FIFTY-SIX

"Can you believe we gotta do this every damn year?"

Jacob chose to ignore Griffith Hope, allowing Louisa to answer for them both, "Give it a rest Griff, we know you wanna be here as much as everyone else."

Her tone seemed smiling despite the condescending words. They all knew she was right, no one would miss the Longest Night Gathering. Jacob let his hand sink to Louisa's waist as Griff responded with his normal wit, "Whatever."

Jacob watched his friend take a sip from an aluminum water bottle before handing it over to him. Keeping one hand on Louisa, he lifted the bottle to his lips and drank a mouthful of the putrid liquid, forcing himself not to wince. Griff's parents called it homemade wine. Some sort of concoction made out of canned fruit, potato peelings, pine needles and whatever else they could find. He handed the bottle over to Louisa.

Jacob knew her very well, but he could never predict when she would join in the drinking and when she would beg off. This evening she took the bottle from him and drank a careful sip. A ripple of excitement rolled over him. She generally accepted his advances more eagerly on nights when she drank. That coupled with this being a special night, gave him hope. He gave her a gentle squeeze as his father, Paul, walked into the Lodge.

The twenty-three people crammed into the Lodge's dining hall broke into spontaneous applause. Paul grinned, moving through the crowd, shaking hands and accepting more slaps on the back.

Once the gratitude for Paul bringing back the supplies died down, Luke noticed Sam had slipped in. A few people quietly shook his hand, but everyone knew Sam did not like public praise, so they gave him the gift of ignoring him. He took up his usual post, against the back wall where the weathered sign him and Griff found as kids deep beneath the porch now hung. The faded, green letters read, "Sychar Lodge and Resort." They all figured it referenced some long-dead owner's last name, whoever ran the place before it became Camp Malden. However, Luke liked that name better than Malden and had filled his childhood with daydreamed fantasies about Sychar being some great hero.

Shaking his head slightly, Griff took the bottle back from Louisa and said, "Man, all they brought back was some soup and a few mangled books."

Jacob knew Sam, and Paul's supply run impressed Griff, and his words stemmed from jealousy. Griff badly wanted to go on supply runs, he wanted to walk into the Lodge and be the one everyone cheered for bringing new and helpful items into their lives.

Jacob responded, "Yeah, pretty nice to get something new to read, though."

Tina, reaching her one arm towards Griff for the bottle, interjected, "I hear that, I couldn't read The Stand one more time without going insane. And Louisa's going back through all those religion books again."

Louisa shrugged, "Some of them have good stories."

Griff handed over the bottle, growling, "A couple of books doesn't mean this place isn't still boring as hell."

The left side of her face twisted by old burn scars and her left eye permanently pinched shut, Tina's grimace after drinking the harsh drink was even more pronounced as she said, "Sure, but I'll take boring as hell with a new book over boring as hell with an old book any day."

Before they could say anything further, Jacob's uncle Leo climbed on the sturdy table in the middle of the room and everyone grew quiet. "Thanks, everyone for coming, especially Paul and Sam who hurried back to bring us treats in time for tonight."

Another round of applause and a few jovial cheers filled the space before Leo held up his hands and continued, "This year is special because, for the first time, a child born at Malden has been selected to do the first reading."

Leo climbed off the table and helped up Paulina, a pale girl of eight with long black hair who always appeared, to Jacob, to be on the verge of crying. Tonight, standing on the table and opening the Diary, Jacob thought it cruel how nervous they were making her. She managed to get the Diary open to the first page and, standing in the rustic room lit by candles and firelight, the girl began to read in a soft, almost whispering voice.

"February 4, 2036. We drove all night, going too fast for the icy roads. All the time we were driving I hated Morreign. She yanked my family into her crazy fantasy. I could barely speak to Leo, so mad at him for agreeing to go along with the stupidity. Then it happened. A huge explosion behind us lit up the entire sky. Morreign saved us, she saved us all. I don't even want to think about what happened at Thule, can't think about it."

Paulina turns the page and continues, her voice growing slightly stronger as nervousness recedes and confidence grows. "February 6, 2036. This place is in ruins, and it's always freezing, impossible to get warm. Now that I can't be mad anymore all I have left is the fear, the fear of me and my children dying of cold or hunger or some other unseen danger. Paul and Leo somehow remain cheerful, even keeping the kids mainly happy while fixing things up as best as possible. Morreign is putting on a strong face, but I think she's as afraid as I am. We all need to keep appearing strong, but I'm tired, very tired."

Another page turn. "February 13, 2036. Yesterday a strange man named Sam and his dog without a name showed up out of nowhere."

Even though everyone had heard this story told many, many times and even the children had it memorized, there are scattered claps and a couple hoots at the mention of Sam before Paulina continues, "Of course, Morreign invited him to stay without talking to any of us about it. I was worried about having a stranger here, but I guess I trust her, trust her instincts, she's been right before, and this Sam guy seems to know about the woods and that sort of stuff, knowledge we desperately need. I'm too tired and cold to write more."

Tina handed the metal bottle to Jacob. He took a painful swig before slipping it to Louisa as the girl continued to read from predetermined spots in his aunt Ainsley's diary. Telling of the arrival of the Hopes and the Walkers interspersed with more mundane but equally important occurrences such as harvesting the first garden, the return of a large supply trip, the signing of the Seven Rules, the day the fuel ran out, the marriage of Ram and Emmanuelle.

Then a heaviness took over the room as everyone knew Paulina had reached the last page of the Diary with writing on it. They had all seen the Diary and could picture the strained handwriting that replaced Ainsley's usual neat, looping style. "March 2, 2041. I think the baby is coming. I don't know why or what but I think something is wrong, the pain is different this time, and my body seems to know this isn't right. I want to tell Leo, but it'll only worry him, and there's nothing that can be done but let whatever is going to happen happen. I don't think I've missed anything from the past as much as I miss the idea of a clean, well-lit hospital full of arrogant doctors. I keep thinking back to that first night, that first day with nothing but the collapsed huts, four exhausted kids and four clueless adults pretending to be tough. I don't know how but through all our hard work and cooperation and luck we managed to rebuild life here, not only for us but for many others. I hated this place, this horrible, barren, frozen lifeboat in a sea of trees, but if the birth goes wrong, I will dearly miss this place and the community we've built."

Ainsley's intuition had been right. The baby came breach. Both mother and child died the next day in a flood of blood, chaos, gore, and agony. Every year different passages of the Diary were chosen, key ones being picked more often than others, however, every year the reading ended with that last entry. Years ago Jacob asked his mother why they always finished the reading that way, and she told him it was a reminder of all they lost building this place, a reminder they should appreciate their good fortune for being in Malden and a reminder of danger still existing.

A moment of awkward silent reflection as Paulina climbed off the table. After a minute or two, Jacob's mother's voice, strong and clear, broke the quiet. "I'll say my piece, but I'm too old and battered to get up on that damn table.

•　　•　　•

The dinner at the Longest Night Gathering was not fancy, it never was, but it was hearty and plentiful, which made Morreign glad as she watched familiar faces eating through smiles. When they first got to the Lodge, they commemorated the fleeing on its anniversary back in February but the deep, dreary winter month with everyone cold and hungry meant the event lacked a celebratory tone. People campaigned to move the party to June when fresh food and sunlight existed. As the setting sun cast the room in a pleasant glow and she felt contentedly full, there could be no question they were right to make the change.

Despite the filling meal and her husband's safe return, for some reason, Morreign felt woebegone. She felt the impulse to ruminate at length about those they lost and all they endured. Regardless, she kept her speech succinct, because tonight was not a night for mourning and, instead, she spoke easily of winter finally passing.

After the speeches, came the reading of the Seven Rules. No violence tolerated. No theft tolerated. The Committee to determine the allocation of supplies and work. The Committee determines acceptance of strangers. Location of Malden not to be disclosed. Committee members to be elected every Longest Night and two-thirds of adult inhabitants can call for re-election of Committee members at any time. The Committee to determine all punishments.

Next, they held the annual election. Everyone lined up and dropped their well-used slips of paper into Leo's well-used hat. There was a nervous moment at the beginning when he pulled out the first two votes and read out that they were both for Griffith Hope but, with the way some of the youngsters were trying to suppress giggles, Morreign figured the jokester put up a couple of the teenagers to vote for him. In the end, he only received three votes, and the Committee remained the same as it had been for the last four years: Morreign, Leo and Boris Walker.

The election rules were extremely simple. Every person over the age of fourteen wrote two names on a piece of paper which went into the hat. The three people whose names showed up the most formed the Committee. Every adult was eligible to serve and once elected they were required to sit for the year. Everyone, except for Sam. They all said they exempted Sam out of respect for his other talents but Morreign knew everyone knew they could not force Sam to do anything he did not want to and he would not want to sit in meetings about rationing and work details.

Morreign's hip ached miserably, so she was glad when the kids started clearing the dishes. She stood. The ache did not go away, but it spread out and lessened. For the thousandth time, she cursed herself for not being more careful on that measly strip of ice. Years of facing countless dangers and she wrecked her hip walking across the Clearing with an armload of firewood. She leaned against the wall with a sigh.

People were beginning to mill about, patches of conversation forming. Soon Leo would break out his harmonica, then RueAnn would open her guitar case, and a couple of ad hoc drums would be set up as the sparse furniture was moved aside. The adults and kids would dance as the teenagers snickered. When the mediocre musicians and clumsy dancers needed a break, people would take turns telling the funny, happy stories they all heard a thousand times before.

Morreign used to love nights like these. They reminded her why they did all the hard work, why they grew so many blisters and why they sacrificed so much. Tonight, though, she only felt tired. Despite what she told Paul, their supplies were adequate but dwindling. Malden could not survive on puny potatoes grown in a too short season and the occasional squirrels Sam trapped. If they could no longer supplement the food they grew and hunted with items looted from the past, not only would life be grim, she feared serious nutritional problems.

Boris Walker leaned against the wall next to her, interrupting her thoughts. "How's the hip?"

She smiled and answered, "Annoying."

Boris arrived in the second spring after the attack. Him and his girlfriend, Samantha. They were doing government research on the impact of climate change on tundra growth. They referred to it as a weeklong boondoggle designed to get them out of the office and into the fresh air. Getting out of the office saved their lives. However, they had left their daughter behind at Thule with a babysitter and, to this day, a deep, guilt-laden depression hung about the couple.

Before long, they realized the world was not going to be revived, and they could not stay in their motor home outfitted for research barely surviving off trapped prairie dogs forever. Packing up the remnants of their supplies on to their aluminum boat, they set out on the river with no idea where they might end up. Luck led them to Malden where they settled and gave birth to a second daughter, Paulina.

"I bet. Nothing of mine is broken, and I'm still sore all the time from chopping wood and turning dirt."

For a long moment, they stood in companionable silence. Boris, tall and lean with a grey beard seemed to be taking in the scene like an anthropology professor surveying a lost tribe. Morreign found him overly cerebral but respected him, a practical person without the need to joke or fill every silence with small talk. They watched the kids hurriedly clean up the dishes, all of them wanting to get done so the party could start.

As the last dirty bowl scurried into the kitchen, Boris said, "Sometimes I think some things out here might actually be better than back in the old world. I remember when I was a kid, my mom had to scold, threaten and bribe to get me and my sister to simply put our dishes into the dishwasher."

"It is different that's for sure. I made the mistake of mentioning dishwashers to Jacob a while back. Try explaining a machine that sprays super-hot water on plates to a kid who hauls water from the river and heats it over a fire before washing his face. He looked at me like I was insane."

"Yeah, there were some battered magazines in the stuff Paul and Sam brought back. One had these pictures of a football stadium packed with fans. Paulina asked if everyone in the world got to go to the game. They're our kids, but we're from different planets."

Looking over at her son, his arm possessively tight around Louisa's hip as they laughed with Griffith and Tina, she pondered this thought. When she was his age, her life revolved around text messages, one hit wonder boy bands and lip gloss. Jacob's life revolved around collecting firewood, re-reading worn out novels and not starving. Seven years old at the bombing, he vaguely recalled the past world but never really lived in it. Morreign figured this to be for the best, he could not pine for what he did not remember. Still, a part of her wished he remembered more. A family should have a history, a culture and a past they can share.

This world was more his than hers. Jacob grew up in it, she came to it late in life. His lifelong experience equipped him better than her. He carried none of the biases from the future turned past, and he lacked the desire to force things here and now to work like things in that other place and time. Further, the harshness which filled Jacob's entire life hardened him in a deep and practical way. She and Paul were merely toughened up enough to survive the radical change from a once soft lifestyle. They were forced to rapidly grow a hard crust over soft insides, they were eggs. Jacob's life made him hard through and through, he was a stone. Morreign felt useless to Jacob in this new world as any advice he sought from her would be a local asking a tourist getting off a train for directions.

Weary of her maudlin thoughts, she moved stiffly from the wall before saying to Boris, "I think I better go home and try to stretch out this damn hip before it completely ceases up. Please tell Paul when he comes looking for me that I went to lay down."

•　•　•

Hale's back ached, and the nest of blankets felt suffocating, the heat of Kinma's naked body filling the tight space despite the coldness of the room. The powerful smell of sex between unclean bodies wafted out of the bedding every time he moved. When he first came back to Thule with Kinma, Hale felt awkward sleeping with her, his reason for going to get her coming from a sense of concern about leaving a human alone in the wilderness, not desire for an indebted slave. However, after a time, she became the initiator and, with no TV or internet, sex quickly became a favorite pastime of theirs.

Despite their intense activity, Hale could not fall asleep. To be fair, he did not really want to sleep. He merely laid there, in the tangle of blankets, trying not to think as ideas raced through his mind as he listened to Kinma breathing softly, enjoying the feel of her hot skin and the smell of her hair.

Of course, dawn did not care about what Hale faced, and it arrived undaunted and undelayed. Hale managed to creep out of the blankets without waking Kinma. He did not know what to say. She knew everything he could tell her, she must know by now. However, he stumbled pulling on his heavy boots, and one thumped loudly against the wall.

Wrapped in a blanket, her long black hair a pretty, tangled mess, she smiled at him. He opened his mouth to speak, but no words came. She stepped forward and kissed him gently on the cheek, saying, "I love you."

"Me too."

"I'll miss you."

"I'll miss you, too."

She let go and stepped back, holding the smile on her lips even as her eyes filled with tears. Hale knew she was afraid. She would be left here, alone, in the grungy darkness surrounded by a band of deviants severed from humanity and led by a sociopath. He also knew she was afraid for him. He could not speak, not only because he did not know the words to say but because his own fear would be clear in his voice and worry her even more.

He nodded and smiled back slightly before turning the knob and stepping out of the apartment that once belonged to a woman he only briefly knew, a woman named Rosa. Standing in the dark hallway, he tried to remember the night he first came here ten years ago to sleep with a stranger he picked up at the bar but he could not. That night occurred in someone else's life. With a deep breath, he walked away from his decade-long sanctuary.

•　　•　　•

The harsh, crab apple wine made Jacob's stomach ache and his head swim. With the party winding down, the young men and women of Malden snuck off to the woods behind the Lodge. They built up a fire, another bottle of wine showed up from somewhere and, as always, Griff loudly led the conversation.

"All I'm saying is that it should be the young guys, me and Jacob and Hurley, going out there. We've got more energy, we can travel farther and can come back with more than scraps. Go out and find things that'll really make a difference around here."

Louisa and Jacob knew it was pointless to argue with Griff when he was in this mood but Jacob's cousin Emma always let his ruminations get under her skin. She poked at an old wound, "Yeah, like last time? Maybe you can get so sick you need to be carried back again."

Griff had gone on a scouting and hunting trip in the fall but, after a few days of sleeping rough, he caught a fever. The others on the trip ended up putting him on a makeshift litter to bring him back to Malden. He appeared to shrug it off, but Jacob knew his friend's pride was irreparably wounded.

As Griff began to provide his familiar retorts, Jacob, feeling emboldened by the wine, took Louisa's hand and gently led her away from the firelight. Once they were several steps away, she said, "Don't understand how those two can have the same argument over and over."

The usual gossiping held no interest for Jacob tonight, and he kept walking, responding aloofly, "Yeah, I'm tired of it."

In behind the Lodge, on the edge of a gully, stood a clump of willows with their curving branches arching above them to make a hidden alcove. Tonight, with the white moon massive in the sky, the dewy grass shone like silver, and the budding leaves made a soft rustling sound all around them. Jacob gently turned Louisa to face him.

A head shorter than him, she stepped in close, sliding her face in under his chin. Jacob knew this move, even though they were closer he could not kiss her and if he could not kiss her, the evening could not progress as he wanted it to. He sighed with barely masked frustration as she said, "Hold me, hold me for a minute."

For, what seemed like ages, they merely stood in the glistening woods listening to the leaves in the breeze. Finally, Jacob could take no more delay, and he stepped back, lifting her chin with his index finger. They kissed, chastely at first but Jacob pushed forward. Slowly, cautiously, like a child trying to pet a frightened puppy, Jacob moved his hand up inside her loose jacket. She did not stop him when his cold hand touched her warm, smooth skin and he grew bolder.

It felt clumsy, his hand cupping her surprisingly heavy breast under the layers of clothes but the pleasant sensation made him bolder. He pulled her tight, pressing into her waist which sent a tremor into his gut as he reached around to squeeze her backside. For a time he enjoyed holding her in each hand as they kissed sloppily. She let out a sigh and shifted against him causing a powerful sensation to ripple through him as she rose up on her toes to nuzzle his neck.

Taking this as a profoundly positive sign, Jacob dropped his hands to her hips, fumbling with her belt buckle. He managed to open the belt, but before he could undo her jeans, Louisa pressed in again, sliding her head back under his chin and locking his hands between them. He tried to step back so they could continue but she held him fast, whispering through her heavy breathing, "I'm sorry."

Pained frustration immediately replaced excited eagerness. He thought, this time, would be the time. An odd rage coursed through him but he tried to hide the anger in his voice as he knew it would do no good. "Why not?"

He hated the tone in his voice, the whiny sound. Talking into his chest, she said, "I'm scared. I don't know how to explain, I'm simply scared. I want to, I really do, deeply, but, I don't know, I'm scared. Scared about after, about us after, I guess."

"Scared? Of what? I love you, you love me. We are obviously meant to be together, how can you question that?"

The words were true. When he first saw her, terrified and lying silently on that musty bed in the Lodge, Jacob knew. Despite them only being children, he knew he would be with her forever, knew that as clearly as he knew the sun would rise and the poplar leaves would fall. Every minute of the millions of minutes they spent together since that first moment reinforced the certainty of that for him. Tonight, however, his words sounded shallow, accusatory and pleading rather than caring and truthful.

"No. No. I don't question that. I don't know. I try to explain, I want to explain, I really do…"

Jacob knew he should interject, console her and remain patient. But he was tired of being patient. He let her trailing words die on the breeze, not letting her off the hook. She continued, "You belong here. Hell, your family created here. I'm, I'm alone here. Alone everywhere I suppose. It's different for me."

Jacob heard this before, but every time she tried to explain he could not understand. She was not alone, being with him kept her from being alone, yet she always stopped. He did not want to have this debate again, not tonight. He stepped away.

"I'm going back to the fire. Stephanie was going to tell me about her plan for setting up a rabbit hutch."

With that, Jacob turned and strode out of the willows.

CHAPTER EIGHT

JUNE 7, 2046
DAY THREE THOUSAND SEVEN HUNDRED AND FIFTY-SEVEN

From his balcony, Harrison watched the group of fifteen men preparing to leave in the early morning light. He felt something he figured to be akin to jealousy at the way they listened to Hale, eagerly carrying out his commands while laughing and joking with one another. Harrison always received obedience but never so willingly or happily.

Uncertainty never troubled Harrison for long, he now knew, without doubt, he wanted Hale to fail. Success would mean a new source of supplies, buy him time for everyone to adjust to being more self-sufficient. However, it would also mean more respect for Hale making it harder for Harrison to retain his control. Having lived a decade being in charge, a decade of never taking orders or needing to ask permission, Harrison knew being relegated to a pawn was not an option.

Failure would remove Hale from the equation. Failure might also mean fourteen others being killed. Reduced numbers used to be a great concern as it meant fewer men for protection and for going to find supplies, but now Harrison figured fewer numbers meant less need for supplies and less strong men to oppose him internally. Regardless, if they all died that would not be best, never good to lose useful soldiers especially if their deaths could be blamed on him, so Harrison decided such an outcome should be avoided but, if necessary, it could be tolerated.

"You wanted to see me?"

Clarence's voice came from behind him, the fact that someone actually startled him was more startling than actually being startled. Harrison needed to regain his alertness, maintain his focus, the strain of running the Bank was starting to show. He turned from the window and said, "Come in. We need to talk about this trip."

Clarence sat on a stool by the counter. Ever since Harrison killed the Colonel and led Clarence out of that frozen forest, the helicopter pilot followed him loyally, realizing Harrison to be the sole reason for his survival, covering him in the cloak of a savior. Harrison rewarded him well for that loyalty, but he knew the others did not respect the pilot in the slightest, allowing him to exist at the Bank only because of Harrison's protection.

Years ago Clarence tried to take a woman, but a scrawny original member named Bautista already had already claimed her as his own. Clarence ambushed Bautista, attacking from behind like a coward but, despite the surprise, Bautista immediately overtook Clarence, landing a flurry of blows as the pilot turtled on the floor. Harrison needed to physically step in and throw Bautista off. Since then Clarence was seen as nothing but Harrison's dog.

Regardless, Clarence was fast thinking and generally got things done as ordered. He asked, "Sure. What's the plan?"

Harrison calmly said, "A win. But not a complete win."

•   •   •

Barely out of the rubble and remnants of Thule and Hale's legs were already aching. Before the gas went bad, he only rode a bike as a child, laughing internally whenever he saw an adult in their stupid tight pants and plastic helmets. Now, he needed to pedal.

"Come on, it's going to be a goddamn month 'fore we get anywhere at this pace."

Milo and Taco rolled up next to Hale, they were both pulling loaded carts behind their bikes, yet they were not even breathing hard. They were both originals at the Bank, former military men who came with Harrison back to Thule from the destroyed base. They had spent much of the last decade on patrol, pedalling was like walking to them.

Hale answered Milo, "Yeah, I guess I'm out of practice."

Milo said, "You mean, you fat."

Taco laughed his distinctive cackle before speeding a dozen feet or so up ahead. Hale laughed as well, "Ain't no one fat anymore."

"True that. Man, I miss worrying about how many calories stuff had," another chuckle and he continued, "Remember when we took over that farmer's house way back when?"

Of course Hale remembered. Besides sex and fighting, storytelling was the main form of entertainment within the Bank and tales of successful patrols were the favorite genre. The tale of the farmer's house got heavy play.

Taco, his bright blue jacket flapping in the breeze, circled back and pulled in beside Milo. Without looking back, Hale could sense a few of the others creeping up closer on their bikes. He knew they were worried. Going on a lengthy patrol to face an extremely nasty foe when the guy in charge pulled himself out of the killing business years ago had them all concerned. This was Milo's way of helping.

"Sure, I remember. Hard to forget that one."

"All those jars of crab apples and raspberries in the basement, we ate ourselves sick."

The version of the story told to the Bank en mass was somewhat censored. Even though common practice, speaking of how patrol members ate their fill of the choicest supplies before returning was considered taboo. Hale caught the hint Milo was dropping, time to bring the other men on this patrol into their full history, remind them this was not Hale's first trip, let them know that he would not hesitate to do what needed to be done.

Hale said, "Taco threw up all over the damn place if I remember right. I didn't get many of the apples."

Milo took up the cause. "Yeah, yeah. We pulled that arrow outta your leg and set your busted arm. Me and Taco ate all night while you slept."

One of the men behind them piped up, "I thought it was a crossbow bolt?"

Falling into a familiar rhythm, Milo told the tale. Gas was still good back then, and they were in a truck when they found a snowmobile track winding its way off-road. Unable to follow by vehicle, they split up, the other men stayed to guard the truck while Milo, Taco, and Hale followed the tracks on foot. Unfortunately, a storm blew in, freezing the men and obscuring everything.

If they found something, the plan was to turn and head back to the truck, get the others and return in force. However, with the blowing snow, they got too close to the farmyard without knowing it, and the damn dogs caught their scent. Three massive, hairy beasts, bounding through the drifts in a snarling, barking mass. Hale drew his bow but let the dogs get close, Milo and Taco crouched next to him and followed his lead, shooting right after he did. The dogs collapsed, but their warning barks echoed about them.

An arrow thunked into the snow, an inch from Taco's foot, followed by a second and a third. Running back was not an option, they would be easy targets for whoever was up in the windows. Firing blindly at the windows would be useless at this distance, a waste of their arrows. Hale, without hesitation, slipped his bow onto his back and charged the house, trusting Milo and Taco to follow.

Hale took over the telling. Describing how projectiles screamed past him as he ran through the deep snow. Somehow he reached the narrow porch without a puncture but, unsurprisingly, the door was locked. He drew his belt knife, reared back and kicked at the sturdy wood. Nothing moved. As he kicked again, Taco and Milo both darted past and crashed into the door in unison. It splintered inward, spilling all three of them into the house's foyer.

A woman's scream came from their left, and an arrow flew high above their heads as they stumbled to regain their feet. A man yelled, "Don't move, turn and leave right now or I put this one in your guts."

Looking up, they saw a heavyset man in a ski-doo suit with a high-tech hunting bow leveled at them, his arm shaking from the tension. Next, to him, a woman fumbled at trying to nock an arrow in her fiberglass bow, more of a toy than a weapon but probably effective enough at the close range. If they turned, surely the arrows would be immediately buried in their backs. From his crouch, Hale charged forward like a Pro Bowl nose tackle.

The man fired. An arrow pierced his left leg, but Hale's momentum carried him into the amateur archer, taking them both to the floor. From atop the man, Hale stabbed downward repeatedly until his foe moved no longer. Behind him, he heard the wet sounds and screams of the woman being killed by his companions.

Hale's sense of relief that the violence was over proved short-lived. Thumping footsteps sounded above, at least two people moving quickly. Their options were limited. If they tried to leave they would be easy targets from the upstairs windows. If they headed upstairs, their opponents would have the high ground.

Forcing himself onto his injured leg, Hale looked at Milo and Taco who merely nodded their agreement, best to be the attackers. Milo moved to try and take the lead, but Hale ignored the pain and subtly stepped in front of him to slowly climb the narrow stairs as he stowed his knife to draw his bow.

Hale reached the top step without being attacked but, as his toe touched the upstairs' landing a glimpse of movement came from his right, and he instinctively turned to shield himself. A heavy shovel smashed into his arm with a sickening crunch, but he managed to maintain his balance enough to swivel back and loose the arrow. An elderly man in overalls slumped to the floor, struck by a lucky shot to the throat.

A floorboard creaked, and Hale instinctively leaned back as a crossbow bolt sunk into the wall where his chest had been. He dove over the body on the floor, crashed into the wall across the landing and came up in an awkward stance before rapidly pulling the arrow from the old man's throat, drawing back his bow and firing the bloody missile in one practiced movement before immediately nocking a new arrow.

A woman, also elderly, stood in a dirty parka, a homemade crossbow hanging limply from her hand, blood seeping around the arrow buried in her heart. She stared at him and opened her mouth to speak but no words came; she merely sunk to her knees and fell onto her face.

Behind the fallen woman stood a frail girl of about thirteen in a grimy, yellow coat. Tears made trails down her dirty face as she shook with fear and pointed a kitchen knife at him with a trembling hand. Straining to hold back his bowstring's sixty pounds of draw with his ruined arm, this girl's bleak future flashed through Hale's mind in an instant. He might be able to protect her from the men during the trip back to Thule. But, even if he did manage to keep the patrol members off her, there were few women within the Bank, and they spent most of their time fulfilling the disgusting desires of the roughest and meanest of the men. Harrison would view this girl as spoils of their victory, another supply to be used for increasing the morale of the men. Hale let loose his arrow and did not miss.

As the men now pedaled towards another violent encounter, Hale and Milo both left out the dead girl at the end of the story, jumping ahead to talk of gorging themselves on preserves.

•　•　•

The ingenuity behind the sawmill continued to impress Jacob despite the endless hours he toiled over it. A canal dug out from the river bank created a channel of fast-moving water, well hidden behind thick willows and reeds. Built on a base of stacked stones, a wooden waterwheel dipped into the channel to turn a series of gears which eventually turned a circular saw blade.

Malden members told and re-told the story of how the sawmill came to be. Early on, Leo and Sam were out scavenging on the snowmobile and came across an abandoned, backwoods lumber operation. Extremely tired of the extreme effort needed to prepare firewood, the two discussed hauling the saw back to Malden. However, without a power supply, the system would be useless, and they immediately discarded the idea. The next morning, however, when they reached the river on their return trip to Malden, the plan struck Leo like lightning, and he made them return to get the heavy blade.

The waterwheel instantly became invaluable. When the river ran fast, two men could section three sticks of firewood a minute, a task that could take half an hour and a lake of sweat using regular handsaws. Regardless, the morning after the Longest Night celebration, Jacob was cursing the machine as its clacking wooden gears rang like hammer blows inside his throbbing head.

"Quit trying to force the damn thing, you're gonna bust something," Griff snarled at Jacob as they fed a stubborn log into the saw.

Jacob barked back, "You worry about your end and I'll worry about mine."

Even though she was a few years younger than Jacob and Griff, Tina persisted in wanting to spend her time with them, even if their work was more physically demanding than what might be otherwise assigned to a fully able-bodied girl her age. Now using her one arm to sling the cut wood onto the sled, Tina called out, "Enough. I'm tiring of you two bickering all bloody day."

The two boys returned to silently working. Despite his response, Jacob knew he was trying to hurry the process because, if they managed to work through the pile of logs the men falling timber upriver floated down to them, they could take a break, and his sore head could use a rest. Moving with the silent choreography of men who worked together repeatedly, they re-set the log to let the saw do its work three more times and were done.

Jacob said, "Something must've gone wrong up there, haven't sent anything down in a while."

Griff answered, "Probably as hungover and tired as us after last night."

Tina tossed the last of the wood on to the sled as she laughed, "No one is as hungover today as you two fools."

They moved down to the riverbank to wait for more timber. Griff plucked up the lightweight, yellow handled axe he somehow managed to co-op as his own years ago and tossed it between his hands as he asked, "You talk to Louisa this morning?"

Jacob normally ate breakfast in the common room with the other single people, but he did not want to face Louisa, so he snuck out early to eat with his parents this morning. "Nah. Did you see her?"

Griff answered, "Sure. She didn't say much though. How bad a fight was it?"

Griff's perceptiveness would surprise most people in Malden. His loud, occasionally abrasive, nature made him come across as rude and uncaring but, normally when they were alone, he could talk smartly and with profound insight.

Today, however, Jacob did not want to discuss Louisa. He was no longer mad, but he was not yet ready to eat his dignity and apologize once again. He mumbled, "It's alright."

Griff asked, "She still not overly welcoming?"

Tina flung a pebble at him, "Hey. Mind your own business, oh, right you ain't got no business."

Jacob picked up a handful of his own rocks and threw them at the ice bobbing down the river instead of responding, letting Tina and Griff fire barbs back and forth at each other.

"Careful there Tina, not like the world is filling up your dance card. And don't blame your melted face, I think it's all about your personality."

Looking down at the stump of her arm before looking knowingly at her own right hand, Tina responded, "You're right, I guess you at least got one more girlfriend than I do."

That crudeness got Griff to laugh. "Good one. But I'll have you know I'm currently in intense negotiations to get with your mother."

"Great, I'll be happy to tell her that news, she likes a good laugh."

Griff spun the light axe, lifted it over his shoulder and flung it easily at a poplar tree. Shorter than a normal axe, longer than a hatchet, it perfectly flipped end over end twice before burying into the soft wood with a satisfying thunk. Griff said, "Sure, go ahead, women find my sense of humor very attractive."

Tina moved to retrieve the tool turned toy from the tree, and looked to Jacob and said, "It is your business Jake, but I wouldn't push it. She'll come 'round soon enough, and you'll both be happier if she can get there on her own terms."

Of course, Griff interjected, "Andas I've told you, you're a lucky asshole. You don't want to be stuck with the scraps I have to pick over."

This was a common refrain from Griff. Other than Louisa, and Tina who was too much like a sister to Griff and Jacob to be considered romantically, the list of available women around their age only included two more names, both of which despised Griff. This meant his prospects were essentially nil. The fact that he still advised Jacob to act properly in order to keep Louisa should have been taken as a sign of his true friendship but, instead, Jacob found the advice annoying.

Instead of joining the conversation, Jacob stepped in front of Tina to pull the axe from the tree. He turned and flung it at a log near the bank. The three of them played this axe throwing game for endless hours and, while Griff was best, it was rare any of them missed easy throws anymore, this time, however, the axe head glanced off the birch wood and clattered into the shallow water. As they hurried to retrieve the valuable item they saw them. An elk cow with two calves emerging way down the river on the far bank.

For a long moment, the three merely stared at the half ton of meat calmly drinking in front of them. Game was scarce. Big game like elk was practically extinct.

Griff whispered to Jacob, "Too far?"

Understanding he was asking if they could make a bow shot from that extreme distance, Jacob shook his head. Their bows, based on Leo's design and carefully crafted out of scavenged rebar and pulleys leaned against the nearby wood sled as they always kept them close. However, even if they lucked into hitting something, at that distance, an arrow would not come close to penetrating elk hide. They would only be scaring away the meat.

The aluminum boat brought by Boris and Samantha to Malden, now with numerous patches, was stored up by the tree line. Griff grabbed the axe from the water and tossed it up onto the grass as Tina and Jacob hurried towards the trees. They carefully and silently moved the simple craft back to the rushing, freezing water.

As they climbed into the boat, the powerful pull of the fast-moving river became obvious to Jacob. He shared a look with his friends, knowing they would have the same worry. Griff whispered, "Do we have to try?"

Jacob and Tina both mouthed the same answer, "Yeah."

"Water's really moving."

Fear and uncertainty filled him, but Jacob only nodded sternly. They simply could not let that much meat get away. Jacob considered telling Tina she should wait on shore, but he knew she would not listen. He pushed the boat into the current and jumped in.

They immediately got sucked out to the middle of the river, instantly moving at an alarming speed. It was difficult to keep his balance, but Jacob pushed down his panic, moved into a crouch and leveled his bow at the elk as the boat rapidly neared them.

For a heartbeat, the animals merely looked at the strange sight hurtling down the river then, with a shiver, the cow turned and darted out of the water, heading for the brush with one calf immediately behind her. The smaller calf, front legs in the rushing water, stayed confused for an extra breath and Jacob fired.

His shot was off slightly, the arrow sinking into the animal's shoulder rather than its neck. The calf tried to turn but stumbled, falling into the fast, frigid river. The stampeding water grabbed the fallen elk and pulled it in despite its struggles. Griff cursed, "Shit."

With the excitement of the hunt, Jacob forgot their own peril as he nocked another arrow and commanded, "Hurry, get us in front of it."

Using the boat's oars, Griff and Tina fought the current with all their strength, managing to pull the boat over a few feet, so they passed near the flailing elk. Jacob fired into the frothing water and then fired again. The struggling animal stilled, floating calmly along the speeding current. Jacob said, "Ok, I got it. Slow us down."

Panic filled Tina's voice, "Slow us down? Are you kidding?"

Jacob hurried to sit next to Griff and grabbed onto Tina's oar. Plunging the wood into the water, it took all his might not to have it yanked out of their hands, however, the extra drag did slow the boat enough to let the elk catch up to them. "Ok, it's getting closer. Hold on."

Through gritted teeth, Griff said, "You know we're very quickly getting very bloody far from home."

An obvious point. They would need to get the boat and the elk back to Malden and, at this crazy speed, the upriver return distance was getting long in a hurry. But Jacob could see his kill floating behind them, and that's all that mattered to him. He imagined dropping the carcass at the door of the Lodge as everyone came rushing to clap him on the back and to thank him for the fresh meat. He could hear his dad's praise and see his mom's approving look. More importantly, he could picture Louisa seeing him as a man instead of the boy she grew up with.

He growled, "We're getting that goddamn elk. Pull on the damn oars."

•　•　•

Harrison watched from the corner, hidden in the deep shadows left by two weak lanterns. He knew the twins were not actually stupid, they simply chose not to waste energy thinking too deeply, finding it more fun to live on pure impulse.

Harrison found them two weeks after the Bombs, living in the rubble of the officers' quarters, burning furniture and files for heat while drinking bar supplies for sustenance. Despite their difficult situation, the two heavily muscled men with long blonde hair and standing nearly seven feet, remained shockingly fit. Also, they did not seem concerned that strange men were pointing rifles at them. Harrison immediately knew they could be valuable additions. Thankfully they both agreed to his proposal of joining with matching shrugs.

Initially, they stayed to themselves but seemed contently loyal to Harrison mostly because he made sure they were well fed and well rewarded. Over time, they talked more with their European accents Harrison could not place and, while they only spoke in vagaries, it became clear they were military trained by some unnamed entity and were sent to places where conflicts erupted to engage in unnamed tasks.

Upon seeing their highly skilled violence and the innate way the twin brothers fought together as one massive beast, the other men gave them a wide berth and were especially careful to not offend them. Harrison remembered the night, after a particularly savage encounter with a truckload of survivors which the twins dominated, a brave soul, overcome with the adrenaline of winning a fight, took one look at their immense, blonde beards covered in the blood of others and nicknamed them the Vikings. The other men laughed, but the twins merely glared at this attempt at inclusion before both striking drown the man in perfect unison and stomping him to death. Only after the murder did the twins discuss name between themselves and decide it was acceptable.

Despite the occasional outburst like this, Harrison figured they were content at the Bank. They clearly enjoyed violence and were smart enough to realize life at the Bank put them in a great position to engage in that pastime with little chance of any negative repercussions. Plus, Harrison knew enough to ensure the tasks he had them perform involved indulging in the instinctive behaviors they craved.

Tonight, the Vikings had cornered Kinma at the end of the second-floor hallway which served as the makeshift laundry room. In the dimness, Harrison could not make out her features, but it appeared that she was doing a decent job of maintaining her composure despite the massive threats moving in on her. One twin, chuckled, "You think Hale'll make it back? Them Survival pricks are pretty tough. Got lotta of guns too."

The other Viking took a step forward, shoving a clothes' rack out of his way and added, "I'm ok that he up and decided to leave us at home like a fool, for sure he gonna get killed without us there. Suppose he wanted us to look out for his wifey wife while he was away?"

Kinma casually ducked under a line as she stepped back, the hanging blankets providing only pretend protection as she quipped, "Nah, I think he left you two guys behind because you'd eat too much out there."

Impressive banter considering the situation. The Vikings were proud of their appetites despite it being an odd thing to take pride in when food was scarce. Her friendly jab a smart attempt to dissuade the impending attack. While both brothers laughed, they continued to move slowly toward her.

There was nowhere for her to go. They could have easily rushed her, but Harrison figured they were enjoying the stalking, a form of entertainment. Moving in unison, as usual, they knocked the clothesline down, the damp blankets crumpling to the floor, leaving Kinma standing with her back to the wall and nothing between her and them.

For a moment, both merely stared at her hungrily. She looked tiny as she tried not to cower. Harrison ensured the two brutes never lacked for female companionship but, like most, they always desired that which they had not had before. One feinted to slip out to her left causing her to turn and kick out at empty air with a pathetic, feminine grunt. The other Viking, anticipating his brother's move, slipped in behind and pinned her arms to her sides as he lifted her into the air.

Feet dangling, Kinma struggled in the huge man's grasp and managed to land a booted foot against the other's chest. One brother laughed at the other as he struggled for a moment to catch his breath before laughing himself and then perfunctorily punching Kinma in the stomach. She doubled over but kept weakly kicking.

Having witnessed innumerable struggles since the Bombs, Harrison could tell the difference between one borne from panic and one borne from rage. Strangely, this struggle seemed borne of both. Kinma managed to stomp the Viking holding her with a boot heel, cutting off his laughter.

With both now struck an annoying blow, they were done playing for fun. The Vikings roughly slammed her against the wall as if they were slapping a freshly caught fish against the side of a boat. Each grasped the neck of her shirt, pulled her back up and, together, ripped the worn fabric apart. Her sweaty skin shone in the dim light, and she let out a scream of frustration. One Viking clapped a heavy hand against her throat, pinning her to the wall while the other fought to loosen her belt as Kinma pumped her knees like pistons.

Another punch, more pressure on her throat, a harsh slap. The jeans were pulled down. Finally, her legs stopped struggling as rough hands pulled down her underwear. Sobbing. Harrison heard sobbing. He stepped from the shadow.

"Alright guys, that should be enough."

He spoke calmly but used a commanding tone. The Vikings stopped and looked over their respective shoulders at him. Identical confusion clear on their identical faces. One of them said, "What are–"

Interrupting, Harrison said, "You head on out of here. Leave her with me."

The Vikings must have been wondering if they had been set up. Harrison casually rested his hand on the sidearm on his hip. His gun held their last seven bullets. Normally the gun stayed locked in his room with the invaluable ammunition always in his pocket as he did not need to constantly remind people of his power. Today he wanted the reminder, clear and visible and obvious.

"It's ok. Go."

The hulking men slipped by Harrison but hesitated to tower above him for an instant, a silent indication from the violent men that they were dissatisfied. A year ago such a display would not have been dared, even by them. Harrison would need to do something to repay them for his deceptive tease of telling them to attack her and then stopping them. However, that was a problem for a later time. He turned his attention to Kinma.

In the brief delay, Kinma managed to pull her underwear and pants back on, and she was standing defiantly.

"You injured?"

She merely glared at him. Kinma would know he put the Vikings up to the attack as there was no reason for him to be in the laundry area. He was sending a message, telling her he could do whatever he wanted with her. Harrison moved forward and said, "He's not coming back."

Wrath filled her face as she spat out, "You don't know that. You don't know."

"I do know. And you need to decide, right here, right now, how you are going to deal with that certainty."

The hatred in her eyes could almost be felt physically. Perhaps he misjudged this woman, underestimated her spirit. Perhaps she would not bend as he hoped. Her popularity was not as powerful as Hale's, but she was well-liked for her common sense, her strength and her link to Hale. Further, he could not merely exile or kill an attractive woman, the men would revolt at the wastefulness. Her voice might become even louder when Hale became a martyr so Harrison decided he would be better off if she spoke in unison with him.

Her rage seemed to dissipate somewhat underneath fearful concern, her hands moved to cover her chest, and she asked sternly, "How do you know? How do you know he's not coming back?"

"I know. It's taken care of."

Lowering her gaze slightly, Harrison was surprised when, instead of arguing, Kinma calmly asked, "What are my options?"

"You don't speak out against me, and I pair you with a decent man. You say anything I don't like, and you become communal property with no protection from me."

Her eyes flicked up to his. The life of an unpaired woman was beyond miserable. Those women abandoned into communal purgatory became living, breathing tragedies. For a moment, they merely looked at one another before she lowered her gaze, gathered up her clothes and hurried away.

CHAPTER NINE

JUNE 7, 2046
DAY THREE THOUSAND SEVEN HUNDRED AND FIFTY-SEVEN

With a soft thunk, the elk's hoof hit the aluminum of the boat. Through force of will Jacob, Griff and Tina had managed to slow the boat enough. Now they needed to get the animal onboard.

Releasing the oar he shared with Tina, Jacob said, "Ok, hold as best you can, I'll try to haul it in."

Tina put the oar in her armpits, wrapped her good arm over her stump and hunched over the oar as she grunted her ascent.

Moving carefully to the prow of the boat, Jacob knelt, but, with the icy water rushing about, the elk kept disappearing and reappearing. Leaning far over the hull, his heart pounding, he plunged his hands into the water and managed to get his freezing fingers around a foreleg. Pushing against the metal of the boat, his legs pulling with all his waning strength, the elk slid out of the moving water, landing on top of Jacob as he fell back.

He heard Griff cheer as he tried to catch the breath being pushed out of him by the weight of the wet, dead animal. They did it. The calf would not be a lot of meat but it enough for a decent feast, a feast where Jacob would be the man of honour. He began to struggle out from under the corpse when it twitched. Then it twitched again.

The once dead calf, apparently rejuvenated by being out of the icy water, started kicking and clamouring. A hoof struck Jacob in the stomach and then in the thigh as the elk made its way onto uncertain feet. With a lurch and a jump, the terrified calf charged straight over Griff, bounded off Tina's back and into the water.

Unsure what happened, Jacob stumbled to his knees and crawled to Griff who had slumped over. Blood gushed from a gash crossing his forehead. His friend appeared conscious, but his eyes did not seem to be focussing. Panic atop of panic. Grabbing his friend by the shoulders, Jacob shook him, gently at first, then harder.

Tina moved beside him, apparently unhurt. "Careful, don't shake him too hard."

Jacob stopped, and Griff's blurry eyes blinked a few times as he muttered, "Enough, damn it, enough, my head's gonna split."

Relief as Jacob asked, "You ok?"

Griff wiped at the blood pouring down his face, looked at his red hand and said, "Doesn't look like I am, but I think so. You two?"

Soreness in his ribs and leg but Jacob did not think anything was broke. "Hurt but ok."

Tina said, "Going to have a decent bruise on my shoulder but that's it."

Sitting back up Griff, asked, "What the hell happened?"

Jacob pulled off his scarf and started to wrap it around Griff's head. "Guess the elk was only stunned or something. Once he got out of the water and felt something solid under him, he decided to bolt."

Tina asked, "Damn it, where're the oars?"

"What?"

Looking around, she said, "The oars. I dropped my damn oar, and I don't see Griff's."

Frantically looking around, Jacob could not see them in the boat. Looking out into the water, he could see the elk behind them thrashing about the ice floats as it vainly fought against its new found freedom, but the oars were nowhere to be seen. With a sigh, he said, "They're gone."

Holding the scarf to his damaged head, Griff said, "Yeah. That went about as shitty as possible, didn't it?"

Tina, looking back towards Malden, responded, "Yeah. I hate agreeing with you, but I think that's a fair assessment."

With no oars and the boat in the middle of the wide river, they were helpless to stop. They sat in silence with their injuries and watched the trees on the distant banks speeding by, the powerful current inexorably pulling them farther and farther away from home.

• • •

Closing the door of the apartment behind her, Kinma locked the deadbolt knowing it to be pointless as Harrison kept keys to every lock in the Bank. She leaned against the wall and let herself slip to the floor. Fear or anger or humiliation should have been the dominant emotions, but they were all absent. All she felt was a deep loneliness.

She came north as a teenager with her mother, a strong single parent who took a job cleaning work camps in the frozen dark because it paid slightly better than cleaning hotel rooms in the city and, more importantly, because it would remove her rebellious daughter from the bad influences of urban life. At the time, Kinma hated the idea of moving to the wilderness, away from her friends and civilization but, once she got over her adolescent rage, she came to appreciate the outdoors. Life was far from easy, but she tempered the hardships with camping, fishing, and hikes. The night the war started, she was sleeping next to a robust campfire, nestled in a thermal sleeping bag inside a cave-like crevice a good four miles from Thule. She heard the Bombs and knew enough to stay put, far away from the chaos.

Two scared soldiers, wandering about confused and hungry, found her a few days later. Kinma would have viewed them as a threat, but they seemed far more interested in the soup of dried lentils she was making than any type of malice. They explained to her how the world had ended and all hopes of finding her mother painfully faded.

One of them was heavily feverish with flu and died within days. The other soldier seemed to have been entirely numbed by whatever horrors he saw before escaping the attack. She and the traumatized young man stayed in the cave, living off her wilderness skills for almost a year.

The attackers from the Bank came at dusk. The firefight brief. The young soldier firing blindly as a half-dozen men shot him down from all directions. Kinma immediately scurried deeper into the crevice where she remained hidden while the men looted her friend's corpse and took all their supplies. Huddled as far back as possible she saw a flashlight beam wave across the cramped space.

A man's face. A scruffy, reddish beard and grey, icy eyes. Their gazes met, and Kinma feared she was about to be killed or, likely, worse. He lifted his finger to his lips, telling her to remain silent and then stepped back.

For three days after she struggled like never before. Completely alone after burning her companion's body and, with the stores, she set aside, and winter deepening, it became clear to Kinma she would not survive to see spring yet she could think of no option beyond staying put. The image of the man with piercing eyes replayed in her tired mind each night when she tried to sleep. Then, on the fourth morning, the face with the reddish beard magically reappeared in the crevice opening and introduced itself as Hale.

They remained together ever since. There were only two other women in the Bank back then, but Hale told Harrison that Kinma would be staying with him and him alone. Kinma never learned what that demand cost Hale, but she was certain it was not a cheap bargain. Like a miracle come to life, the man with the grey eyes continually treated her with kindness even while surrounded by immense cruelty.

Now, all alone again, alone in a place far harsher than even a frozen cave and all she could think about was how much she missed him. Tears were starting to escape her eyes when a soft knock on the door startled her.

"Hello, Kinma?"

A quiet woman's voice. Her first instinct was to ignore the knock, pretend she was not there, but then she looked around the dark, empty apartment and slowly rose to her feet. Opening the door revealed Seanah.

The petite woman held Kinma's bright yellow toque with the wide, black band. Seanah's bottom lip was split, but an injury on a woman did not even register as noticeable within the Bank. Kinma did not know Seanah well, she used to be a nurse of some sort, arrived two years ago and spent most of her time working in the kitchen while Kinma dealt more with repairs and making things. She lived with three of the men under some sort of arrangement which seemed tolerable from a distance, at least in comparison to how some women were treated.

"Hi Kinma, I found this in the laundry area. It's a good hat, I know you like it, didn't want it to go missing on you."

Instinctively, Kinma touched her hair. Feeling foolish she said, "Oh, thanks, it must have fallen off, you know, while I was hanging things up..."

The angry red mark on Kinma's cheek must have been obvious and the moisture filling her eyes was unmistakable. She was never mean to Seanah, but she supposed she always knew the younger woman looked up to her and she realized, now, that she did little to help make her life better. And Seanah knew nothing like the loving relationship between Kinma and Hale. Kinma figured seeing her knocked off her lofty podium probably gave the mistreated woman joy.

Dumbly, Kinma reached for the silly looking hat but, instead of handing it over, the frail woman stepped forward and wrapped her skinny arms around her. Feeling the touch of another person caused the impending tears to burst forward. Seanah whispered, "He'll be back, don't worry, Hale's strong and smart, he'll make it back."

Sobbing without control, Kinma asked, "But, if he doesn't?"

"You'll be ok, you're also strong and smart."

Seanah released her and stepped back, handing over the bright yellow hat before turning to go. Kinma took the hat, not sure if she could ever wear it again without recalling the attack, but then she quickly put it on and called out softly, "Seanah, want some very weak tea?"

•   •   •

"What do you mean they're gone?"

Morreign wanted to keep her tone calm, but the words came out overly harsh regardless of her intent. Leo's hulking frame filled most of the porch, but he shuffled his feet like a scolded child as he said, "They were working the saw. We came up for lunch, and they weren't up here, so a couple of the guys went to check. And, well, they're gone."

"Gone where? I mean, how?"

"The boat. The boat is gone, as well."

This confused Morreign. The river was running extremely fast with the spring runoff, no one would take that creaky craft out there. "What? They took the boat?"

"We think so, I mean, Jacob's bow is gone as well. Weirdly, that yellow axe they're always playing with is there, lying on the ground like it got dropped. And Griff's bow was there. Something compelled them to rush into that boat and with the current..."

"Why the hell would they get in the half-wrecked boat? They're not kids anymore, they know better than to do something that dumb."

Leo said, "I don't know Morreign. I really don't know-"

Sam, standing silently a few paces behind Leo, interrupted, "Game. There's been some elk around and a bull moose. Found a deer carcass yesterday, think coyotes got it. Only Jacob'd need his bow, he's the better shot so Griff would've been on the oars with Tina."

It took her a second to understand, but then she agreed. They might have risked getting into the boat if huntable game appeared on the other bank. She looked Sam in the eye and said, "Go. Find them."

He nodded, then turned and strode off. Paul stepped forward and put his arm around her shoulder. "They'll find them. Sam'll find them."

Morreign appreciated the sentiment, but everything felt wrong. Regardless, she said, "Yeah, they're probably already hiking their way back, maybe even with some meat."

"Right, we'll all be joking with them about this before nightfall."

"After I scold the hell outta them and double their work duties. You should go, go help Sam and them look."

"Sure, of course, you'll be ok?"

"I'll be fine."

A kiss on the cheek and he left. Morreign picked her knitting back up, sat on her porch chair and watched Paul move across the muddy Clearing. She pictured Jacob that morning, cramming potato pancakes into his mouth, in a bad mood, tired and hungover. He only wore his denim jacket, normally she would have suggested a heavier coat, but she decided not to nag. Now a powerful worry gnawed at her, something she could not name, but it was there sharp and obvious nonetheless. Her instincts were rarely wrong, her keen instincts were why they were here at all. She would not be seeing her son at nightfall.

•   •   •

When they came to a turn in the river Jacob, Griff and Tina tried to steer the boat towards the bank with their hands, but that only served to make them wetter. And being wet was now a serious problem as the sun sunk and a growing chill filled the air. They were facing a frigid night huddled in the hull of a metal boat on near frozen water with only thin jackets and no fire.

"Jacob?"

The question surprised Jacob. Griff hadn't spoken in an hour, an eternity for him. They all sat side by side having moved closer and closer together as the temperature dropped. Tina seemed to have fallen in a fitful doze between their bodies while Jacob and Griff silently scanned the moving water, hoping for something, anything, that might end their unplanned trip.

"Yeah, Griff."

"Are we gonna die?"

"Everyone dies."

"Are we gonna die in this damn boat?"

So far they only saw one decrepit bridge far too high to be of help and, even that false hope, passed hours ago. Chunks of ice constantly floated by but they were too light to effectively push off of when they did get close enough. Other than that, only more rapidly moving water and banks filled with trees blurred by and, it seemed to Jacob, they were actually going faster now.

He started to say their chances were not looking strong when he heard a distance grumbling sound. Griff also heard it and asked, "What's that? A bloody waterfall?"

Squinting, Jacob's keen eyes could see spray up ahead, he said, "I think something's blocking the river up there."

Their movement stirred Tina awake. "What? What's going on?"

Jacob answered, "I don't know, but it looks like there's something up there. Let's get ready."

Worry filled Griff's voice as he asked, "Ready for what?"

"Hell if I know."

They all carefully crept to the front of the boat as the roar of angry water grew louder. After a moment Tina, amazed, said, "A goddamn chance."

Turning a slight bend, they saw a thin island splitting the river. Chunks of ice had piled up against it making a partial dam on one side. They were headed right for it. Jacob said, "When we hit-"

Griff interrupted, "- we jump. Got it. Tina, you go first."

Her voice sounded surprisingly strong and sure as she said, "Yeah. I'll pull you guys up."

Jacob's legs felt stiff and frozen and strangely heavy. He worried they would not work when needed. But when the hull of the boat cracked into the ice, Tina leaped without hesitation. Following her lead, Jacob pressed against the aluminum hull and flung himself out of the boat.

He crashed down hard, and the ice beneath him dipped, but he managed to scramble forward, driven by drowning fuelled fright and the icy cold all around him to keep moving. Quickly throwing himself forward with the hope of more solid ground farther ahead, he clawed at the ice while he eagerly willed it his weight. Behind him, he heard cursing and splashing.

Looking over his shoulder he saw Griff, clinging to the ice as he struggled to kick his way to safety. Spinning on his belly, Jacob moved to help his friend, but Tina scrambled back over him, pushing his ice float down and flooding it with even more icy water. Unfazed, Tina threw out her one hand. Griff missed on his first attempt but then managed to grab hold on the second. Jacob slipped out from under Tina, crawling backward as he took hold of her ankle and pulled. Together, the trio half slid, half lurched off the ice and onto the muddy earth of the narrow island as the boat bounced over the frozen dam and speed off back down the river.

Through panting breath, Jacob asked, "You guys ok?"

Griff said, "Think I sprained my ankle but not too bad."

Tina made it to her feet first, saying, "I'm ok. Let's get a fire going before my last arm freezes off."

•   •   •

Hale's legs were aching, and the bike seat caused his ass to go numb long ago, but it actually felt slightly good being out and away from the darkness of Thule. If not for being constantly worried about Kinma, he might be enjoying himself.

Being in the woods meant not having to conserve wood so, choosing to ignore potential dangers in exchange for feeling true warmth, the patrol built a massive fire out of deadfall, and they all reclined on their packs, taking in the rare heat. Milo dropped down next to him and handed over a tin cup of pine needle tea, saying, "It's bitter as hell but hot."

"I miss coffee."

"I don't even remember coffee."

"That's probably for the best since I doubt we'll see any more of it in our lifetimes."

Milo put his feet near the fire and took in a deep breath before continuing, "Probably shouldn't say this, but this beats that mess back at Thule, even if it means a gettin' shot at a bit."

Hale knew what Milo was getting at, but he still asked, "How you figure?"

"Right, like you don't know. Fine, you want to play innocent, I'll say, it can be somewhat oppressive 'round there at times. Hell, you're the asshole who put these complex thoughts in my simple mind, to begin with."

A companionable silence filled the space between them. Across the flames, Hale could see Clarence arguing with two other men about something. To his left, he could overhear others debating the relative physical merits of various women back at Thule. The mundane normalness of men around a campfire. Men he needs to march to pick a possible fight against unknown foes on orders from a man Hale now figured to be a complete sociopath.

When he and Luke the orphan first moved in with the Bank, Harrison impressed Hale. Clearly in control, clearly thinking in strategic terms, clearly making business-like decisions on how to ensure the group's continued survival. For a while, Hale even considered Harrison a friend of sorts as they spent hours discussing how to best safeguard their group.

Over time, however, as they grew into a sustainable society, Harrison's actions seemed more and more draconian, more and more sadistic, as he worked to maintain his position and control. Any semblance of a friendship with Hale rapidly disappeared beneath Harrison's continuing cruelty. Within the last year, the sadism and paranoia seemed to exponentially deepen and overtake Harrison's last lingering humanity to the point he seemed to no longer think nearly as clearly as he once did.

Out on patrol, away from the chaos of Thule, sitting by the fire and looking back, Hale could not help but wonder if they wasted an opportunity by relying on a madman. Unseen forces reset the world with the Bombs, a nearly clean slate left for survivors. Early on, the niceties of culture and properness needed to be moved aside in favor of meeting primitive needs, Hale understood that. But, within a dozen months, the Bank became established enough so those left alive need not worry solely about surviving as immediate concerns over food and shelter were largely taken care of. Still, Hale and others allowed themselves to defer to Harrison and his unnecessarily brutal control and approach.

He told himself he allowed this to protect, at first Luke, and then Luke and Kinma. However, he knew his deference also came from a form of laziness. Easier to follow than take charge, easier letting another lead than being responsible. They were all well cared for as they took what they wanted from others. Fighting Harrison or taking on the risk of leaving would mean taking on additional hardships in a time when hardship already dominated.

When women were first allowed to join the Bank, Hale spoke up weakly about how they were mistreated, but Harrison easily talked him down, supported by the rougher men wanting their debauchery. Harrison only needed to point out that women ate as much as men but produced less to easily justify them being used. When he rescued Kinma and took her into his apartment, he lost the ability to argue at all with Harrison about the practice of women being seen as Bank property, partially because he would appear a hypocrite and, partially as that was part of the deal made to keep Kinma away from the others.

Lately, though, he found the want to revolt to be undeniable and now, with some distance from home, he could no longer suppress the growing need to stand up. Thinking back though, Hale supposed it was Luke who unwittingly provided the final tipping point as the orphan placed an image in his memory he could not shake.

At first, when they joined the Bank, the child was justifiably terrified, but he managed to settle into the routine of doing chores during the day and taking in whatever slim education Hale could provide him in the evenings. As he grew older, the evening lessons became shorter and shorter until they ceased altogether as Luke began spending his free time listening to the stories told as the men played cards. By the time he became a teenager, Luke was well versed in the informal languages of rig workers and soldiers but he, at least, remained willing to listen to Hale's advice.

About two years ago Luke went on his first patrol. Hale wanted to oppose this, but he knew any attempt by him to delay the inevitable would only cause Luke to endure mockery and feel disdain for him. And Luke was so excited by the prospect that Hale's opposition would be pointless as the boy would go regardless. The patrol turned out to be bloody and successful as the Bankers stumbled across a caravan of oilfield workers trying to find a new place to settle. Bloody and successful were the best sort of patrols, and afterward Luke would no longer listen to anything Hale said, seeing himself as a properly hardened man reveling in the celebration of slaughter and camaraderie.

Hale could ignore such a change, telling himself that such toughness was required to survive in the harsh new world. Plus, he could not expect an adolescent boy to ignore the excitement of those around him and, Hale supposed, rebelling against a parental figure made sense for any teenager. However, one recent evening, he witnessed Luke harassing one of the women in the main room. She pushed him away, and he casually backhanded her. The men in the room howled with laughter as she scurried away with a bleeding lip. For a moment, Luke seemed confused by what happened, but then he seamlessly joined in the laughing and rude comments.

The scared boy in the closet, the one he chose to save, the one who beat him at checkers in that freezing apartment, the one who cried when the fat grey cat died, the one who wanted to help the men down below, now instinctively hit women for amusement. This was the society they were building, the one they were passing on. Since then, the plans to fix things began to form in Hale's head, and his subtle discussions about revolt started. Now, with Kinma trapped back there and him out here, Hale realized protecting Kinma and Luke should not have been an excuse to go along with Harrison's cruelty, it should have been a reason to oppose him.

Turning back to Milo, Hale asked in a low tone, "Really, you think it could be different?"

Milo laughed. "We don't need to dance around out here. Ain't no one listening."

"Alright, you think we can fix this mess?"

For a moment, Milo stared into the flames and thought before quietly answering, "Nah. I mean, so many of them guys like the way it is now, it'd be hard to convince 'em to live any other way. Once down a road like that, hard to get guys to turn back. Might be too broke to fix, I guess is what I'm trying to say."

This brought forth an ancient memory that made Hale smile. "One of my first jobs was out on the rigs. Not even old enough to buy a beer in the damn bar and I find myself out in the middle of the night throwing chain with the roughest of the roughnecks in a damn blizzard. Miserable as miserable can be, I'm leaning against the stack in the middle of the night, trying to muster up the energy to quit."

Milo, also an oil worker in his past life, nodded. "Been there."

"Yeah. Well, this old Newfie derrick hand, a tough as nails, perpetual asshole type, comes up to me and asks if I'm hurt. I expect him to bark at me for being lazy or whatever but I'm well past the point of caring. When I say I don't think so, he leans up next to me and takes his time lighting a smoke in the wind. Then, he says, 'You know, when you've got kicked in the cock as hard as bloody possible, you can spend the rest of your life pretending ya gotta pussy where your balls used ta be and let people screw it, or you can turn around and let the world kick ya' in the ass, knock your dick back into place and get back to work.'"

A scoff of a laugh. "Witty. That speech got you back to work?"

"Nah, I quit that night, got on a Greyhound bus and ran straight back to school."

Milo laughed.

"But I never forgot the speech, and after a year or two of growing up I went back to work and was able to stick it out."

"Your point?"

"If this road is ruined, maybe we need to turn around, come up with a new road."

Milo merely nodded as they settled back into watching the fire as they calmly discussed what they would want the new world to be like.

•   •   •

Tina let out a strange squeal of relief when the spark finally caught, and a tiny flame came to life. Jacob carefully placed wood shavings on to the glowing tree fungus. Only smoke at first, and he feared he smothered the premature fire, but then orange light burst forth from the haze. He and Tina rapidly tossed on twigs, and the fire mercifully grew.

"You did it?" Griff asked sleepily.

"Yeah, yeah, we did. Another of Sam's tricks. That fungus stuff."

Griff, his ankle already purple and swollen, slid across the muddy ground towards the meagre warmth. Even with the added heat, Jacob felt deeply damp and entirely frozen.

With the river running so high, the island was only about ten feet wide at its widest. There were a half dozen willows and a couple of stunted spruce shrubs trying to grow out of the cold mud which provided nothing in the way of shelter. The rushing water crashing against the ice sent up a constant frigid, misty spray. A truly miserable place to be stranded.

The fire not being the sanctuary he hoped for made disappointment clear in his voice as Jacob said, "We need to get some cover."

Tina said, "Yeah. Don't think there's enough wood on this rock for us to ever be close to warm. Damn it, I almost burned to death, and now hypothermia is going to do me in."

Shivering, they managed to set up a few pine bows on an angle around the sturdiest willow, creating a lean-to of sorts. The three of them looked at their pathetic shelter for a moment before Jacob said, "You two go ahead and get in, I'll see what I can find to burn."

Griff struggled to climb under the branches, saying, "Yeah, and see if you can put together a nice venison stew with biscuits."

Tina piped up, "And chocolate for dessert."

"No problem."

Crisscrossing the narrow space, Jacob managed to collect a pathetic pile of damp sticks. Building up the fire somewhat, he took a moment to stare across the dark river. He knew Malden existed upriver but, in the black, his home might as well be the moon.

As he tried to build up the tiny fire, a horrible thought entered his exhausted mind. Even if they did manage to make it home, it would not be for days. Louisa would have no idea what happened, where he was if he was even alive.

The image of her weeping in her tiny room, realizing her worse fear of being all alone again, filled his mind and guilt overtook him. He could not leave her like that. Staring into the blackness between him and Malden he pledged to himself that he would get back.

CHAPTER TEN

JUNE 9, 2046

DAY THREE THOUSAND SEVEN HUNDRED AND FIFTY-NINE

Two whole days and no sign of Jacob, Tina, and Griff. When they fled Thule all those years ago, Morreign thought that night was the longest she ever endured and then she thought the night spent watching Huck die in her arms was the longest, but now it felt like she was trapped in both those nights going on multiple days now with no sign of an ending. Emotional and physical fatigue pulled at Morreign and, looking at the faces around the table, she knew the others felt similar. It would be important to keep tempers in check.

"Everyone here?" she asked.

Nods and murmurs all around.

"Ok, Leo, where we at?"

The humongous man kept his eyes on the chipped mug wrapped in his heavy, battered hands. A long sigh and then, "We're nowhere. We've trekked up and down the riverbank. It's tough sledding because the river's right up to treeline, but there's no sign of 'em. Without a boat, we can't get across to check the other side."

Boris Walker interjected with his usual abrupt logic, "It's obvious, they got in the boat, and the fast running river took them downriver."

While she disliked the idea, Morreign knew it was the only reasonable explanation. Leo and Paul and Sam and everyone else spent the last forty-eight hours searching, but she knew they all saw it as a futile exercise merely being conducted to fill the time with something other than worry.

"How fast's the river?"

Leo said, "By my math, five miles an hour."

Silence. At five miles an hour, they could be a lifetime away. She asked, "Where might've they stopped?"

Everyone instinctively looked at Sam who said, "There's a turn about four miles down if they leaned on the oars they might get to the far bank there."

"But you don't think so?"

Sam shook his head.

Even deeper desperation began to fill Morreign as she softly asked, "Anywhere else?"

He thought for a second, shook his head and then said, "A sandbar island. Thirty miles or more but it'll be thin with the river this high. Hard to hit but possible."

Paul interjected, "We go to the turn. Check it out. If they're not there, we hike on to this island and find them there."

Leo added, "I agree."

Again everyone looked over at Sam. He merely shook his head once. "Can get to the turn easy enough. Island is far, horrible terrain."

The unsaid statement clear, it would be a difficult, dangerous trip using up a lot of supplies and energy with little or no chance of success.

Matt Hope spoke up, "We need to go, at least to the turn. We can't leave them out there."

Tina's mother, Fiona, tears on her cheeks, merely whispered, "Please. Please, go."

Everyone looked back to Morreign. She trusted Sam's instincts and knowledge. Sending out a group would be pointless except it wouldn't be, it would give her, and maybe some others, hope. A false hope she could pretend to be real which meant not having to admit her last child was lost.

"Sam, we need you to stay here and keep hunting while the hunting's good. Only two people go and only to the turn. Volunteers, please."

With that, she stood on her aching hip. Debate broke out over which two would go as she slowly crossed out of the Lodge. Matt and Paul, as the fathers of the missing, seemed to be taking the position they should go, but Leo and others were arguing they were needed here to support their families. Morreign was too tired and sad to care. They could sort it out.

As she opened the door to leave, she glimpsed Louisa sitting on the top of the stairs. The girl had been listening in on the meeting. Realizing she was seen, the girl moved back into shadows.

•　　•　　•

The patrol arrived at the Survivalist settlement near midday and Hale laid along the same ridge where he had surveyed the scene years ago. The collection of well-maintained buildings remained along with some additional pens and structures built out of mismatched, scrap materials. Only a couple of women were moving about, and he saw no children. None of the women seemed to be speaking, focussed on their mundane chores. The place appeared to be flourishing, but something different hung about it which Hale could not put his finger on.

Taking it all in, Hale wondered if he could find someone to speak to without being immediately attacked. See if these people may be amenable to adding a few more to their number, giving him and Kinma a place to escape to.

Clarence shuffled up next to him, interrupting his thinking. Hale handed over the binoculars saying, "Seems off to me."

He looked for a moment before saying, "Wow, quite the place, lots of storage space. Don't see any men. We should go now."

"I'm sure they're down there somewhere."

"Maybe they're off hunting or something. This could be our chance."

"No, we watch first. Make sure we know what we are running into."

Clarence lowered the binoculars and glared at Hale. Annoyed, he merely stared back, forcing Clarence to break the silence. Finally, the lapdog said, "You have orders."

"Yes, I do. And your orders are to follow my orders. We wait."

"You can't bail this time. Harrison made it clear, we are to put an end to these bastards."

"Go make sure everyone is settled under good cover. Send Milo and Taco up here."

"We are not going back empty-handed this time. With or without you, I'm making this happen."

Hale dismissively shook his head at the pointless threat. Clarence's delusion of self-importance stemmed from nothing but his close relationship with Harrison and this frustrated Hale to no end. The fool adopted the worst parts of Harrison, arrogance, cruelty, dominance, and greed, without having any of the intelligence or charisma to back up acting that way. Unwilling to push the matter too far, Clarence began to move down the ridge but could not leave without adding, "Don't forget why we're all the way out here Hale."

Without thought, Hale reached over and grabbed the man by his sleeve, pulled him closer and glared down at him and said, "Don't forget you're out here without your protector."

Clarence opened his mouth to respond but, apparently considered the look on Hale's face and, instead, hurried off without another word. Hale went back to watching the Survivalist yard as he told himself not to let the fool get under his skin.

Taco, his bright blue jacket turned inside out, crawled up beside him with Milo right behind and asking, "Hey boss, what's up?"

"Not sure. Got a bad feeling."

Milo joked, "Something you ate?"

"Something I'm seeing, or maybe not seeing, I don't know. Place seems off, maybe the way the women are moving about."

Milo took the binoculars and gave the scene a quick scan before responding, "They are shuffling. Don't know, maybe we got lucky, and they're all depressed, suicidal, and we can talk'em into putting on nooses."

"Doubt it. Let's go down and take a closer look."

Staying low, with bows notched, the three men moved into a thick, pine forest beside the settlement. They could hear the distant sound of axes and the occasional voice. Sharing a look, the three of them silently agreed to get a better vantage, and they scurried deeper into the woods.

A cart with two patient mules sat in the middle of a clearing as half a dozen people worked with axes and saws, falling and preparing firewood. The mundane scene soon morphed from straightforward to bizarre. Two men were standing to the side, watching the workers with rifles in hand. Taking a second look, Hale saw the workers' legs were loosely chained together so they could take a step but could not run.

Milo, crouched next to Hale beneath pine boughs and whispered, "What the hell?"

Hale, realizing his plan of possibly making friends with these people, was evaporating, said, "Not sure, but I think they're prisoners, maybe some sort of slaves."

• • • •

Willow bark tea tasted awful and sleeping under a pathetic lean-to was uncomfortable. These were all the lessons island-life taught Jacob so far. Griff limped over, sat next to him and accepted the ad hoc cup they carved out of a piece of driftwood when Jacob handed it over. "Thanks, I was craving some super bitter water."

"I threw in some pine this time. Give it a wintery undertone."

Griff took a drink, wiped his mouth with his sleeve and said, "Not bad."

They spent hours drinking miserable tea even though it had no nutritional or caloric value because the flavoured warmth sometimes tricked their stomachs into thinking they were not starving to death. Griff handed the cup back to Jacob who asked, "How's the ankle?"

Pulling up his grimy pant leg, he showed an inch of purple skin above his boot and responded, "Same. Sore but no worse."

Jacob knew his friend was downplaying the injury. It did not seem the ankle was broken, but the sprain appeared severe.

"Keep it elevated. Never know when a dance might break out."

"Right. How's Tina doing?"

"Sleeping, think the fever's gone down but she's pretty sick."

Griff merely nodded.

With limited conversation topics, they returned to sitting and watching the never-ending water rush by. Jacob was dozing, nearly asleep, when he heard it. A crunching noise followed by an aggressive creaking sound. They startled and looked at each other confused.

Griff asked, "What the hell now?"

Jacob had no clue but said, "I'll go look."

As he got to his feet, he noticed the constant sound of the water changed, less of a rumble to it now. Up ahead, at the ice dam, water now poured over the ice instead of going around. Something significant had changed. Maybe a chance.

"Get up and come see this. Hurry."

With a grimace, Griff limped forward as the new scene became clear to Jacob. A massive chunk of ice had come downriver and got wedged against the bank, extending one side of the ice dam. With the new structure blocking the current, more floats piled up until they all became perilously jarred against the bank. The dam, for the moment, had become a bridge. A perilous ice bridge. It led to the wrong bank, taking them farther from home, but it provided a way off the miserable island which was all that mattered.

With real concern in his voice, Griff said, "Shit, it's gonna be tricky."

He was right. Very narrow in places with the water running over slick ice. One false step on the slippery surface and they would be pulled into the frigid river. A certain and awful death. The massive, keystone chunk of ice shifted, rising up half a foot before falling back into place with a crunch, letting them know that if they were going to go, they needed to go now.

"Yeah, but it's a chance. Might be our only one."

Not sounding overly certain, Griff said, "I'm in if you're in."

"Your ankle?"

"It'll hold. Has to."

"Tina?"

"We can help her if we need to. Have to get off this mud."

Getting ill Tina out of the lean-to was difficult but once she saw the possible escape route she rapidly came around, eager to get away. Showing her usual stoicism, she said, "I'm in. Let's go."

Without another word, they moved out onto the ice. Jacob, the most healthy of the trio, went first to test the path and pick the best route. Cold water immediately rushed over his boots, numbing his feet. At first, he was more worried about his friends, but the treacherousness immediately required all his focus be on moving forward as fast as possible while keeping his tenuous balance. Finally, with sweat pouring down his back from the strain, Jacob reached the last of the ice. It shifted awkwardly as he stepped and he fell to his knees, frozen water rushed about him, the cold shocking and for a breath he merely stayed there, unsure how to proceed.

From behind him, Tina cursed, "Jesus man, just crawl."

Jacob followed the instruction and made it to the bank, his friends right on his heels.

•　•　•

Tedium proved to be a problem for Kinma. She tried to stay busy, keep her mind focussed on the immediate to avoid thinking of her dread-filled future. However, her chores did not take all day and, without Hale to spend time with, she often found herself sitting on the balcony staring off to the horizon and worrying. This evening, not wanting to fill herself with stress, she ventured down to the kitchen, seeking any sort of distraction.

The kitchen existed in an outbuilding, set up with an immense wood stove made out of scrap metal and grills pieced together from scavenged barbeques. A table ran along one wall with cabinets above it, and two tall basins filled one corner with embers glowing beneath them to keep the water warm. A pang of remorse struck Kinma as she realized much of the equipment in the kitchen was designed and built by Hale.

Seanah stood over one basin, scrubbing a pot while another woman named Alice kneaded a dark dough. As she stepped inside, Seanah saw her and said with a smile, "Oh, hey Kinma, how are things? Lookin' for something?"

"Hi. No, no not really. I guess I was looking for something to do…"

Without hesitation, Seanah tossed Kinma a well-used dish towel and pointed to a stack of dishes. The women worked in silence for a while before Alice, a former military computer expert, told Kinma, "Walter and Ranger brought in a couple of skinny porcupines. Going to have 'em for dinner tomorrow."

Seanah shook her head saying, "If the men around her spent more time trapping and less time bickering with one another we'd all be a hell of a lot better fed."

Alice added, "They all say it's boring. Walking around out there like that, looking for rodents."

"Right, 'cause washing dishes all damn day is nonstop excitement."

For an hour, the three of them gossiped and joked as they went through their tasks. Gratitude filled Kinma as the pointless conversation buried her unpleasant thoughts. They were laughing about how one of the older women kept hoarding matches even though there were numerous, nearby flames burning at any given time when a loud knock on the door interrupted them.

They all turned to see Tall Tony standing in the doorway. Tony was in his late fifties with rotten teeth, a weepy eye and an aversion to soap. Kinma sensed Alice and Seanah tense up. His eyes flitted over Kinma as if he was checking out a used car on a sales lot before, unashamedly, he pointed at Alice with a grimy finger which he curled slowly.

As Alice took her time wiping her hands, Seanah softly rubbed her back. Eventually, Tony said, "C'mon. Hurry up."

Alice moved out of the kitchen with the dirty man and Seanah began to softly cry. Wiping her eyes, she said to Kinma, "Sorry, sorry. It shouldn't make me cry after all this time but it does."

Unsure how to react, Kinma dumbly asked, "Does that happen often? I mean, does that sort of request come up a lot?"

Seanah, her eyes moist, looked at her with astonishment on her face and said, "Yeah, of course. Couple of times a day at least. It's awful, at first you hope whoever shows up will choose any other woman in the room, so you don't have to go. And then, when they do pick someone else, you get this great sense of relief because it's not you, but then, this powerful guilt at feeling relief over someone else's suffering hits you."

Seanah dabbed her eyes with a sleeve and continued, "I get off a bit easier 'cause I got men to stay with but doesn't make me immune, I get picked once in a while, normally when someone wants to piss off someone else, a pawn in a juvenile power struggle. Anyway, I guess I should be glad. But, you know, though, it's kinda funny, the act actually gets easier over time, I mean you don't want to do it, but you learn to go numb or whatever. Guess your dignity can only take so many beatings before it dies... But the guilt at wanting the awfulness to land on someone else, well, that hurts every time."

Unsure what to do, Kinma put her arm around Seanah. "I think that's natural. You've been thrust into a horrible situation, of course, you're going to look out for yourself, that's only fair."

"No. None of this is fair."

With that, they went back to the chores, but now worked in silence with Kinma often glancing at the empty doorway.

•　　•　　•

For a long time, Milo, Taco and Hale watched the scene in the woods without speaking. The two guards occasionally barked a command at the workers but, in general, the toil was done without speaking. Finally, Hale crawled back from under the pine and the three of them moved around through the forest to the ridge where the others waited.

"So, what's the plan?" Clarence asked immediately.

Everyone gathered around to listen as Hale crouched down and explained, "They seem to have captured some survivors and are using them as slaves."

Hale and Milo explained, as best they could, the scene they witnessed as Taco nodded along. When the tale finished, Clarence jumped back in, "Great, maybe we'll have some allies. Let's get moving."

Milo interjected for Hale, "Didn't you hear? They got rifles, and we don't know how many of 'em there are yet."

Using hushed voices, a ridiculous debate amongst the men broke out. Hale knew the patrol did not have enough information to make a decision, but he let the discussion play out, hoping to give the illusion they were all involved in the process. Eventually, he broke in and said, "We wait. We spread out, stay out of sight and watch. Count their rifles, try to keep track of where they are. Also, watch for anything you think might let us turn these prisoner folks to our advantage."

Clarence started to protest, but Hale cut him off, "Milo, get everyone organized, circle the settlement. If any of you get seen, run west to that fork in the creek and hide there. When we think it's safe, we'll come get you there."

Milo took over the more detailed instructions, and Hale crawled back up the ridge to resume his watch and to try to understand the strange village.

CHAPTER ELEVEN

JUNE 10, 2046

DAY THREE THOUSAND SEVEN HUNDRED AND SIXTY

The clear, silver disc of a full moon hung over the river. Jacob figured their luck finally changed when they stumbled into a patch of early spring clover and dandelions as soon as they escaped across the ice bridge allowing them to feast until their stomachs hurt. Plus, with an abundance of deadfall around, they were able to build a massive fire to burn away the chill ingrained in their bones.

With their stomachs full, freezing to death no longer a threat and getting home now a possibility, humor-filled relief took over as they laid by the huge fire, staring at the star-filled sky. Griff laughed loudly, saying, "Man, I thought you were gonna stay out there forever. Kneeling on that mini-iceberg with water running all around, not sure if you should shit yourself or fall off before Tina reminded you that crawling is a thing."

Not willing to take the ribbing silently, Jacob fired back, "My favorite memory of all of this is you hanging off that ice dam, kicking like a kid learning to swim and before Tina pulled you up like a half-drowned rat."

Tina, hugging herself as the fever continued to send chills through her scrawny body said, "And, not a word of thanks from either of you bastards."

Jacob moved next to her, saying, "Yeah, yeah, I guess I owe you a thank you for that."

Griff said, "Put it in the ledger."

They moved on to discussing what their story to Malden would be, knowing they needed a great explanation for why they lost the boat. Jacob leaned back and listened to Griff's powerful imagination run. He instantly came up with a story of them seeing a ragged woman being attacked by bandits on the other bank. That idea got tossed aside for a story of them seeing a child on a log floating by. Deciding that was unbelievable, Griff moved on to a tale about them fighting off river pirates come to attack Malden.

While the tales were entertaining, none were helpful. Jacob knew, when they made it back, they would tell everyone what actually happened. Griff might be able to live a story, but he and Tina could not keep up that sort of deception. They would be forgiven for their mistake, mainly because their return would be seen as miraculous but, also, because the others would appreciate the value of attempting to get meat. Probably, after time passed, they would be chided for losing the boat but the mocking would be good natured, and they would have a great story to tell and re-tell.

A smile grew on Jacob's lips. None of it matter. He would make it home, and he would see Louisa again, hold her again, make her laugh again and kiss her again. Perhaps, most importantly he would get to apologize for his behavior and ensure his last words to her were not "rabbit hutch." More than warmth and real food, more than his bed or even his parents, he missed her, missed her with physical pain. He would make it home, and he vowed never to take anything about her for granted ever again.

When Griff finally ran out of funny stories justifying their departure, Tina returned them to reality, asking, "What're we gonna do about being on the wrong side of the river with no boat?"

Griff answered, "Shit, as soon as I smell the stew pot in the Lodge, it won't matter how fast the river's running I'll be able to swim–."

The crack was sharp and sickening. Jacob bolted upright in time to see Griff slumping over. He scrambled to his feet, but before he could take a step to help his friend, his head erupted in blinding pain. He stumbled forward. For an instant, he felt intense heat from the huge campfire pushing up against him but before he could fall into the flames a stern hand grabbed his shirt collar, yanking him backward.

Jacob fell to the ground and lights swam around his eyes as powerful agony filled his head. He tried to force his wobbly legs to stand, but he heard someone calmly state, "No." before a fresh agony smashed into his head and everything went black.

•　　•　　•

Taco, always able to sleep anywhere, softly snored next to Hale. The silver moon now huge in the sky, making him worried they would be too easily seen. He knew he should give up and try to sleep as well. For over two hours now they had seen no one outside. But in the long house in the middle of the settlement, weak lights remained burning, and he could see the occasional movement of silhouettes in the windows. Plus, if he strained, he thought he could hear something. Maybe singing. Maybe talking. Maybe only leaves rustling in the breeze but the sound intrigued him.

Without warning, the wide door opened spilling the glow of firelight into the yard. Blinking fatigue from his eyes, Hale moved his binoculars up to watch. Eight people, some carrying lanterns, walked slowly out. Now Hale could hear that the sound was a low, throaty chant. Following the first eight, a man in thin nightshirt was led out by an elderly woman with gleaming hair running down her back which looked silver in the moonlight. She held a thin rope tied around the man's wrists. Trepidation seized Hale's stomach, certain he was viewing an awful scene about to get worse.

He elbowed Taco, wanting another witness, and whispered, "Are you seeing this?"

Shaking himself awake, Taco silently took the binoculars, looked for a moment and then let out a low, whispered whistle.

The man with the tied hands appeared oddly heavy, the once familiar sight of even a slightly fat person now completely foreign after ten years of humanity living off the scraps of destruction. He could not tell his age in the shifting shadows, but he guessed past middle years by the way he cautiously moved at a shuffle.

The soft chanting stopped, and they formed a tight circle around the captor before gently pushing him to his knees. The white-haired woman seemed to be speaking, but Hale could not make out words. After a minute of this, one of them stepped forward and pulled the shirt over the man's head revealing shockingly pale skin while the white-haired woman moved behind him and drew a heavy blade. It glinted for a second in the lantern-light and Hale had to catch himself from screaming out a warning.

Without hesitation, she raised the blade and swung, then quickly swung again, then again. Hale could not see the impacts through the shifting crowd but, when they dispersed, the naked man lay on the grass, his head five feet away from the rest of him. Blackness surrounded his white flesh as dark blood poured out onto the grass.

He did not want to see any more. He tried to hand the binoculars over to

Taco, but he merely shook his head, smart enough to know he did not need a closer look at the horrendous scene. Hale reluctantly lifted them back to his eyes.

Leaving the lanterns sitting on the grass, the chanters silently and solemnly walked back inside as others came out. These new people, two men, and two women, strode with strange hopping strides, their ankles apparently tethered like the workers in the woods. They each carried a knife and plastic containers. Following the workers, came two unfettered men, each casually holding rifles.

The riflemen stopped twenty feet from the headless corpse, merely watching as the others silently knelt over the body. He did not want to acknowledge that he knew what was happening, but Hale knew even before they began the gruesome butchering.

Taco silently looked at him with confusion in his eyes, Hale could only whisper, "Jesus Christ. Where the hell are we?"

• • •

Greyness. Jacob opened his eyes but saw only blurry greyness. He could hear voices but could not focus enough to understand words. He lay on the damp ground, curled on his side. He tried to move, to get up but discovered his ankles and wrist were tightly tied. Confused panic flooded into him. After a few moments of forcing his breathing to slow as Sam taught him, he managed to force the fear down as he squeezed his eyes shut and concentrated, trying to remember what happened.

Eventually, the memories came. He recalled crossing the ad hoc ice bridge. He recalled finding the clover and dandelions. He recalled building the massive fire with Griff and Tina. They stayed up talking and enjoying the heat. Something hit Griff, and then something hit him.

"Griff? Griff, you here? Tina?"

The words came out scratchy and quiet. Jacob opened his mouth to try again, but something smashed into his back thrusting every ounce of breath from him. "No talking."

His eyes popped open at the blow, the pain chasing the blurriness from his vision, but he only saw ground. Sucking in dirt and pine needles, he tried to get air into his lungs. Someone laughing. Laughing at his anguished struggle.

When the weight left his back, he managed to pull in one breath, then another. Jacob rolled and forced himself to his knees. For a second he thought he would vomit as the world turned and tilted awkwardly around him but, after more deep breaths, reality righted itself. Three strangers. Two men and a woman. Two carrying rifles, one casually leaning on what appeared to be an axe handle.

Jacob stared at them. He could not recall the last time he saw a person whom, for all intents and purposes, he had not known all his life. Strangers, they were called strangers in the stories. Unknown people. He used to daydream about meeting strangers, about hearing of their life outside Malden. Dreams like these were relied on to break up the mundane days. Now he wished for nothing but for the strangers to go away.

Not wanting to stare at the unpleasant trio, Jacob carefully scanned the area. Ten feet away, curled in the fetal position, laid Griff. Not moving. Tina, her one good arm tied to her waist, was sitting up, looking down at her lap, her head nodding slowly. Jacob instinctively began to move towards his friends, but the woman hefted the butt of her rifle above him and asked, "You a slow learner?"

For a heartbeat, Jacob met her eyes. They were grey, metallic in the dawn light. Steel Eyes. Her skin tanned, her completely black hair cut short like a boy's. He guessed she was not much older than him. Pretty but in an intense, unhappy way. Steel Eyes growled, "Stay on the ground."

Not sure if he could endure another blow, Jacob sunk back down and lowered his head. But, when he figured the immediate threat passed, he risked a sideways glance over at Griff. His chest seemed to rise and fall minutely. At least he was breathing

For an eternity, he lay, his bound hands aching, his legs going numb, his eyes kept low. His attackers spoke to one another, but Jacob could not hear what they were saying. He occasionally caught a glimpse of them moving, and it sounded like they were eating, maybe passing a jug back and forth.

Finally, Griff let out a groan, miserably soft at first then louder and more agonized. Daring to lift his head a tiny amount, Jacob saw one of the men roughly pull Griff to his knees. His hands were tied behind his back, making him lean forward with his shoulders rolled back awkwardly. Dried blood covered his face like a mask making his eyes and teeth look freakishly white as he grimaced with pain. The man grabbed a handful of Griff's red hair, tilting his face up as he said, "Alright, enough fun? Gonna behave now?"

For a second, Griff glared up at the man. Jacob silently pleaded with his friend to not do anything stupid. With a slight twist, Griff pulled away from the man's grasp but lowered his head and nodded slowly at the dirt.

"Good. Real good. Maybe now that ya' are awake we can have a little talk. Sound nice?"

It did not sound nice to Jacob. The man talking was a massive monster. Shorter but with a thick body and a gigantic head that seemed to sit on his shoulders without the benefit of a neck. His face was covered by a black beard, and a mane of messy black hair poured out from a battered ball cap. The sight reminded Jacob of the lion in an old picture book they had at Malden, one he read and re-read a thousand times as a child. Jacob's dizzy mind decided to name him Aslan.

"He asked you all a question."

This came from the other man. Wiry and older with a matted, greying beard and a pointed nose holding up thick eyeglasses. His heavy, grey, duster-style jacket hung off thin shoulders down to his boot tops. This one reminded him of another book from his childhood where forest animals were the characters. Jacob's dizzy mind decided to name him Mr. Badger.

Jacob merely nodded. Griff gave a noncommittal grunt. Tina appeared to be dozing. Aslan pointed at Griff, Mr. Badger and Steel Eyes roughly picked him up, hauled him over next to Jacob and dropped him down. Aslan calmly stepped over and, looming above them both, said, "So, we've got two young men and an amputee girl, well fed, wearing nicely mended clothes. No settlements 'round here that we know of, but you must've come from somewhere, somewhere people cook and sew for you."

New fear piled onto Jacob's panic filled mind. These thugs wanted to find Malden. Cruel strangers with rifles wanted to find Malden. Neither he nor Griff spoke.

"Ahh, you see, that was meant to be a question, implied I'd guess you could say. Let me ask it slow and clear like. Where the hell are you from?"

Again, neither of them spoke. A strained silence hung amongst the distant sound of the river and the chirp of a squirrel. Aslan sighed and nodded to Mr. Badger. The axe handle whirled and cracked into Griff's bad ankle before instantly swinging back around to smack Jacob across the shoulder.

"I'll ask again but only one more time. Where did you come from?"

When they hesitated, Mr. Badger lifted the handle over Jacob's head. Jacob wanted to tell Griff to shut up. Keep the assholes from Malden, keep them from Louisa. But, before he could react, Griff blurted out, "Upriver. Long way upriver."

The axe handle was lowered as Aslan continued, "Good, good. Apparently, you upriver guys are fast learners. How'd you end up down here?"

The story spilled out of Griff as he continued to look at the ground and used a whispering, defeated tone Jacob could not believe came from his generally cocky friend. They were brothers, Tina a girl their father rescued after the Bombs. Their sickly, starving parents sent the three of them out from their farmhouse in search of food when spring finally came. Unable to find anything near home, they decided to make the three-day hike to the river in hope of catching fish. After spending an hour on the bank with no luck, they ventured downriver where they came across an old aluminum boat washed up on an ice flow.

Thinking their fishing chances would be better out in the deeper current, Griff explained how they tethered the boat to a tree and ventured out into the raging river. All day they caught jackfish with almost every cast, laughing as they filled the boat with protein. As the sun set, they grabbed the rope to pull themselves to shore. Straining against the current and their aggressive pulling, the weathered rope broke. In an instant, they were speeding downriver with no way to stop.

All night and most of the next day they traveled. Eventually, they were stopped by the island and ended up here. Shaking his head as if he were fighting off tears, Griff finished by saying, "After all this time, our parents are probably gone, too sick and too hungry to last long. They died, they died thinking we abandoned them on purpose."

Jacob watched as Mr. Badger and Steel Eyes shared a look while Aslan squatted down in front of them, stirring the grass between his feet with a twig. It took great effort not to speak, to not try to convince this man of the truth of Griff's lie.

Finally, Aslan took the twig, placed it under Jacob's chin and lifted his head. Glaring at him, the beast of a man asked, "That what happened?"

Knowing he was very bad at lying, that he could never tell tales like Griff, Jacob decided to keep his mouth shut and merely nodded, trying to look solemn. Aslan rose back up.

Aslan said, "Ok, I believe your little story. Guys stupid enough to build a fire big enough to signal everyone for a hundred miles while laughing like loud jackasses are definitely stupid enough to get stuck in a runaway boat for a day and a half."

Despite the pain and fear, a sliver of relief slipped through Jacob. Griff had done it. The thugs would not be going to Malden. Louisa. His mom and dad. Sam. Uncle Leo. All the kids. They were safe.

"Our friend, she's sick, we need to take care of her, try to get her home. Can we go?"

Griff's question elicited a snort of a laugh from Aslan. He shook his massive head and said, "No son. You can't go. We don't let people go."

• • •

"They were cutting her up for food, no question."

The patrol regrouped behind the ridge at sunset as planned. Predictably, Hale's story was met with disbelief. Milo stammered out, "Eat the body? I mean, how do you know?"

Hale looked over at Taco who, nodding, softly said, "Butchered her."

Clarence pushed forward, "Makes no matter. We came to destroy these vermin anyhow, now we've got an extra reason to end them."

For once, Hale agreed with Clarence. "Yeah. But we've counted six rifles and at least ten men. That's what we've seen, there could easily be more. We can't simply storm that many guns with only our bows."

With a hint of fear in his normally demanding tone, Clarence said, "You're supposed to be the expert on this. What's your plan?"

Most of the night, while lying up on the ridge, Hale pondered how to proceed. Divide and conquer seemed to be their best option.

"We can't barge straight in, but I think we can take them down one or two at a time. Hopefully, they go for more firewood like we saw yesterday. If they do, we ambush the guards and hope the workers don't do anything stupid. If it goes as planned, we end up with two of their rifles and maybe get some allies with information."

From there, a lengthy discussion of logistics and roles occurred and, in the early morning, when the guards left the longhouse with half a dozen tethered people following the mule cart, the Bankers were silently moving through the trees alongside them. They reached the clearing unseen, spread out and remained hidden to wait, letting their targets get into the rhythm of their work. When the sleepy looking guards were sufficiently lulled into the tedium of the routine, Hale let out a low chirping noise.

Taco slipped from behind a pine tree like a shadow with a knife in hand. In three quick, silent strides he grabbed one guard and slit his throat to the spine. Before the blood-covered man could sink to the ground, five arrows thudded into the other guard. He started to let out a throttled yell, but a final arrow buried itself into his ear, sharply cutting off the noise.

The workers looked at Taco with his inside-out jacket, holding a bloody knife. They took in the fallen men with wide eyes and mouths ajar. They did not call out or try to flee, but only huddled together. Hale stepped into the clearing, showing his empty hands as he approached the frightened group.

"Hello, I'm Hale. We're from Thule. Help us and no one gets hurt."

A young, terribly gaunt man moved slightly forward. He managed to make eye contact with Hale despite any fear. "What do you want?"

His tone actually carried a defiant edge. Despite the scene, perhaps the man was not actually scared. Hale thought it might be more correct to see the man as desperate enough to no longer care. "We've come here to put an end to this place and take their supplies for ourselves."

Behind him, Hale could sense the other Bankers moving into the clearing, expertly disarming the dead guards and surrounding the others. Despite this show of force, the worker in his tattered coat and with a dirt-smeared face, let out a scoffing laugh. "So what? We help you then you take off and leave us to starve and freeze? Or maybe you decide t' eliminate us as well?"

Before Hale could respond, Clarence charged forward, sticking a finger in the captive's face and growling, "You've got no choice. Help us do what we need to do, or it ends here and now for you."

Enough became enough. Hale grabbed Clarence by his collar and yanked him to the ground. Predictably, Clarence threw his hands up to protect his face before curling into a ball rather than fight back. As the others quietly chuckled, Hale calmly said to the turtled man, "Learn how to control yourself before you get someone hurt."

Returning his attention to the captives' apparent leader, Hale said, "Sorry, ignore him. What's your name?"

Maintaining the distrustful glare regardless of the commotion, the man said, "Marvin."

Hale extended his hand, and Marvin reluctantly shook. "Well Marvin, I have no interest in killing innocent people. We only want to be rid of these assholes and their rifles, they're the threat, not you. How many captives are there?"

After a moment of reflection, he responded, "Us six plus three others back there."

At this a woman touched Marvin's elbow, prompting him to correct himself, "Sorry, two others back there. We lost Dean last night."

"Yeah, I saw that. What the hell's going on here? What is this place?"

With a sigh, Marvin said, "Well Hale, they call this place Gergesa and I'd say it's the home of pure evil."

CHAPTER TWELVE

JUNE 10, 2046

DAY THREE THOUSAND SEVEN HUNDRED AND SIXTY

The knock was so soft it took Morreign a second to realize someone was at her cabin. She left her breakfast of stale corn mash on the table and limped the two steps to her door. Expecting it to be Leo coming to check in on her, seeing Louisa on the porch surprised her. The girl lifted her head and pushed the hood off her glowing, yellow hair, showing Morreign her perfect, angelic beauty.

"Hi, I was wondering, if, you weren't busy if maybe we could talk."

As Jacob's closet friend and without a family of her own, Louisa practically lived with them. Louisa often ate dinner with them or played cards or merely visited in their cabin until the late hours of the night. However, except for a few fleeting moments, Morreign could not recall spending time alone with the girl. In fact, Louisa might be the only person in Malden with whom Morreign expended no effort getting to truly know. The sad realization made her wonder why she avoided no one but this lonely child.

"Of course, sure. You have breakfast? I have some extra corn mush. It's bad but filling."

"Sure, thanks. I just, I don't know... guess I couldn't sit around the Lodge any longer, you know?"

The child took off her jacket revealing a body no one would mistake for that of a child. Appreciating, for the first time, Louisa as a grown woman made Morreign realize Jacob was very far from being a boy. She supposed, living isolated, made it easier for parents to keep their children, but in many ways, at Malden, she supposed kids grew up faster than in the past.

They were expected to work and contribute from a young age and whining was not tolerated. Further, true threats like hunger and deadly disease hung about them, replacing previous worries like bullies, low self-esteem and acne. However, the kids were never truly outside the embrace of Malden, never more than a holler for help away from caring adults they knew all their lives. Now, with her last child out somewhere in the wilds, Morreign wondered if raising children sheltered in such a way was a mistake.

"Yeah Louisa, I think I know what you mean. Come on in, have a seat."

With a slightly awkward silence mingling amongst them, Morreign spooned up a bowl of corn and poured a cup of tea. Setting the sad meal before Louisa she said, "The tea is only dried dandelion, not very good but I like it better than the dirty taste of the river water."

"Thanks."

They made small talk about the weather and the gardens as she ate. Then, as Morreign moved to clear away the dishes, she noticed a tear slipping down Louisa's pink cheek. Cursing herself for not thinking, she put the dishes aside.

Louisa obviously did not come for bad food and chit-chat. The girl came to her because she was suffering and knew Morreign likely was suffering in much the same way. Morreign sat beside her, wrapping her arm around her. After a second of hesitation, Louisa hugged her back, and the tears came in earnest.

When the roughest of the crying finished, Louisa looked up at Morreign and said, "Sorry, I'm sorry, but I'm... I'm scared. I keep asking, 'what happened to him'? To them, I mean."

Morreign's instincts wanted her to lie, to placate Louisa's suffering with niceties about how they merely got lost and were probably hiking back right now. But she knew lying would not work. Louisa was smart enough to know better and tough enough not to let herself believe comforting falsehoods. "Honestly, Louisa, I don't know, I wish I did, but I don't."

More sobbing followed by her weakly saying, "I need him to come back. I can't, I can't be alone. Not now, now that I know what life could be with him."

Forcing herself to sound firm and sure, Morreign said, "Look, I don't know what happened to them but Jacob is out there, and I know he'll do everything in his power and then some to get back here, back to you. I know this because, for all these years, I've seen the way he looks at you. I ignored the look, or at least tried to ignore it, I think because acknowledging it would mean I'd need to admit that Jacob was no longer only mine. But I saw it nonetheless, and it was there always. Any man who carries that look will risk everything and more to get back, and that's especially true for a man like Jacob."

"The last night, the night of the celebration, we fought. Not fought exactly but I, well, I disappointed him, and he was mad."

For the endless hours, since they went missing, Morreign's mind continually found its way to imagining her life if Jacob did not return. With both of her children gone, going through all the difficulties of creating what they were creating at Malden would seem pointless. She doubted she could go on if that became her reality. While knowing it to be very thin, she clung to the hope he would come back, convincing herself he would make it back and now another motivation for him returning came to her.

"I know Jacob as well as anyone, not only does he love you as deeply as it's possible to love someone, he'll want to come home so he can tell you he's not mad. The idea that you'll be worried or upset will drive him crazy. He's too damn considerate to do otherwise."

This got a brief chuckle from Louisa, "Yeah, you're right he'd swim cross that icy river twice to apologize for even a perceived slight. Too polite for his own good."

•   •   •

Hale figured it best to befriend the frightened workers. Some of the Bankers were lazily chopping away at trees so the sound of axes would carry and no one would think to check on the work crew. This allowed the captives to sit and rest while eagerly eating the patrol's supplies.

Marvin, spooning canned beans into his mouth, sounded more cooperative now as he explained, "They always call themselves The Prepared of Gergesa. We call them Preppers but only when they can't hear. Listening to their chatter, it seems they're all bunch of survivalist nuts who got lucky when the world actually came to an end. I think they were probably a good bit insane before the war but, now that they think they've been proved right, they've gone totally nuts."

Hale said, "We came by this place about eight years ago. Didn't want to take it out back then 'cause they seemed like nothing more than families. Well-armed families but families all the same. Lots of kids running around."

This got sideway looks from the captives. Marvin stopped eating and said coldly, "Those kids you let live turned into cruel, murderous cannibals."

It never occurred to Hale that his choice to leave people alive could've been a mistake, but he figured it best to move the discussion away from this problematic past, so he said, "Yeah, but I'm back to correct that. With these two guards gone, how many are left to deal with?"

"That leaves ten. Six men, four women. Women shoot as good as the guys. Three more are out ranging somewhere, been gone for a while but not sure when they'll show back up."

"Guns? Ammo?"

"They've got enough guns that each of 'em can carry three with extras leftover. Not sure on ammo but there are cases in the basement, so I doubt you'll be able to run them out. Remember, these assholes devoted generations to being ready for an apocalypse."

Hale cursed under his breath. When the ammunition at Thule ran out, most of the men were despondent, but the idea of a world without guns appealed to Hale. Before the Bombs, gun control escalated to the point that, essentially, no one but military and native hunters were allowed to keep them. Unregistered rifles undoubtedly existed but the penalties for having one were so strict that they were confined to cellars and attics. He could only wonder at how these Preppers managed stockpile such an arsenal, but he supposed zealots could always find a way.

"Ok, give me the complete lay of the land. Who sleeps where and when? Who watches what?"

Marvin, with the help of the others, detailed the operations of the Preppers while Hale and Milo carefully listened. Finally, when it seemed all available information was provided, Hale asked, "If these guys are so well prepared for the end of the world, how'd the cannibalism come about?"

Marvin shrugged and said, "They were already into that 'fore they caught me. There's a tinge of religion 'round it, treating it like a sacrifice or something, but they only decide to go that route when other meat ain't around, or they got more workers penned up than they need. Also, they always pick the person that's the least helpful in getting things done and fatten them up. Have to say, it's a decent motivator to keep us working hard."

Thousands of other questions about this freakiness poured into Hale's mind, but there were more pressing matters to deal with. He asked, "How long before you all are supposed to go back?"

Scraping out the last of the beans and checking the sun, Marvin said, "Oh, damn, yeah, you don't have long. Normally around noon two Preppers come out to spell the guards."

After glancing at the sun and thinking for a moment, Hale said, "Good, gives us another ambush opportunity, limit their numbers so more."

Marvin shook his head, "Nah, they normally call from a long ways out and expect a response from their friends, these bastards are cautious, well-trained and serious. You got lucky on these guards, they were the younger ones and sleepy from being up doing their bullshit chanting and feasting last night. The others, they ain't half as sloppy and will be rested, won't get caught in an ambush."

Sharp pain shot up his knee as Jacob stumbled for the hundredth time under the weight of a heavy pack they had loaded on his back. Steel Eyes roughly grabbed the rope tied around his raw wrists and pulled him to his feet. Ahead of him, Griff limped stoically onward, a canvas bag strapped to his back as well. Behind him, Jacob could hear Tina heavily breathing under her load. For hours they marched like this through rough, heavy brush as mosquitos and black flies feasted on them. Jacob realized they were following a trap line as they had come across two snared squirrels, he could only hope it was a short line with something better at the end.

Aslan harshly whispered, "Stop."

The sad caravan ceased as Jacob, Tina and Griff were roughly sat down amongst low pine boughs. Steel Eyes loomed above them, standing guard while Aslan and Mr. Badger slipped off into the trees. Jacob felt clueless, but he did not care, content merely to be off his feet.

Griff, apparently not content with simply resting, asked the hard looking young woman, "Why they leave you back?"

She growled, "Quiet idiot."

"I'm only saying, seems they boss you around pretty good."

Jacob winced, expecting Griff to receive at least a kick. Instead, Steel Eyes growled again, "Shut your damn mouth. Don't make me hurt you."

Griff gave Jacob a watered down version of his mischievous look. Despite the fatigue and pain, his friend still tiredly poked at their captors, perhaps looking for a weakness to exploit or, maybe merely being his usual difficult self. Tina kept her distance from their captors as much as possible, Jacob also had no interest in talking to the strangers. Instead, he watched, intrigued by having new people to observe. Even though smiling was the last thing he wanted to do, Jacob managed a weak grin of his own, knowing it easier to go along with Griff than to lecture or persuade him to change behaviour.

For half an hour, they merely sat, listening to the muffled sounds of the forest. When Aslan and Mr. Badger returned, they were dragging a scrawny man with a yellowing beard and rough clothes made of hides. They set him down next to Jacob and, with scary efficiency, tied the new captive's hand and tethered his ankles.

With their work down Aslan clapped Mr. Badger on the back. "How's that for trapping a trapper? He'll probably be tough as hell to chew but might be a good worker."

Steel Eyes asked, "He out here by himself?"

Aslan answered, "Seems like. My guess is, we follow the line; it'll lead us to a cabin or house or something."

At this, the old trapper raised his battered face and spat out, "No cabin out here, assholes."

This caused their guards to chuckle. Griff, for some reason, laughed along with them as he said, "Yeah, assholes."

The chuckles stopped, and Aslan nodded subtly to Steel Eyes. She quickly cut a switch off a nearby willow and, without a word, began whipping Griff with the stick. He curled up and wiggled on the ground, trying to avoid the stinging blows as the others loudly laughed at his torment. When she finally stopped, Jacob looked over at Griff to see if he was ok, but he only got a vacant stare back, all sense of mischievousness and cockiness left his face.

Jacob could not worry about his friend's psyche though as his thirst overtook all thoughts. He watched with silently pleading eyes as the three guards passed a plastic water jug back and forth. They each drank deeply, ignoring the thirsty people tied up beneath them, before putting the lightened jug into Jacob's backpack and pulling them to their feet to recommence the sad trek.

After an hour or so, the trapper marching behind Jacob whispered to him, "You three... you youngsters, you from that there old hunting lodge? Camp Malden?"

Shock overruled Jacob's fear of being caught talking, "How you know about that?"

"Kid, you think you can build up a place like that out there without the trappers 'round here knowing? Hell, you must be extra foolish, even for town folks."

A fresh worry filled Jacob, piling up on top of the fears and torments already coursing through him. This old man knew about Malden. He could tell their attackers. "How do you know we're from there?"

"Tended clothes, cut hair and you're big, dumb fawn eyes like you're seeing the world for the first goddamn time. Heard rumors there was a community up there now. Thought about paying you all a visit this summer, do some trading."

"These people, these people with the guns, they can't know... they can't know about Malden."

The responding whisper carried a slightly mocking tone to it as the man behind him said, "Think these guys'll let me go if I give up a fat prize like your home? I think so, you probably got lots to eat up there, not to mention some nice, young, clean ladies, I imagine."

Jacob stumbled over a root. "Please, don't tell them. My family, a girl -"

Jacob's sad plea was cut off by Mr. Badger laughing out, "No cabin, eh? That there looks pretty cabin like to me."

Up ahead, tuck neatly amongst some massive pines, sat a low, log cabin. Aslan harshly cuffed the trapper across the face. "That's for lying old man. Now make your houseguests feel welcome."

Screams of the wounded could now be heard coming from his left and his right. Hale reached into his quiver. Two arrows left. To make things worse, for some time now, he heard no gunfire coming from his men with the two rifles while a nearly constant barrage continued to come from the Survivalists.

Returning to the settlement from the woods, the patrol spied a handful of people moving about, but they could not account for everyone. Hale placed his men as close as possible without being seen and opted to wait until the Preppers moved to spell off the dead guards. As soon as the replacement guards entered the woods, the patrol attacked.

Hale had given one plundered rifle to Milo and the other to Wilson as they were the best shots. Unfortunately, they were out of practice with guns, and their first volley missed allowing the Preppers to scatter for cover. The more familiar arrows found their marks better, taking down the startled replacement guards, but another Prepper managed to get in behind a shed while two more made it back to the longhouse taking away any advantage of surprise. A lengthy standoff followed with the patrol trying to encircle while the Preppers fired from their ensconced positions.

Clarence snarled at Hale, fear obvious in his voice, "This is a disaster. We're almost out of ammunition and no closer to taking them."

"Stating the obvious is no help."

Unfortunately, the walking annoyance was right. They needed to do something soon or, with the sun setting, the Preppers would be able to reorganize under cover of darkness.

"Seems you missed the obvious here as you've screwed this up completely. What do we do now?"

"Gather our people to the east," pointing, Hale added, "Meet me behind those willows."

It took a few minutes for the patrol, now with four injured men, to collect behind the bunch of trees. The low sun glared behind them, casting long shadows. Hale detailed his improvised frontal assault plan.

Together the eleven of them charged, hoping the setting sun would blind their enemies. Hale led, forcing his legs to keep pumping as the crack of gunfire rang all around. He jumped over a rail fence of a pen but stumbled on the landing, falling down as others managed to rush past him. He heard a snap as a bullet splintered the wood behind him. Hesitating would be fatal. A twisted knee ached, and his heart threatened to explode from his chest, but he barely noticed, pushing himself up and only caring about moving forward.

Wilson fell as they ran, crashing wounded or dead in the grass and Hale slowed to scoop up his rifle. Eight of them made it, running fast, pushed by their comrades' screams of pain. They charged into the yard, darting between the buildings. While the others flattened themselves against the long building so the rifles inside could not find them, Hale and Milo turned a corner at full speed. Their arrows took out the Prepper hiding behind the shed as he fumbled to reload his rifle.

With no hesitation, the remnants of the patrol kicked in the door of the longhouse. Two Bankers hurled lit lanterns inside, smashing them against the back wall before moving to the side of the door. A slight hesitation then the whooshing sound of kerosene erupting into flames. Preppers fled the flames through the only door in the building and were met by a flock of arrows.

Jumping over the bodies, Hale led the patrol inside the fiery building. The woman with the white hair and an elderly man remained huddled in a corner, holding up blankets against the heat of the flames. Hale ordered everyone to ignore them and put out the flames. In the matter of a minute, the building with all its supplies was safe. Heavy casualties but the settlement of Gergesa was there's.

CHAPTER THIRTEEN

JUNE 17, 2046
DAY THREE THOUSAND SEVEN HUNDRED AND SIXTY-SEVEN

Morreign could feel a deep, awkward angst hanging over Malden with three of their youth now gone ten days. Paul and Matt had returned from searching, tired and defeated, having seen no sign of their sons or the boat. On their return, the quiet talk of holding funerals began, people seeking closure of the issue so they, and the community, could move on.

Morreign discussed a funeral softly and vaguely with Paul. He dodged making a definitive decision but gave the impression he could accept the idea, having, on his lengthy, depressing hike back, come to grips with the fact that his last child was gone. She, however, found it beyond difficult to turn her mind to saying a final goodbye to Jacob, certain that clinging to painfully thin and senseless hope was all that kept her sane and functioning. A funeral would destroy that mirage and, surely, grief would overwhelm her.

Walking through the Lodge's common room, Morreign suffered curious stares as she nodded to the handful of people finishing their dinners before she limped up the stairs. Raising her pale fist to knock, Morreign rapped quietly.

Louisa's eyes were red with tears. Clearly, the news of Paul and Matt's failure had reached her. Without a word, she moved aside to let Morreign into the narrow room.

Morreign never visited her room before. The cramped space only held a skinny bed, a worn out chair, and a thin table. Regardless, Louisa obviously took pride in the simple space. Yellow drapes made out of dyed sheets brought in color while a wide mirror made of carefully flattened and polished tinfoil made the place seem bigger. Decorations of dried flowers and handcrafted hangings covered the walls. A rug of knotted, colorful rags softened the plank floor. A home, the girl, had turned the tiny cell into a cozy, welcoming home.

"I have a couple cookies left. One of the benefits of people pitying you is extra treats. They're the dry kind Shelia makes but better than nothing."

Taking the treasured rarity felt wrong to Morreign but denying the gesture would be rude. Sitting on the rickety chair and biting the cookie, she agreed they were dry but tasty. Butter no longer existed but she doubted Louisa even knew cookies were supposed to have butter in them.

Louisa sat cross-legged on the bed, and they nibbled in companionable silence, savoring the delicacy before Morreign asked, "You've heard Paul and Matt got back?"

"Yeah, can't say I'm surprised, but it still hurts to hear it for certain."

After a moment, Morreign, numb from the onslaught of despair, said coldly, "People are talking of holding funerals."

Louisa merely looked at her, pondering this idea before she eventually shook her head. "I don't know about Griff and Tina, but I don't think Jacob would want a funeral. Not like this."

A stab of guilt pierced Morreign's chest like an ice pick. She only thought about what her reaction to a funeral would be, she had not thought about what her son would want. Realization quickly followed. Louisa was right, Jacob would not want people sitting around crying and remembering him.

"You're completely right. If he we were here, Jacob would say no thanks."

Surprisingly this got a snort of a laugh from Louisa. She covered her mouth with her hand. "Sorry, sorry. I shouldn't laugh. This all feels surreal. I mean, if they're dead they won't care about damn funerals, and if they're alive, they're going to be struggling, dealing with far more serious problems than whether we get together and talk about them."

The reaction made Morreign laugh a bit herself and, for the first time in days she enjoyed a minor sensation of relaxation. The ache, which had been constantly residing in her stomach, faded slightly, and she let out a long breath.

"Louisa, I have to say, I appreciate how you first thought about the funeral from his perspective. I feel awfully selfish. I was only thinking about how horrible the funeral would be for me."

"Funny. For days now, I keep telling myself that I'm selfish."

"Really? What makes you think that?"

"Well, if I truly believe he's alive then I have to believe him, and Griff and

Tina are out there with no gear or food, starving and freezing."

This thought had not completely escaped Morreign, but she worked hard to push the idea of her hope that they survived also meaning her child was suffering somewhere in the wilderness to the deep back of her mind. She merely nodded.

Louisa continued, "Right. But instead of worrying about him out there or missing him, all I really find myself doing is getting angry about all I dreamt about for so long now not happening."

The idea that Louisa thought about a future with Jacob should not have been surprising but now the idea intrigued Morreign, and it provided a chance for a change of subject. "What sort of things do you dream about?"

Picking at the frayed hem of her jeans, Louisa sighed, "Nothing strange or anything, simple things. We talked about building a new cabin, maybe kind of removed away from the rest. Not too far, but maybe closer to the river. Jacob even worked on some basic plans. They looked pretty rough, but I figured Leo could help with the details when it came time to start."

A smile crossed Morreign's lips at the realization young people in Malden thought about building lives together the same as young people in the past did. She asked, "Really? He was going to put up a cabin?"

"Oh yeah, multiple rooms and a cellar. I pictured putting in another garden, you know, in the stretch between the poplars and the creek. I've been thinking about trying multiple crops. Spring onions and then late fall potatoes, or whatever so we could get two harvests. Something everyone could benefit from.

"I saw us spending the days working, side by side. Then, in the evenings, we'd sit together and eat dinner while laughing at silly jokes before climbing beneath a warm quilt to fall asleep in each other's arms. At some point, a pudgy baby with curly hair like his..."

Tears were now running down her cheeks to her chin before falling on to the girl's lap. Morreign moved to sit next to her on the hard bed. She had been pitying herself, but now she felt intensely grateful for all the life she had been lucky enough to enjoy fully and easily before the harshness came. Louisa knew nothing but hard times, hard times which seemed destined to constantly get harder.

• • •

Griff looked awful as he tottered on his ruined ankle. Tina's fever had let up some, but her pack seemed to be pushing her into the ground with every step. Jacob wondered if he looked any better himself after being forcibly marched for seven days with almost no food and minimal water. The hunger pains disappeared a while back but the incredible, overwhelming thirst persisted, and his muscles ached intolerably. Now every movement made him feel dizzy, and his throat felt like fire, and his own load sent painful shocks down his spine. As the sun got higher and his head became dizzier with fatigue he gratefully pondered how this might be his last day alive.

As usual, they stopped midday so the guards could torment them by eating and drinking their fill while the captives watched, lucky to get a quick mouthful of water before being moved along. Today though, Mr. Badger tossed them a half-full jug of water saying, "We'll be home before supper so you fools might as well drink this one up."

The influx of unexpected water eased the agony in Jacob's throat but the news they would soon be done marching truly rejuvenated him. Once their prisoners became too exhausted to flee, the guards became less watchful providing them the opportunity to talk if they could muster the energy. For the last two days, Griff barely seemed conscious and not up for conversation. Tina initially tried to raise spirits but, eventually, her jovial nature fell on deaf ears, and she too retreated into her own misery.

After giving in to Jacob and agreeing not to help their captors find Malden, grunting that he'd probably seen enough killing in his life to not need to cause some at the end, the trapper generally did not talk much, appearing to have resolved himself to an unfortunate finish. However, Jacob decided to try again now that they were close to stopping.

"Hey, you hear that? We're getting to wherever we're going today."

A scoff.

"We'll be done walking soon."

Another scoff. Jacob was about to give up on conversation when the old man turned slightly and asked, "And you think that's good news?"

The question confused Jacob, and he responded, "Yeah, I guess. Has to be better than walking and starving all day."

"I'd reconsider that."

"You know where we're going?"

"Got a pretty good idea."

Curious dread about their destination overfilled Jacob, and he blurted out, "Where?"

The trapper glanced over at the kidnappers who seemed uninterested in them before he whispered, "I'm not sure, but I think these are some of the crazy survivalist types. They set up a settlement about thirty years ago, and all of us up here learned to give them a wide berth. Heard a rumor couple years ago that they all gone completely insane after all civilization went away."

It didn't seem possible but Jacob's worry actually deepened. "What do you mean?"

"They keep slaves."

"Slaves?"

"Yeah, lock people up, put chains on them and use them to do work."

Not a pleasant thought but Jacob figured a chance to escape would arise once they were able to rest up some. "Could be worse."

"Rumors say it is."

"What rumors?"

"That they're cannibals."

Confused, Jacob asked, "What's a cannibal?"

"Means they eat their dead. Actually, I think they make people dead so they can eat'em."

The words were unbelievable. "No one would do that."

"Like I said, only rumors but persistent ones."

"No one could be that insane. No one could..."

"Before you left your little camp, you think anyone be insane enough to starve four innocent people and force march them through the woods? I learned long ago, evil resides in many people and when too many of those evil hosts ban together it pours out in unpredictable and undesirable ways."

Jacob could not ask anything further as Steel Eyes moved over to get them back on their feet. As they trudged, Jacob's exhaustion would not allow him to think about what he had been told. Thankfully, when he tried to get his addled mind to contemplate the horrors whispered to him, it refused to focus on anything more complex than his next stumbling step and cool water.

As he dreamt about getting another long drink, a scream erupted nearby. For an instant, Jacob thought it may have been him screaming, but then Steel Eyes collapsed to the ground and rolled about in agony, clutching at her stomach. An impossibly loud cracking followed, it took a second for Jacob to recognize the sound of gunfire from childhood memories and fear caused him to instinctively fall to the grass and awkwardly crawl beneath a pine tree.

Pressing his face into the grass, Jacob could not see but, from the various sounds and yells, he figured a brief attack occurred followed by the sounds of an agitated conversation. Lying there, trying to breath slow and silent, Jacob pleaded with unknown deities that his captors would lose and the new attackers would entirely overlook his existence.

However, their bad luck continued unabated as Jacob saw heavy boots move under the pine boughs and a calm voice called down, "Alright, we've got a rifle trained on you. Come on and crawl outta there nice and easy like."

Choices were nonexistent, so Jacob fought his bindings to get his battered body partially out from under the tree before hard hands grabbed his shoulders and helped him onto his swollen feet. A middle-aged man with a blue cap and military style jacket gave him and his bonds a once over before asking, "These folks capture you and your friends?"

Frightened, Jacob could only nod.

He flinched as the man drew a long knife. Seeing this, the man quickly said, "Don't worry. I'm only tired of people being tied up around here."

He knelt and cut the ropes from Jacob's ankles and then from his hands. In a dry-throated whisper, Jacob said, "Thanks."

"No problem," he pointed at other men standing amongst the trees, "I'm Hale. This here is Milo, and that's Walter. Over there is Grey."

Griff, Tina, and the trapper were being helped up as well. Ahead of them lay the bodies of Steel Eyes and Aslan with Mr. Badger kneeling in the grass, a rifle pointed at his back. The sight unabashedly pleased Jacob, perhaps their nightmare had finally ended. He wheezed out, "I'm Jacob."

Hale handed him a canteen. Jacob drank deeply, coughing in his rush to guzzle the water before handing it back empty. Hale smiled and asked, "Ok, you alright to walk on up to the house? It's only about three hundred yards or so."

At this, he wanted to laugh. Three hundred yards. It felt like they walked three hundred miles, a few more yards would not matter. He nodded again.

With Griff being helped by Milo and Mr. Badger being prodded along at gunpoint, they all moved forward. Hale sauntered slowly next to Jacob and curiosity and worry over the trapper's rumors caused him to ask, "Can I, well, ask a question?"

"Sure Jacob."

The minor polite friendliness after a week of endless cruelty almost caused Jacob to breakdown and cry, but he managed to remain composed enough to ask, "Where are we? I mean, what is going on? Who are these people?"

A chuckle from Hale as he said, "People might not be the right term. These demons are part of a group that called themselves The Prepared. Survivalists set up before the war. Because they were planning for the end of the world, they had superior weapons, shelter, and supplies when things went to hell. They used their better position to enslave desperate survivors to work for them. My guess is you all were to be added to their stable of workers."

Trapper was at least partially right. Jacob was too scared to ask the other question in his mind about what would happen to them now. Instead, he hopefully asked, "And who are you guys?"

"We're mainly made up of ex-military people who survived the bombing and its aftermath by setting ourselves up in one of the only buildings left standing in Thule. These Prepared folks were causing us trouble, so we came out here to put an end to those troubles."

His heart sunk. More violent men. Jacob wondered if everyone outside Malden were killers. "Now you guys have taken over their place?"

"Yes, but we'll be leaving soon. Miraculously none of us were killed in the attack, but some were badly injured, and we need to wait until they're able to move 'fore we can head back to Thule. Plus, we were told those three who captured you were out here, and we were hoping to deal with them before we left, that's why we were watching for their return."

The important question almost caught in Jacob's throat, and he sounded like a child as he asked, "What happens to us?"

A shrug of the shoulders before Hale said, "First a decent meal and a night's sleep in a real bed. We'll figure out the rest after that."

The lack of certainty should've scared Jacob, but the idea of food and rest was so wonderful he did not care about the future beyond. He urged his ruined feet to move faster.

• • •

Re-reading it for the hundredth time did nothing to help Harrison figure out what to do. Hale had sent Taco hurrying back to Thule with the brief, childish letter, explaining how they took the settlement but suffered five serious injuries and some of the enemy remained at large, so they were going to wait to return. The report vaguely indicated they captured food along with a number of firearms and ammunition. He questioned Taco, but the near-mute fool only told bizarre half-stories about slaves and someone being eaten.

The firearms worried Harrison. Another mistake. He figured the Survivalists might, at most, have a couple of rusty rifles with a handful of bullets, not an arsenal. Early on, he managed to maintain control when guns were plentiful, but that was with everyone scared of the new, unknown world. Now, the unknown was known and painfully routine, merely being willing to make the hard decisions and ensure no one froze to death would be insufficient to keep command if his sole gun became one of a dozen or more.

Having survived a major firefight to get new supplies for the Bank, the men on the patrol would be returning heroes with few remembering it was Harrison's idea to take the risk. He could envision talk of holding elections and establishing governing committees starting up. Especially if the cowardly Clarence failed and Hale made it back. In any event, he needed to be ready.

Something would need to be done to re-solidify his position before any opposition could act. Unfortunately, sitting at his desk, staring at the letter by candlelight, all ideas crossing his mind were discarded as too desperate or inefficient. He folded the note and slipped it into a drawer, but before he blew out the candle, he pledged to himself to watch diligently for any opportunity to turn the situation back to his advantage.

As he climbed into bed, he heard the barking of laughter from somewhere below, and the idea occurred to him: he was not dealing with the most intelligent, long-range thinking people. Maybe a grand, complex scheme was not needed. Something immediate and memorable might be sufficient to consolidate his position with the men at Thule before the others could return.

A knock on his door. He almost forgot he had summoned Seanah. Even after all these years, she was more reluctant than the others, and he liked how, on some nights at least, she put up a fight. He let her in, growling, "Took you long enough."

     •   •   •

"Sherman and Brady're doing better. Won't be fast moving but, one day, maybe two and we can head back," Milo reported to Hale as he took a handful of stale crackers out of the box on the table.

The second floor of the longhouse was divided into cramped apartments which the patrol members gladly took for their own. The main floor was an open, communal space and the low ceilinged basement served as storage with a metal pen area for captives at one end. Hale gave the slaves freedom to move wherever they wished as the three surviving Preppers took their place in the cage.

Marvin was correct about there being a lot of ammunition boxes and guns, however, and to Hale's amusement, the boxes were mainly empty leaving less than twenty rounds. Food supplies were better, their best find in years. Sacks of dried vegetables augmented by canned and boxed goods from before the Bombs. Disgustingly, a smokehouse behind the main building was busily persevering fresh meat which they promptly buried.

Despite their success, or because of their success, Hale was tormented. He wanted to go back so he could see Kinma, oddly he could not remember ever missing anyone, but now he knew the constant physical yearning in his chest meant he missed her deeply. However, leaving here meant he needed to decide how to deal with the prisoners and start the fight to repair the ongoing disaster back at Thule.

The rule regarding foundlings was to dispose of anyone who would not provide a significant benefit to the Bank. None of the slaves met the requirement, and no one would agree to sparring the Preppers. Hale knew his only real option was to leave them all behind, but he also knew leaving them behind with no supplies could be tantamount to a death sentence.

Hale answered Milo, "Alright, I think we've earned an extended vacation but let's also get ready to move so we can roll first thing day after tomorrow."

Milo, his mouth full of dry crackers, said, "Ok, how many of us will be going?"

His old friend knew the dilemma facing him. Hale looked him in the eye and shrugged, "Don't know yet. Thoughts?"

"I got no problem leaving those cannibal bastards in their cage, when they get hungry they can flip a coin to see who gets ate by who. The other folks though, I don't know. I've been talkin' with 'em, and nobody is going to be a great help back home, but they all seem decent enough."

"Rule is we leave 'em behind."

"Rule is we eliminate them," Milo corrected.

"Right, but I think those days are done for me though."

Milo took another handful of crackers, "Yeah, not sure how much I care about any of the damn rules anymore wither."

"I hear you, but I'm not sure we can defy Harrison that openly without it coming to immediate blood."

This got a shrug from Milo. "We got the guns now."

Hale had already done the math on this suggestion. With Taco gone to report back, and the injuries, the once powerful patrol now consisted of nine able men. Clarence ensured he stayed near the back during the attack and, as a result, he, of course, remained unscathed. He would not agree to overthrow Harrison, and a few of the others might think they would be better off sticking it out under the old, familiar regime especially now that they would be returning as heroes. The rescued prisoners might be up to fighting, but Hale could not assume they would be willing to act with them rather than act against them, plus they did not strike him as fighters. This all left him with only a handful of people.

While Harrison only had one gun with ammunition, the Bank remained lousy with other weapons. When he went through the population at Thule and counted the fors and againsts, Hale determined his coup force would be outnumbered by as much as three to one. The advantage of guns over bows would not level those odds.

And there was Kinma's safety to worry about. He could not presume Harrison would be unaware of the threat, he was too paranoid not to be expecting something, even with him having sent the calming note. Any suspicion of a rebellion and Harrison would either take Kinma hostage or execute her immediately.

Hale said, "I've thought about it. Don't think it'd work, too many unknowns. We go back and work on getting change once we're there."

"Alright, I'm with you I guess, but we gotta bring the guns back."

Nodding Hale said, "Yeah, can't really leave them."

"All this talk doesn't answer what we do with the poor sad sacks they captured."

Standing, Hale said, "I know, I know."

"And there's the cannibal bastards we didn't kill in the attack? Surely we can take them out?"

Hale sighed, "I don't know, feels like we've drank from the killing cup too many times already, it don't seem to quench anymore."

"Poetic. Alright, you're the boss. I'll get stuff ready and organize like everybody is coming along."

Hale took the crackers and said, "Ok, now let me think in peace."

•　　•　　•

The rough, kid-like handwriting made Kinma smile. Taco slipped her the tight roll of paper on his return. Her eyes roamed over the letters, not really reading because she knew the words by heart. It explained how Hale's trip was successful, but he needed to wait before returning. Then he briefly and, somewhat awkwardly, spoke of how much he missed her. The statement seemed out of character for the normally reserved man, and she could not help but grin as her fingers touched the ink.

At the end, he wrote, "I have witnessed what happens when cruelty is left unchecked. When I get back, we need to act to improve the situation there. Give this thought, I will need your help but keep it to yourself for now. Burn this once you've read it."

Not the most romantic of sign-offs and Kinma could not come close to bringing herself to destroy the letter. She knew Hale often thought about changing life in the Bank, but she also knew these thoughts were rolling about his mind for years now. Reading the words put on paper made his ideas seem concrete, and she felt this meant they would act firmly on his return.

Coincidentally, the same thoughts and pressure to act were occurring to her. Seeing the cruelty more acutely since Hale left, Kinma fully hated going blindly down the horrific path Harrison was laying for them. For days her mind toiled over how to turn the Bank onto a better path. Simply killing Harrison would not work, too many loyal followers, too many men who enjoyed the easy depravity of their lives to support a sudden change so such a frontal assault would only throw everything into violent chaos. The change must be smarter and more subtle.

A knock on the door startled her, instantly scattering her thoughts. She hastily stuffed the paper into her pocket as she called out that she was coming. Opening the door revealed Seanah with a swelling bruise on her cheek. Painful sobs were shaking the woman as tears poured down her face. As she let her new friend inside, Kinma found herself hoping even more that Hale would get back in a hurry so they could start improving this hell as soon as possible.

CHAPTER FOURTEEN

JUNE 19, 2046

DAY THREE THOUSAND SEVEN HUNDRED AND SIXTY-NINE

With the patrolmen, the captives, Jacob, Tina and Griff all together, the common room of the longhouse was crowded. Surrounded by so many strangers made Jacob greatly uneasy and his body ached everywhere from the forced marching. Still, after eating his fill and sleeping the sleep of the exhausted, he felt remarkably better than he had in the past days.

The food and rest returned some of Griff's stinging verbosity, and he quietly growled, "With our luck, they'll now want us to run to the goddamn moon."

Tina, seeming especially nervous amongst all these people, her eyes shifted around as she said, "I've never thought I'd want to be back on that muddy island with you fools, but I'd be happy to be there right now."

Jacob whispered, "I met the guy I think is in charge. Right when they found us. I think he's ok. I mean, I don't think he's like those others."

Griff muttered, "Maybe the prick'll carry us home."

Annoyed at Griff ruining his hope, Jacob said, "Maybe he'll let us go home at least."

At that Griff turned to look at him, a striking harshness in his eyes. "Can you even point in what direction home is? Can you even point towards the bloody river?"

Griff was right. Even if they were set completely free, they had nothing and no idea how to find their way back. He was not even sure how many days they were forced to hike, let alone what direction they were going in. Jacob had planned to ask the trapper, hoping he would give them directions back but the old man seemed to have disappeared in the night leaving him with no idea how to find home. Despite Griff being right, Jacob did not appreciate being reminded of their predicament. For now, he was warm and fed, and he could tell himself he would somehow make it back to Louisa.

Before he could express this to Griff, Hale walked inside, and everyone grew quiet. He stepped to the front of the room, the wall behind him blackened with char from a recent fire. He calmly said, "Alright, I'll get right to the point. Everyone's mainly back on their feet so the patrol will soon be heading back to Thule."

A man from the back called out, "Better get eating double-time then."

This got a few laughs which Jacob did not understand. Another called out, "Hope them women back home all got a good rest."

More laughs.

Hale cut off the laughter by raising a hand and continuing, "Ok, it'll make for a long trip but, by using that firewood cart and the mules, I think we can take all the supplies–"

"What about us?"

The shouted question came from the back of the crowd. A couple men began to tell the interrupter to shut up, but Hale interjected and said, "Fair question, Marvin."

"It is, and we could use a fair answer."

Hale took in a deep breath before saying, "Right. Unfortunately, it's not all that simple, but I decided it's not right for us to free you all and then leave you with nothing. Anyone who wants to come back to Thule with us can. Otherwise, you can remain here, and we'll leave some perishable supplies to help get you through to harvest."

Confused chatter filled the room. One of the patrolmen loudly called up to Hale, "We can't bring 'em back. Harrison won't allow adding a bunch of useless mouths."

Again, Hale lifted his hands, "Alright Clarence, that'll be my problem, not yours. You newcomers need to appreciate that when we get back to Thule, the leader of the Bank may not accept you. You'll have to prove that you have value and if you can't do that you might be left outside. Every Banker needs to pull their own weight and then some. I won't lie, life there is not exactly easy. I suggest you speak with myself and the men from the patrol to get a sense of what coming back with us will mean to you. You may choose to stay here or strike out to on your own instead of trying to join with us."

With that Hale stepped down from the front of the room and people broke into conversations. Jacob looked at Griff who said, "Ok, you were right. I guess we can head home."

"Problem of not knowing where to go still's a problem though."

Tina added, "I don't know. That guy sounds like he'll help us maybe. We ask how to get to the river and head upstream 'til the scenery gets familiar. Maybe they'll even let us take some food and gear."

That made sense to Jacob but recent experiences kept him concerned for Malden, he said, "Right, right. But I'm worried, I mean these guys are better than the others but they're still killers and looters. We start asking about how to get home, they're going to ask questions and I think they'll realize there's stuff at Malden worth going to get."

Tina said, "Might be right. But, we could stay here for a while, at least there'll be shelter to rest up in, and then we can figure out how to find the river on our own."

The torture of the march remained centered in his mind. And, even without kidnappers, the idea of wandering around in the woods, starving and freezing again did not appeal to Jacob. He said, "I'm not sure, we'd be pretty lost out there."

Griff nodded. "You know, I gotta say when that guy said we could go with them, the thought of seeing Thule struck me as interesting. We could see the ruins of the legend. Rest up there and more carefully figure out how to make it back home. It might mean waiting longer, but it's better than starving to death in the woods. Plus, it'd make for a pretty cool story when we get home."

An intriguing idea but Jacob remained wary. "I don't know, you wanna trust these guys?"

Tina added, "Yeah, I don't like being around strangers like this."

Griff shrugged, "No, but I don't want to stumble around in the woods starving to death either. We've all had enough of that lately."

Jacob was pondering his response when one of the patrolmen sat down across the battered table from them. Through a mouthful of the pasta he spooned into his face from a massive bowl, the man asked, "Hi there, you three feeling better today?"

For a second, Jacob considered their new company. More slender than the others with straight dark hair. Predictably, Griff answered for them, "Yeah, quite a bit better. I guess we owe you guys for saving us from those guys."

Setting down the heavy bowl the man handed them each a fork and said, "Good timing for sure. I'm Clarence."

The three awkwardly introduced themselves, Tina, unable to even look up from the table as she muttered her name. However, they all eagerly shared his rich breakfast as Clarence asked, "What happened to that old guy who came in with you?"

Griff said, "Not sure, he was a trapper those guys caught on our way here. Think he took off, back out into the woods I suppose."

Clarence nodded and grunted his understanding as he ate.

Chewing the wonderful food, Jacob nervously asked, "You're from Thule?"

Throughout his life, Jacob was enthralled by thoughts of Thule. His father and Uncle Leo would sit around the table in the dark nights of winter or out on the porch in the cool air of spring and endlessly discuss all the amazing luxuries they used to enjoy. Jacob would ask questions about his forgotten hometown and bask in all the older men would tell him. The idea of actually seeing the mythical place never occurred to Jacob as a possibility, but now it seemed shockingly close.

Clarence swallowed a mouthful and said, "Yeah. I'm the second in command there."

"Really? Hale is in charge?"

"No, he's only running this patrol. There's a brilliant guy named Harrison back at Thule who leads us. I'm his right-hand man. Together we decide who gets in and who doesn't. You guys thinking of coming back with us?"

Griff quickly said, "Considering our options."

After a pause for more eating, Clarence asked, "Where you come from?"

Clearly, they could not tell these men the truth about their home. So, with no reason to come up with a new story, Griff told an abbreviated version of the tale about them being sent out to find food by their sickly parents when the boat took them far away. For a long time, Clarence looked at him and Griff and then he said, "You two don't look like brothers."

Jacob did not understand this, he did not think brothers looked any different than any other people. He asked, "What do you mean?"

Suspicion filled the man's face as he answered, "He's a curly redhead, you're dark and taller. Obviously strange to have that big a difference in siblings."

Griff shrugged, "Don't know about all that, but I know we're brothers."

A laugh which somehow sounded both fake and chilling was followed by, "Maybe your mom spent some time with the mailman."

With no idea what he was talking about, they all gave bad fake laughs of their own. Apparently realizing they should change the topic away from their lie, Tina asked, "What's Thule like?"

"Thule? It's pretty much nothing but rubble that nature's spent the last ten years growing over. But, we've carved out a nice bubble of civilization. We got an entire apartment building the Bombs missed."

As they ate the pasta, Clarence enthusiastically told them about the place, focus on the abundance of not only food but of comradeship, hinting about willing female company. With their stomachs churning through the unusually heavy meal, surrounded by impressive men joking and laughing, the Malden residents listened intently, soaking in the stories of a place they thought of as myth. Finally, done describing, Clarence, asked, "So, you got any skills that'll make it easy for me to recommend letting you in?"

Hearing about Thule and all it had, the idea of not going with them faded somewhat. Even though he desperately wanted to get back home, Jacob told himself it presented a possible opportunity. They could go and learn about this other civilization and, upon returning to Malden, they could tell everyone all about it, perhaps bring new ideas, maybe even make some allies of a sort.

Plus, Jacob had to admit, spending time in a well-supplied group seemed far superior to more cold nights wandering alone in the woods. Jacob shared a look with Griff and, his lifelong friend managed to express the same thought with a slight shrug. Tina, however, shook her head slightly with a confused and worried look on her face.

Before the trio could come up with a response, the captive who spoke up, stopped at their table, putting his palms down and leaning over them. "What's your name?"

His stomach immediately tensing with worry, Jacob answered, "Jacob."

"Well, Jacob, I wanted to let you know, before these guys leave with all our food, that you and your friends are not welcome to stay here with us. I suggest you tag along with them because, once they're gone, there will be promptly be nothing for you three here. Understand?"

Jacob, tired and overwhelmed by all that had happened, was not sure he entirely understood what the stranger was implying but the words were abrupt and harsh, making it clear how he should reply. He said, "I understand."

With that, the captive gave a quick nod and strode back into the crowded room. Clarence, plucking up the now empty bowl, stood and laughed, "Guess that'll limit your options somewhat."

•　　•　　•

Enjoying thoughts of seeing Kinma again, Hale eagerly packed his travel pack, carefully wrapping two absconded boxes of cookies for her in his extra shirt. Milo knocked and walked into the small room. He immediately and exaggeratedly averted his eyes, pretending not to see the valuable supplies being squirreled away.

"Think we're all set for dawn, boss."

"Great. Any change in the tagalongs?"

"Nope, all the captives decided they don't want to come. They're going to try to make a go of it here. Sounds like they dislike the idea of living under someone else's control again after what happened here. Can't blame 'em."

"And the new ones they were bringing in?"

"That old timer they brought in took off on his own, disappeared back into the woods, so we don't got to worry about him. I think those two young guys and the one-armed girl, the walking dead trio, are thinking of coming with us."

This surprised Hale. They seemed scared of everyone. He asked, "Really?"

"Yeah, I think Clarence told them life in the Bank was nothing but parties and ice cream."

Hale figured, all in all, this was not a horrible outcome. The idea of dragging all the captives to Thule only to have Harrison turn them away or worse did not appeal to Hale. The news that Clarence apparently encouraged the kids to come troubled him as they seemed very naïve, plus, everything Clarence did worry him, especially when he did not understand his motivation.

The boys were battered, but they were young and, by the time they made it back, they would be healthy enough Harrison might view them as worthwhile enough. The girl with the burn scars would likely be accepted simply because she was a youthful female, but Hale figured her treatment at the Bank would be especially unpleasant given the scars and amputation.

Regardless, Hale figured he could get the three alone on the trip back to Thule and educate them about the realities of their choice. He could slip them supplies and convince them their best option was to disappear into the night with his help. That would allow them their freedom without anyone knowing he let a young woman go.

Hale said, "Alright, like I said, leave some of the perishable food for those staying behind, maybe those wrinkled up carrots. Give 'em something to start off with."

"You think that's necessary?"

"What do you mean?"

"I mean, do you think them slaves might be considering turning the tables on their former masters, making them into jerky?"

Hale knew things would not go well for the remaining Preppers being left behind with their former slaves, but his mercy could only extend so far. He merely shrugged and said, "I'm gonna be glad to leave this messed up hell hole behind. Thule ain't all rainbows and puppy dogs but at least no one's getting eaten there."

Milo used his serious tone, "You know, at some point, we need to talk about what we gonna do when we get back."

Hale knew this was coming. "Once we're on the road. I need some time to think about it now that this mess here is settled."

"Ok. But, I've been thinking already."

Throwing one of Milo's usual jokes back at him, Hale asked, "Oh yeah? Did it hurt?"

"Not too much. One idea kept coming through the fog: we might be better off if Clarence didn't make it back with us. You know he's going to be a problem no matter what we do. Plus, he's almost as evil as Harrison. We could make it look like an accident or something, and then we've got one less enemy to worry about."

The reality of what they were discussing struck Hale again. A violent coup within the Bank meant people, people they lived and worked with, getting hurt and killed. He pulled on his parka and said, "I'm still hoping for something more, well, subtle, I guess. A compromise of some sort."

Milo shook his head and said, "You know how crazy Harrison is, I doubt he's the type to make any sort of sensible deal."

Moving to the door, Hale said, "You're probably right. Let me think on it tonight. I've got to go relieve Wilson on watch."

As patrol leader, Hale did not need to take a turn on watch, but he always did. It improved morale, and he enjoyed the peace and quiet.

Clapping him on the shoulder as he walked by, Milo added, "Ok, but now I'm actually worried that, with all this thinking we're doing, we might actually end up hurting ourselves for real."

•　　•　　•

Setting the book on her chest, Louisa let out a sigh. She had read the novel before, a half-dozen times at least, and it was unable to distract her. Downstairs she could hear people talking, probably doing those odd jobs that never seemed to get finished like knitting scarves, darning socks, and mending tools. She used to enjoy these communal past times especially when it resulted in something useful being made or fixed.

Now, however, her mind would not quiet during repetitive work. Before long she would be missing Jacob or worrying about Jacob or both. Books were a better distraction, but only barely, they always failed to hold her interest before long. For a while, she tried working on her crafts, weaving a basket out of willow branches, but she always ended up realizing the best part of those hobbies was getting to show her silly projects to Jacob.

She got off the narrow bed. Walked three paces one way and three paces the other. Stared out the window. Walked three paces, thought about opening the door, walked three paces the other way. She could go downstairs to join the others, however, everyone looked at her oddly now and she knew they twisted the conversation to make sure not to upset her. She did not like her grief ruining their night. She thought about going to see Morreign but she was at her cabin that morning, and another visit would be imposing.

Louisa sat back on the bed and realized the rare problem of boredom used to be alleviated by merely going to find Jacob. Her hands went to her face, and she began to cry. Not fair. A thousand times a day she saw something, heard something or thought something which made her immediately plan to tell Jacob about it when she saw him only to then have to realize she would not be able to see him. Her whole life, since early childhood, involved Jacob being with her, so it was no surprise that, now, everywhere she looked at was a memory or thought of him. Her life became a throbbing agony of repeatedly remembering then missing.

The tears dried up fairly quickly, the crying jags still started easily, but they lasted less time these days. As if her tear supply was running low and rationing was in effect. She laid back down, picking up the half-read book when there was a knock.

She wiped her face with her sleeve and opened the door to reveal Sam. Louisa spent time with him when she was a child, learning the basics of survival from the silent teacher alongside all the other kids but, once she crossed into her teen years and no longer needed the lessons, she hardly spoke with him beyond polite greetings, figuring that was how he preferred things. Staring at her with stony, black eyes he said, "Full moon, lots of animals moving around. Going to see what I can catch. You should come help."

CHAPTER FIFTEEN

JUNE 19, 2046
DAY THREE THOUSAND SEVEN HUNDRED AND SIXTY-NINE

Alcohol was technically banned in the Bank. An unpopular rule but, after a handful of unfortunate events, no one could logically dispute its necessity. Despite the rule, brewing of discrete batches of hooch occurred. Plastic buckets of fermenting fruit hidden under beds and in closets. Harrison surely knew of this practice, but Kinma figured he looked the other way to maintain morale so long as no one became a drunken problem.

Today, however, Harrison ordered the Vikings to conduct a search of the building and confiscate all the alcohol. People became deathly worried as rumours circulated about Harrison cracking down but, instead of punishment, everyone received an invitation to the common room to partake of the confiscated goods. Before the indulgence started, Harrison, with an unusual grin plastered on his face, explained that, since the patrol was undoubtedly gorging on the supplies they found, those working hard back home should also get to enjoy themselves.

At first, the celebration remained tolerable as the men seemed uneasy about blatantly breaking an ingrained rule, like the children of strict parents being told they could eat as much candy as they wanted. They sat around sipping while Rodger with his guitar and Walter with a harmonica, badly played the few songs they knew. Kinma, knowing it would not be acceptable for her to hide in her apartment, took a seat at the least offensive table and was given a cup of thick drink.

It smelled like an infected wound, tasted like rotten yeast and her first hesitant sip caused her stomach to immediately revolt. Given the awfulness of the beverage, she thought that the night might not disintegrate into craziness as she figured no one could stomach much of the putrid concoction. But the drinking continued unabated under Harrison's watch, each glass emboldening the men who seemed able to ignore the taste as the horrible, homemade booze disappeared.

The women without permanent partners became the predictable entertainment for the roughest, drunkest men. They were groped and grabbed with impunity. A couple of the women played along somewhat, probably to ease the treatment while the others tried vainly to fend off the assaults. Eventually, clothes were roughly removed from the women, and they were lifted on to tables for the amusement of the guffawing fools.

Kinma wanted to do something, anything to stop this painful spectacle but every time she moved to interject she saw Harrison standing off to the side with his unfeeling eyes on her. He merely shook his head slowly. Regardless of the unsaid threat, as the men mocked the scrawny, naked human beings shifting about on the messy tabletops, she couldn't take any more.

Stepping forward, pushing between two of the men, she handed her jacket up to one of the girls. Drunken boos were flung at her. She turned, raising her hands, saying, "We are better than this. We are meant to help one another, not hurt -."

The protesting grew louder, cutting her off but, through the mass, she made eye contact with a few of the men she thought to be not as horrendous as some of the others, starting with Luke. Even through the haze of too much drink, they seemed to partially understand, a feather of humanity remaining and causing them to recall the existence of shame. Eyes lowered under her gaze. Thinking she might accomplish something, she opened her mouth to continue, but Harrison called out, "That's enough. Go ahead boys, she's up for grabs now."

For a moment, no one moved but, certainly, they understood him. Up for grabs meant Kinma was no longer with Hale, she became communal property. Obviously, Hale would be furious if anyone touched her but they would presumably have the protection of Harrison, plus in their drunken, aroused state she doubted any of them would be thinking that far ahead.

Comprehending the situation before the drunks understood, Kinma bolted, but four strong hands grabbed her almost immediately. The Vikings. One on each side. Her feet left the floor as she kicked and screamed. They easily carried her out of the room as the others cheered and whistled encouragement.

•   •   •

Louisa's back ached and she wanted to shiver with cold, but Sam remained stock still next to her, so she remained unmoving in the moonlight. Sam had already bagged two rabbits, and Louisa felt a minor thrill at having been a part of helping to the community, even if her involvement was entirely irrelevant to their success. She also found herself enjoying the distraction of silently learning hunting techniques from Sam and needing to intently focus on the tiny signals being sent out by the springtime woods.

In an instant, the calm forest erupted into action. The thrum of a bow. The crashing of underbrush. The squeal of an injured rodent. All of it seemed to happen at once and, before Louisa could even make her frozen, cramped muscles start to work, Sam had bolted out of their cover and buried his knife into the wounded porcupine as it waddled out of the grass, an arrow in its side.

Moving beside him, Sam said, "Best to end them clean."

"Right. Of course."

He looked over his shoulder and, in the glimmer of moonlight, Louisa thought she caught the glimpse of a grin as he said, "Not much meat on this one, hardly worth carrying back."

Louisa caught on to what he was implying and grinned back with a nod.

In typical Sam fashion, within fifteen minutes, he had skinned and roasted the wiry animal over a small fire, doing all the tasks without a word but in a manner so Louisa could watch every step of the process. Regardless, she was certain she could not skin the porcupine without getting a thousand quill pricks even though Sam managed to expertly avoid them despite chilled fingers and dim light. He used his knife to pluck the meat from the fire, handed her half of the thin carcass and sat across the fire from her.

Tearing into the charred meat, eager for the simple treat even though she felt tinges of guilt for not sharing with the others, Louisa asked, "You do this often?"

"Sometimes. At night. Everyone sleeping."

Expecting the laconic Sam to merely shrug at her question, Louisa was shocked by all the words coming from the shadow across the fire. It took a moment for her to reply, "Right, fair enough. I mean, you must get tired of doing so much for everyone."

He took a bite of porcupine. "I do my share, everything I can. Only way it works."

Louisa took a bite, but her mouth felt suddenly dry around the food. Softly, she said, "Not sure I'm doing my share these days, not even close."

A pause hung over the little, crackling fire. Louisa figured the brief conversation was already ended and she let tears creep from the corners of Louisa's eyes. When they started to trickle onto her cheeks, Sam's voice came back, "That's the point."

"Pardon?"

"The point of being together."

Wiping a tear off a cheek with the back of her glove, Louisa couldn't understand and asked the darkness again, "Sorry, what do you mean?"

"I was alone lots, I get living together now. Someone gets hurt, people help them, they get better and can then help others when they get hurt."

Not liking this analogy, Louisa said, "I didn't break my leg or get sick. I'm... I don't know what I am. I should be sad. Or maybe even angry. And I am, but there's something more, deeper, worse."

This time Sam spoke immediately. "You're afraid. Afraid to be alone."

Louisa was stunned by the insight from Sam and contemplated for a moment before realizing he was perfectly right. She whispered. "Yeah, that's it."

Apparently, done with his snack, Sam tossed some bones into the fire as he stood and said, "Don't be afraid. I think they find their way back, those three, but, no matter what, you won't be alone. This place don't work like that. Morreign don't work like that."

Louisa wanted to sit there by the fire to take in what Sam said but he was already striding through the pines, disappearing into the branches like a breeze and she did want to be left behind in the woods. With no choice, she clenched the last porcupine leg in her teeth, got to her frozen feet and followed after him, feeling a minor sense of revived energy in her steps.

CHAPTER SIXTEEN

JUNE 19, 2046

DAY THREE THOUSAND SEVEN HUNDRED AND SIXTY-NINE

Pitch black sky. Heavy clouds completely hid the moon and stars. Hale wondered if he should give up on the watch and go to bed as a herd of drunken elephants could go by without him seeing a damn thing. Deciding that, after one more slow lap around the settlement his shift would be over anyway, Hale began to turn but then sharply collapsed to the ground as his legs instantly crumbled beneath him, a puppet getting its strings cut.

No pain, no anything, simply lying face down on the damp, cool grass unable to move. Reaching around to his back, Hale discovered the problem, the shaft of an arrow stuck in the middle of his spine. An attack. He opened his mouth to yell out an alarm, but someone landed on him, grabbed his hair and roughly pulled back as Hale tried vainly to free himself. A voice growled directly into his ear, "No one can help you now, you cocky asshole."

Clarence. Not an attack. A one-man mutiny. The asshole chuckled and then searing agony erupted across Hale's exposed throat. He attempted again to yell, but it came out a wet gurgle as gushing blood engulfed his last breath.

As Hale's life poured out into the night, an eerie calm came over him, and he stopped struggling; only lying there and breathing in the damp earth. Before the black of final sleep overtook him, he pictured Kinma's beautiful, laughing face and silently told her he was sorry, completely and utterly sorry, for leaving her alone, for leaving her in such an awful place, all alone.

CHAPTER SEVENTEEN

JUNE 20, 2046

DAY THREE THOUSAND SEVEN HUNDRED AND SEVENTY

Predictably, the drunken party ended abruptly when a clumsy fight broke. Now, only Harrison and Luke the orphan remained in the dark room. Harrison saw an opportunity.

Harrison sat across the mess-filled table from the young man, his sparse beard, a source of amusement for the other men, held some dry vomit but, in the dying firelight, he looked more tired and ill than drunk. Despite his age, Harrison figured Luke tended to understand more than he let on as, when he was relaxed, a quick, concise wit came through. Also, mainly because he did not carry the thinking of the past world which was full of easy-to-use technology, he managed to come up with inventive solutions to problems of the new world. His best idea amongst a bevy of impressive ideas involved taking the old gas that could no longer sustain combustion in a vehicle and mixing it with engine oil so it burned at a placid, useable rate. Their lanterns now all ran off the mixture.

The more foolish men would not pay any attention to the young man, but the keener people in the group realized taking cues from him could be worthwhile. As Luke aged, he would become more and more of a force within the Bank. It would be for the best if Harrison could keep the orphan on his side. Hale and Luke's relationship was fractured somewhat, no longer as close as they once were, and Harrison figured it was Luke's willingness and eagerness to fight running counter to Hale's more passive views which partially caused this rift. However, now Hale had successfully led one of the most dangerous patrols in recent history, and Harrison figured Luke might revert to worshiping his rescuer. Smart to keep a wedge in place between them.

Looking down at the table, with a slightly slurred voice, Luke quietly said, "I know, I know we ain't supposed to question stuff 'round here, but I don't get why you'd take Kinma away from Hale like that. Especially when he finally went back out there."

"That's right, you're not supposed to question. But in this case, I think you're entitled to know what's occurring."

This got the young man's attention, and he looked up from the table with glossy eyes. Harrison continued, "Hale had the chance to take these Survivalist bastards out a long time ago. He decided not to. Now important men of the Bank are badly injured, and many could have been killed. When you factor in the headaches those assholes caused us over the years, I don't think Hale should be rewarded for making that mistake all those years ago."

At this Luke nodded slowly but he clearly was not convinced. The kid was smart, he could sense the deception. Harrison decided he needed to be more upfront.

"You know what's going on around here. You're not an idiot, quite the opposite. I know people are talking about changing how things're run. I'm ok with that, change is fine. But I'm concerned men like Hale, men who are smart enough but who hesitate or shy away from the hard, necessary decisions, will end up in control and then we're all doomed. You know life out here is difficult, it's defined by hardship. You were raised in it, made by it. We need men like you and men like me, men who are not nostalgic for a time of kindness and excess where life and death choices did not exist on a daily basis."

The words hung over the filthy table. Harrison could tell the young man was trying to force his drink addled mind to properly contemplate the words and appreciate the hint of an offer of an alliance with a man in charge. Harrison leaned back, giving him space to consider, and calmly looked around the dim, foul room.

The space used to be the lobby of the apartment building before they turned it into their communal area. In the fading lantern light, the open doors of the useless elevators looked like the openings of menacing caves. An eclectic and bizarre collection of artwork both scavenged by looters and created by bored, uncreative people, covered walls and filled shadowy corners. The juvenile art focussed on the three themes: the female form, angry animals and sports cars. It reminded Harrison of a high school boy's bedroom or a clubhouse for delinquents. The silliness of it all disgusted Harrison.

Back in the early days following the frozen night in the crashed helicopter, he had envisioned creating a society, an efficient and powerful society constructed in his stoic image. Surrounded by the stench of yeasty drink, body odour and vomit, Harrison knew that the image became horribly mutated. He needed to rethink his plan, return the image to its proper form.

He had consciously tried to keep them all isolated, only venturing out to loot and steal without making any real contact before scurrying back to the insular safety of Thule. This was touted as important for everyone's safety, but Harrison also knew this kept outside influences from corrupting the Bank and threatening his rule. However, if the core was rotten, encircling it would only allow decay to spread from the inside. Perhaps the Bank needed to stretch out and expand beyond the confines of the filthy building, move beyond its borders and away from the festering rot of this place.

Before Harrison could complete his thoughts, Luke got uneasily to his feet. As he stumbled away, he said, "Sorry, I need to sleep, I need to sleep and then to think."

Harrison called out, "Oh, and Luke, one more thing: you can move in with Kinma."

That got him to turn around. Early on Harrison realized managing access to sex was an important key to maintaining control, second only to divvying up food. Others in the Bank might be perturbed by this decision to give an attractive woman over to young, largely untested man, but this would destroy any connection between Luke and Hale. And Luke would become Harrison's to control as he would not want to risk losing his prize. Plus, if he was being honest, Harrison worried that putting such a strong woman with anyone else might end badly, she may tolerate life with Hale's relatively kind protégé who she helped raise.

Confusion crossed Luke's fatigued face. Harrison smiled and said, "Don't worry, the Vikings will be done with her soon, they bore easy. And I'll take care of Hale, he won't stop any of this."

The orphan swayed on his feet, but he managed to nod and mutter, "Ok. Good. Thanks."

•　　•　　•　　•

Yelling. Lots of yelling. In the strange place, Jacob was sleeping thinly, so he sat up abruptly when he heard the noise. Tina asked out of the darkness, "What's happening?"

Jacob answered, "I don't know. Something's wrong."

Climbing out of the bed, Griff sighed, "Of course there is."

They got up, pulling their battered boots on to their sore feet. Before they could put on coats, Clarence burst into their room carrying a lantern, bows, and quivers. Excitedly he said, "Come on. Time to show you can earn your keep."

Tina asked, "What happened?"

"We've been attacked."

"Attacked?"

With an angry, mocking tone Clarence responded, "Yeah. You know, when bad people come and try to hurt you. You two hurry up. You with the one arm can stay up here, out of the way."

Fear and confusion holding even Griff's tongue, they grabbed the proffered weapons and followed Clarence, leaving Tina standing, bewildered, in the middle of the small room. Jacob could only look at her and shrug. Speeding down the stairs, they rapidly found themselves outside in pitch black but for a handful of lanterns rushing about in the dark.

Without a word, Clarence moved off to the left. Jacob pulled out an arrow and managed to notch it with shaking hands as he followed, trying to be minuscule, nonexistent even, unsure where they were going, what they were to do and what unknown threats waited for them now.

For half an hour they moved, apparently aimlessly, through the inky dark. They could hear yells from others and see their lights, but Clarence seemed intent on staying away from them. Occasionally, Clarence would stop, inspect the ground or a branch in their lantern's glow. Sometimes he would listen to the breeze, asking them if they heard anything which they never did. Finally, he pointed at a muddy spot between two pine trees where no grass grew.

"Look, look. Right here, look. I figured we'd find a sign."

Jacob and Griff bent down. In the dim light, Jacob thought he could see the outline of boot prints in the soft earth and he said, "Guys out on watch?"

With an immediate fury, Clarence grabbed Jacob's neck, pushing his face nearer the wet earth. "No, look, look close. They're moving away. No man on watch would push his way through trees like that. The attackers came in and then fled off through here."

Pretending to examine the marks, his face being forced lower and lower, Jacob said, "Yeah, yeah. I think you're right."

Clarence turned to Griff who seemed wholly confused. The question came out harshly, "And you, red? What do you see?"

"Uh, the same. Men, probably two, sneaking away through them trees."

This seemed to please Clarence. He let go of Jacob's neck. Moving back towards the buildings, he said, "Good. Now come with me. We have to tell the others what we saw, Hale was obviously killed by some cowards out in the dark."

•   •   •

The cramped room smelled powerfully of unclean bodies. Kinma was huddled in the corner, naked but covered by an itchy, wool blanket that desperately needed to be washed. Her throat ached both from thirst and from screaming. Her body ached from numerous torments. Her mind ached from forcing herself to not think of what was occurring, while constantly pushing herself to fight back regardless of its futility.

Carefully, slowly and on shaky legs, Kinma managed to stand. She could hear their voices, speaking in their strange language, eating and laughing. She knew the layout of the Vikings' apartment was the same as hers. Three steps to get out of the bedroom, three more to get through the living room, two steps down the hall and then out through the apartment door. Eight steps in total. She thought she could manage that, although they might see her crossing the living room. Regardless, she needed to try.

Looking about the dimly lit, nearly empty bedroom for anything helpful, she saw little. She pulled out the drawer in the nightstand and dumped the useless junk onto the mess of blankets. The drawer was not much of a weapon given the beasts out in the kitchen but clutching a flimsy box of wood in her fists felt better than going out with nothing.

Moving quickly to avoid losing her nerve, Kinma kicked through the mess and got to the door. Shadow filled much of the living room, but she could now hear the men more clearly. If they looked, they would see her despite the shadows. Struggling to make her racing breath quiet and slow, she slipped out of the doorway.

Creeping along the wall, she tried to hurry without making noise. One of the twins yelled something, causing Kinma to freeze in place, holding back a startled yelp. Laughter and a banging noise. She cautiously continued her short journey.

A minor trickle of relief when she reached the hall, hidden from the kitchen. Two quick steps and she reached for the door's handle.

"No, no... no, you don't."

A heavy hand grabbed her shoulder spinning her back. Without thought,

Kinma blindly flung the drawer. It landed with a satisfying crunch, the corner catching one of the Vikings right above his eye.

He let out a foreign language curse and covered his now bleeding face. Kinma turned and lunged for the door again but, amidst a chorus of laughter, the other twin grabbed her hair and roughly pulled her back. She stumbled back, the strong grip not letting her move.

"Come on girl. Back to the room. We ain't done yet."

The other one merely dropped his hand and grinned down at her through his blood smeared face.

CHAPTER EIGHTEEN

JUNE 20, 2046

DAY THREE THOUSAND SEVEN HUNDRED AND SEVENTY

Grey light filled the yard, the short grass gleaming with silvery dew. Jacob stood off to the side, not wanting to be noticed as the men loaded supplies on the heavily laden cart. It had been a long, sleepless night and he needed to think.

After seeing the faint marks in the mud, Clarence dragged Jacob and Griff in front of the other men where he prompted them to describe what they saw. Not sure exactly what he had seen but not wanting to anger anyone, he explained that he thought he saw boot marks between the trees, possibly from men sneaking away. Griff had backed this up, sounding more persuasive than Jacob thought he had been.

This caused the frayed group to break into a heated, yelling argument with much of the ire being directed at Clarence. Griff and Jacob were ordered to go up their room, which they gratefully did, wanting to be far from the unintelligible conflict. However, for much of the night, they continued to hear the arguing continue downstairs.

This morning, the men seemed more subdued and Jacob figured the outrage of last night was largely the product of the shock and rage over their friend being killed. He had noticed freshly turned earth under a spruce tree and he deduced that a funeral for Hale had been held in the night. Perhaps, with the nastiness behind them, the men would be calmer now.

Tina, carrying a cup of steaming liquid, walked out of the building and stepped over to him, saying, "You're up early."

She handed over the cup and leaned next to him, looking tired and small.

Jacob said, "Hard to sleep."

"Do you have a plan?"

Jacob knew this question was coming and resented it. Tina would want him to decide. Griff would feign annoyance at him deciding but would go along with whatever choice Jacob made without ever pushing for his own choice. Neither of them wanted to step forward and declare a position, preferring to put it all on his shoulders and merely follow his lead, free from any blame.

He turned, planning to chastise Tina for foisting all of this on him. But she was looking up at him, her weary eyes full of worry and Jacob instantly realized, by some cruel twist of fate, it was clearly up to him to make this decision, to lead whether he wanted to or not. He sighed, "I would prefer to stay here for a while, but we have been informed we are not welcome. I think we need to go with them."

She looked back at the men hauling supplies. "They worry me. They're all so mean to one another."

Jacob scanned the dark pine trees surrounding the yard, recalling the endless torture of the marching, and said, "Yes, they are a bit of an unknown, but we know for certain we will not do well in the woods. We were out there for less than a day and were captured by people far more nasty than these. Plus, someone killed Hale last night. Someone is out there, and I doubt they would hesitate to hurt us. We'll be safe if we go with them and, only once we are safe, can we learn how to get home."

Tina hesitated and then said, "Ok, if that is what you think is best."

In his heart, Jacob wanted nothing but to take the chance and try to find their way back to Malden as directly and quickly as possible. The need to see Louisa pulling on him like the deepest hunger he ever felt. And, even though he once dreamt of meeting new people, he now wanted to be away from strangers and back amongst friendly faces. Yet he knew doing what one wanted was not always the wiser course, putting off undesirable chores only made them worse on the morrow. He needed to take the smartest path even if it was not the desired one.

Trying to sound more sure than he felt, Jacob said, "I do. Go and tell Griff, for better or worse, we are heading to Thule."

•   •   •

A lone rabbit hopped across the Clearing and disappeared into the underbrush. Morreign stood on the narrow porch, wrapped in her blanket, looking down towards the river like she did every morning, trying to will three missing children to come walking back up the path. This morning felt different though. Most mornings she knew it was highly unlikely they would magically appear in the dawn mist, but she still hoped. This morning, she knew they would not be appearing.

Paul stepped up behind her and handed her a mug of pine tea. Noticing the familiar tears on her cheeks, he put an arm around her shoulders and softly said, "They will make it back. They will."

She wanted to tell him that he was mistaken, that she could sense that they were now going the wrong way, moving away from Malden or, perhaps, were already gone, moving away from this world entirely. But she did not. Her intuition was given a great deal of weight in this world so her worrisome instinct about the children would be taken as gospel and she could not bear that happening.

Morreign merely nodded and quietly said, "I know."

PART THREE

CHAPTER NINETEEN

JUNE 22, 2046
DAY THREE THOUSAND SEVEN HUNDRED AND SEVENTY-TWO

Laughter cascaded up the hill towards them followed by someone cursing at people to shut up which was then followed by more laughter and louder cursing back. Jacob rolled over, trying in vain to find a position to lie in on the hard ground that did not annoy his sore muscles. Jacob, Griff, and Tina had spent most of the last two days trying to learn how to ride a bike. Much to the amusement of their traveling companions, the learning process mainly involved falling.

Despite the bruises, strained muscles and troubling company, the travel was generally tolerable. The men shared their wealth of food fairly easily, so thirst and hunger were not issues. Warm breezes blew, and the sun remained high in the sky late into the day, as summer made its brief foray into the north. Dormant plants and silenced animals came to life, filling the air with chatter and sweet smells. While he knew every day in this short season should be cherished, it only made Jacob yearn for home more as he felt he was wasting these salad days filled with angst rather than joy.

A whispered question in the dark, "Can't sleep?"

It was Tina, lying a couple feet away. Jacob slapped at a persistent black fly and sighed, "Want to but too sore. You?"

"Same, plus, I don't know - this feels especially wrong tonight."

While they traveled, Tina repeatedly tried to voice her uncertain concern over the idea of going to Thule, wanting them to go off on their own instead of being surrounded by all the strange men. Griff, somewhat annoyed by her vagueness, tried to convince her to push her worries aside, repeating all the wonderful things at Thule which Clarence had told them about while pointing out their full dinner plates. However, the farther they went and the more time that passed after Hale's murder, the more Jacob noticed the looks the men gave Tina.

Despite being filled with innumerable worries about their predicament, concerns over Tina's safety often pushed themselves to the top. Everyone at Malden knew her story because everyone knew everyone's story. When Tina was a toddler, her and her mother, Fiona, came north to visit her father. They were alone, playing with dolls in his work camp unit when the Bombs came.

The camp immediately erupted in fiery explosions. Tina became trapped in the room, her mother screaming from outside, pleading with her to run through the fire but she was too scared. An oil worker darted into the ruins, jumped through the flames and carried her out as her flesh burned. More and more fire rained down as they ran into the frozen wilderness.

When they finally stopped, Fiona saw that Tina's arm was nothing but a mess of charred blood and bone. Tina's mother was forced to hold down her screaming child as an overwhelmed medic from the production site severed the remnants of her daughter's arm. With no choice, Fiona wrapped up the horribly injured girl as best she could before fleeing further into the woods.

Fiona told the story of them moving aimlessly through the freezing woods as the toddler screamed endlessly. Starving and freezing, the oil workers with them eventually grew weary of Tina's noise and all the extra risk it brought so they slipped away one night. Exhausted, Fiona walked aimlessly through the woods and stumbled across the frozen river. Clutching the feverish child, certain they would be granted the mercy of death before too much longer she limped pointlessly along the ice. Instead of dying, she was spotted by Leo and Paul who were out hunting.

With no doctor and Fiona's salvaged antibiotics running out, everyone figured the burned and mutilated girl would soon succumb to her injuries but, instead, she rallied, improving each day under the care at Malden.

Thankfully, Tina was young enough that she did not remember the intense agony bestowed upon her, but she confided in Jacob that she was often tormented by nightmares of being burned alive.

Jacob rolled onto his back, looking up at the star-filled night sky. For the hundredth time he wished beyond wishing to that he had not gotten into that leaky boat to chase that scrawny elk. All three of them went but it had been Jacob's choice, they would not have gone if he said it was foolish. He rationalized the decision by saying they needed the meat but that was a lie, there was plenty of food, he had wanted the glory. And, now, because of his need to stoke his pointless pride, Tina was lying terrified in a field surrounded by a mass of men who wanted to do horrible things to her.

He wanted to apologize, to say how sorry he was they ended up in this position but he could not find the words, worried speaking too truthfully would only worry her more. He softly responded to her, "I know, it does seem off, but I don't know what else to do. I wish I did but I don't know. We didn't fare very well out on our own, we almost froze to death before being kidnapped within, what, an hour of being off that damn island. Not sure how far we'd make it if we venture off."

"The way they talk, the way they stare, it -"

A stifled chuckle nearby interrupted her. Jacob's heart started pounding as he sat up and strained to hear more in the dark. A scolding tone, more a harsh whisper really, off to their left, broke the silence. "Get back down there, nothing for you two up here."

"Screw off Milo, we ain't gonna hurt her or nothing."

"Yeah, you ain't the boss. Can't tell us what to do."

The first voice, even sterner, "Want to test that theory?"

A hesitation, then some unintelligible grumbling as the voices moved away down the hill. Tina asked in a hushed whisper. "What was that?"

Jacob thought it best to downplay the situation, so he said, "Nothing, I think. Some men talking. They went back down."

"Oh."

"I think we should try to sleep, tomorrow will be another long day - these guys don't seem big on breaks."

Her voice sounded tiny as she whispered back, "Ok."

Jacob slid over, so his body was next to hers. After a moment, Tina wrapped an arm over him and pushed her face into his chest as she sobbed. "Sorry, I miss home. I miss my mom. I miss everything."

In all the endless time they spent together, Jacob could not recall Tina ever crying, even when they were kids. Awkwardly rubbing her back, and feeling more worried and guilty than ever, Jacob muttered, "I know, me too. Me too."

•   •   •

Morreign wrapped her sweater tight as she sat on her chair in the night air. Bright, clear stars filled the sky. She always tried not to think back to the times she came here as a teenager, before the Bombs, the memories of her parents and brothers always hurt too much. But, tonight, looking over the wide expanse of the Clearing, she could not stop remembering.

She thought of her dad grilling burgers. She thought of her mother calling them in from the river for bedtime. She thought of running through the tall grass with no destination. She thought of the endless games of lawn bowling with her brothers. Everything was so simple, so easy, the biggest worry was running out of soda or forgetting to pack an extra swimsuit.

A gust of wind blew across the porch, cool in the night air, bringing Morreign back to the reality that all of those people and that simple world were completely gone. Now, sitting in the darkness, she needed to grapple with having lost three young people.

Survival after the Bombs had always been hard, but Morreign thought they had managed, through intense labor and persistence and good luck, to carve out a bastion of civilization where they could be relatively safe. They had shelter. They had gardens. They had firewood. Now, being reminded that, despite all those earned accomplishments, they existed in a world of complete uncertainty, made it seem far too hard. Fatigue, guilt, and despair all pushed in on her.

Morreign unconsciously muttered angrily into the summer breeze, "It's not fair."

Hearing the basic statement coming from her own mouth surprised her. The clearest memory of her mother was on an early morning at their home in Edmonton. Morreign, twelve years old, maybe eleven, wanting to go somewhere with her friends, she couldn't recall where, but her mom refused. When Morreign whined about it not being fair, her mother laughed, which only made pre-teen Morreign more angry and whiny.

She could still picture the scene perfectly. Sun coming in through the dusty kitchen window. Her mother in her canary yellow dress, turning from the sink, wiping her hands on the faded dish towel with the strawberries on it. Morreign, sitting on the counter in her usual spot, her coltish legs tucked under her, covered in the bruises and scratches of summer. Her mom looked straight at her, her serious gaze cutting off her childish complaints before she calmly said, "The sooner you realize there's no magical force in this world making everything fair for everyone, the better off you'll be."

A cough. Then another. The sound carrying through the crisp night air, across the Clearing from a cabin to the West, distracting Morreign.

The cough was probably from Boris. He had been dealing with a nasty chest cold for weeks now. Morreign forced her aching hip to bend and got up off the chair. Limping back to her bed, she made a mental note to bring Boris the last of the honey to add to his tea.

• • •

The inventories were in a bad state, the worst in over eight years. Harrison knew the ledgers by heart, but he continued to scan the lists of supplies regardless. He told himself he continually went over inventories and made detailed plans out of a sense of duty to those he led. However, he knew the true reason was that he enjoyed the process.

The strategizing, the calculating, the basic bookkeeping, it reminded him of running his trucking company. The late nights in the cramped office in the trailer beside the loading dock. The TV in the corner playing muted sports highlights on a loop. The space heater ticking annoyingly by the door. A bottle of diet coke and a bag of salty cashews for dinner. Back then he could control his business, make decisions and put plans into action. And he was certain he would soon accomplish great things, every minute he spent to toiling at his desk seemed like a step towards that, towards establishing an empire.

All of that hope was taken away by that one unforeseeable accident. Looking back, like he had done innumerable times before, Harrison always thought he should've taken precautions, moved slower and kept some cash in reserve for emergencies. The Bombs made it all moot anyway but, still, he wished things would've gone differently.

Taking a sip of pine needle tea, Harrison stood from his table and stepped to the darkened window. In the starlight, the overgrown rubble of Thule was merely shadows of shadows. Nothing forever in every direction. Something needed to change, the Bank could not continue to operate the same way for long.

He put his hands on the cool glass and leaned in, staring into the endless blackness. He managed to carve out an oasis for the hint of a civilization, a sliver of an empire for him to run. He wondered if his failure at the trucking company tainted his views of how to manage in the new world. From day one, he had been cautious. Limiting the people allowed in. Not expanding beyond the one building, not venturing out too far. Keeping it all compact, not wanting to overreach.

The attack was an unmitigated disaster but from disaster is borne opportunity. Harrison knew that, but he had not taken full advantage. He could have used all the emptiness created by chaos to create a new world. He should've thought bigger, taken greater chances and made something more worthy of his control, something more in his image, something more than this ramshackle gang of thugs constantly near starvation.

Turning from the dark window, Harrison grabbed the map and unfolded it. Paper maps were a rarity, but they had managed to scavenge this one from an army truck. Very detailed, showing every road and creek with the numerous creeks far outnumbering the few roads. Over the years, Harrison carefully added to it, writing in the places where they had found supplies and encountered other survivors.

Leaning over the table, scouring the map, taking it all in for the thousandth time, he knew there must be other survivors out there, other places, colonies he could add to his isolated and battered empire. He would wait until the patrol returned, see what they encountered and if Clarence handled Hale. Then he would dictate a new mandate: expansion.

CHAPTER TWENTY

JUNE 25, 2046

DAY THREE THOUSAND SEVEN HUNDRED AND SEVENTY-FIVE

With the injured men, the cart and piles of supplies, it took six days for the patrol to reach Thule. A thoroughly unenjoyable six days for Jacob. The youths from Malden eventually mastered bike riding, discovering it to be an efficient but painful way to travel. The tension inflicting the group after Hale's death never completely receded while the lecherous looks and comments regarding Tina increased daily. Now, though, the end was near, and Jacob forced his tired legs to push harder, pedaling up next to Tina.

"Hey, they say an hour, and we'll be there."

Tina, working extra hard to balance the loaded bike with her one hand, said, "Not sure if that's good news or bad. My ass is beyond numb, and I want to get off this damn thing for good but, Jacob, I'm worried about what things are going to be like there. I doubt these men come from a welcoming place."

With Jacob unable to think of anything reassuring to say, the two rode in silence, their breathing heavy as they pushed the bikes up the rough trail. Jacob's initial excitement about seeing Thule had quickly faded as they traveled as he too grew more and more concerned about his traveling companions and those they were going to meet.

The night Hale was killed, he and Griff were brought by Clarence to stand awkwardly before the others to tell them about the tracks they saw in the mud. Occasionally, as they traveled, they were grilled by a furious man named Milo who clearly did not believe them as he asked accusatory questions and scowled whenever Clarence tried to intervene. Jacob had never been part of such an intense situation, and he needed to muster all his fortitude to keep from running away.

Thankfully, no one but Clarence and Milo seemed overly interested in talking to Jacob. Some of the men seemed to enjoy Griff's jokes, but they did not answer his questions about Thule, merely shrugging them off and saying they would see when they got there. Jacob got the impression that the men thought saying too much might anger one side or the other of the unseen battle.

As Tina had worried, the men did have an especially keen interest in her. She tried to keep her distance as much as possible and always stayed close to him and Griff. But Jacob figured, given their staring, it was only Milo's interventions and threats that kept the others from being overtly abusive. After the night, when he heard the men coming up to where they were sleeping, Jacob raised his concerns over Tina's safety with Clarence, and he said that, in Thule, Tina would be allowed to stay with Griff and Jacob if that's what she wanted as if this statement explained completely.

Back then, the comment placated him but, over time, worry that Clarence might be misleading them soaked into Jacob's consciousness. The others seemed to hate him, or at least not respect him, often mocking or outright berating him while his answers to questions about Thule became more and more vague the closer they got. And, on the rare occasions when someone else started to converse with Jacob or Griff or Tina, Clarence always appeared and ruined the conversation.

They crested a slight rise on their bikes and one of the men up front called out, "Home sweet, home."

Unconsciously stopping his bike and almost toppling over, Jacob stared. For his entire life, he heard stories of Thule. Fictionalized images mixed with his blurry childhood memories and a few faded photographs to create an awesome vision of the place. Buildings of steel and glass, taller than the tallest trees. Bright lights coming on with the touch of a finger. Heat poured from holes in the walls without wood or smoke. Places where a person could get whatever they want to eat or drink merely by asking. An unbelievable marvel of mystical proportions. This place laid out before him appeared nothing like the magical pictures filling his mind.

Of course, he knew of the attack, of the Bombs. The story of his family's escape on the Longest Night was Malden's purist legend, and other survivors told similar tales. But he thought an attack meant, at worst, a forest after a fire with some trees standing but burnt. Now, laid out beneath him was a grassy plain dotted with short, scrubby pines and shrubby willows amongst the occasional collapsed wall or twisted metal tower. Far off he could make out a few squat structures standing grey and lifeless.

Tina sighed, "We should have tried to go home."

Griff pulled up beside them and let out a low whistle, saying, "Really? This is it? Malden's got more buildings than this mess."

As they surveyed the debunked myth in near shock, Clarence appeared from behind without them noticing his approach. Jacob worried the strange man heard and understood Griff's careless comment as Clarence merely said, "Not much to look at, is it? You guys probably got nicer buildings back at the farm with your parents, hey?"

Trying to sound casual, Griff answered, "Yeah, there's a house and couple of outbuildings. Whatever. It'll be nice to get under any roof again."

"Well, you haven't been let inside yet. But as I said, I think you three could be helpful to us so I'm going to talk to Harrison for you. I'm sure he'll take my recommendation. Oh, and people might have more questions about what happened to Hale out there, but as long as you tell the truth about what we saw like you've been doing that'll all go fine for you."

Confused by the last statement, and deeply wondering why he ever listened to this man in the first place, but out of other options, Jacob said weakly, "Ok, thanks."

• • •

After five days, the bruises and soreness had faded, and Kinma could now move without flares of pain constantly reminding her of the ordeal. Regardless, the memories burned brightly in her mind, both when she was awake or asleep.

She had known the Vikings would not injure her too badly because that would anger Harrison as she was now a commodity, ruining her would be like breaking an important machine or spilling a stew. So, the Vikings' repeated abuse did not cause her to fear for her physical wellbeing. Instead, the true fear came from worrying that shame and disgust would rob her of all dignity, strip her of an identity such that she would no longer truly exist.

After one night and half a day, the Vikings tired of her and Kinma had crawled out of the filth, wrapped a crusted blanket around her battered body and, with uncontrolled sobs of relief and despair wracking through her, she ran stumbling through the dim halls to her apartment. Opening the door to her former sanctuary, she wanted only to be alone, however, she discovered Luke sitting at the table, peacefully reading a book by the window.

While Luke clearly viewed Hale as a father figure, Kinma was not so foolish to think he thought of her as a mother figure. She saw the way he looked at her when he thought no one would see and it was the way of men looking at women, not the way of sons looking at mothers. Regardless, she thought it was only teenage lusting and that he would never harm her out of respect for Hale. However, when she entered, clutching the filthy blanket to her chest, smelling heavily of sex, her legs and shoulders bare, the young man looked at her like a starving man eyeing someone else's dinner.

After endless hours of vainly fighting monsters in order to retain a sliver of pride, she could not handle fighting a perceived friend. Enough was enough, and her last vestige of adrenaline-fueled energy disappeared. She fell to her bruised knees as a wave of intense crying overtook her. Apparently seeing the normally strong person so suddenly vulnerable shocked away Luke's animal instincts. Instead of doing whatever he had been envisioning, he hurried forward and helped her inside the apartment.

That first day, Luke had prepared her a basin of warm wash water and brought her dinner before graciously leaving her alone when she asked. Later, he clumsily explained how Harrison decided they should live together with the new arrangement being explained to Hale on his return.

Hale. She had push all thoughts of him away during the abuse but now he flooded back to her. Kinma's tormented mind could not contemplate all the angles, but she confidently knew in her soul that, instead of being the one dealt with like Harrison and Luke planned, Hale would deal with them, all of them. And she would eagerly help.

At first, Luke continued to give her distance to heal and recover, but after a few nights, he climbed into the bedding nest in the bathroom with her. She was able to politely fend him off by saying she remained too sore, but his fumblings became more aggressive over time. She mainly used a technique of sleeping at odd times coupled with lengthy trips into the woods to avoid him as much as possible. She knew Luke could not complain to anyone about her lack of cooperation as this would make him look terribly weak. She also knew, before too long, his desire and pride would overcome the vague remnants of his polite morality, and he would take by force what Harrison had granted him by decree.

After surviving the Vikings, the idea of this child, a child she helped raise, mistreating her could not be tolerated. She knew she would do everything in her power to stop him. If Luke wanted to take what Harrison thought he could give away, it would cost the boy all she could deal out. Still, she knew such an attack would not end well for her so she continued to avoid Luke as much as possible while silently pleading with all the unseen forces in the universe that Hale would get home before she needed to act.

This morning, with the pleading mantra constantly running through Kinma's mind as she worked on making candles in the apartment, a quick knock on the door was preceded immediately by a breathless Seanah bursting in. Excitedly the woman squealed, "Kinma, Kinma! They're back. They've been spotted up on the hill."

Her silent plea answered, Kinma darted towards the door, but Seanah stopped her and said, "No, Harrison ordered me to come and tell you to stay in here."

Confusion and anger struck Kinma. "Why?"

"'Course he didn't tell me why, but I'm guessing he wants to talk to Hale right away, get an inventory of the supplies or whatever. They got a whole wagon load with them."

Seanah bolted back out of the apartment as quickly as she had come. A sharp pang of fear struck Kinma. She greatly doubted Harrison's motives were so banal as wanting to know how many potatoes Hale had found.

The Bankers all poured out of the building, gathering out front to welcome back the patrol and check out the new supplies. Harrison stood to the back, allowing the crowd to congratulate the returning men. Murmurs of conversation increased to yells of excitement as the heavily laden patrol moved into view.

Harrison instinctively counted heads, but with injured men not on their own bikes, he could not be certain of the number. Plus they may have brought back a woman or someone of skill which would skew the numbers, again Harrison cursed the vague message Hale sent back with Taco. However, as they neared, he saw to his satisfaction that Hale did not appear to be leading them back.

The cheers of the Bank increased even further as people moved forward to help the patrol the last hundred yards. However, celebration turned into rumblings of concern as they realized the leader of the patrol was absent. Angry, worried questions were flung about. Milo dramatically climbed off his bike to loudly tell the story, a herald making a practiced proclamation to the whole village.

"Hale, always one to do his duty, went to keep watch the night before we left. When he did not return, we went out and found him, only fifty yards from where we slept, an arrow in the back and his throat cut. We hunted in the dark, seeking the cowardly attackers but found nothing."

Milo turned his gaze to Clarence and continued, "Someone shot an arrow into his back and then slit his throat, someone no one saw coming or going-"

Harrison cursed under his breath as Clarence, the fool, stepped up, lifting a hand to interrupt as if announcing himself to be guilty of the accusation, and exclaimed, "Your claim we saw no sign of attackers is false. We came across tracks of men clearly fleeing. Surely we missed some bastardly Survivalists who came back to seek cheap revenge for our massive victory."

Milo countered, "No Survivalists were missing, and all we saw were some scuffs in the dirt that you happened to be the one to find."

Angrily, Clarence said, "No, again you lie. These two, these two right here discovered the tracks with me."

With that, he pointed at two strangers. Teenagers. One darker complexioned, one redheaded and pale. Well dressed and thin but not with the normal gauntness of feral survivors, looking especially frightened and wide-eyed. Standing next to them was a girl who stared at her feet, hair falling over her face, her left arm ending in a stump at the elbow. Harrison shook his head, the idiots brought back children.

"Sure, sure. Those scared forest mice with you said they saw the tracks you found. That's all worth a handful of fresh shit as far as I'm concerned."

Understanding the import of the ad hoc trial happening before him, Harrison strode forward, slipping through the grimy crowd before Clarence could continue losing the debate. With calm coolness, Harrison said, "Alright, obviously, the failure of Hale to return is a great loss for the Bank. A founder of our society and friend to all of us, a true leader we could rely upon is gone, and we'll mourn his loss. However, we knew this was a dangerous mission and let's not overlook his last victory, a victory all of you who did return deserve congratulations for."

With that, the Bankers moved forward at his urging and began unloading the eagerly awaited supplies. Soon, going through the new found treasures overwhelmed any sadness or questions over Hale. Harrison caught Clarence's eye and pointed with his head up towards his apartment. Despite looking very tired, the pilot nodded his agreement before giving Harrison an odd, annoying smirk.

•   •   •

Luke strode into the apartment. The seriousness on his face looked out of place, an upset toddler trying to hold back a tantrum and appear tough. Waiting impatiently, Kinma heard the too-brief cheering from below and then vainly strained to hear anything further, unable to see from the window. Worried, she hurried over to Luke, asking, "What happened? Where's Hale?"

With sharp coldness, he said, "He's dead. Killed on the patrol."

She heard the words but could not believe them. "No, you're lying. Taco came back. He was fine. He wrote me. You're a liar!"

Luke grabbed her wrists as she began to hit his chest. Not a sizable man but well-built from a lifetime of labor and Kinma was unable to gain any freedom from his grasp. Sounding distant, he said, "I don't lie. Dead. Shot in the back, throat cut. Milo said it himself."

"No. He was fine. He is fine."

With annoying ease, Luke pushed her into the apartment. Enraged by this treatment and baffled by the horrible news, Kinma yelled, "Stop. Stop! You need to tell me what happened."

"Hale is gone. That's the reality. You're completely mine now."

His voice sounded terrifyingly inhuman. Luke spun her around and roughly pushed her against the kitchen counter. Kinma's yellow toque tumbled off her head to the floor as the edge of the counter dug into her stomach. Luke pushed down on her, bending her over before he clawed at her pants while growling, "No more waiting. No reason to."

Rage overtook her grief, focusing her mind to a fury sharpened point and, despite being pressed into the countertop, Kinma responded with a calm tone, "No, wait, wait. If Hale's gone you don't need to do this, we can do it proper."

The pressure on her back eased somewhat as he seemed to be considering this, but then he leaned back against her, growling into her ear, "Enough of your tricks. I waited out of respect but now none of that bullshit matters, nothing here ever matters. I'll take what I want."

"I know, I know, I wanted you to wait, needed you to wait. But, I agree, all of that is passed, without, well, without…"

She could not say Hale's name, her words trailing off. Luke returned to struggling with her jeans. She resumed, "No, listen, I'm not tricking you. Think about it, do you think I want to get used by everyone else out there. I'll do anything to be spared that. I want to be with you now, it's my best option, you're my best option. We can still have something better, something together."

This got him to pause, and she thought her desperate plan might be working so she continued, trying to push a hint of sultriness in her tone, "Trust me, Luke, it doesn't need to be like this. It can be better, much better when both parties are interested. Let me turn around and show you."

His weight shifted, moved off her slightly, and she took the opportunity to turn over. He still loomed over her and roughly held her shoulders, but she looked him coyly in the eye as she slowly hooked her thumbs into the waistband of her pants and pushed them down. Luke released her and gaped down stupidly. Kinma leaned back, put her hands on the counter and lifted herself up, so she was sitting before him.

The half-grown orphan looked intrigued by the sight but also stunned, so she twisted a half-smile onto her tight-pressed lips and pulled her feet up onto the counter to improve his view. He remained laser focussed as primal instinct caused his hands to fumble at opening his own belt and allowing Kinma to let her right hand slowly creep to the edge of the counter. He managed to open his jeans and pushed towards her, but she playfully put a foot on his stomach before leaning back to make a show of pulling her shirt over her chest with one hand as her other hand blindly searched for the knife block.

Before he tired of the view, her free hand managed to grasp the handle of a paring knife. When he pushed towards her again while letting out a creepy, soft groan, Kinma's right fist pounced with all her power at his exposed neck. The knife was short, but sufficient as it found its vulnerable mark, impaling the flesh of his throat as she stabbed, and then stabbed again and then again.

Kinma pushed the young man's bulk away with her foot, letting the dying body fall sickly to the floor like a half-filled bag of rice slipping off a table. As Luke, fear filling his panicked and confused eyes gurgled for help, she plucked up the yellow toque before it could be soiled by the expanding pool of blood and placed it on her head.

She knelt down to make sure he could hear. With wide eyes, he stared up at her in complete, abject fear. For a heartbeat, she felt remorse. She had watched Luke grow up. Blaming him might have been wrong. He had recently learned his father figure was dead. Raised in a den of filth surrounded by unthinking brutes what could she expect him to become, how else could he react. Then the familiar image of Hale reading with the boy by candlelight flashed into her mind. Unthinking brutes, but one man of integrity who cared for him.

Leaning in close to his contorted face, she softly said, "He pulled you out of that frozen closet. He took care of you when no one alive even knew your name. He took care of you when people were not taking care of one another. You could have chosen to be like him. You could have chosen to be a proper person, he gave you that lesson, that opportunity, that gift. Instead, you chose the easy way. You chose to indulge your foulest needs despite all he showed you. You chose this. You chose this death."

Standing up, Kinma walked away. They had not stolen her dignity, they had not stolen her identity, they had only hardened it.

CHAPTER TWENTY-ONE

JUNE 25, 2046

DAY THREE THOUSAND SEVEN HUNDRED AND SEVENTY-FIVE

Sam stepped out of the trees lining the main garden. Definitely not unusual for Sam to silently appear, normally he was carrying a rabbit or a grouse. However, this time was very unusual as a woman Morreign did not recognize walked beside him.

The others, weeding between rows of freshly-sprouted potato plants, stopped to gape at the stranger. Morreign, who liked to try to slowly help in the gardens as it loosened up her hip, leaned her hoe against a tree and limped towards them. She took her time, partly because of her limp but also to give herself a moment to prepare. A trickle of hope rose up, this stranger might have seen Jacob. Morreign had to tell herself this was unlikely and she needed to be strong when the disappointment came.

As she approached, Morreign counted back. Six years. Over six years since the last visitors came to Malden. The Seven Rules, specifically Rule Four, clearly addressed how newcomers were to be dealt with. The Committee would meet with them, if they were deemed not to be threatening to the proper order of Malden and they agreed to live by the Seven Rules, the newcomers were invited to stay. Beneath that formality, however, Morreign knew of an unwritten rule which was making her uneasy.

Managing to sound sure of herself, Morreign said, "Afternoon Sam, who do we have here?"

Leo and Paul would describe the woman as linebacker-like but probably not to her face as she wore an unimpressed scowl on her thin lips and looked with a harsh glare. Wrapped in hides and coyote furs despite the warmish weather, Morreign guessed the woman was actually more wiry than stout under all the bulky clothing. The grey hair braided into a thick rope coupled with the wrinkles on her weathered face made Morreign think she was in her late fifties.

Not surprisingly, Sam ignored the question and walked off after merely saying, "She's alone."

Morreign put out her hand and said, "Hello, I'm Morreign, welcome."

The stranger overtly scanned her, reminding Morreign of a dog sniffing over an unfamiliar dog. Finally, she took her hand, made eye contact and with a gravelly voice, said, "Marge."

"Nice to meet you, Marge. By chance have you seen two young men and a girl in your travels?'

Marge hesitated just long enough to let the hope in Morreign grow before she shook her head. "Sorry, no."

Morreign had expected this but the disappointment still stabbed her in the chest. Forcing the pain from her voice, she said, "Ok. Please, come with me to the Lodge. We'll get you something to eat."

This seemed to confound the newcomer. "Really?"

"Sure. Nothing fancy but decent enough."

"All simple and easy like that, you just invite me in?"

"Of course. Why not?"

This got a bark of a laugh from her. "Maybe you folks with your nice gardens and cozy cabins and all haven't noticed, but Armageddon happened a while back. Plus your friend there didn't strike me as overly friendly."

Morreign gave a laugh of her own and said, "Oh, Sam's quiet but harmless unless you're a rabbit. And, yeah, I heard something 'bout the Armageddon. Even so, I think we can spare a few beans for an innocent traveler. "

"I got an ex-husband might not call me innocent, assuming he's still breathing somewhere, but I'll take your beans, all the same, assuming, of course, I'll be free to leave after eating."

Morreign's stomach tightened as she gave a curt nod. The visitor gave her a penetrating look so Morreign added, "We do have some questions we'd like to ask, and then you can decide if you want to leave. I mean, we don't get many guests out here and grow tired of telling each other the same old stories, be nice to hear something new."

Another hard look, then a shrug. "Guess I can answer some questions in exchange for my meal, but I doubt it'll be tasty enough to get me to want to say. No offense but I'm sort of a loner, either by choice or curse, I can't decide."

As they walked to the Lodge, the woman talked continually, apparently enjoying the stretching out of her unused vocal cords. Rambling stories about storms, trapping and rare encounters with humans. Malden residents openly stared at them as they passed, baffled by the vision of a stranger, but Marge did not let this attention slow her speaking. Morreign figured the woman, despite her contention of being a loner, was deeply lonely and this gave her hope the newcomer would decide to stay.

•   •   •

Harrison watched from his window on the third floor as his people moved about below. The hedonistic, alcohol-fuelled party had definitely increased the morale of the men, and they all seemed content, especially when he hinted at such events occurring again. He hoped, when the returning patrol members were told of the festivities, they would not be angered over being excluded but instead would look forward to the next one.

A soft knock announced Clarence's arrival. Harrison turned and silently pointed to the couch before he took a seat in the armchair. His lackey looked tired and battered from the road but also annoyingly pleased with himself.

Dealing with Clarence all these years, Harrison knew the former helicopter pilot to be quite smart with technical and planning matters but quite clueless with inter-personal matters. Through their conversations, Harrison gleaned the diminutive man felt he got mistreated by the rougher elements of society and now enjoyed being able to act under the safety of Harrison's protection.

He reminded Harrison of those people who were picked-on in high school, and then when they got to participate in any small way with the cool group, they were overly excited and grateful. As a result, the best way to get him to blindly follow orders was to keep him guessing as to whether he was pleasing or disappointing, make him worried about losing that emboldening protection and, subsequently, any chance at inclusion.

"You managed to get rid of Hale?"

Nodding eagerly, the former pilot answered, "Yeah, yeah. He was out on watch, all by himself in the pitch black. I snuck right up on him. Pretty easy actually."

Shaking his head in response, Harrison said, "But everyone suspects you did this easy job and if they suspect you, they'll think it was my plan."

"Sure, I suppose, I mean they suspect, but they don't know."

"The fight with the Survivalists sounds like it was bloody and chaotic. You couldn't have taken care of it then?"

Lifting his hands slightly, Clarence said, "No, no. I thought about that, of course, but I couldn't get near him, and it was so crazy I figured he might get taken out anyway, the way he was charging right at 'em. When he made it through the attack, my only option was to take care of him when he was alone."

Harrison knew Clarence was not brave and, more importantly, he knew Clarence also knew this. Harrison decided to poke at that soft spot. "Right, I imagine it was hard for you to get at him during the fight when you were way in the back."

Opening his mouth to refute this, Clarence seemed to decide against arguing and meekly said, "I got done what I was told to get done."

"And now I've got another mess with everyone thinking I ordered the killing of one of their bloody heroes."

The defensive hands came up again as Clarence began speaking quickly, "I know, but I covered myself pretty well. While we were out there at that settlement, a few of those Prepper guys brought in captives. Those kids that came back with us were with 'em. They're so scared and rattled they don't even know which way is up. When everyone was running around looking for whoever killed Hale, I got the two guys and took 'em out with me.

"I pretended to be hunting for the intruders, eventually bringing them to where I left some fake tracks. I convinced the terrified idiots they were proof someone came into the settlement and then ran off. They parroted this to the others. I think most of them bought it."

For a moment, Harrison sat quietly, letting Clarence stew before he said, "Some of 'em might have bought that bullshit but not all. Not Milo, certainly. Anyway, what's done is done. I'll fix it like I always fix your mistakes. I need to get down there and supervise the sorting of supplies. Anything else I need to know?"

Surprisingly, the chastised pilot said, "Yeah, maybe. Those kids, the ones that were brought to the settlement-"

Harrison ordered, "Out with it."

"There's something shady about them. I think they're lying about where they come from. Might be worth looking into."

This was actually interesting. "Explain."

Clarence leaned forward, excited at the new opportunity to please. He said, "They told a story about being brothers from some isolated farm, but they don't look like it, and I doubt there's any farms way up here. Plus, their clothes are well tended, and they look pretty well fed for being secluded on some farm for all these years."

"But you've only got speculation?"

"Yes, one of them, the redhead, said something about a place when they didn't know I was listening. He called it Malden, I think it's a village or something."

"Malden? Give me the context."

"When we came upon Thule, them seeing it for the first time, he said that Malden had more buildings."

Very interesting. "Did you ask them about this?"

"No. I figured it would be best to wait and see what you wanted to do."

Harrison thought for a second. Finally, a turn of good luck. An opportunity, one that perfectly fit his new plan, his mandate to explore and expand. An established settlement which had been overlooked.

"Ok. Make them wait outside until tonight. No food, no water, no company. Then bring the boys up to me for a talk at sunset."

• • •

"Getting really tired of these people out here in the big, wide world. We should've bolted when we had the chance."

Griff paced diagonally across the rocky area, stepping over random items littered about to kick a plastic bottle. After their arrival at Thule, Clarence told them they would need to wait outside before the leader could meet with them. Taking in the impressiveness of the building and their new surroundings kept them occupied for a while but that soon gave way to worsening angst.

Laying on the ground, using his coat as a pillow, Jacob resisted the temptation to point out that Griff was the one who wanted to come to Thule. Griff continued, "Shit. They could've left us something to eat, some water at least."

Tina muttered, "I don't think our comfort crossed their minds."

With a defeated sigh, Griff sat down on a bin, put his head in his hands and asked, "What the hell is going on? I'm so damn tired, I can't even think. I'm scared and worried all the time. Is this nightmare ever going to end? When do we get to wake up?"

Strange to hear his normally arrogant friend talking in such a manner but Jacob could completely understand, all the fear and torment was threatening to erode any toughness they carried from Malden. Jacob sat up. "I know what you're saying. Maybe we should simply run. Bolt into the woods and take our chances. Sam taught us, we'll be ok and we'll be smarter this time. After all this facing an angry bear in a thunderstorm is preferable to dealing with one more stranger."

Nodding, Tina quickly said, "Makes sense to me. Completely."

Griff, however, only shook his head, his usually cocky gaze fixed on the floor. It worried Jacob to see his friend so despondent, the last setback of seeing Thule in ruins apparently one obstacle too many. Griff only muttered, "I don't know. I don't know anymore. What if -"

The apartment building door abruptly opened, interrupting the conversation as Clarence walked out with two massive men who looked shockingly similar: long golden hair, huge beards, and glaring eyes, a mirror image of menace in the setting sunlight. Clarence said, "Come on. Harrison wants to see you now."

Jacob looked down at Griff who was looking back and forth between the mountainous men with pure fear in his eyes. No way they could chance running away from monsters like these, so they all silently stood. Clarence lifted a hand. "No, she's gotta stay out here."

Confused, they merely stared. Shaking his head, Clarence said, "The girl. She stays out. For now."

Tina pulled on Jacob's sleeve pleading in a whisper, "Don't leave me. Don't leave me alone."

Jacob looked at her, "No. We won't."

Before he could protest, one of the blonde-bearded men, stepped down and grabbed him. Moving remarkably quickly, the huge beast hurried him inside, the other one roughly dragging Griff along. Risking a look back, he saw Tina. She stood stock still, staring at him, an equal combination of terror and disbelief on her face as she clearly fought back tears.

Jacob could only blindly hope she would be safe as struggling against the man's powerful grip would be like trying to snap iron. They were led through the building, the two silent masses lumbering them along. Even in the dim light, the smooth walls, shiny tiles, and copious glass were visible enough to be impressive; nothing like this existed in Malden. If he was not terrified for himself and worried about Tina, Jacob would have marvelled at the sights.

They walked up numerous stone stairs before entering another hallway. One of the beasts grunted, "In there."

After sharing a leery look, Jacob and Griff stepped inside. Light filled the space. A lifetime where, once the sunset, the world became a dim place, forced Jacob to take a step back from the bizarre brightness. Composing himself, he moved into a narrow entryway, shoulder to shoulder with Griff. Candles and lanterns glowed everywhere and, even full of fear, his first instinct was to rush around, putting them out to stop the wastefulness.

A calm voice beckoned them, "In here."

A kitchen area filled one side while an area of comfortable looking furniture ran along a wall impossibly made entirely of glass. Across from some sort of padded bench, sitting in a wide armchair, was the man who must be the leader. He did not look physically imposing to Jacob, especially compared to the matching brutes who brought them there, but, in the copious firelight, his eyes shone and his penetrating gaze almost hurt.

He did not get up, merely pointed to the bench, inviting them to sit. "My name is Harrison. You are Jacob and Griff?"

They both sunk on to the incredibly soft seat and nodded.

With a cold tone, the man calmly said, "I understand you, and your one-armed friend down below wish to stay with us."

Unsure what to do, Jacob nodded, Griff doing the same next to him.

"That's fine, however, we -"

A knock on the door interrupted the man. He called out, "Come in."

Two women carrying trays walked into the room. Both were wearing short, thin dresses and Jacob smelled a hint of flowers in the air as they moved by. He chanced a look up at them. He could not recall ever seeing a woman for the first time as, until this painful adventure, everyone he ever knew he always knew. The sight of unusual females caused an instant pleasurable ache to float up despite his intense fear. One of them, tall with freckles, a few years older than him, apparently noticing his dumb stare, flashed a brief, uncertain smile. His face grew hot and he promptly stared back down at his feet.

"Ladies, these young men are Griff and Jacob. They are thinking of joining us. This is Alice and Andrea, great examples of the lovely women you'll get to know here."

The women murmured hasty greetings as they set down the trays. Griff and he managed to meekly say hello. Then the women stood before Harrison as if waiting for orders. He turned his palms up to the ceiling and said, "Can't we show these young men some hospitality, they've traveled long and far. Let them see what they can expect to enjoy here."

They reluctantly turned to face them. Peering up through his eyelashes, Jacob saw the hems of the dresses lifting. He could not help himself, he glanced up at the unfamiliar, naked flesh. When the cloth was bunched up under their chins, Harrison said, "Give them a turn."

Slowly, the naked legs caused the naked torsos to turn, but Jacob shied away, averting his gaze from the scene. Finally, in his steady tone, Harrison said, "Thank you, ladies. That will be all."

Thankfully, with his stomach aching with hunger and his throat parched, Jacob could immediately forget the awkwardness and turn his attention to the food now covering the low table. There were items he recognized, roast potatoes, beans, and dried venison. Amongst those were a couple of items he did not know but looked wonderful, however, his eyes were first drawn by thirst to the tall pitcher.

Harrison apparently recognized this look and poured them each a glass of the cool water which they greedily drank. He then handed them each a plate and said, "Go ahead gentlemen, help yourselves."

Jacob took the plate and carefully dished up some of everything as Griff did the same. Harrison added, "Take as much as you like. We've got plenty."

Even with the invitation, Jacob did not completely fill his plate, not wanting to look gluttonous to this composed stranger. Jacob said, "Thanks, this looks great."

Griff, already starting to eat, said, "Yeah, thanks."

A smile touched Harrison's lips, but it did not seem to reach his unchanging eyes. "You're welcome. While you eat, we may as well discuss what joining the Bank means. Perhaps, most importantly, everyone here is family. Must be that way for things to run smoothly, to allow us to continue to survive as we have. A key component to maintaining a family is trust."

He stared especially hard at each of them as if to punctuate before continuing, "This also means we can have no secrets or lies within the Bank. Everyone who comes in must be open and honest upon their arrival and every day thereafter."

Jacob glanced sideways at his friend but, unusually, Griff seemed too uncertain to speak. Not sure what to say, Jacob muttered, "Sure. I get that, makes sense, sure."

"Ok, good. Now, why don't you two start by telling me where you came from."

Thankfully, Griff managed to gather himself, apparently made bolder by getting to tell their story again, he sat up straighter as he said, "We're brothers. Jacob and I. Tina was taken in by our parents -"

Harrison lifted a hand, cutting him off. "Actually, Jacob you tell me."

Nervousness instantly stole away Jacob's appetite when the stranger turned his cold gaze on him. He tried to sound composed as he choked down a mouthful of food and said, "Right, ok, well, like Griff said, we lived on a farm with our parents. After the attack and all, we, well we were able to live off the land, you know, it was tough, but we got by. They took in Tina. The five of us managed, barely, but we got by. But then, last winter, things got worse."

Jacob knew he was awful at lying and he knew his tale sounded stilted, and this knowledge made him even more uneasy. He took a drink, trying to calm himself. Griff's story had length, peppered with helpful details and descriptions but Jacob decided to shorten his telling and get it over with.

"Both our parents got sick, very sick, and our supplies ran out. When the weather finally cleared up, they sent us three, they sent us out to find food. We didn't have much luck, so we hiked down to the river. On the bank there, we found an old boat stuck on the last of the ice."

He tried to grin like Griff would at this part, but it felt ridiculous. "Not sure what we were thinking, desperation makes idiots I guess, but we got in that boat to try and get out where we could fish better. The current was super strong, and it took us downriver."

Griff, apparently unable to hold his tongue as Jacob massacred the story, jumped in, "Yeah, it was fast. Before we had time to think we were miles away. Couldn't stop. Thought for damn sure we were done for."

Harrison merely turned his focussed glare on Griff, the message clear that he did not appreciate the interruption. Instead of a witty retort, Griff stopped talking and sheepishly looked down at his plate, and Harrison looked back to Jacob, silently telling him to continue.

"Right, well, we got lucky, sort of anyhow. We crashed into an ice dam thing and were able to jump out of the boat there. We hiked for a couple of days, trying to make our way back home. Then, when we were sleeping, those, well those people, I guess they were called Preppers, they found us and made us go with them back to their buildings. That's where we met up with Clarence and those patrol guys."

Jacob forced himself to look Harrison in the eye, trying to make him think he was telling the truth but also trying to figure out if he believed him or not. The steady look he got in return revealed nothing.

•　　•　　•

An interesting day to say the least. The return of the patrol. Critical questions surrounding Hale's death. A pair of liars and an amputee girl. On top that, before he could address that multitude of issues, Harrison had been told about Kinma killing Luke. When it rains, it pours.

Murder was not unknown to the Bank, but it was rare. Early on, two men were killed when a brawl broke out and Harrison exiled the perpetrators. Later, one man killed a woman after she bit him and he was summarily executed. Another killed a newcomer for stealing beef jerky, and Harrison cut him to half rations for a month. The Vikings killed a man for no real reason, and they were not punished at all. His rationales for these different penalties were kept purposefully vague so no calculation of the risk could be done by potential killers. Plus, Harrison could then favor those he wanted to if need be.

This uncertainty, however, meant Kinma's crime created a dilemma. Harrison could not allow women to think they could kill men when they did not like what was being done to them or no male in the Bank would be able to sleep safely. Plus, Luke was well-liked so the others would want a steep penalty imposed. However, women were in short supply, and they were valuable pieces in the chess match he was playing to maintain control. Right now, there were too many unknowns to address the dilemma smartly, and he had learned long ago to avoid making final decisions in chaotic situations. In order to buy himself time to think and strategize, Harrison ordered her locked up.

Now, these idiot boys were clearly lying to him, making things more difficult. He had hoped that putting girls in front of them would have them falling over each other to get in his good graces. However, that had been misguided, the nakedness seemed to scare them even more than the Vikings did. He glared at the one named Jacob and said, "That is quite a story."

The nervous kid, his fork halfway to his mouth, merely nodded. Normally, Harrison would torment the liar for a while, toy with him by asking questions until he knew he was completely cornered. Tonight, however, other duties pulled at him and he was keen to know where these people came from, he wanted this done.

"Unfortunately, I don't believe it. Not a word of it."

Intensified fear seemed to seize both of them, but, surprisingly, the dark haired one gathered himself fairly quickly and said, "Sure, I can understand that, it is pretty unbelievable, but it's all the truth."

Harrison nodded and asked, "So, if I gave you and your friend each a paper and pen, tell you both to write down the names of your cherished parents, you'll both write the same thing?"

At this, he let the two fools share a look as he enjoyed watching them try to silently come up with a solution to this simple conundrum. Plucking a dry cookie off the table, Harrison took his time to eat the morsel, expecting the kids would cave and confess. Instead, Jacob emphatically shook his head at his friend, and they both returned their looks to their plates.

Deciding to try one more tactic, Harrison said, "Fine. Be defiant. That's your choice. However, I cannot let you stay here if you choose to lie. We have plenty of food, plenty of room and plenty of women. Liars like you, though, get exiled to the forest to freeze or starve or both. Last chance boys, tell me the truth of where you came from, and I will let you and your friend downstairs stay. Utter one more lie though and I'll have you immediately escorted from Thule with nothing but the clothes on your back."

CHAPTER TWENTY-TWO

JUNE 25, 2046

DAY THREE THOUSAND SEVEN HUNDRED AND SEVENTY-FIVE

In the darkness, Kinma rubbed at her skin. Luke's dried blood had stuck hard, and she was filled with disgust as she tried to frantically scratch it off.

After killing Luke, with her mind racing and panicked emotions coursing through her, she tried vainly to plan an escape. Somewhere to hide the body, some way to explain Luke's disappearance, fleeing into the wild. But, before she could do anything, to Bankers walked in looking for the recently deceased. They observed the obvious scene and, with alarming speed, she was seized and locked in the narrow storage room that served as their jail cell, a thin chain on her ankle holding her to the wall.

Sitting in the corner, her knees clutched under her chin, she tried forced her mind to think through the scenarios of what Harrison could do to her and how she might outmaneuver him; however, every time she ventured near intelligent thought, only Hale came to mind.

In the blackness, covered in Luke's blood, the shock at realizing she would never be able to speak with Hale again morphed into an intense, all-encompassing pain that coursed through her body and mind as she screamed into the nothingness.

•　　•　　•

Sweat rolled down Jacob's back under Harrison's stern, angry gaze but he actually felt relieved. Getting to leave this demented outpost unscathed sounded perfect to him, regardless of what hardships they might face in the wilderness. More importantly, Jacob realized their foolishness created a greater problem than risking their own safety, they had made these dangerous men aware that a place existed somewhere which might be a great prize for them. If they were free of this demented group there could be no more slips of information and these cruel men would not be able to go looking for Malden.

Griff beat him to speaking and quickly said, "Oh, ok, but what we told you is what happened. I get why you don't believe us, it's crazy, but that's what happened. It's probably best if we simply go."

For the first time, emotion reached Harrison's face. Jacob recognized the change to his mouth as the physical act of smiling but it did not reflect happiness in any way, and this scared him even more.

Jacob hurriedly set his plate with his half-eaten meal on the table and got to his feet. "Sorry, obviously this was a mistake, I mean, a mistake by us. I'm sorry to waste your time and thanks for the dinner, but I think we should go now."

Griff, probably sensing their chance to escape, returned to his senses and set his plate down as he said, "Yeah, all this here looks great, but I don't think we'd fit in."

A brief bark of a maniacal laugh escaped from Harrison despite his eyes remaining harsh. "Sit back down."

Taking a step away from the couch, Jacob said, "Thanks, but I think we've wasted enough of your-"

"Sit down."

Jacob kept moving. "No, we are just going to leave."

Harrison let out a sharp whistle. Griff and Jacob sped up their exit but, before they got far, the two massive men with the blonde beards stepped inside, easily blocking the way. Jacob turned back to Harrison and said, "Oh, thanks, we don't need an escort or anything, we can find our own way."

The leader spoke calmly behind them, "I gave you fools a chance. I treated you nicely. Gave you good food and water. But you chose to lie and then defy me. Now, you're going to tell me the truth, all of it and right now."

The mountain-like men easily walked them back to the couch where they were roughly seated. With the silent, imposing men standing over them, Harrison leaned forward in his chair and calmly said, "I am not an idiot. I can see the two of you are not related, and you're not starving. You are not from some isolated farm. You are from somewhere established, somewhere with people, food and supplies. Somewhere that has managed to escape our attention up to now. Tell me where you are from, or I will make you tell me."

Jacob, realizing the pleasant threat of exile was only a ploy, opened his mouth to reply but, with fear, both for himself and for his home, filling him, no words came.

•   •   •

The sturdy defiance surprised Harrison, he expected the terrified kids to crumple immediately. Frustrating but he figured it would make no difference in the end. When the threat of true harm became reality they would not last long.

He nodded to one of the Vikings and a huge fist immediately smashed into the redhead's ribs. He gasped for air as Harrison turned his attention back to the other one. His eyes were now wide as he looked at his friend doubled over. "Ok, how about now? You smart enough to play along? Where are you from?"

The kid's lips moved but, annoyingly, no words came. One of the Vikings cuffed the redhead in the back of the skull, knocking him to the floor. Finally, the one named Jacob looked down at his feet and said, "I can't. I can't tell you. Sorry."

Harrison reached over, lifted the kid's face back up by his hair. "Why? Why can't you tell me?"

"My family is there. And, and, a girl, my friend. And, beside, there are rules. The Seven Rules."

"Your rules don't matter here son, you'll see that soon enough. Get that one up on his feet."

Without a word, one of Vikings grabbed a handful of red hair and dragged the boy to the counter where he held him upright. No struggling, the redhead merely stood looking baffled and scared.

Harrison sighed. He was fine causing physical pain to people, and the Vikings would surely enjoy helping. However, Harrison viewed such steps as undignified and rudimentary, he preferred to use his wits to cajole someone into cooperating. He said, "Alright Jacob, maybe you and I can make a deal before this gets out of hand. You say there's this girl back home, I understand you don't want to put her at risk. You've got a friend right here, not to mention the burned girl down below, who are both at serious, immediate risk. But I think you can keep them all safe if you handle this proper like."

A hint of hope flashed into his frightened, darting eyes and Harrison continued, "You tell me where this place is, and I won't torture Griff here, you won't have to listen to him scream in agony all night, and you won't have to watch later while my massive friends here do what they wish with the one-armed girl. Then, if we decide to go to this place you're from, I promise I will ensure your family is not harmed and I will make sure that girl you want is yours and yours alone. You can live out your little lives together in bliss."

He paused to let the idea sink in, but the kid kept his gaze on his feet and shook his head with annoying immediacy. One of the Vikings tore open the redhead's shirt, exposing his pink skin. With the terror in the room now palatable, Harrison leaned in, "It's going to get extremely unpleasant. Tell me now and tell it true."

More head shaking with some muttering through sobs about seven rules and someone named Louisa. Harrison grabbed Jacob's hand and slapped it onto the counter. Jacob struggled slightly but did not free himself. Drawing his belt knife, he pressed the blade against the boy's finger and stated, "I cannot tolerate people lying to me, cannot allow it under my command. One last chance."

Tears leaked from the boy's eyes but he shook his head. These morons were not going to make it easy on themselves. Harrison pushed down on the knife, slicing along the finger as a scream pierced his ears.

•　　　•　　　•

Marge the trapper reminded Morreign of an adjective her mother used to use: spunky. With the arrival of a talkative stranger carrying a mind full of fresh stories, the entire community came out to listen and, as long as they kept bringing her food, Marge seemed more than content to keep telling tales.

With Marge half-way through a funny story about how her son tried to tame a fox using peanut butter, Morreign suddenly could hear no more of this woman's life, she needed to leave. She stepped outside, hoping the cool, fresh air of the night would help relieve her discomfort. It did not.

Limping off the porch, she heard the question from behind her, "She going to leave?

Turning she saw Boris Walker stepping out of a shadow.

Morreign nodded.

"You sure?"

"I'm sure."

"Tomorrow?"

"I don't know."

"We'll need to know."

"Probably tomorrow. She might stay longer if I ask her to."

"Her staying longer will not make it easier."

She sighed. "I know."

He nodded and walked away.

Suddenly, feeling too tired to even make the short limp to her bed, Morreign leaned back, feeling the footstep-smoothed wood of the porch under her calloused hands. She stared at the crystal clear stars, pure white points in a perfectly black sky. Taking a deep breath, she wondered if she needed to do this. Did it matter any longer? Her children were gone, did she need to take such a drastic, horrible step out of a vague need to possibly protect what remained here.

More laughter poured from the Lodge. She thought she could make out Paul's chuckles and definitely heard Leo's loud bellows above the others. Somehow they could still laugh. After all, they've been through and were going through, they somehow laughed. Maybe that was worth protecting but tonight she was not certain it was worth protecting at whatever cost.

Another round of laughing. She pushed herself up from the porch with a sigh, knowing all along what she would decide. Regardless of how she felt about her life, she could not stop protecting them. With a nod, she muttered to herself, "Tomorrow."

CHAPTER TWENTY-THREE

JUNE 26, 2046

DAY THREE THOUSAND SEVEN HUNDRED AND SEVENTY-SIX

"I'll tell you. I'll tell you. I don't care about the Seven Rules. Stop. Just stop. Please."

At first, Jacob thought he had spoken the words. Screams filled the room. Griff's screams, or his own, Jacob could no longer tell. Harrison grabbed Griff by the hair, pulling back his head so he could glare down in his eyes. He snarled at Griff who was bloodied and bleeding, "Yes? Enough?"

Griff nodded. They released him, and he collapsed onto the floor. It had been Griff speaking. Jacob did not think he cared. He was lying on the floor, in a gruesome puddle and, for the moment, no one was hurting him and that was all that mattered.

Rough hands grabbed him, lifted him and dragged him easily across the slick floor before setting him onto a hard chair. Harrison handed him a cup of water. For a moment Jacob merely stared at, it looked foreign in his blood-covered hands, and he was unsure what he was supposed to do. A drop of his blood fell from his chin into the water, and Jacob watch as it floated about, making a pretty pattern before Harrison gently moved the cup up towards his mouth and Jacob remembered how to drink. His lips were split and bruised, and the cool water caused a cracked tooth to let out a jolt of pain but the simple, normal act of drinking felt wonderful regardless.

Setting down the empty cup, he watched as the massive men lifted Griff and set him in the chair next to him. His eyes remained closed, and Jacob figured he had died. He knew, intellectually, that he should care but he hurt too much to care.

Harrison spread a colorful paper across the table and slapped Griff in the face. His friend started and mumbled something. Not dead. Jacob was unsure if that was good or bad. Harrison put a pencil in Griff's hand. "Ok, you two put up an impressive fight. Lasted longer than I figured you would. Now show me."

Jacob stared at the paper. There was an atlas at Malden, a huge book full of maps. When they were ten he and Griff became, in the way of young boys, obsessed with the maps. They had poured over the pages, talking about all the towns, rivers, mountains and lakes with strange names they would go and see one day. He recognized this paper as being a map like those, and he guessed it represented the area they were in.

Jacob could not tell this evil man. He wanted to tell him everything and anything to make this end but he couldn't, Louisa was there. Looking at the map, Jacob thought he could lie, but the man seemed to see their lies better than they saw them themselves. Lying would only illicit more punishment.

Harrison slapped Griff across the face again, and he came to slightly. "You, tell me where this place is, do it right now, or I'll take out your eyes and cut off your useless tongue."

Griff, his mouth gaping open, merely stared at the map. Apparently sensing confusion, Harrison snatched up another pencil and pointed, saying, "This is Thule. This, up here, is the settlement with the Preppers."

A map with places he had actually been to. In any other circumstance such a marvel would intrigue Jacob to no end, now it terrified him. Harrison continued, using the pencil to point at thicker blue lines as he said, "This is a river, the Pembina River. Here's another one. And another, further north, here."

That got Griff's attention, and he mumbled, "Right, right. River. A river with a crooked tree."

Jacob, perceiving through the fog of agony what was about to happen, said, "No, Griff, don't –."

Grabbed from behind, Jacob and his chair suddenly crashed down onto the wet, sticky floor before one of the massive blonde men put a heavy boot on his neck. Jacob heard Griff muttering up above, "Yeah. The story about the boat, that was true, well, mostly true. We got swept downriver."

Smelling the blood and feeling sharp pain everywhere, Jacob decided he did not truly care. Griff could tell them. Then, as he gasped for breath beneath the weight of the thug's boot, an image of Louisa, standing under the silver willows in the moonlight as he stupidly marched away, leaving her, flashed into his mind.

If they told him where to go, this evil could find its way to Malden, to Louisa. He needed to get home, needed to tell them all of the horrible nature of the outside world and, most importantly, he needed to get back to Louisa. Apologize for everything. Make her smile one more time. Make sure she is safe.

He roughly twisted out from under the boot on his neck and sputtered out, "Don't Griff. You can't."

A soft pleading voice that did not sound much like his friend came back, "Sorry, I can't take this, I got to, Jake, I have to end this."

Realizing Griff did not have a Louisa to think about, Jacob said, "Your mother, your father, your sister. Picture them."

Rough hands pulled Jacob back to his feet, surely preparing him for more abuse. He watched as Griff looked over at him, their pain filled eyes meeting, and Jacob said, "We're dead either way."

Griff looked away to stare back down at the map and then lifted his blood covered hand. He slammed his palm down on the paper, smearing dark red across the carefully drawn details, ruining much of the map. A shockingly loud, crisp and pure cackling laugh escaped from Griff, startling Jacob.

Harrison stood stalk still amongst the strange laughter, and Jacob cringed, worried the psychopath, having not gotten what he wanted truly would kill them both now. But Harrison merely turned away as he said to one of the huge men, "Go get that girl."

•   •   •

The hoe felt wonderfully substantial in Louisa's hands even though her recent break from manual labor meant blisters were already forming where the callouses earned from a life of work had softened. Last night, hearing the noise of revelry down below, she had left her room and sat on the stairs to listen as the stranger told stories to the rapt audience. Before long, the scene evolved into an ad hoc party with children scurrying about the laughing adults. Seeing her sitting alone on the steps, Paulina had hurried up to her and climbed on to her lap.

Before Jacob's disappearance, the eight-year-old spent a great deal of time playing and cuddling with Louisa. However, after Tina, Griff, and Jacob disappeared, the child clearly sensed Louisa's mood and avoided her. Sitting on the stairs, the doe-eyed girl twisted on her lap and looked up at her, "Were you sick?"

This made Louisa smile. "Sort of, I guess."

"You better?"

"Sort of, I guess."

A few of the other children scurried past. Paulina wrapped her arms around Louisa's neck. "That's good. Wanna play dolls again tomorrow?"

Knowing she could not say anything else, Louisa answered, "Sure."

With that, the girl happily squirmed off her lap and joined the small mob of kids. For a while, Louisa watched the scene from the staircase, but Emma spied her spying and waved for her to come over. Louisa's instinct was to politely shake her head, but the idea of slinking back up to her room all alone seemed daunting. She slipped off the stairs and moved down to the main table.

Silently sitting down next to Emma, a few people noticed her and gave tiny smiles or nods of welcome but quickly returned their attention to the visiting storyteller. Emma, not taking her eyes off the visitor, who continually chatted away, casually leaned her cheek against Louisa's shoulder.

Long into the night, they listened to Marge talk about life out in the woods. She fended for herself, trading from time to time with others on the rare occasion she encountered someone, but otherwise taking care of everything on her own. Her stories were meant to be humorous, but Louisa found them heavily tinged with profound loneliness. Looking around the table crowded with familiar faces and at the content children now sleeping in a massed heap on the cushions in the corner, Louisa realized, even without Jacob, she still lived amongst people that knew her and cared for her.

After the stories, when she laid on her cot back in her room, Louisa had decided she had wallowed in her sorrow long enough. Thinking about it, she realized, while she did not feel good, she had felt best after hunting with Sam in the woods. Being valuable, being productive, truly helped. She would continue to think about Jacob, to miss him and worry about him, but she would no longer let those thoughts and that pain engulf her entirely. It was past time to that she return to pulling her weight, pay her due.

In the pre-dawn morning, after a short night's sleep following the storytelling marathon, she ate a breakfast of carrot biscuits in the common room while the others silently welcomed her back to the world of the living. When they left to start in on chores, she walked out with them, happily taking up a hoe.

Now, standing in the middle of the huge garden, she spit in her palms and rubbed them together hoping to keep the blisters from growing worse. As she was about to turn her attention back to the freshly turned earth, she saw two people on the path heading to the creek. Far away but the limp made it obvious that one of them was Morreign and she guessed the other was Marge, heading back to her solitary life in the forest.

Strange the visitor chose to return to loneliness rather than stay amongst everyone at Malden, but Louisa figured there were all types of people. Hoping the interesting woman would return soon with more stories, Louisa looked back to the weeds and hacked away.

•　　•　　•

"Leave me alone, let me go."

Jacob, sitting on the floor, unable to contemplate the various pains emanating from his various wounds but glad for the brief respite, spun at the sound of Tina's pleading voice. One of the massive men was dragging her in by her arm as she struggled mightily to stay outside. He and Griff had walked into this horror willingly, Tina, far smarter than them, at least tried to stay out.

When she was thrust further inside, she saw him and Griff. She stopped pleading as her mouth fell open in shock at their bloodied and beaten appearance. The genuine concern in her eyes made Jacob want to stand up and apologize, to tell her everything would be fine even though he knew it would not be. Regardless, when he tried to move one of the thugs easily pushed him back and Jacob could only mumble through swollen lips, "Don't tell them, Tina, don't tell -"

Harrison, slowly walking into the room, casually backhanded him before he could finish. Tina's eyes started darting around the well-lit room, a cornered rabbit looking for a direction to bolt. The psychopath, having washed and changed into a clean shirt, calmly approached her, his palms facing forward. "Don't worry, these boys were foolish and lied. I don't tolerate liars, but I hate the idea of hurting them further, so why don't you do us all a great favor and simply tell me about the place you three came from."

She looked down at Jacob and asked, "Jake, what... Jake? What do I do?"

He wanted to save her the horror, to save her the agony, and tell her to let them know everything. But he couldn't. They would destroy Malden and everyone there would suffer, better the three of them here than everyone back home. He shook his head and looked down as he said, "Don't say anything."

It had been a long night. Harrison did not actually enjoy inflicting pain, although it did not bother him like it appeared to bother some others, it was merely a chore. However, the persistence of these country bumpkins to remain silent despite his best efforts was wearing Harrison's patience very thin.

Looking at the terrified girl, thirteen or so he supposed, with deep burn scars shiny in the candlelight, he decided to get right to the point. He pulled the cover off the largest kerosene lantern, its oily flame swaying lazily and a glance told him his instinct had been right, she did not like fire, not at all.

"All I need to know is where you three came from. Simple as that. You give me that, and you can all go on your merry way."

Her eyes focussed on the flame as it moved towards her, the girl slowly shook her head.

A few feet from her, Harrison paused, "Ahh, but you see, if you don't tell me, I scorch - "

"Stop it. Goddamnit, stop it."

One of the boys yelling. Harrison didn't take his eyes off the girl who remained transfixed. "I'll burn the flesh off your fingers, I'll cook the soles of your feet. I suggest you speak up before -"

Without preamble, the thin girl turned and immediately darted at the window. She crashed her bony shoulder into the glass with a powerful crack, but it withstood breaking. Without hesitation, she stepped back and charged again. A boy screamed. Another crack, spider web lines now visible in the glass as she stepped back.

Harrison barked, "Idiots, grab her."

The nearest Viking lunged forward, grabbing at her shirt but the girl was stronger than she appeared and she tore free, crashing into the glass again. The window shattered into a million pieces.

For an instant, she stayed there, only her toes on the window ledge, suspended in open air for a heartbeat. The Viking lunged further, trying to catch her but swinging desperately, he missed.

The girl, despite being on the cusp of her death, seemed utterly calm as she looked at the massive man before her, now leaning completely off-balance. As she started to fall, she threw out her one hand and grabbed the Viking's meaty paw as if she were eagerly meeting a business acquaintance. Then she yanked at the same moment her tiny feet left the ledge, hurling her out into the grey dawn light. The Viking cursed as he took one big booted step, slipped on the glass covered floor and tumbled out after her.

Harrison stepped to the opening. Three stories below, on the cement walkway, lay a mangled mess of human parts with the tell-tale pool of redness spreading out from beneath them. He heard the remaining Viking yell in a foreign language before he ran out of the apartment to check on his brother, but Harrison was certain neither of them survived the fall.

Fury overwhelming his usual calm, Harrison spun and grabbed Jacob from where he sat looking battered and stunned. Holding a handful of the young man's blood-soaked hair, he leaned him out of the smashed window, his feet scrabbling on the precipice.

"Tell me. Tell me, or you meet the fate of your friend."

Struggling to get a footing on the glass covered floor, the boy looked down for a second and then, his struggles stopped. He turned and looked Harrison in the eye. "We'll never tell you. Kill us or let us go home, those are your only options."

Harrison was about to let gravity bring an end to the fool but, after the boy spoke, a better idea suddenly struck him. He pulled the child back inside and stoically said, "Fine, you win, I give up."

CHAPTER TWENTY-FOUR

JUNE 26, 2046

DAY THREE THOUSAND SEVEN HUNDRED AND SEVENTY-SIX

Dawn filled the summer forest with beams of shimmering light, the air smelled earthy and fresh, a perfect morning for a hike. Marge walked next to Morreign who struggled to limp along.

"Thanks again for all these supplies, like I said, I'll come back by some time when the trapping's been good and share my take with all of you all."

"Oh, yes, that'd be great."

Marge continued to talk as they walked, discussing how she thought this fall would be a good one for catching gophers because she knew of a clearing running thick with pups. Morreign actually caught herself thinking of how Marge bringing back some meat would be helpful when she saw the footbridge up ahead and remembered why they were out there. Beneath the plank bridge, a wide creek rushed, filling the forest with white noise as they neared.

As she stepped onto the worn planks, Marge said, "Wow, don't see a lot of bridges way out here. Did you folks build this or was it -"

The arrow silently pierced through her chest and the woman collapsed mid-word. Her knees made a heavy, hollow thump on the bridge before she toppled over on to her side. While the sight revolted her, Morreign knew her role in this sick play. She drew her hunting knife and rushed, not wanting the woman to suffer. Bending over her, she felt Marge's neck. No pulse, no breath. Morreign let out her held breath in a sigh of relief as she gratefully put away the unused knife.

Boris Walker, bow in hand, stepped out from the trees and walked purposefully onto the other end of the bridge. Without hesitation, he calmly pulled the arrow from the woman's ruined skull, wiped it in the grass and put it back into his quiver. He then opened the sack Marge carried and began taking out the supplies Morreign had given the lone woman.

A candle. Two jars of pickled carrots from last fall. Some old magazines. A patched-up sweater. That was all. The talkative woman near ecstatic to get these simple items. Items, ten years ago, Morreign would have mindlessly tossed out if they were in her way. Now, set out next to the dead woman, they reminded her how hard and horrible life became. Exhaustion struck her, and she sat down on the wooden bridge.

Boris remained unmoving and silent for quite some time, apparently waiting for her to get herself under control and back on her feet. When it became clear that this was not going to happen, he squatted down next to her. He did not look at her, he kept looking straight out at the rushing water.

"I hate this, I truly do, but it had to be done. She wouldn't stay. She would have told others about us, likely a lot of others given the way she talked."

Angered at the horrible situation, she barked back, "We don't know that. We don't know that. We could've explained…"

"We do know."

She turned on him, but he continued to look at the water. She said, "You know, way back when we first got here, I could have killed Sam. He came out of nowhere with a gun on his shoulder. Leo and I were up on a roof and had a rifle trained on him. There was no pledge from him about staying. How well do you think we would've made it through all this without Sam? I could have killed him."

"Could have."

She waved at the corpse. "How's this any different than that? How's this different?"

Boris answered with annoying ease. "Back then you were desperate. You needed to take the chance that he might be able to help. Now, you need to protect what you've built. Situations dictate decisions, not wants. You made the right decision at the right time, both then and now."

Her anger retreated. Boris was right. But it did not make this easy. She asked, "When? When can we stop protecting and struggling? When can we merely live the life we've built?"

Instead of answering, Boris asked, "Can I tell you a story?"

For an instant, this made Morreign want to lash back out, she did not think it was the time for storytelling, but she also did not want to return to dealing with the body, so she merely nodded.

"When I was a teenager, like twelve or so, we lived on the edge of a town. My mom, my younger brother and me. We didn't have much of anything but my mom worked in a store and I did odd chores in the neighborhood after school so we had groceries and the lights stayed on. Can't say it was easy, but it was nice. Really nice. We played games. We cooked dinners together. Curled up on our worn out couch in the evenings to watch old movies.

"As a kid, you don't understand much about adult things. But, after some time, I think my mom, she wasn't as content with the simple life as us kids were. She started saying she was going to get us a nicer place, nicer things. She let her guard down and started dating the boss from her job."

Boris plucked a pebble off the bridge and tossed it into the rushing water before he said, "A mistake. At first, it was ok. He brought us things and got her better shifts at work. But the man was married, and his wife found out about his dalliance. My mom got fired, and we couldn't afford rent. I was lucky, I came up here to live with my grandfather, and he got me interested in nature and science. My brother had to go live with a great aunt who could barely care for herself and he ended up in the army. I never saw my mom again."

Boris turned and looked at her. "Life here is not easy, it's not perfect, but it is good. Every decision, every choice has to come from that thinking. Will doing or not doing something risk what's here?"

He pointed back at Marge's body and said, "Unfortunately, that was the right decision."

Boris stood and helped Morreign to her feet. They returned to their unpleasant but necessary task.

•　　•　　•

Kinma tried to get the unknown man to talk, but he was fading in out of consciousness. She tried to give him a drink, but the water mostly dribbled onto his chest. The only light in the makeshift cell came from the thin crack under the door so she could not determine the nature of his injuries, but his murmuring unconsciousness made it clear they were extensive. When the door swung in again, the flood of light into the tiny room blinded her but, from the size of the looming silhouette, she knew it was one of the Vikings.

She pleaded, "Please, he's really hurt. He needs help."

No response as someone else was pushed inside. The newcomer stumbled over them, crashing into the wall, the Viking slamming the door and sending them back into darkness. The man with his head on Kinma's lap let out a groan and the new one, in a tired, distant sounding voice asked, "Is he going to die?"

"I don't know. I can't see a damn thing in here. He's not talking."

The only response from the shadows was a quiet, "Oh."

Carefully laying the injured man onto the floor, she slid over to the newcomer. She put the water bottle in his hand, saying, "I'm Kinma. Are you hurt?"

He slowly took the water, and she heard him drink before he said, "My name's Jacob. I'm hurt, but ok, I think. Bleeding but ok."

The arrival of strangers confused her. If someone arrived and Harrison did not want to allow them in they were immediately escorted away or killed, not tortured and kept. She asked, "Where'd you guys come from?"

The unseen person snapped back, "Why does everyone need to know that?"

His voice carried an edge of anger, but he sounded young, more like a petulant child than an enraged man. She said, "Calm down, calm down. Only curious about how you two got here and what happened."

"Oh, okay, sorry. We came in with the patrol, they found us after those survivalists people kidnapped us."

Hale, this person saw Hale. She wanted to ask about him but decided this was not the time. She said, "Interesting trip. Harrison did this to you guys?"

Kinma sensed him nodding in the darkness and asked. "Why?"

She could hear the desperate worry as he answered, "Our home. He wants our home. We wouldn't tell him where it is, and he hurt us. Our other friend, Tina, she died."

Kinma had no words to comfort this unknown boy. If Harrison thought they came from somewhere worth finding, he would not give up until he got what he wanted. And, if got what he wanted, it would likely go very badly for whoever was at the boy's home. A hopeless situation she could relate to.

They merely sat in the dark and, eventually, the quiet was replaced by the slow, sputtering breathing of the newcomer's exhausted but uneasy sleep. Huddled back in her corner, alone again, curiosity over these strangers pulled at her. She stared at the crack under the door. Would they be delivering another person? Was there some other boy upstairs being tortured because he knows something Harrison wants to know? Or would the monster do that to her next? Or would he merely let her rot in this dark room?

CHAPTER TWENTY-FIVE

JUNE 30, 2046

DAY THREE THOUSAND SEVEN HUNDRED AND EIGHTY

Everyone gathered outside, standing before their building. Harrison stood atop the steps in front main doors and looked out over the silent group.

Earlier, he had Clarence go into the ad hoc cell that, for the last four days, served to hold the boys and Kinma. He reported back that the darker man was fairly well recovered while the other was in bad shape. Predictably, Kinma remained unbent by her confinement.

This meant there was no reason to wait, the redhead might never recover, and he only needed one of them. The murmurs amongst the Bank were growing louder and louder, no longer murmurs really. All of it made worse by the death of the Viking and Milo's constant harassment of Clarence over Hale's death. The Bank was becoming a powder keg. Harrison decided to put his plan into action.

Speeches were rare in the Bank, Harrison preferring to lead through silent fear and occasional, drastic action, rather than words. As a result, he knew everyone awaited his message with great anticipation. He spoke with a strong, clear voice, "We've grown soft. After the Bombs, we were strong, venturing far and wide to take what we needed to survive in the new world. We were built to thrive through strength. Over time, however, we became complacent, allowing the ease of a life, safe and warm at home, to seduce us."

He could see ripples of concern in the crowd as even the dullards realized this did not sound like a preamble to good news. However, Harrison also saw hard glares, some men, tired of his command, did not like being chastised like children. He could not push too far, not like in the past.

"I am as much at fault for this development as anyone, more so even. But, regardless of where the fault lies, we are in a dire position. Even with the return of this last patrol, our general stagnation has created a perilous situation that hampers our ability to become the great society we should become, that we deserve to become."

A few mumblings. None knew the actual state of their supplies as Harrison kept that information segregated so only he held the complete picture and dire might be overstating the problem given the supplies taken from the Survivalists, but he knew imparting a sense of desperation would make people more willing to act as he needed them to.

He lifted his hands and said, "Thankfully, we have been granted an opportunity. The very opportunity we need. Three young strangers returned here with the last patrol. Myself, with Clarence's guidance, suspected they carried useful information."

Harrison looked out over the grimy crowd. A few scowls remained, others looking with worried anticipation, but everyone paying attention. He took a breath, time to bet on his bluff.

"They are from a secluded community where many survivors have established themselves. Stores of dried fish and meat have been put aside, heavily planted gardens are waiting to be harvested along with stockpiles of gathered goods. We are going to go and take what, as the strongest survivors, is rightfully ours."

This got people talking amongst themselves, more excited murmurs than worried murmurs. He continued, "Do not think this will be easy. We are talking of traveling a far distance to attack a substantial, well-supplied community with the men there protecting not only their lives but the lives of their families. Regardless, I am sure we are better equipped and, as always, better in a fight. We will succeed, but it will take a great effort from all of us working together as it will be the greatest endeavor we've ever undertaken. But with this success, we will be re-established, ready to flourish as we deserve. Who amongst you will take on this challenge?"

Harrison carefully watched the gathering. Most cheered with true enthusiasm. A few cheered but seemed to be slightly hesitant in showing their support. A few merely stood and stared up at him silently. This response fit with his estimate and his plan.

He raised his hands to silence them and continued, "The trip will be lengthy and arduous, moving over unexplored territory. Many will need to go, and we will need to take much of our remaining supplies with us, leaving only a brave handful behind to maintain and protect what we've built here for our return. This will clearly stress our group as it will require as much from those remaining here as from those traveling, but I know all of you and I know all of you will do what needs to be done. Because of this, I am certain we will emerge stronger than ever."

Turning his back on the group, Harrison listened to them cheer, as he strode confidently back inside.

• • •

Difficult to tell but Jacob figured they had been locked in the cramped room for three days, maybe longer. They spent much of the endless time trying to take care of his and Griff's injuries. Jacob was hurt, but his wounds were relatively minor cuts and bruises. Griff, however, was far worse off, likely having suffered a severe concussion. In the dim light with no supplies, there was little they could do for him but, fortunately, he seemed to be slowly improving nonetheless. He awoke occasionally, but he did not really speak, mainly he muttered and moaned, only taking water when a cup was pressed to his lips.

While not tending to Griff, Jacob and Kinma passed their waking hours talking into the blackness. She told stories from growing up in an actual city. She told stories about years in and around work camps. And she told a couple stories of living amongst the rough characters of the Bank. A few times she tried to talk about Hale, who Jacob learned had been her husband of sorts, but grief would always have her stop before long.

Jacob felt guilty, certain his tales were far less entertaining in comparison. He could only tell the dull tales of growing up and living in Malden where most days were filled with gardening, schooling, fishing and wood chopping, with the evenings passed knitting and cooking mixed in with the occasional card game or rare party. Regardless, Kinma continually asked for more descriptions of this simple life, especially prodding him about his relationship with Louisa.

At first, Jacob was reluctant to talk about Louisa. He never talked to anyone about his feelings towards her, other than the occasional, guarded comment to Tina. However, once he began to talk, the words came faster and easier until they poured out freely. He found reliving the numerous happy moments with Louisa addictively enjoyable in a bitter-sweet way, like poking at a sore tooth with your tongue. Now, sitting on the floor next to Griff, listening to his slow breathing and staring through the darkness, he was telling the story of their first kiss.

"The snow was starting to fall, but it was still sort of warm, so it came down heavy and wet and slow like it does. I remember thinking how strange it was that everyone was inside dancing and laughing, celebrating the last of the potato and carrot harvest when all I could do was dread the oncoming winter. Back then, I was eleven, I hated winter. Dark all the time, no more fishing, no more soccer games, a hassle to go outside and do anything. Now, I appreciate that getting the food in and safely stored greatly alleviated stress for the adults because having it all in the bins safe from bugs, weather and disease, meant not starving to death. I learned that lesson the next winter when an early frost hit and we all got very hungry."

Kinma responded out of the black, "No need to retell me that one, I've dealt with enough hunger and, you tell stories so well, listening to it again will make my stomach hurt."

Jacob felt his cheeks warm at the minor compliment as he continued, "I could hear music coming from the Lodge, muted already by the thickening snow, as I sulked. I was mad, you know that kind of stupid, directionless angry kids get? Not wanting to face another winter was probably the main reason I was pouting but my dad also told me I'd been given firewood collecting duty for another Turn. I'd asked to be put on trapping, but the Committee decided I was too young.

"I didn't hear her coming, she's always been good at moving around real quiet like. She silently slipped her mittened hand into my gloved hand. Her face was shadowed 'cause the only light was that coming from the Lodge's windows and she kept looking straight forward. For the longest time, we merely wandered, not talking or anything, only shuffling slow circles through the fresh snow.

"Finally, when we heard people leaving the Lodge to head to their cabins and we knew we needed to head back or they'd come looking for us, she asked, 'You know what I like most about winter?' I think I growled something about there being nothing to like but she turned to look at me and continued with a shy smile, 'At night, when the air has that crisp coldness to it, cuddling up together feels even nicer.'

"My pre-adolescent mind failed to understand. She was used to me not understanding things though, and she turned to face me and leaned forward, her cheeks glistening with melted snow. She rose up on her toes and kissed me. At first, our lips were cold but they warmed fast, and I managed to come to my senses, wrapping my arms around her waist and holding her as we pressed together. It probably lasted less than five seconds but a lifetime happened before she softly broke it off, spun away and skipped off into the snowy night."

"And that's when you knew?"

Wrapped in the memory, Jacob missed the question, "Huh?"

"That's when you knew you were meant to be together?"

"Oh. No, I knew long before. When I first saw her, when she first came to Malden, I knew. She was distraught, not talking and her mother was too exhausted to help her. Even though I was only a kid, I wanted to take care of her, more than anything I wanted to make sure she was ok, make sure she got better. I held her hand, I talked to her, read to her, sometimes I only sat next to her bed. That moment she first spoke to me, my heart beat differ-"

"Jacob? Tina? You guys here? Where the hell are we?"

Griff, his voice raspy but surprisingly strong after his recent mutterings. Immediately flung from the pleasant memories back to their current nightmare, Jacob moved over, putting his face close to his friend, "Hey. Hey Griff, welcome back. How do you feel?"

Sounding scared, he said, "Feels like I've been beaten with a bat. Everything hurts. Where are we?"

Thinking it not best to tell him of their horrible predicament right away, he said, "We're ok. We're still at Thule."

Griff flinched when he heard Kinma move closer. "What the hell? Who else is here? Light a candle or something."

"That's Kinma. She's a friend. Sorry, we don't have any candles right now."

She said, "Here, drink some water."

He took the cup and then they carefully moved him to sit up against the wall as comfortable as possible. Sipping water and carefully chewing, he asked the question Jacob anticipated but did not want to hear, "Where's Tina?"

•   •   •

Kinma could hear the heartbreaking sadness in Jacob's voice as he told his friend about how the girl died. She could feel the intense grief and guilt the two young men were enduring, knowing they would never be the same as they pondered what had happened.

Finally, in his pained tone, Griff rasped out, "Ok, what do we do now? I mean, that crazed asshole is going to ask us about home again and again until we tell him what he wants to know or he kills us."

Jacob responded, "I've been thinking about that. We need to come up with a new, more believable story, send them on a goose chase or pick a place really far off so they won't bother looking. We'll memorize it together, so it becomes reality to us. Then, when they come we tell them, we give up -"

Griff interrupted, "No, no, no, I can't. If that monster thinks we're lying, he'll be even worse..."

Jacob sounded defeated as he whispered out, "I know, I know."

For days now Kinma listened to the surprisingly talented storyteller paint perfect scenes for her which she gratefully fell into to avoid the current horrors of her own life. Before hearing of the world, Jacob came from she could not have believed such a place of harmony and humanity could exist in this world. It was the place that Hale had wanted to create.

Initially, Jacob's stories of simple meals eaten together in peace, of men and women working side by side in gardens and of old-fashioned celebrations with no fighting gave her a glimmer of hope. The glimmer kept growing and growing as he told more in-depth tales of newborn babies, of reading books to children, of developing traditions and of his perfectly blossoming love with Louisa. She did not know how she could possibly get to it but, if she could not have Hale back, all she wanted was to at least see that life with her own eyes.

Kinma's words came without thought, "Look, it could be worse."

Changing from afraid to angry, Griff said, "I don't know you, you're only a voice in the dark to me, but I'd like to hear how you think this could be worse? I'm lying here in a prison cell after being beaten so bad I can barely move. Tell me, voice in the dark, how could it be worse?"

"Harrison hasn't killed you yet."

•   •   •

Harrison enjoyed being surrounded by paper, he enjoyed making notes of his plans with a sharp pencil. He carefully reviewed the list, wrote another name and wrote the new number. He erased the name off the other list. He examined both lists side by side.

If the plan presented to the Bank was what he actually wanted to play out, he knew he should be leaving more men behind to guard Thule but, privately, he hoped it would not be necessary to return. Over the last few days, Clarence had been situated outside the storage closet, eavesdropping on the boy and Kinma. Hard to make out everything being said but he caught enough to give Harrison the idea that the three young people were from a very well-established community. The boy told stories involving other families, making it seem there were a fair number of people, and he mentioned gardens, cabins, fishing and a lodge.

If they found what he thought they might find, they could take over the place and re-established themselves there. This re-settlement option appealed to Harrison on a number of grounds. For one, he could merely leave members of the Bank he found to lack usefulness or to be troublesome behind. Potential problems like Kinma would only be vague memories. In a new place, anger over Hale's death would fade while re-settlement provided a rational trigger point for transitioning the Bank from violent pillagers to colonizing farmers.

Harrison even had a fresh idea. The patrol's stories of the Survivalists keeping slaves intrigued him, perhaps such an arrangement might work as these far off farmers with families might be easily cowed into toiling for them. This slavery arrangement would ease the transition even further as the tedious, unfamiliar work could be carried out by others.

Finally, by taking everyone useful from Thule to a new, desirable land of plenty Harrison would be championed as a prophetic leader. His command would become unquestionable once again.

He reviewed the lists. One more name needed to be added to either side of the ledger. Harrison, however, could not decide whether to bring or leave Clarence. He generally trusted the lackey but this trust was based solely on the coward's fear, if he ever grew a backbone it could be a problem as he now knew too many secrets best left unknown. And Clarence would want some recognition for his role in discovering the settlement. Plus, if the mission failed, Clarence might actually have the wherewithal to keep the building in Thule standing while they were away. It made sense to leave him back.

For an instant, Harrison considered if a sense of loyalty to his companion of the last ten years mandated he not abandon the man but he quickly pushed such considerations aside as irrelevant. He wrote "Clarence" on the short list of people to remain.

Clarence would not be happy being left behind, especially since he knew what they were likely to find at the end of their trip. He might even be smart enough to realize Harrison did not plan to return. Turning an ally into a sudden enemy, especially one who would be at his back, even a coward like Clarence, might be problematic in a time of drastic change like this, adding another wild card to the already uncertain deck. He decided he would tell Clarence he was being given command of Thule until his return as he needed someone he could trust for such an important role. The praise and promotion would likely placate him.

Thinking it best to get the scheme implemented as soon as possible as Harrison long ago learned that time kills all plans, he stepped into the hall and called out. Within a minute, a young woman appeared out the gloom, nervously asking how she could help him. Harrison coldly said, "Get Clarence."

Returning to the table, certain the summoned patsy would arrive shortly, Harrison decided that giving Clarence more distraction would help ensure he stayed put after they all left. Reviewing the lists again he saw the name 'Kinma' at the top the list of people to be left behind, and the idea came to him as Clarence hurried into the apartment, still chewing the last bite of his dinner.

Knowing small talk was not necessary the former pilot asked, "What's going on?"

Harrison had already told Clarence about his general plan, allowing him to get right to the point, "I need to go on the trip as much can happen over such a distance and length of time which will require leadership and immediate decision making. That means I need someone smart and trustworthy to stay here and manage things while I am away."

Recognition crossed Clarence's features, and he lifted his hands as he responded, "Wait, I'm the one would found out this place even exists, I deserve to go."

Harrison understood why someone would protest being left out. Not only would he miss out on any rewards they found, but he would also be robbed of the glory of being mentioned in the numerous stories to be told afterward. However, Clarence lacked any hint of bravery so missing a fight would appeal to him. Harrison merely needed to give him a replacement for the benefits while reminding him he would not need to face the difficulties.

"I know what you have done, and it is appreciated. When we succeed I will ensure everyone knows it was your insight that led us there, the story will not be able to be told without mention of how you brilliantly ferreted out the opportunity."

This only got a pensive look as Clarence apparently pondered so Harrison continued, "While you will not be taking part in the long march or the ensuing bloodshed, everyone will appreciate the key role you played."

That seemed to help as Clarence nodded slightly.

"On top of that, by having you stay here, everyone, myself included, will know that our home base is secure for our return. You will be in complete control with discretion over all matters including rationing of supplies."

Harrison added this last part so the conniving fool would know he could be as greedy as he wanted while everyone else was away. More nodding and Harrison figured it was time to seal the deal.

"Also, Kinma is a problem. I cannot merely dispose of her, she's seen as too valuable by the men. But she is far too unpredictable to bring along. So, while we are away, she will be yours and yours alone."

They shared a look. Harrison realized Clarence might actually be afraid he could not control the strong-willed woman and would either look foolish or be killed in his sleep. In truth, Harrison doubted Clarence would be able to bend her to his weaker will and he might face the same fate as Luke. He needed to push Clarence over this final hurdle, so he added, "Oh, and I'll leave you the handgun. We have the rifles now so I won't need it on the trip. I doubt you'll have problems, but it will help ensure your authority if there is an issue as you will have the only firearm."

Another nod as he said, "Ok, if you need me here then I'll stay here and run things. Who else is staying?"

They turned their attention to the papers. Harrison felt slightly dirty at having been so complimentary and accommodating to the idiot, but it was for the best. If they needed to return, he could easily take the place back from Clarence. If things went as planned and they stayed away, the fool would likely freeze to death with an empty stomach.

CHAPTER TWENTY-SIX

JULY 1, 2046
DAY THREE THOUSAND SEVEN HUNDRED AND EIGHTY-ONE

The door opened, and a plastic jug of water was slid in by an unseen person. Thankfully, this happened on occasion. Feeling the torment of all his slowly healing injuries, Jacob crawled over to get it when he noticed a crack of light. A crack of light that was not there before. A crack of light running up the side of the door.

When they were first put in the room, Jacob tried the door numerous times, but it would not budge. But then there had not been this crack of light. Jacob forced his battered body to stand and, when he touched the handle, the door moved.

Startled, Jacob pulled his hand away and scurried back. In an intense whisper, Jacob said, "Hey, hey, Kinma."

Coming out of her light sleep, Kinma muttered, "Huh, what?"

"The door, I think it's unlocked."

"Really?"

Moving back towards Kinma, Jacob said, "Yeah. Someone brought water. I think they didn't close it right after."

·　　·　　·

It seemed strange. How could someone simply leave the door open when the whole point was to have them locked up? Kinma sat up against the wall. "Did you see who brought the water?"

Jacob squatted down next to her. "No, they only slid it in."

It probably would've been one of the women. Maybe Seanah or Martha. They might be willing to risk angering Harrison to free Kinma and they would not know about the chain on her ankle. They had spent a lot of time fighting with the chain, the padlock and the bolt holding her to the cement wall, but none of it would give. She would not be going anywhere until someone showed up with a key or a hacksaw. The boys were not chained though, they could leave.

She said, "Might be your chance..."

Griff stirred, coming awake. "What's going on?"

Jacob answered with more enthusiasm and surety, "Our chance. The door's unlocked. We can sneak out, get away."

"What? The door?"

"Yeah, yeah. Our chance, we can get out of here."

With a strange panic in his voice, Griff immediately answered, "No, I can barely stand. They'll catch us. He'll catch us, hurt us. I can't. I want to, but I know... I can't."

Kinma could hear the pain in Griff's voice, now mixed with terror, and she couldn't blame him. She knew he was right if Harrison caught them they would be severely punished. She said, "That's true. Griff's got serious injuries, I can't imagine him walking more than a dozen steps. And Harrison will be especially cruel if he needs to go looking for you."

Jacob said, "It doesn't matter. We need to go. We need to get home, try at least."

"I know, Jake but I can hardly move let alone run through the goddamn woods."

"We need to try Griff. We can't simply stay here and hope for another chance."

Griff mumbled, "I know... I know we can't stay here, but I can't move. There's no way."

Kinma did not completely trust the fortuitously left open door, but she realized it could be the best chance they would get. She knew what needed to happen, the boys probably realized it too, but neither wanted to say it. Kinma said, "You go Jacob. Griff is too hurt. I'll take care of him, it'll be ok. You get back home, back to Louisa."

Regaining his composure somewhat, Griff stopped the sobbing and stammered, "She's right, you go. At least you can tell my parents I love them and tell everyone I'm sorry, sorry for what happened to Tina, that I'm sorry we ever got in that damn boat."

They stayed silent for a moment. Over their time in the darkness, Kinma had come to deeply like Jacob. He was insightful, curious and caring. He reminded her of Hale, but with less experience hiding behind the harder edges of his toughness. Now, Kinma could only guess at the difficult thoughts rolling through the young man's mind.

Finally, Jacob said, "Ok. I'll go on my own."

•　　•　　•

None of it appealed to Jacob. The risk of being caught. Wandering the woods alone. Leaving Griff behind. But the image of Louisa, being able to apologize to her, seeing her smile again, holding her again, talking with her again, made it obvious he would go.

The decision made and his mind focussed, he turned towards Kinma. "How do I get away?"

Sitting on the floor, Kinma quickly explained the layout of the building and where the sentries were normally posted. Thankfully, the storage room they were in was located on the main floor, near the back so Jacob would be able to slip out without having to go through an area where people usually congregated.

Kinma said, "Go to the left when you get outside, you'll go by the kitchen, it's in a stand-alone building. There are often people around but you can sneak up behind some bins put there for garbage. Listen near the door and, if there's no one there, go in and get some food, a knife, whatever else you can find."

Feeling wholly unsure, he said, "Ok, I'll try."

"Now, I don't want to know where your home is, I can't be made to tell Harrison something I don't know, but we need to figure out what direction you should head. From what you told me, I'd guess you came south and east. That sound right to you?"

Griff, always better with directions, interjected, "Yeah, more east than south though. The river mainly runs east."

Jacob said, "Right. I'll use the stars, head straight north, I only have to get to the river and then I can follow it back."

"Sure, but there's more than one river that way. By the sound of it, the one you guys were on had to be pretty wide and fast and, if it brought you close to the Survivalist settlement, my best guess is it's the Pembina. You'll have to cross a narrower river first. Keep heading north from there and then follow the next river you come to, it'll take you all the way home."

It sounded simple but Jacob knew they were talking about huge distances through harsh wilderness filled with evildoers and innumerable other threats. He said, "Ok."

Jacob hurriedly gathered up a soiled bedsheet to use the as an ad hoc bag. Kinma stood, and they embraced as she said, "Be careful. Get home."

"Thanks."

"I will."

Feeling masses of guilt and sadness, Jacob moved over and awkwardly hugged his friend. "I'm sorry, Griff."

"I'm sorry too, I want to come with you, I just... I can't, I know I can't."

Jacob held back tears and tried to sound confident as he said, "It's ok, it'll be ok."

As he moved towards the door, he heard Griff calling from behind him, "Good luck Jake. Tell Emmanuelle she's got to do all my chores now and you can give Sam my bow if he wants it."

He wanted to tell him he would make it home too, that he could tell them all himself, but he knew that would ring far too hollow so he merely answered, "I will Griff."

• • •

The door seemed to open shockingly easily for Jacob and Kinma watched him slip out. When it closed behind, Griff merely slumped back against the wall and put his head in his hands.

Kinma strained to listen for anyone yelling at Jacob or sounds of a commotion. She heard nothing and let out the breath she was holding. If he made it down the hall, he would make it outside and have a chance, not much of a chance but at least a chance. She sat back down on the hard floor.

The dark room felt even more painfully lonely with her own dire predicament closing in on her more closely. She told Jacob she would help Griff, sounding like she was somehow in control of her life when, in reality, that she was chained to a wall with no one coming to save her.

• • •

Following Kinma's directions, Jacob hurried down the dim hallway, ignoring all his aches and pains as terror-laced adrenaline flooded through him. As he moved, he was certain Harrison or his massive yellow-haired beast would step out of shadows and grab him. But, he quickly made it to the metal door Kinma described without seeing or hearing a single soul. For a second he was confused as there was no knob, only a wide bar but, thankfully, when he pushed on the bar, the door smoothly opened, and he stepped out into the fresh air.

The sun was starting to set and, notwithstanding his fear, being out of the horrible tower was a relief. After taking a deep breath, he carefully turned left. He smelled the garbage bins before he saw them, however, now that he could see the trees in the distance, all he wanted to do was run at top speed to get under them where he could not be seen. But, he knew, with no supplies he would not make it very far, so he girded himself.

Creeping behind the foul-smelling bins, he managed to get close to the outbuilding Kinma said held the kitchen where he crouched and listened, hoping to hear nothing. After an immensely long minute, Jacob decided no one was in the building, so he moved along the wall and slipped inside.

In his rushing, panicked state, it was almost impossible to take in all items. Utensils hung from walls. Shelves held pots and pans. Thankfully, a canvas bag sat on the counter. Looking inside he saw dried fish and a dozen potatoes. Exactly what he needed, he plucked it up, threw a small pan and the largest knife he could see into the sack and turned to leave.

The door opened ahead of him, and Jacob's breath caught. He silently watched as a petite woman stepped inside, humming a soft tune. At first, she did not notice him standing there, and Jacob rapidly pondered what to do. Hit her. Kill her. Run. Cover her mouth and tie her up.

Before he could decide on an action, she turned from the door and saw him. He recognized her and her freckles, either Alice or Andrea, one of the women who brought the food and lifted their dresses. For a heartbeat, they silently stared at each other, neither sure as to what to do.

The woman silently pointed to her left with her chin. It took a moment for Jacob's worried mind to understand the simple gesture, but then he looked over. A box of matches sat on a shelf. He plucked them up. When he turned back, Alice or Andrea gave him a slight grin and a nod as she moved to the side. Confused but thankful, Jacob stumbled past her, making it back outside where he immediately ordered his sore legs to run faster than they ever ran before.

•   •   •

Harrison did not look up from his papers as he asked, "It work?"

Stepping into the apartment, Clarence stammered an answer, "Yes, the one called Jacob left. The other one with worse injuries, Griff, stayed behind in the cell with Kinma."

Harrison had pondered letting Kinma escape too but she would be too much of a wildcard and unchaining her would make the ploy too obvious. Plus, Kinma was smart about life in the woods, she would be tougher to track and more likely to notice being followed. He had not been certain if the redhead would be able to flee, but Harrison did not care, one of them leaving should be enough.

"Ok. He find the supplies?"

"Some of them, he took the bag I left in the kitchen and some matches."

"Nice, it'll be even easier to follow the fool if he's lighting fires every night."

"For sure. The Viking and Walter are watching him now. They'll leave markers like we discussed."

"Good. Leave me. I need to get some sleep, we head out at first light."

•   •   •

A cacophony of coyote yipping and howling filled the dark woods, but Louisa barely noticed the familiar sound. She followed close behind Sam, careful not to let her footsteps make a noise as she scanned the shadowy underbrush. When Sam abruptly stopped, Louisa almost crashed into him.

Knowing there was no point in asking Sam why they had stopped, Louisa stood and waited, peering about the shadows to see what he saw. But, instead of looking, Sam seemed to be testing the air, feeling it on his cheeks, smelling it, tasting it. She was shocked when he asked, "You feel that?"

"Huh?"

"Wind shifted, it changed."

Louisa looked at the leaves, they shimmered slightly in the moonlight but did not seem to be moving much at all. "What wind?"

"It changed."

Confused, she asked, "Yeah? Changed for good or bad?"

He started moving again, shaking his head. "Never know."

Following, Louisa took in a chest full of air and thought it did feel different, fresher maybe. She decided she would decide it was a good omen regardless of what Sam said.

• • •

Morreign startled awake, breathing hard. Paul turned beside her, coming awake as well. He muttered, "You ok?"

It took her a moment or two to decide if she was, her heart pounded, and her skin felt clammy, but the sensations were fading. A dream, only a bad dream. She answered, "Yeah, think so. Had that dream again."

Wrapping an arm around her, he asked, "The resort?"

As usual, it felt as much a memory as a dream. Her parents took them to a beach resort when she was eight, not long before commercial air flight became restricted.

Overflowing buffets, tables covered in plates of half-touched food. Obese Americans with too much-tanned flesh barking at the harried waiters. Massive pools of gleaming water to splash in. Huge glasses of sugary drinks abandoned to spoil in the sun once they grew too warm. All of it made her heart hurt, so much excess for the sake of excess.

"Think so."

"Normally that doesn't wake you up."

Paul was right. The dream of her family happy, safe and secure and playing, was bittersweet but it did not frighten her.

"This time it was different."

"Different how?"

Morreign was concerned it might unnecessarily worry Paul if she told him, her instincts having been given mythical status at Malden, so he merely said, "I don't know. Scary somehow. Don't really remember."

"Ok, try to get back to sleep, Leo will want your help supervising to get that new A-frame up in the morning."

As she heard Paul's breathing deepen as easily fell back asleep, Morreign stared at the ceiling, jealous of his ability not to worry. She knew she would not be going back to sleep anytime soon. She did remember the nightmare, remembered it perfectly.

They were at the resort as usual, eating hamburgers in the sun and laughing when they came. Filthy men with tangled hair and matted beards rushed in, climbing over the walls, wading across the pools, and pushing through the carefully groomed hedges. A growling, snarling horde swinging massive, bloody axes as the sunbathers ran futility in every direction. People screamed as they were slashed down and Morreign could only stare with her childhood eyes at the slaughter. The whole time a voice in her head whispered through the yelling and silly music, they are coming, they are coming, they are coming.

PART FOUR

CHAPTER TWENTY-SEVEN

JULY 4, 2046

DAY THREE THOUSAND SEVEN HUNDRED AND EIGHTY-FIVE

It must have been a huge caribou. Morreign watched the men walking out of the trees, each carrying a load of meat to the smokehouse. Large game near Malden was practically nonexistent, their only non-fish protein coming from squirrels, porcupines and the occasional beaver or wayward goose, along with tough coyote meat which everyone hated. Only a handful of times over the last decade had Sam brought down a skinny caribou or a scrawny deer. Recently though, the hunting began to improve. In the last few weeks, they bagged a calf moose and a mule deer and now this caribou.

Paul and Leo, both grinning widely, walked over to her. Paul, his jacket sticky with blood, wrapped an arm around her shoulders and said, "It's about five hundred pounds field dressed."

Morreign smiled back. Despite living off the land for over ten years now, she still got a kick out of her nerdy accountant husband, who used to spend his free time playing fantasy football and reading spy novels, talking like a lifelong woodsman. She said, "Can't believe it, the smokehouse will be bursting at the seams."

"Yeah, we were thinking we should alleviate some of that storage pressure with a good old fashioned barbecue."

While she did not feel like sitting around with everyone happily feasting, she could not think of any rational reason to oppose the plan. Morreign nodded. "Sounds like a good idea to me."

Within the hour, the smell of roasting caribou filled the Clearing.

Everyone ate their fill of the rich, gamey meat, waited for a minute or two and then ate their fill again. The sun took forever to set in the summer, and those at Malden took full advantage of the lengthy, northern dusk, sitting outside the Lodge in chatty groups.

Paul sucked grease off his fingers before leaning over to Morreign and saying, "That was a great idea I had. We should do it more often."

"If the animals are really coming back like it seems they are we might be able to."

"Yeah. Have to say, things feel more, well, settled around here these days."

She turned and glared at him, but he was focussed on the remnants of his third helping and did not appear to notice the angry look. When Huck died of fever, she resented Paul for getting over the tragedy first. He grieved, crying himself to sleep and raging at the unfairness of it, but the lengthy depression that enveloped Morreign seemed to have passed him by. When Jacob disappeared, Paul put all his energy into trying to find him and, when it became clear his son was gone, he grieved but the dragging depression passed by him again as he got back to living his life while Morreign continually wallowed in the all too familiar fog which only seemed to worsen as time passed.

Without looking up from his plate, he coldly said, "I can feel you giving me that look. You give me that look a lot. I don't like it."

This startled her. While it did happen on rare occasions, Paul generally did not get terse with her. Slightly rattled and also slightly angered, she responded, "I don't... I don't know how you can go on being all jokey and carefree, after all that's happened. Jacob's only been gone a month, and you're already kidding around as if he never existed."

He turned his head and looked up at her, his eyes piercing above his scraggly beard. "Because I choose to, that's how, because I bloody well choose to. We've been married for a long time and our marriage has gone through more than either of us could've ever imagined, more than anyone could've imagined. I know you think of me as perpetually happy and, perhaps, foolish. And, to an extent, that might be true, but it's true because I choose for it to be true.

"Every morning I wake up before you, and every morning I lie there with you breathing beside me, and I remember them, Jacob and Huck. I wish they were still here, I wish long, and hard they were still here, that I'll get up, and they'll be sitting at the table playing games or eating porridge, but then I choke back the tears before they can take too powerful of a hold. I force my body to climb out of bed as I silently tell them how I miss them both, and then I start my horrible day. Taking care of you and the others, working and joking, keeping the encroaching thoughts of my sons out of my mind and spending all of the day fighting to keep those thoughts at bay until I can wallow in them the next morning, by myself, in solitude.

"Because I don't brood about in public, full of self-pity and pointless weeping, doesn't mean I don't miss my sons every day. I do. More than you can imagine."

He stood up and took her empty plate from her lap. Before he could take the dirty dishes inside, Morreign grabbed his wrist. Weak tears trickled down her cheeks when she looked up at him. Beard and unruly hair covered most of his face, but she could still see the boy, the cute boy she fell in love with a thousand years ago, the boy who lit up her life and then became her life. Through all of this, he truly had taken care of her, and she did not think about caring for him as he did not seem to need help. Instead, she choose to cruelly resent his perceived easy endurance.

"I'm sorry Paul. I am, I should have thought more about how you are actually dealing with all this. I realize that my being so difficult only makes this harder for you. But I don't know, I don't know if I can do that, force the thoughts away like you can. I can't get past pitying myself, it's become... I think it's become ingrained, become part of me."

He sat back down and rested his hand on her thigh. "I don't want to tell you how to feel, and I know it's not been long since Jacob left, but, one thing, for me at least, that helps is to remember the fun times."

She immediately shook her head and said, "I've tried that, I have, but it's too hard. It hurts, it physically hurts when I realize there'll be no more times like that."

"I know. Nothing about this is easy though. With Jacob I've found starting with thoughts about him as a little kid works best," he looked around the Clearing, seeing all the people clustered about, "Maybe you should tell the story about Bear."

Morreign knew others, at least in the past, viewed her as a decent storyteller. And, in the past, she had greatly enjoyed the attention and liked entertaining everyone. The story was an old favorite, and the thought of it put a tiny smile on her grim face. Maybe Paul was right. She supposed she owed it to him to at least try.

She nodded and said, "Ok, I'll try, but if I can't do it, you have to step up and rescue me, deal?"

Paul seemed surprised by her pleasant agreement, but he nodded back. "Deal."

She carefully got up on the Lodge's porch and gently knocked on the railing so all eyes in the Clearing turned to look at her. Her voice started off soft, but she pushed it louder as she said, "The second winter after the war erupted. A miserably cold day. The kind of cold that freezes nostrils closed and makes skin burn."

She noticed people looking at each other as if they were seeking confirmation of what they were seeing. They probably had expected a speech about work duties instead of a story. She continued, "Jacob, nine years old, impossible to keep inside no matter the weather."

Everyone moved close, ringing the porch.

"We were all working in the Lodge, trying to stay warm but Jacob convinced Griff to go outside with him. I clearly remember Griff rushing back inside an hour later, wearing that bright red snowsuit which was way too big on him. We needed to pull off the scarf which was wrapped repeatedly around his head to figure out his excited squealing."

Using her best kid voice, Morreign exclaimed, "A bear, a bear. There's a bear."

Everyone laughed at this, giving her a chance to take a breath before continuing, "Well, it was the middle of winter, so if there were any bears around they were fast asleep. But, as a mother, the excited words sent a chill down my spine despite the logic. Remember, back then, we were new to this and bears were our monsters under the bed. We thought they were always out there, waiting to maul us all and we jumped anytime we saw anything bigger than a squirrel in those days."

That got a few more chuckles as fear of deadly predators had waned greatly over ten years in the woods.

"Griff said Jacob was fighting it off, so we bolted outside. Crashing through the drifted snow, like a herd of crazed cats. The wind whipping around made it impossible to hear anything, and it blew sharp, stinging snow into our eyes.

"I knew where they'd been playing, working on one of their snow forts, and ran that way, cursing myself for not keeping a closer watch. The wind died for an instant, the blowing snow cleared and I could see Jacob."

The memory old but strong, she could recall the picture easily. "He was heavily bundled making him appear spherical. His tiny arms swinging a pine branch and, at the end of the branch, jumping back and forth, biting playfully at the offending stick, was a dog,"

Even though they all knew the story, everyone laughed. A laugh even escaped Morreign's throat.

"To be fair, he was a small boy, to him the good size dog likely looked massive. Plus, back then, we talked about the threat of bears all the time. And, to his credit, it was black. But, thankfully, the dog was not a menace. In fact, it seemed quite happy to have a boy to play with. I suppose he should have realized bears did not wear collars or have long tails, but I guess, in all the excitement, he overlooked those facts."

A few more laughs.

"When it saw me, the dog abandoned the stick game and bounded over. Jake darted at it, trying to use his branch to protect me. It took me a great deal of effort to convince the child the bear was, in fact, not a bear but a dog which meant us no harm. Finally, he put down the stick and let the beast approach and scratched into its fur behind his ears. I asked Jacob why he did not run away like we taught him and he said he wanted to make sure Griff got away first."

She thought this part of the memory would have choked her up but, seeing everyone smiling up at her, made her recall only the joyful pride she felt at that moment. She shook her head and said, "Of course, we named the friendly dog Bear, and he lived out the rest of his life perpetually at Jacob's side."

•   •   •

Normally, Harrison would not allow a patrol to have campfires in the summer but, with this many men, remaining hidden was impossible regardless and the fool they were following seemed completely clueless. Two scouts constantly tracked Jacob, leaving a trail of string tied to tree branches so the main group could leisurely follow at a distance. They could not let the boy know he was leading them to his home.

Moving a patrol of twenty-five people was proving to be an extensive exercise in logistics. Each man needed to haul their weapons as well as all the food they could manage. Regardless, morale remained fine. Anticipation serving to motivate the group. However, Harrison feared a month or more on the road would wear them all down as the excitement of the mission waned beneath sore legs while stomachs tired of stale potatoes.

Sitting around the fire for another evening, listening to the same eager plans told by the same voices, appealed even less to Harrison tonight than usual. Harrison hated all the unknowns. Not knowing what they would find. Not knowing what they would face. Not knowing what how long they needed to walk.

Realizing frustratedly that he could do nothing to address these unknowns, he decide he needed to at least undertake something useful to distract himself. Harrison tossed his tin plate on the pile to be cleaned and, not wanting to waste valuable ammunition, grabbed up a bow. Everyone grew quiet when he approached the group. He pointed at Walker and Taco, decent bowmen who would not annoy him with inane chatter, saying, "You and you, let's go and see if we can't find some fresh meat."

•   •   •

Clarence opening the cell door had surprised Kinma. Using a serious tone that did not match his nervous, twitchy nature, Clarence unlocked the padlock and explained he was freeing her only on the understanding she was now his. Kinma wanted to laugh, they were passing her around like a whiskey bottle on payday.

Numerous days spent in the darkness filled with fear and worry and grief left her mind muddled and hesitant as she squinted against the bright light of the outside world. Thankfully, the situation she found herself in did not need much intelligent surveying as the place was essentially deserted. Tall Tony, Walter, Link, and the women remained along with Kinma, Griff and Clarence. The remaining Bankers explained that a few days before her release, Harrison took off with a massive patrol to take over some settlement.

Kinma's fleeting relief at being freed and not having to face Harrison, disappeared immediately and her heart fell. She should have known, should have known Harrison's devious nature was at play. He left the door open on purpose and let Jacob escape so he could follow him straight back to Malden. She failed to see this simple scheme and convinced Jacob to go. Hell, she gave him directions.

Clearly, Harrison wanted all the healthy, fit men who could survive the trip in fighting form with him because he only left the weakest behind. Tall Tony, in his fifties, slow-moving and perpetually ill. Link, who she figured must be suffering from lung cancer as he coughed up blood with every other breath. Walter had been shot twice in the leg attacking the Preppers with Hale and remained far from recovered. Most of the women were physically strong enough to travel but years of living tough lives of abuse made it unlikely they could keep up with the patrol, plus they might be unpredictable in the new setting and could cause dispute amongst the men. Harrison must have decided they were not worth the hassle given that they were marching to fresh conquests. The only fully able person remaining was Clarence who constantly strutted around with the handgun eagerly displayed on his hip.

To Kinma it was obvious, Harrison had abandoned Thule for good, leaving those he thought were useless or troublesome behind on the pretence of protecting the home front. Clarence, however, did not reach this conclusion as he continually barked out orders about maintaining the building and storing food in preparation for everyone's return. The others seemed to understand better than him but were apparently content in their less crowded home with decent supplies, so they placated Clarence by slowly following his pointless demands.

The penetrating ache over the loss of Hale was compounded with fresher worries over Jacob and his home. With Jacob's stories filling her mind, she knew she could not simply allow that existing vestige of humanity to burn or rot like this place. If Hale had known about Jacob's home, he would want to save it, needed to save it. Kinma's decision was made instantly and easily.

Being four days behind the patrol meant she needed to move immediately, but she could not simply abandon Griff without a word. She found him sitting alone outside the main doors, a blanket over his slumped shoulders and a plate of lumpy cornmeal on his lap. Surprising he was upright as, in the light of day, it had become clear his injuries were worse than they thought back in the cell.

A wide, deep purple bruise covered his lower back with black bruises along his left side. His piss came out an alarming orange color. A severe injury to the kidneys with internal bleeding along with the remnants of a concussion was her unprofessional diagnosis. Remarkable he survived, and now he clearly needed a long spell of bed rest.

Sitting next to him, she said, "Nice to see you out and about, I thought you'd be laid up for a few more days at least."

Shifting slightly but not looking up at her, Griff winced and muttered, "I've got to get moving. Gotta get going."

Apparently, Griff had spoken with the others too. He forced down a spoonful of the gruel, grimaced and said, "Have to go, have to find Jacob. That asshole is following him. We should've seen it. I need to get to him before he accidentally leads the monsters right to Malden."

Kinma briefly considered the possibility of taking Griff with her, but he could barely even sit up, and they would need to move fast and long. She asked, "You think you're strong enough to chase a patrol cross country?"

He sighed with fatigue and discomfort. "You know, I've been trying to think, but I can't, you know, I can't recall."

"Recall what?"

"Whether I've ever gone a day without seeing Jake. And, I can't, I can't remember a single day. Sounds weird, I know, but ever since we were kids we've spent all our time together, at the very least saw each other every day, even if we were sick or whatever. Seems wrong that I don't know where he is, what he's doing. I mean, I can't even contemplate Tina being gone, not yet anyhow. But I understand being separated from Jacob is wrong, I understand that wrongness requires me to act."

Kinma wanted to tell him she thought Jacob and Malden would be fine, but she could not lie to the battered boy. Not sure what to say, she dumbly said, "I can understand that. You've gone through hell."

He continued with a minor scoff, "And I know Jacob. Funny thing is, the thing I worry about the most, is how he'll react when he realizes he was followed. He'll hate himself even though it ain't his fault. He's the kind of guy who blames himself when it rains. You know anyone like that?"

Immediately thinking of Hale, Kinma felt a hitch in her throat when she said, "Yeah, I do. I did."

"Anyway, I've got to get on my feet again, got to get moving. I never should've let him go alone."

Griff forced himself to eat the mushy cereal and vainly tried to stretch his limbs. Kinma could see the resolve on his face, and she thought back to all she had heard about Malden.

The stories. All the stories Jacob told her as they sat in the darkness, the scenes and the characters coming to life and helping her anguished mind. Children scurrying around the lodge as adults played cards in the firelight. People working side by side in a wide garden full of vegetables. Sleeping in a cabin, warm with family members under thick quilts as snow fell outside. That being eagerly and happily destroyed by a horde of unthinking brutes was unbelievably, cruelly and wrong.

Her contemplation was interrupted when Clarence strode by, the handgun prominently on his hip and Tall Tony following obediently behind. Seeing them sitting there, he said, "Come on now, Kinma, he's still recovering, but you're ok. There are lots of chores in need of doing, let's be useful."

Neither of them responded, but Clarence did not push the matter, pretending the minor disobedience was beneath his notice as he walked past.

Tony, his greying, grimy beard falling to his chest, gave her a lecherous wink and licked his dry lips as they passed. She glared at the sad duo as it disappeared. Kinma could not leave the damaged boy in this damaged place.

She turned to Griff and said, "I'm going after Jacob. Eat up, you'll need your strength if you're coming along."

* * *

Dinner was a handful of unripe berries and the last, shrivelled potato. Jacob's stomach ached with hunger, but he chewed slowly, wanting the tiny amount of food to last for as long as possible. With the sun setting, he was also growing cold, but he felt too tired to build a fire, he wrapped his damp blanket around him and climbed under some pine bows.

After escaping, he had run as fast as possible. The difficult terrain mixed with his sore body and being filled with terror at the idea of Harrison catching him made it a clumsy affair. He tripped and fell and got turned around multiple times, but when the sun finally rose, Jacob figured he traveled enough distance through deep woods to be able to declare the escape a success.

Now, lying, half-starved and shivering under a tree with no idea how much longer he needed to endure, Jacob thought of the elk calf they chased after so long ago. It jumped out of the boat, desperate to get away, never considering that being in the icy river could be far worse. Realizing he may have made the same mistake as the elk, he quietly laughed into the blanket, the sound scaring him slightly.

Jacob doubted he would actually sleep, but maybe, if he managed to push away the aches, the cold and the hunger and he could conjure up pleasant memories of Louisa to fall into.

CHAPTER TWENTY-EIGHT

JULY 11, 2046
DAY THREE THOUSAND SEVEN HUNDRED AND NINETY-ONE

As expected, the trail was easy to follow, two dozen people hauling supplies left explicit tracks. The signs of the patrol were getting fresher all the time making Kinma believe they were gaining on them. Regardless, tired and hungry she currently regretted her hasty decision to leave the comfort and food of Thule. Even though in her past, she spent a great deal of time in the wilderness, not having a stocked pantry, cooler or cupboard drained a person.

Griff handed her a nearly empty water bottle, mumbling, "We need to find water."

Kinma nodded, having already been worried about the water supply for the last day or so. Before long they would be too hungry and thirsty to walk. Perhaps going this quickly was a huge mistake.

She said, "Let's keep our eyes open for signs of a stream or pond. Let me know if you see any willow trees, flocks of birds, things like that."

Griff had shown impressive resolve, pushing through his injuries and keeping up, but he still looked dangerously pale and exhausted. He said, "Ok, guess I'll hope we see some damn birds soon."

Before Kinma could respond, the sound of cracking branches startled her. Dusk made the trees into a mass of infuriating shadows, and she vainly scanned where the sounds came from, the hunting knife in her hand feeling shockingly inconsequential as sharp laughter came from behind her.

Kinma wheeled toward the unseen source of sound.

"Damn it, girl, you two make more noise than a herd of drunk rhinos."

She dropped the knife into the grass, threw up her arms and darted forward. "Milo! You jerk, you scared me shitless."

He leaned back, a massive smile splitting his black beard. "Sorry, too good to resist."

She turned to the other prankster. "Good evening, Taco. You couldn't talk him out of this?"

Taco, in his bright blue jacket, grinned and shrugged as he held up two rabbits. Kinma moved over, hugged Taco and took the offered meat. Griff, looking frightened, asked, "What is this? I mean, what is going on?"

Kinma turned to him. "Sorry. Don't worry, they're friends."

Milo happily said, "Hey Griff. Every time I find you, you look like crap."

Kinma asked, "I thought you went with Harrison. Are you scouting? Are we that close?"

Milo shook his head and said, "Not scouting, deserting. We bailed on the patrol the moment Harrison's back was turned long enough to escape. We were heading back to Thule, going to check on you and deal with Clarence, do a little scavenging before finding a way to ride out our final years that didn't involve Harrison and killing farmers. We came across your tracks up by the cutline and decided to circle back and check them out. What're you two doing way out here?"

Kinma, not wanting to say it out loud, looked over at Griff. Milo, always seeing the angles, started to laugh, "Damn it, you're going to try and stop Harrison from wrecking this kid's picturesque home."

Appreciating why he was laughing did not stop her from being annoyed at the laughing, Kinma said, "Yeah, that's exactly what we're doing out here."

"Doubt I can convince you to forget this foolishness, get you to come and find a nice and peaceful life with us."

She shook her head, "Doubt it."

Milo sighed and looked over at Taco who merely grinned and nodded. Milo turned back to Kinma and said, "I guess then playing at saviour is what we're all doing now."

•   •   •

The last of the men who had been sent out to look returned with no information. Milo and Taco were clearly gone. Disappeared. Harrison would waste no more time or effort on them. He disliked but respected Milo and appreciated Taco's abilities, but he could not say their disappearance overly upset him. The only reason he sent out men to look for them was a vague concern the duo might double back, looking to cause him trouble.

Their abandonment highlighted that desertion could become an issue. The patrol's pace was too slow, the men were getting antsy. Harrison figured the kid would be soft but not this soft. He seemed wholly unable to march with any pace at all. Men from the Bank were expected to travel all day without slowing, or they would simply be left behind. Jacob infuriated Harrison by resting repeatedly or stopping to look for food. To make matters worse, the kid was walking vaguely north but, with no idea of the terrain, he needed to constantly circle around hills, gullies, and overly dense forest.

They made it to the Canzie River a couple days back where the kid turned upstream, and Harrison hoped this easier path would speed their trip. But Jacob only went a few miles before he came across the collapsed bridge where he crossed and carried on, wandering tediously north. Now, the patrol was moving along an overgrown roadway as the kid pushed through the nearby forest, unaware of the much easier trail that existed only a quarter a mile to his right.

His patience waning, Harrison tried to make Jacob's journey easier and quicker. He had the scouts repeatedly leave useful items in his path until the idiot found them. The carcass of a young deer. A water jug. An extra blanket. Regardless, the fool still spent half of the daylight hours napping or foraging.

Pulling out his notebook, Harrison looked up who would be going out next to keep an eye on the kid as he would go out with them. Time to hurry the kid along.

•　　•　　•

Cracking a charred rabbit bone in his teeth, Milo finally asked the question which was hanging over the campsite, "So, you have a plan?"

The realization of how far they were behind Harrison's army worried Kinma as she was not sure they could catch them but, at least, the distance meant they could light a fire without fear of detection. Despite the warmth from the food drawing forth her ingrained fatigue Kinma, grateful for the pleasant company, stayed awake with Milo sitting on the non-smoky side of the fire while Griff and Taco snored underneath nearby pines.

Kinma poked at the embers and said, "Don't really have one, right now I'm only hoping to catch up before they get to this mythical village. If we somehow manage that feat, then I get to worry about step two."

Milo tossed the chewed bone into the fire. She always was jealous of Milo, of his relationship with Hale. The two of them could sit on the rooftop, their feet up on the railing, watching the nothingness below and not speak of anything for hours, neither of them finding this odd. Or, they could be sitting at a table with other people, share a look and laugh at something unknown to everyone else. More importantly, while Hale discussed things with Kinma, it normally came at her prodding, and the discussion always involved explanations. With Milo, conversation came organically with no extraneous explanations needed.

Regardless of this envy, she liked Milo. Smart and competent without being arrogant or competitive. Plus, she knew she could trust him, if not because he cared for her then because he revered Hale.

He sighed, "We'll be able to catch 'em easy enough. They made better time early on, but that kid has led them into some nastiness, muddy as hell on the low ground and too steep to get up on the high ground. We can loop around since we know where he's headed, go quicker, at least until we get past the area where we know the terrain."

Oddly, this news worried Kinma more than it pleased her. If they were unable to catch the Bankers, she suppose she could tell herself she tried while not having to risk opposing them. She said, "Ok, any idea what we should do then?"

He leaned back. "Not really. There's no way we can fight 'em openly and if we show up looking to rejoin in an attempt to work from the inside, Harrison's smart enough to have us shot in the head immediately. I think we do an end around, get to this hunting lodge place before them and see if we can set up a defensive position there."

"I thought about that, but the Griff says the people there are gardeners, not fighters. Plus, we can't set up much in a day or two."

"Yeah, but, if shit works out right, we'll have an advantage: Harrison will think he's attacking unsuspecting farm folk. If we can warn them, take away his surprise and gird these gardeners up a bit, we might be able to turn that against him. And men fighting for their homes can be tougher and meaner than you might expect, trust me, I've seen it."

"You think that'll be enough? I mean Harrison has rifles now, and his men will be very motivated."

She felt him shrug as he said, "You never know in these things Kinma, you take what you think's the best position with what ya got and then unleash chaos. It's always a roll of the dice when the killing starts. But, yeah, I think that's our best chance, maybe not a good chance but our best chance."

For a while they merely stared into the dwindling fire before, finally, Milo said, "Kinma, I'm really sorry I didn't get you out of that bloody supply room. I was trying to figure out a plan, something that wouldn't get us both strung up, but then Clarence started bragging he was being left behind to take care of things and you were going to be his. I knew you could handle that limp noodle once we left and me barging in would only mess it up worse. As soon as we could slip away, we were headed straight back to make sure you were ok."

"I know you wanted to help. You were right though, kicking in the door would've ended badly. Clarence wasn't a problem."

"You kill him?"

The matter of fact nature of the question shocked Kinma, and she turned to look quizzically at Milo. He laughed and said, "What? I think it's a fair question. That's what I was planning to do when I got there."

"No killing, we merely left. I don't think he even bothered to come after us."

"Clarence'd be too scared to leave Thule with no one useful to watch his back. Shouldn't be laughing at the idiot though, he's sitting back there on top of a pile of food and firewood while we're out here sucking on rabbit bones."

"Fair point," she hesitated for a moment and then asked, "Why did you decide to do this? Why risk helping these people, these gardeners, you don't even know? You and Taco could go and take Clarence's spot easy enough or find your own spot to set up."

He took a deep breath and began tossing a pebble back and forth between his hands. Then he said, "I suppose the idea of living out my later years with no one to talk to but Taco did not appeal to me. But, to be honest, when I heard you say you were heading to help these people, only you and that battered kid, I instantly thought of Hale. It sounded like something Hale would do. So, I guess, it's Hale's damn fault."

This made a knot form in Kinma's throat as she said, "Yeah, he was definitely a troublemaker."

"For a while, before we headed off on that last patrol, we talked, you know, around the edges I guess about how, despite the wars and all that, life for those left didn't need to be as horrible as it was. Never really had a plan or even spoke about anything all that concrete, but he put the idea in my head by saying anything obvious, you know, in that way he had."

She smiled at the glowing fire, and said, "I know that way."

"Yeah, then when we were out on that patrol, I sort of brought it up, how we could make Thule more humane. It came out like it was my idea but, looking back, I think the conniving bastard walked me to it like a tired dog on a leash."

"He could do that. In fact, now that you mention it, I realize he slipped those thoughts into my skull as well, making me accept them as my own."

"But after he died, I guess, I don't know, my will to improve things dissipated. Then, over the last days, following that pathetic kid, listening to everyone else talk with glee about all the terrible shit they had planned. I couldn't take it anymore, I told Taco I was fed up with Harrison. We obviously couldn't fight 'em all, best to simply leave. Figured we'd stop at Thule and make sure you were ok and then we'd take it from there."

He tossed the pebble into the dying campfire. "Frankly, I'm embarrassed I didn't decide to try and stop the asshole myself. I guess I was simply content to be rid of the whole mess, wasn't ready yet to start thinking of actually doing good, stopping doing bad seemed to be enough. Not until you said what you were thinking, as crazy as it was, then it made perfect sense. Exactly what Hale'd do."

She sighed, "Exactly what Hale would do."

•　•　•

Jacob did the math on his dirty fingers. The days were muddled and hazy, but he thought he was right, or at least close enough for him to call it right. Today was his birthday.

Only eight on the Longest Night, Jacob could not remember much from the pre-Bomb years, and the memories he held were blurry and uncertain. However, one of his most complete recollections came from his sixth birthday, him sitting at a kitchen table before a massive cake covered in icing while friends held brightly coloured toys all around him. In all honesty, Jacob did not know if he actually remembered the event or if his mind recreated the recollection from a photograph his parents kept, but he liked to think he truly remembered the day.

His mom kept a box with a few photos, pictures of him and his brother mainly, a couple from weddings. She said they took lots of pictures before the Bombs but they were digital so, when the computers died the images vanished. He often asked to look at the faded photos that still existed and, while he flipped through them, he questioned his mother about their previous life, trying to fill in the annoying gaps in his childhood memories.

Jacob, however, stopped these sessions when he grew wise enough to realize the discussions upset her. His dad called it pain-soaked nostalgia. But, to Jacob, the memories were not painful, to him the old world was like a fantasy, a fantasy he actually lived in so his faint recollections could add weight to the daydreams of it.

Lying in his filth-encrusted blankets under an empty sky, Jacob knew it was going to hurt deeply, but, nonetheless, he thought about what this night would be like if he were at Malden. There'd be no cake, but his mother would try to make something special for him out of whatever they had, maybe she would use the last of the honey. The people of Malden, as a group, would give him a few simple gifts. He imagined carefully opening a fishing lure, a scarf, and a jar of crab apple preserves.

Louisa would have her own present for him as well. Maybe a drawing. Maybe a jacket she decorated. Or a carving. The image of her shyly giving him the item, something she made herself in the dim light of her room, caused the intense pain he expected when he started the reminiscing to flow freely.

Before they foolishly got in that damn boat, Jacob had been looking forward to this impending birthday more than normal. For some time, he had pressured Louisa to sleep with him. Gently at first, but, as time passed, he found himself pressing harder even though he knew it upset her. He thought he caught hints, nothing certain, but a vague clue or two when she talked of his upcoming birthday. The longer he had thought about it, the more he turned the nebulous tips into a certainty.

Often, Jacob's pressuring was not even conscious, surprising himself with his actions and pleadings. Other times, he knew exactly what he was doing, carefully conniving to try to get what he wanted. Part of him wanted to have sex, wanted the physical act. However, much more of him also wanted to get it over with it, to get rid of the cloud hanging over them. He wanted to be able to move on, to stop seeing Louisa seeing this way. And, to be honest, he also wanted to be able to tell Griff it was done so his friend would stop pestering him.

Now, lying in the mud, Jacob cursed his stupidity at concerning himself so greatly with such trivial silliness. Right now, he would give up everything he ever had or ever would have, to merely make her laugh one more time or to simply hear her say his name. Realizing he wasted much of their last time together thinking only of his own selfish, wants made him double his resolve to return to her.

For days, he had moved slowly. A sense of despair and self-pitying making his boots extra heavy. He had escaped, there was no need to rush now. Certainly, he deserved some rest. However, now, he knew that was selfish. What happened, to him, to Griff, to Tina, had happened. He needed to stop wallowing and get moving forward, get home, get to Louisa. It was his birthday, he could no longer be a child.

•　　　•　　　•

Sitting on the hard, narrow cot, Louisa rolled the bracelet around her fingers. Hours on hours spent making the square links out of copper wire, polishing them and linking them together. Before the gift had seemed so important, now it seemed foolish and childish.

The calendar pinned up in the main room of the Lodge was re-used every year. On December 31, everyone gathered around, and someone flipped it back to the front, to the first month with its familiar picture of a red tractor. With a pencil, they crossed out the previous year and wrote in the new one. Much discussion had been held about what to do once they ran out of room to write in the new years.

Important dates were marked on the calendar. When planting of certain crops should occur. Celebratory days like the Longest Night, Christmas and the First Potato Harvest. The week when jackfish spawned in the river. Also, everyone's birthday was noted, well, everyone's but Sam's who did not want even that simple recognition. The square representing today on the calendar showed, "Jacob B-day."

All day, Louisa sat on the cot in her room. Not wanting to go downstairs and feel the others looking at her, worried she would utterly break down. She merely sat. Oddly sadness, while present, was not the most powerful emotion. Instead, regret filled her.

A soft knock. She sighed, not sure about responding. Her pouting had been reduced since she started working again. Now, however, on this night, she wanted to be left alone to wallow in her misery. But if she did not answer the knock, they might worry for her wellbeing.

She called out, "Yes?"

"Louisa, its Paul. I have some dandelion tea and stew."

Strange having Paul arrive at her door. She liked Jacob's father, he was funny and good-natured, but she could not recall having spent any real time with him alone. "Ok."

She opened the door, and he handed her a tray. "Sorry, got a bit cold.

Weren't sure if you'd be coming down or not. Tea's not bad though, especially if you like bitter."

His face held a smile, but his shoulders were slumped. He turned to go back downstairs and, without thinking, she asked, "Keep me company while I eat?"

Louisa sat on the bed, balancing the tray on her lap, sipping the not very pleasant tea. Paul took the chair, it creaking dangerously beneath him. For a heavy minute, they stayed silent before he pointed at the links on her blanket and asked, "That for Jacob?"

She merely nodded.

Paul nodded back. "Real nice. I was going to give him my good hunting knife."

Playing with her stew, she asked, "How're you doing?"

This seemed to startle him, and he looked right at her as his eyes grew wet. "Sorry, I expected you to ask how Morreign is doing, that's what most people ask. I honestly don't know how I'm doing. Hard day, especially so soon after they disappeared. I was sort of coming around a bit I think but then this day shows up. Actually, it makes me feel guilty, you know? Guilty I was getting over all of it, starting to move on already."

She knew exactly what he meant, and she said, "I keep trying to tell myself he'd want us to all move on, to not live like this. But now that seems selfish like I'm lying about what he might want only to make myself feel better."

Tears started to spill from her eyes and Louisa wiped at them with a sleeve, wondering how there could be tears left. Paul handed her a handkerchief and said, "Such a great guy. It's tough when it's your own kid to think of him being a man, but I think he was becoming quite a leader. Guess that'd make him more like his mom than me but that'd be fine, too."

"That leadership stuff might come from her, but he definitely has your sense of humour. Remember him secretly teaching that trick to Sam's dog?"

A muted laugh, "Yeah, right. Every time anyone said Lodge, Dog would bark. Drove Sam nuts. That's something I definitely would've done in my younger years. I guess I'm supposed to miss him as my kid, but I keep finding myself missing him more as a friend. I catch myself wanting to tell him something or talk through an issue with him or just joke with him."

Hearing his father talking about Jacob as a full grown colleague caused a stab of guilt. She had treated the young man like a whiny child. Sobs overcame as she mumbled out, "I was so mean, so mean to him…"

"Huh, you? Mean? No, you were wonderful with him. You were everything to him. I saw it each day."

"No, no. He wanted to move things forward, but I made him wait. I don't even really know why. Sort of scared, I guess, we were such great friends, he was my whole life, and I didn't want to risk ruining that but, I don't know, I might have also liked having that bit of control, you know?"

A sigh. "Yeah, I know. Sometimes, out here, I forget you kids go through the same messes we all did back in the old world. I should've explained to him how those things aren't all that important in the grand scheme and that he should be less worried about making it happen and let life take its course. But, I don't think he'd resent you or be mad about something like that, he's not that kinda person, you know that. Young men sometimes say crap in order to get what they want without appreciating what they're saying. Hell, sometimes old married men do that too."

Louisa could only cry softly as Paul continued, "I wish there was something, anything I could say or do to make this better but I can't. Eat your dinner, breathe and keep breathing. Someday it'll be better. It has to be."

CHAPTER TWENTY-NINE

JULY 11, 2046

DAY THREE THOUSAND SEVEN HUNDRED AND NINETY-ONE

Milo set a fast pace. Having decided that they needed to get to Malden before Harrison meant that any time they made up was more time they would have to prepare, more time to improve their chances of surviving the onslaught.

When they told Griff their plan, initially, the boy was defiant, he wanted to find Jacob, wanted to protect his friend first. But, when Milo explained that they would make a concerted stand at Malden, this girded the worn out Griff somewhat. The idea of getting to fight back, of getting to stand up to Harrison seemed to make him rise up straighter and step quicker, staring towards his far-off home with a set jaw as he struggled to keep up with the new pace despite his injuries.

Tonight they built no fire, Milo concerned they might be too close to Harrison to risk the smoke. It was not cold, but Kinma found it strange to be sitting on the ground with nothing to look into as they talked.

Milo stretched out his legs, leaning back on his elbows. "We got time but no need to wait."

Griff, already half asleep, sat up slightly, "No need to wait for what?"

"Plans. Let's talk about what we've got ourselves into here. What're we going to find at this land-of-milk-and-honey of yours? Any sort of defenses set up?"

Taco shifted over, apparently eager to hear. Having listened to Jacob, Kinma was confident the answer would not be what they wanted to hear. The settlement she heard about relied solely on isolation for protection.

"At Malden?"

"Yeah."

"Defences?"

"Right, you know, guns, walls or ditches or pickets, anything like that."

Griff thought for a moment before his exhausted mind seemed to understand what Milo was getting at and he sadly shook his head. "No, there's nothing like that. Morreign managed to smuggle out two guns before the Bombs and Sam had his hunting rifle, but we ran out of bullets years ago. No walls, only the river."

Kinma thought of the Bankers' building at Thule. All the ground floor doors could be sealed and barred in an instant. Sniper holes were placed in strategic places where a man with a bow could fire endless arrows without worry of counter-attack. A dozen barrels of gas-infused oil sat on the roof, waiting to be lit and rolled off on to anyone foolish enough to try to break in. There were even rope ladders coiled up to allow for escape from the balconies in case of the security down below being breached.

Milo glanced at her and then sighed, "Alright, let's step back a bit. How's the place set up?"

Using twigs and leaves, Griff laid out a rough map. A hunting lodge, a wide clearing ringed by cabins, a couple of outbuildings, a path down to the river, thick pine forest all around. As he spoke, Kinma could hear the combination of pride and longing for his home.

He set a pebble down, saying, "Here's where the waterwheel is. It's set in from the bank, there's a canal all covered by willows so you can't see it from the river."

Milo chuckled, "A waterwheel?"

"Yeah, Leo designed it. Mainly runs a saw blade for firewood but it can be set up to grind corn, but that don't work so well."

"Jesus, we're walking right into a pioneer village."

"Huh?"

Pointing at the layout, Milo said, "Don't worry about it. My guess is Harrison will circle around, come in from behind the lodge to avoid being caught with his back to the river, probably split into three groups to increase the chaos. They'll stream down from the trees, crashing on the pioneers like a hoard of hungry vampires."

"Vampires?"

Milo asked, "You don't know about vampires?"

Griff shook his head. "No, sorry, we don't have 'V' or 'K'."

Confused Milo asked, "Pardon me?"

"The encyclopaedias. We don't have the book for 'V' or for "K". They were missing from the set."

Kinma and Taco chuckled slightly as Milo said, "Of course, should've known that. Anyway, we can explain vampires later, tell me what's out there, behind the lodge."

Griff detailed the terrain, right down to every minor hill and fallen tree. Finally, Milo said, "Alright, might be a spot or two we can set up an ambush out there, funnel them along the creek bed. What about the people? What'll we have to work with?"

"There's twenty-five people, well, I guess twenty-two now, with me, Jake and Tina not there anymore. Six are kids though, they won't be able to help much. And Morreign, she's the person in charge, but she busted up her hip falling on some ice so she can't move much."

Milo gave Kinma a knowing look before he turned back to Griff, "Ok, fifteen able-bodied people. Any of them fighters?"

Griff eagerly ran through a list of the people. None of them were former soldiers, but he described many of them as hardened and good with bows. Kinma decided it could be worse.

Milo sighed, "Alright, hopefully, that'll be enough if we can use surprise and if Harrison's guys are tired out some from the long trip."

Griff said, "And there's Sam."

"Sam?"

"Yeah, Sam."

•　　　•　　　•

Jacob, having decided he needed to get back to Malden as soon as possible, made good time all day, pushing himself to cover as much ground as he could. At one point near noon, he thought he heard the river but, after darting up a rise, he saw the rushing water was only a stream crashing over cement rubble. While he was disappointed about having not reached the river, he forced himself not to pout, sticking to his mantra of no longer acting the child. He drank the cool water until his stomach could hold no more, filled his jug and then drank some more before carrying on.

By dusk, his legs and back ached badly, but it felt more like being sore after a long day chopping wood than having endured misery. The accomplishment of having covered miles helped, he could tell himself he was closer to home.

He hurriedly moved around a narrow clearing, collected two handfuls of pine kindling and dried leaves. Having learned the lesson that massive fires brought unwanted people, he created a tiny fire using twigs. Dinner would be simple as he did not spend any time foraging, but he had stumbled across some dandelions and rosebuds. He threw the rosebuds into his pan to make a tea while he slowly chewed the dandelion leaves, trying to keep his loneliness and worries at bay as the evening shadows deepened.

A strange sound. A cracking noise in the trees. Seemed far off. Probably nothing. He chewed some more. Then it came again. Maybe closer. Jacob got to his tired feet, hoping it was only the breeze in the branches or a young buck testing new antlers as he did not think he could run a handful of steps if he needed to get away.

Then he heard a different sound. He strained further, his hope fading. A voice. Voices.

Jacob scrambled, his exhaustion disappearing as he scurried to gather his few belongings. Remembering the chains, the never-ending march, the all-encompassing thirst, he moved with ever increasing speed. He glanced around, looking for an escape route through the thick trees and heard someone call out, "Over here. I smell smoke."

Close. Very close. Too close.

Another voice, off to the side, responded to the first, "Ok, move in."

With no time to pick a path, Jacob simply darted through the trees, the branches whipping him as he ran.

· · ·

Leo was easy to find as he was constantly tinkering away in his ad hoc workshop behind the Lodge.

Morreign asked, "What's the nutty professor inventing tonight?"

The large man turned from his bench, pliers in his paw-likehand. "Oh, hey, Morreign. No inventing this time. Fixing the pulley, it got bent putting up the A-frame."

Leo's recent project was putting up a granary, the Committee having decided that living from crop to crop was too stressful and risky. He designed a tall pyramid structure, and they were all working to get it built. The kids, all very familiar with Malden's well-read copy of the book "Native American Indians of Canada", were already calling it the Tee-Pee.

"Guess we're stronger at pulling than we thought."

"Cheap metal."

Morreign leaned against the rough slab wall, taking her weight off her ruined hip. She had pondered and re-pondered whether to broach this subject. She didn't want to unnecessarily worry people, and she didn't want to expend resources or energy needlessly. Still, the dream of the horde of men storming the resort stuck with her, itching the back of her mind.

"Look, I want to run something by you but don't want it to become a whole big thing."

Even after ten years of hardship, Leo could still break out his boyish grin. "I'm flattered but think I'm too tired to be starting in on an affair with my brother's wife this late in life."

She grinned back, "My hip couldn't handle it anyway. No, I was wondering, you ever think of what'd we do if we were attacked?"

Leo looked at her quizzically, trying to figure out where this was coming from. He asked, "That Marge woman tell you something? Something going on out there in the world?"

Raising her hands, worried that bringing this up might have been a mistake, she quickly answered, "No, no, nothing like that, only the silly worries of an old lady. The thought dug itself into my head one night when I couldn't sleep, and now I can't get it out."

Leo leaned his haunches against the workbench. "Figured we all sort of silently agreed not to think about attacks as there wasn't much we could do about it, especially with, you know, freezing to death being a real and immediate threat. Then, after we got by for so long with nothing happening, we seemed to have decided it would never happen, that there wasn't anyone like that left out there, at least no one close enough to matter."

"Right, I know, and I don't think it'll happen, not really. But with things getting more established here, I guess I need something new to worry about. Or maybe it's the kids going missing. Either way, humour me, what do you think?"

Leo picked up a wrench and fidgeted with it as he answered, "Ok, I'll humour you, but I doubt you'll like it. Honestly, I don't know there's anything we could do, practically speaking. A handful of armed, determine men decide they want to come and take this place, not sure we could stop them. We'd run out of good arrows very fast. Only place we could hold up is the Lodge, and they'd be able to smoke us outta there in a couple minutes. Frankly, best chance we'd have is to run for the hills."

Not a surprise as Morreign had come to the same conclusion. "Yeah, that's about where I got to too. Any thoughts on what we could do to better prepare?"

"Prepare for something we don't think'll happen?"

"We're just talking."

He shrugged his massive shoulders. "I mean, if we wanted to devote a bunch of time and effort we could build a wall using logs, but it'd be a helluva a project, and I doubt that it would do much but slow attackers down. Or, maybe a watchtower type thing, up in a tree perhaps, might help to give us some warning, but could also signals we are here. And, I suppose we could set up traps, create some sort of rudimentary minefield, but they'd more likely catch one of the kids rather than bad guys."

Walls of logs. Men up in tree houses. Bear traps littering the woods. All ridiculous. Not sure what she was thinking, Morreign pushed herself up from the wall. "Right, I guess we better keep hoping the Bombs did in all the assholes who might want to come for us."

Leo picked the bent pulley back up, as he said, "Yeah, or at least they're too busy trying not to starve to come hunting for us."

"Alright, thanks. Oh, and let's keep this talk to ourselves. No need to add to people's worries."

"Sure."

As she walked back to her cabin, Morreign did not feel any better, and she startled when two of the kids tumbled out from between two trees, laughing as they chased one another amongst the shadows, engaged in some complicated game of tag. Stopping her walk as they darted past, she scanned the looming pines, deep and imposing.

Her instincts poked at the back of her mind and it reminded her of back before the Bombs, when she noticed worried looks on people's faces around the office and every secret meeting made her more certain something was coming, something to be afraid of. Why would this new, seemingly foolish, worry not leave her? What was out there?

·   ·   ·

The plan worked. Maybe worked too well actually. Harrison and two of his men had flushed Jacob out before he could go to sleep, got him moving again, moving fast. Stumbling and falling through the darkness, the terror-filled idiot made it to the overgrown roadway they were herding him towards and then they managed to turn him north so he could follow the easier route. However, he must've been more frightened than Harrison thought as he continued to clumsily run along for hours after the men called out to each about how they were giving up on chasing him.

Now, as they caught back up to him, Harrison saw the kid laying in a heap.

The fool had run himself to the point of collapse. He turned to his men and quietly said, "Ok, keep eyes on him. Let him go at his own pace from here for a while."

He turned to go, thinking he best get back to the main group or a fight would probably break out over the last pancake. But one of the men tentatively said, "Uh, boss?"

This was JR, an army mechanic who stumbled into Thule about a year after the Bombs. Not much of a fighter but he carried his own weight, had been good with engines which as helpful when they had usable gas to burn, and the others seemed to like him. Harrison said, "Yeah?"

"Well, I was thinking and, you know, this kid's soft as cotton, don't think he's used to being out here like this."

At least he could agree with that point. Harrison prompted, "And?"

"I think he might do better if he had a friend."

Irving, the other scout, put a hand on the younger man's shoulder, saying, "C'mon JR, let's find a good spot in the cover to wait for this guy to wake up like we was told to."

Obviously, Irving wanted to protect his comrade from Harrison's wrath over the apparently silly notion. But, maybe the idea had merit. Jacob did not know all of the Bankers, he only met those on Hale's patrol and the Vikings. One person, no rifle, being all friendly, pretending to be a solo hunter merely headed the same way, not asking any questions, that might not scare the kid too much. Remembering their impressive resistance in the apartment, Harrison was sure Jacob would not disclose where he was going, but he might accept some short-term company. And that company could help him make his way a little quicker.

Harrison called over, "Hold up JR."

CHAPTER THIRTY

JULY 15, 2046

DAY THREE THOUSAND SEVEN HUNDRED AND NINETY-FIVE

The chittering chatter of a squirrel, not quite right but close. Taco signaling from off to her left. The buck was coming her way. Kinma drew the bow, enjoying the familiar, minor strain in her shoulder as she tried to calm her breathing against the rush of adrenaline. They had been surviving off the minimal fare they could find while Milo rushed them through the woods, a deer would be a huge improvement and, when they spotted the tracks, they could not resist.

Crouched behind some deadfall, she watched the animal cautiously step through a clump of willows. Thin but a decent enough size. She forced herself to wait. Let it get close. Let it turn. Let its neck get sideways to her. She loosed.

At the last moment, the skittish animal started, hopping slightly. The arrow missed the neck and buried into its shoulder. Jumping into the air, it bolted into the underbrush, crashing through branches, disappearing into the foliage like a fish tossed back into the water.

Hurrying after it, Kinma called out, "He's running. North, straight north."

She thought she heard Milo cursing to her right and saw the flash of Taco's blue jacket to her left as she ran, ignoring the pine branches scratching her face. Pushing through some willows, she stepped into a narrow clearing and spotted the wounded animal limping in the tall grass. Not a great angle but she fired again anyway, burying another shaft in the deer's rump.

It lurched forward, making it to the trees before she could notch another arrow, but Kinma felt certain it would not make it far now. She ran after, now wanting to put the buck down to end its suffering.

She leaped past some poplar trees and found the deer lying in a tumbled heap in a muddy ditch. However, she barely noticed the animal because, right there, sitting on a log, his ass hanging out, his breeches around his ankles, was Bono.

For a strange moment, they each simply stared at the other. He was a Banker, and he was very loyal to Harrison. He was a problem. But her mind could not seem to completely comprehend what the situation meant or how to handle it. Bono appeared to assess the matter quicker as he bolted off the log, yanking at his pants as he tried to rush away.

But, before he made it a half dozen stumbling steps, Taco flew out from the trees, a flash of blue across the green. He lowered his shoulder and caught Bono in the chest with a perfect tackle. The Banker, already off-balance, crashed into the pines as Milo swooped in, grabbing Bono by the collar of his coat and hurling him to the ground, jumping on Bono before he could figure out which way was up and covering his mouth as he tried to scream out for help. He twisted and bucked, but Milo held strong until Taco pressed his knife point against Bono's neck. He instantly stopped struggling and looked at them with bulging eyes.

Milo sounded calm despite his heavy breathing as he said, "Ok Bono, not a sound or it'll go bad. We understand each other?"

Their captive nodded, and Milo took his hands from his mouth. Bono's dry, colorless lips parted, and Kinma worried he might yell out regardless of the threat, but Taco pressed harder, a drop of blood trickled out from his cheek, and Bono shut his mouth. Without a word, they got Bono on to his feet.

·　　·　　·

It didn't matter. Jacob decided it didn't matter. He thought the voices, the men in the woods, must be far off by now. Regardless, it didn't matter. Now he needed to rest. Needed to stop.

No way he would risk a fire now and he was too tired to build one anyhow, so Jacob crawled in under a pine tree, wrapping himself around the trunk, his blankets left behind when he ran. He wanted to think of Louisa, wanted to escape all the hunger, cold, fear and fatigue with memories, but all he could do was strain to hear if anyone was coming. He collapsed after running from the unseen men, his body simply giving up but, after catching his breath, he managed to get up and started moving again and, with thoughts of dying of thirst at the end of a chain pushing him or another endless night of torture in a strange room, he hadn't stopped until now.

Despite the immense fatigue, he could not sleep, he could only lie on the dry pine needles and worry over every minor noise, pleading it was nothing but the breeze.

"Hello?"

For a moment, Jacob wondered if he had spoken to himself. He did not think so.

"Hello? You ok in there?"

Not Jacob speaking to himself. All of him wanted to run, wanted to roll out from under the tree and bolt but his body no longer had the energy to respond to fresh influxes of terror. When he tried to order his muscles to move they simply refused. He could only hang onto the pine trunk, waiting for some new horror to grab onto his ankles and pull him out.

"Alright, your choice, but I'm going to set up camp right here. Got dried corn meal and half a porcupine left, none of it much good but got enough to share."

Weird. Probably a fresh type of evil trying to trick him by being friendly. He pressed tighter against the trunk. Then... nothing happened.

Jacob could hear sounds. A man building a fire. Water being poured. The clanking of a pot. Then whistling. His uncle Leo whistled, this whistling not as good as Leo's but not bad. He smelled wood smoke. Nothing grabbed at his ankles.

The idea of warm food was compelling. Jacob could not recall the last real meal he ate. Even more than the food, it was the pleasantness of the man's tone and the idea of a friendly conversation which pulled at Jacob. In Malden, conversation and storytelling was a key source of entertainment. Long nights were spent in the Lodge, sitting around the main fireplace, working on small projects or crafts as people happily talked into the night. Often a deck of cards was broken out, or the chess pieces Boris carved would be set up, but conversation always continued over the games. Huddled under the pine bows, Jacob craved those nights as much as he craved an end to his perpetual hunger.

Without thinking too deeply, Jacob crept to the edge of his makeshift burrow. Peering through the spring grass and green branches, his nostrils full of the smell of earth and pine, he took in the placid scene. A man in a thick jacket of rabbit skins and pants of deer hide with hair and beard clipped not too long ago and no obvious weapon in sight and no obvious companions.

The stranger did not look up from the simple campfire but must have sensed Jacob's eyes on him as he calmly said, "I don't bite. Come out and have something to eat at least."

While the man looked somewhat travel weary, he clearly was in better shape than Jacob. If the stranger wanted to do him harm, huddling under a tree would not stop him and running away on his tired legs was not an option so Jacob figured he might as well take his chances and he slid out from under the branches.

Moving cautiously, Jacob's exhausted eyes scanned every shadow for an anticipated attack. Nothing came, and he gingerly sat across from the stranger. The man handed him a tin bowl with a wooden spoon and said, "I'm JR. Cornmeal. Pretty tasteless but warm and it'll fill you up some."

His unused voice coming out as a gravelly whisper, Jacob took the bowl and said, "I'm Jacob. Thanks."

As he ate the gruel, Jacob expected JR to ask him what he was doing out here, ask him where he's from but, instead, they simply sat and spooned bland food into their mouths. When he finished, JR used a handful of grass to wipe out his bowl before putting it in his pack. He added twigs from the nearby stack of sticks to the dwindling fire and laid out beside it, pulling his battered ball cap over his eyes and using his bag as a pillow. He muttered, "Long day, I'm going to crash. Put on more wood if you get cold."

Confused, Jacob dumbly watched the man calmly fall asleep across from him. Jacob figured there would be no way he could sleep mere feet from a stranger with concerns about others being nearby still lingering but, before long, the heat from the campfire, his powerful exhaustion and the belly full of dense food caused Jacob's eyelids to droop. With no real choice in the matter, he lay on his side and let his eyes close, a deep, dreamless sleep overtaking him.

•　　　•　　　•

Kinma was surprised by how calm Bono was. He went along peacefully with them to their campsite, Milo never more than a step away with his knife out. They sat Bono on the ground and Griff, who stayed back to rest while they tracked the deer, worriedly asked, "Who's this?"

Kinma said, "One of the Bankers. Stumbled across him out there."

Griff looked confused. "Another guy defecting? He gonna help us too?"

Milo shook his head and crouched down in front of Bono and said, "Nah, my guess is poor Bono here caught a case of the shits and couldn't keep up."

Bono merely grinned up at him with yellow teeth.

Milo continued, "Right, Harrison don't wait for the sick or injured, so you got left behind. You followed them as best you could, hoping your guts would straighten out in a couple of days and you'd be able to catch back up."

Smiling, Bono said, "Woulda been back with'em in half a day but for you cowardly pricks."

Milo stood back up, and they stepped away from their prisoner. In a whisper, he said to Kinma, "Now what do we do with the fool?"

"I don't know, I mean, can't we simply leave him?"

Milo shook his head. "Bono's as loyal to Harrison as anyone. He'll do everything he can to catch the group and rat us out. And, frankly, I don't like him being at our backs. Guy like that will sneak up and cut our throats while we sleep without a second thought if it means he can present our heads to Harrison."

"Ok, but can we simply kill him? I mean, he's awful, but we know him."

Milo glanced back at Bono sitting in the grass before whispering, "I know, but we can't very well drag him along with us."

Not sure what to do, Kinma said, "Maybe we could tie him up somehow, leave him with water and whatever..."

"That'd be an even worse –."

Milo stopped talking as Griff purposefully walked away from them. Kinma watched as the skinny boy plucked up Milo's hatchet from next to the remnants of their campfire. Without hesitation, he smoothly swung the tool turned weapon and buried the thick blade in the top of Bono's skull.

Bono did not have a chance to react. He did not even make a sound. He merely toppled over on his side.

Griff stared down at the body for a heartbeat. Then he turned back to them and said, "You said he was loyal to that horrific bastard. He was marching to my home to hurt and kill people, my family, people he's never met, people that never did anything to him. He was going there to take all they worked for because he was too lazy to work for it himself. That's evil. Pure, simple evil. I may not know much about this world out here but I've learned a great deal in a short time, and I know you don't barter with evil, you don't tolerate it, you end it."

The boy tossed the bloody axe onto the grass and walked off into the trees. Kinma, shocked, looked over at Milo and Taco. Milo calmly said with a shrug, "Guess that solves that problem."

Milo and Taco went to collect the deer, leaving Kinma to search Bono's foul body for anything useful. As she rummaged in pockets, Kinma realized Griff was right. They had tolerated Harrison and his brand of evil and that tolerance let him get ensconced and established, allowed the evil to grow. Their tolerance had brought them to this intolerable place. Griff didn't know what a vampire was, but he understood the nature of evil better than the rest of them combined. She muttered to herself, "From the mouth of babes."

•   •   •

Moonlight glinted off the inky black river. Morreign did not know exactly why she had decided to limp down to the river, but she had been unable to sleep and could no longer lie in bed.

Thinking the cool, fresh air may have done the trick, she was about to turn back to make the hike back to her warm cabin when a trickle of movement to her right caught her eye. Heart suddenly racing, worried her bizarre instincts were proving unfortunately right again, she peered through willows. Two people on the bank. She took a few careful steps closer. A man. A woman. Another cautious step. Sam and Louisa.

Morreign, generally aware of most things occurring within Malden, knew Sam and Louisa were sending more time together. She figured some of the more gossipy people would be carefully implying that, perhaps, Sam was not acting with the purest of intentions since his attention in the girl arose after Jacob's disappearance. She also figured those people were either fools or were purposely spreading false rumors to alleviate boredom. She knew Sam, as well as anyone could know Sam and she knew he was not acting out of personal motivations but out of his usual unconscious kindness.

A loud whisper, "Hey Morreign, come over."

She wanted to get back to bed, somewhat confident she could calm her mind enough to sleep now that she had seen the wide, protective river running between her and the rest of the world. However, curiosity over what the duo was doing won out, and she awkwardly moved down the bank.

Louisa and Sam had both waded out up to their knees in the frigid water. Sam held a long willow branch with a net at the end, hovering it over a complex collection of sticks protruding out of the water. Louisa stood to the side and put a finger to her lips as she waved Morreign over.

The idea of stepping into the icy river did not appeal to her, but her curiosity was even more piqued now that she could see the odd activity. Having given up on lace-up shoes after her hip got wrecked, Morreign kicked off her sandals and rolled up her well-worn pajama pants. For a shocking instant, the freezing water hurt her feet but the pain quickly subsided into a pleasant numbness.

As she managed to step carefully across the rocky bottom, she wondered how long it had been since she was in the river. The first summers in Malden involved a lot of swimming time, the cool water a key form of entertainment for the children and refreshment for the adults. They would wait for sunset and stay close to the trees to avoid detection. She had spent endless hours in the dim light watching Jacob and the other kids splash around. On occasion, she and Paul had even snuck down for a midnight skinny dip as the cramped cabin did not provide much in the way of privacy. The memories felt as good as the refreshing current moving over her calves.

She reached Louisa, and the girl put an arm around her shoulders as she leaned in to whisper, "We built a fish trap. Sam came up with the idea and I made the net. We put some bait in there, where the sticks form that funnel. The fish swim in with the current and eat away, but they can't go any further downstream, so they get stuck, too dumb to turn back."

Sam slowly began to lower the net downwards. Louisa said, "That's my cue."

In a blur, Sam dropped the net down at the end of the sticks, apparently blocking the exit as Louisa hurried to the other end of the trap, splashing loudly. Morreign noticed a few silvery flashes of fish leaping out of the water and over the sticks before Sam flung the net upwards, this time heavy with writhing creatures.

Morreign wanted to let out a small cheer, more at the impressive innovation than at the actual success. The people around her, especially Louisa, had every reason to make excuses and wallow in their hardship but, instead, they persevered by coming up with more and more ways to improve life. However, since they did not seem to be celebrating, Morreign merely followed them up the bank where Sam dumped out the catch of three decent sized fish and a few minnows.

"That's great. Amazing, really."

Sam handed Louisa a filleting knife and said, "Too many still get by the net, jumping over or going under."

Louisa picked up the largest fish and began gutting as she asked, "Make it bigger?"

Sam grunted an agreement, "Need a stronger pole then. I'll talk to Leo."

With that, the two silently worked to clean the catch as Morreign mainly watched, impressed by the efficient cooperation. When they finished, Sam picked up the net and buckets before striding off into the darkness without another word. Morreign would have felt slighted if she did not know this was Sam's usual manner of exiting. Louisa looked over at her with a grin. "Care to join me in a snack."

They sat near the water and gently picked at the leftover raw fish flesh. In the not too distant past, the idea of eating the uncooked meat of an animal she saw flopping around on the mud a moment before would have been unthinkable. Now it felt luxurious.

After a moment of silent eating, staring at the stars, Louisa calmly said, "They're talking about funerals again."

Morreign knew this. People were not discussing them directly with her, but she could sense the renewed rumblings. Griff's parents wanted the closure and figured it would only happen if they came together as a community and all decided the kids were gone forever. Tina's mother did not seem to care much, the grief over her lost daughter, her only family member, had entirely overwhelmed her and made her totally despondent and she now moved about Malden like a ghost. Others seemed to hope the closure would help her, maybe allow her to get back to living some semblance of a life but Morreign doubted it would matter.

Morreign answered, "Yeah. I know. I've heard the whispers."

"What do you think?"

"I don't know, Louisa, I really don't. It has been so long, I wonder if funerals are even needed anymore."

They ate a while longer. When the fish was gone, they silently agreed to leave, stood and walked slowly back up to the Lodge. When they reached the porch, Morreign felt wrong leaving Louisa to go upstairs to spend the rest of the night alone in the dark, and she did not like the idea of lying sleepless under her quilt, staring at the ceiling and pondering funerals for children.

Louisa apparently did not want to go to bed either as, without discussion, they both sat on the porch steps.

·   ·   ·

Louisa was glad Morreign did not leave her alone. The late nights hunting with Sam followed by full days of chores had her thoroughly exhausted, but she still did not think she could sleep. It was now five weeks since they disappeared and it became harder and harder to tell herself to keep believing Jacob would be back any moment, that her life would be back. She needed to prepare herself to at least be able to attempt moving on in case he never returned home.

She leaned back against the steps, looking up at the sky full of bright stars. Wanting to delay heading to her empty room and, without planning to, she asked, "What do you think happens when you die?"

Embarrassed at the bold question, Louisa was about to claw it back, when Morreign let out a slight laugh and said, "Weird, I was wondering the same thing. Every time I think about funerals, I remember a time when I was younger, about thirteen or so, and my grandmother was dying. We all returned to my small hometown, and we'd take turns sitting with her in the cramped hospital room. Mostly she slept so you'd simply sit there, listening to her trying to breathe while flipping magazines or watching the fuzzy TV."

In Malden, discussing one's past, especially one's former family, was a prominent topic. Louisa never really understood the urge as she never really knew her family. Regardless, hearing the stories normally warmed her slightly even if they also brought a profound sense of jealousy.

Morreign shifted on the hard steps before continuing, ""Bout three days into the waiting, I was in there alone, and Grandma came to. I did what I'd seen the adults do, fluff up her pillows, let her sip some juice through a bent straw, dab at her face with a cloth but the tough old lady quickly waved my fussing away. Normally, in those last days, when she did talk, it was babbling, nothing coherent, but this time she looked me square in the eyes, her glassy, grey pupils boring right into me.

"Her toothless mouth smiled, and she confidently said, I'm ready, I'm going to Heaven now Mo, and I'm going to see my Henry. With that, she closed her eyes and never woke again."

The story told with no emotion, confused Louisa. She had no way of knowing what to say in such a situation. She muttered, "Oh, I'm sorry."

"No, no, it's ok. I think of that moment fairly often, especially after the Bombs and it makes me wonder, what if whatever you think the afterlife is then that's what it is?"

Louisa enjoyed the intellectual discussion, it reminded her of conversations she used to have with Jacob. Eagerly, she said, "You mean you can imagine your own afterlife?"

"Sort of, yes. If you truly think there's a heaven when you die then your consciousness's last action is it to tell itself you're in heaven and it plays out your idea of heaven for you for eternity. If you think there's nothing after you die, then your consciousness tells you there's nothing, and it is all over. Only an idea, but I sort of like the idea."

The thought was intriguing, but Louisa was not sure she could wrap her mind around it properly. Years ago, Sam had found a number of religious texts in a weird church out in the woods. The Old Testament. The Quran. The Torah. The Rig Veda. Most people at Malden ignored them, but Louisa dug through them, trying to understand the ideas while enjoying the stories. Something in them seemed to gel with Morreign's idea, the commonality of faith.

Before she could voice her vague thoughts though, Morreign awkwardly got to her feet. "Sorry, my old bones are aching. I should find my bed."

Louisa got to her feet. "Ok, but do you think, sometime later, we can discuss this some more. It's way more interesting than talking about the weather or weeds all the time."

Hard to tell in the dim light but she thought she saw Morreign grin at her as she said, "Of course, I'd like that. Weather talk bores me too. Goodnight."

Louisa sat back down, trying to remember if Jacob ever told her what he thought happened when you died.

•　　　•　　　•

Too many days. Far too many. And to make it worse, Harrison could not even guess how many more days were left.

He should be sleeping, but he wasn't. As usual, Harrison laid off to the side of where the men congregated, but he stayed close enough to hear. And there was a fair bit to hear. Only low grumblings but a number of them, all predictable. Complaints about food. Complaints about boredom. Complaints about no women.

JR had contacted their prey, and the initial report from the scouts sounded promising. Jacob did not flee or fight when JR approached, instead, he merely ate then laid down and slept next to his fire. Given this, Harrison was confident JR would be able to help lead the kid. He instructed JR not to ask him questions, simply be a companion who happens to be traveling the same way while finding easier paths. If the subterfuge shortened their trip by even an hour, JR would be soundly rewarded for his ingenuity.

Despite all of that, he knew he needed to be diligent. Mutiny became more and more possible with each day that passed without any pillaging or excitement, but they were getting close to solving all their problems, he could not let it slip through his fingers now.

As if on cue, someone yelled at someone else to have sexual relations with themselves. Someone else yelled back. Normally they would be afraid to wake Harrison, they usually walked on eggshells around him. They were hushed up by the others, but the message remained, his authority was waning.

Harrison decided it was not the time to be a disciplinarian and rolled over onto his side.

CHAPTER THIRTY-ONE

JULY 26, 2046

DAY THREE THOUSAND EIGHT HUNDRED AND SIX

Something seemed off. For five days now, Jacob had walked with the stranger he came to know as JR. The man was polite but did not say much about anything. He had merely explained that his wife passed away over the winter and now he was heading to the river, hoping for better hunting along the waterway. He never even asked Jacob why he was wandering around in the woods by himself, half dead. Most of their minimal conversation was about weather or game. But Jacob figured this silence merely a product of the man's lingering grief.

Jacob initially took this as a positive. Glad the stranger was not interested in him or where he was going or where he was from. Plus, Jacob had bigger concerns, he had come down with the flu or a cold or something. His chest ached, and he could not stop coughing as chills shook his body.

A day ago, they had reached the river. On seeing the wide ribbon of clear, rushing water Jacob could not control himself. Despite the sickness and fatigue, he darted forward, wrecking the remnants of his left boot on the sharp rocks, as he crashed into the river. The cool water felt fantastic but nowhere near to how wonderful it felt to know he was close to home, that he would now be able to find Malden without getting lost forever in the wilderness, that he would now make it back to Louisa.

They made good time moving down the river bank, but Jacob soon began to worry. JR continued to travel with him, still not asking anything, still not saying much other than gently prodding him to move along despite his illness.

And, he seemed to be looking around more than before, often scanning the far bank for some reason. As they first hiked, Jacob had thought he might be able to take JR all the way to Malden, let him settle with them. However, once he started to wonder, he could not stop wondering.

They sat on the bank, watching the river rush by as they shared a jackfish. The curiosity and worry had become too much, and Jacob asked, "So, you going to settle in around here somewhere?"

"Don't know. Want to go down away further first."

Again a vague answer and he never bothered to ask Jacob how much farther he planned to go or what his plans were at all. Strange. Jacob decided to keep pushing. "You been in this area before?"

"Nope."

"Why'd you want to come down here then?"

Only a silent shrug before he stood and walked down to the water, dipping his two wooden bowls in the current before coming back and handing one to Jacob. Two bowls. Why would a man traveling alone over such a great distance bother to carry two bowls? Actually, he had two of many things.

The thought came fuzzily at first, simply a sense of ingrained wrongness that came like a bad smell. Then it sharpened, pieces fitting together like the jigsaw puzzle of the penguins back at the Lodge they had all put together so many times.

The realization crashed down like a bucket of ice water poured on his head. Harrison had let him escape from Thule. The deviant bastard was determined to find Malden, he would not have let one of them walk off so easily. Surely, a building full of men like those who took out the Survivalists would have been able to track one stumbling, injured kid. The locked door of his cell helpfully left open. The bag of supplies sitting in the kitchen as if packed especially for him. The woman merely nodding at him instead of calling out. Harrison wanted him to get away. But why?

More of the puzzle pieces moved, turned and twisted until they fit together. The strange noises in the woods. The odd things he found in his path, a water jug, an old blanket. The men who chased him but then gave up. They were following him. Moving towards Malden so they could swoop in and claim it as their prize.

Jacob looked over at JR who seemed to be working hard to ignore him as he picked at a tooth with a sliver of wood. All the prodding to continue, why did this man care if he stopped or not? It came to Jacob, Harrison sent this "hunter" to act as a guide, to move him along, point him to easier paths and make sure he succeeded in getting to Malden.

He tightly gripped the fork in his hand, one of two that JR had, holding the sharp metal against his leg. He knew he should end the man right now, not risk him finding Malden but, with his hand trembling with tension and his fever making his muscles weak, he knew he could not do it. Instead, with an overly dramatic sigh, Jacob said, "This is a nice spot. I'm beat, think I'll camp out here for a few days, catch jackfish and rest."

The man's head snapped around sharply, and he stared at Jacob with his mouth agape as if trying to think of what to say. Jacob became certain, Harrison had sent JR to move him along. "Really? Why?"

The man did not know where Jacob was going, or if he was even going anywhere, so his confusion over the desire to stop was wrong. His throat feeling especially dry, Jacob answered, "Sure. Might as well, not in a rush. Don't worry, you can carry on. Thanks for all the help and stuff but I'll be fine here."

Having said he wanted to travel on, it would seem strange for JR to now decide to stay with the stranger he had barely spoken too. JR hesitated, so Jacob pushed, "I mean, you said you wanted to go further, check things out. Maybe, in a few days or so, I'll come along and find your campsite."

After a long pause, where JR seemed to contemplate his options, he resigned himself to merely nodding which relieved Jacob as it meant no immediate confrontation. With the silence growing awkward, JR slowly packed up his meagre items and prepared to set out alone. Before he left, he handed over half a bag of stale biscuits, "Here, I don't need these."

Their eyes met as Jacob accepted the treasured gift with a muttered thanks. As he waited for JR to walk away, Jacob nibbled a dry biscuit and looked into the dark woods behind him. The trees were now full of invisible evil. Worse, Jacob needed to contemplate the new reality of how, with what he now knew, he could never go home. He would never see Malden again. Never see Louisa again.

CHAPTER THIRTY-TWO

AUGUST 1, 2046
DAY THREE THOUSAND EIGHT HUNDRED AND ELEVEN

From behind thick pine boughs, Kinma, through Taco's worn our binoculars, watched the mass of men, moving along the river bank. It was hard to be sure, but she thought, in the middle of the mass, she saw Harrison, back straight as he marched, continually confident and in charge.

She hated the evil beasts and knew she should be glad they caught up to them but, seeing the rough group, many with rifles on their shoulders, she only felt foolish. Knowing what she chased and actually seeing it were different realities, the vision slammed her desperate plan into painful perspective. How could they get gardeners armed with arrows and knives to possibly stop this motivated, violence-infused army?

Milo squatted down next to her, peering through the pine boughs and, apparently reading her mind, he whispered, "Guessin' a frontal assault is out of the question."

"I have no idea how we even delay them, let alone stop them."

"I say we cross the river right here, move fast along the other bank and try to get ahead of them unseen."

With a despairing tone, she asked, "What good does that do us?"

Milo shrugged. "Cheer up. We ain't dead yet."

She laughed, "Very reassuring."

After building a simple raft to carry their minimal supplies, they all stripped down and, carefully pushing the fragile raft ahead of them, waded in. Extreme cold engulfed her and Kinma's breath caught in her throat, but she forced herself to move forward. Once the water became waist deep, her body seemed to accept the frigid temperature and, after weeks of living rough, the sensation of cool, clean water moving around her felt entirely wonderful. Apparently, the others felt the same as even Griff, while trying not to stare at her nakedness too blatantly, splashed about as they slowly moved across.

When they reached the far bank, they scrambled to get dressed in the cool air, and Kinma glimpsed Griff. Over the last week or so, Griff's physical state improved. Instead of slumping and meandering along in obvious discomfort started to march much of the time with a set jaw and his eyes on the horizon. She noticed that, when they talked about defending Malden, a conversation they often used to pass the time, Griff became increasingly resolved even if worry showed in his eyes. Now, dripping wet and naked, he looked painfully childlike, gaunt and pale with yellowed bruises covering much of his scrawny back.

He surprisingly knelt in the grass, leaned forward and pressed his forehead to the ground. After a moment, he got back to his feet and noticed Kinma watching him acting strangely. He blushed and answered the question on her face. "I don't know. Suppose I never believed I'd actually see this side of the river again, the home side."

She smiled. "I get it."

He lowered his gaze. "It's strange though, as we get closer, I can now risk imagining walking back into the Lodge. Seeing my family, all excited because I'm back. My mom and sister crying, my dad trying not to cry. Everyone happy. Everyone wanting to hear the story, my story."

Griff looked off into the woods, upriver. He continued, "Then I realize that's all wrong 'cause, right away they're going to ask where Jacob and Tina are. They're going to look at me with hope in their eyes, and they're going to ask, and I'll have to say Tina is gone and that Jake is being likely stalked by a torturing psychopath. And, if that is not bad enough, this monster and his army are coming to attack Malden, to destroy everyone and everything."

While the tired boy stared off in the direction of his endangered home, Kinma got a blanket, walked back and handed it over. He wrapped it around his too-thin shoulders, covering his bony, hairless chest covered in partially healed cuts before he looked over at her with watery eyes. "Do we have a plan?"

She shrugged and smiled. "Nope. But we'll do all we can."

An impish smile crept onto his face as he started to get dressed and said, "Ok."

•   •   •

Jacob knew what he needed to do. Harrison was out there, in the trees and the shadows, watching him, following him, waiting for him to lead them all to Malden. But, if he suddenly changed directions after discarding JR, Harrison would know Jacob figured out he was being followed. He needed to keep going along the river and then go straight past Malden, leading Harrison and his band of evil-doers off into the endless wilderness.

The decision obvious, not even a decision really, but intensely difficult all the same. He could not go home. He would die in these woods, alone and miserable. Continuing to trudge, sick, hungry, tired and sore, proved to somehow be far more arduous when he could not imagine seeing Louisa at the end of his ordeal. But, if it meant keeping Louisa and the others safe, Jacob knew he would manage to walk on.

As he turned a bend in the river, he thought the scenery looked familiar, but he told himself it was not. Ever since reaching the river he kept thinking places looked familiar, but they always turned out to not be. Like in the stories of nomads in the desert chasing oasis that did not exist, he taught himself to not let his mind trick him any longer.

Then, as the sun began to set, he saw it and it could not was be denied: the crooked tree. Far in the distance but Jacob was sure. He had broken his wrist there when Griff dared him to swing off the outstretched branch into the river. When his dog, Bear, got old and could no longer hear Jacob calling for him, more often than not, he could find the dog laid out under the tree watching the water go by, sniffing the breeze. On hot evenings, he and Louisa would climb to the first fork and dangle their feet out. That was the tree. That was Malden.

• • •

Unusual for Harrison to experience self-doubt but, standing above the river, watching his weary gang stumbling along the muddy bank it began to creep in. When they left Thule, the caravan moving swiftly down the remnants of the road, everything seemed certain. Follow the fool to the village, overwhelm the farmers, take what they needed, enjoy what they wanted, decide on staying. Simple.

Now, he wondered if he had miscalculated. The men looked battered, slumped and angered. Tempers erupted more and more often, but no one was bold enough to direct their temper straight at him, regardless, overt dissension became more likely every day they trudged. If a choice few decided to revolt he was uncertain which way the mass would lean, the men were eager for a fight and fighting him might suffice.

The distance was a problem. The terrain was a problem. However, as always, time was the main problem. Time kills all plans.

The men could handle discomfort and tedium, they could handle hunger and exertion. But not knowing for how long they needed to endure, with no visible endpoint, made it exceptionally difficult. For a moment, a brief one, the arrival at the river quelled their irritation. But, once they bathed and drank their fill of the icy water, the drudgery of marching ever forward promptly returned, bringing back their irritation even stronger.

As he moved along the running water, he wondered how many more days he could force this march before a mutiny erupted. He needed to shrink the time. They could not move faster than the boy, but maybe he could shrink the perception of time. Put the idea of the prize in the forethought of the men's minds, make it seem close, make it seem imminent.

Harrison let the march continue until sunset. As the men finished their simple suppers while complaining about the ration size, he ordered more wood to be put on the dying fire, building it up into a roaring blaze. Weeks of the mundane made even this minor change interesting, and all eyes were on him as he strode out of the shadows.

Up until now, in order to manage expectations, he had kept his plan slightly vague and the prize they were seeking somewhat ambiguous, mainly because he did not truly knew what they would find. He decided it was past time to put a more concrete vision in their deviant minds. He calmly said, "Many of you have heard rumors about where we are going, about what we are going to find there but mainly you have trusted me. Trusted me blindly and completely. Your trust has not been misplaced, I know we are enduring much but I also know the reward is worth the ordeal, but now I want you to know for certain this is worth your impressive endurance."

Seeing intense interest but also some smirks of annoyance on the faces of his men, he continued, "This fool we are following is going to lead us straight to an established and unguarded settlement the likes of which we have never had the good fortune to find before."

With as much pomp as he could stomach, Harrison entered storytelling mode as he detailed the bulging food stores, the numerous young women and the comfortable shelter they would enjoy as the men cheered and laughed.

•　　•　　•

Jacob knew he needed to keep going, but the illness worsened with each passing hour, the fever intensified and he could not keep what little food he ate down, even water ran right through him. His left boot had decomposed to nothing and his foot became a swollen and scraped mess. He knew he would not make it much further in this condition. Jacob needed to keep going, get some distance from Malden before he could walk no further, but his body refused his mind's commands to move him away from his home.

He merely stood and stared across the familiar water. So close. The river remained wide, and it still ran fast, regardless, Jacob knew he could swim across it in a heartbeat, even as exhausted as he was, because Louisa waited on the other side. So close and so simple, ten steps, a couple hundred strokes, ten more steps, yell out, and he would be quickly surrounded by his family, his friends. And Louisa. He would be safe and without pain again, the lonely nightmare over.

Instead, he needed to say goodbye, say goodbye to everyone and everything he cared about. Deciding to start with the easiest part of the unbelievably difficult task, he silently resolved himself to never seeing the Lodge again, to never sitting in the common room, laughing and talking. He concluded he would never feel the deep satisfaction of finishing a day of working in the gardens or chopping firewood alongside his friends. Never again could he enjoy the easy pleasure of sitting on the porch of his parents' cabin, sipping cool tea and reading a novel while happy kids ran after one another in the Clearing.

Letting go of everything good in his life hurt but it was a soft brushing of his cheek compared to the pain of what came next. First, he said a final goodbye to all his friends. Then to Sam, imagining the solemn nod the man would give him in return. Then to his uncle Leo who would make some joke and his cousins. Then, with tears starting to slip down his cheeks, he said goodbye to his father, thanking him for all the delightful laughter and all the heartfelt lessons. Then he started to cry in earnest as he told his mother he was sorry, sorry for being so foolish when she went through so much to save him and protect him against all odds. He thanked her for all the comforting, all the joy and all the strength and then he said goodbye to her.

It took great effort to fortify himself as he came to the worse of it. He thought of the routine times with Louisa, merely enjoying the simple contentment at being together, of having found one another. He thought of the sad times they endured together, taking comfort in caring for each other when hardness entered their lives. He thought of the wonderful, joyous times together, reveling in the pure glee of being in love. Finally, he whispered his last goodbye to Louisa.

Turning, he forced his ruined feet and weary legs to carry him away, wondering how far a beaten and sick and heartbroken man could travel once all hope had left him.

CHAPTER THIRTY-THREE

AUGUST 3, 2046

DAY THREE THOUSAND EIGHT HUNDRED AND THIRTEEN

No moon, not even the glint of a star. Morreign sighed. Why did these things always happen on the blackest of nights? She wearily climbed the steps up to the Lodge and opened the door.

The Committee sat around the table as others filled the space behind them. Only one candle and one lantern burned, leaving gloomy shadows. As she limped in, Morreign figured this setting matched the mood perfectly.

Two more young men were missing. Richard and Errol. They went out to check trap lines and, when they did not return by dinner, others were sent to find them. The sun set and the searchers returned without finding any helpful signs. Now, in the black of night, they needed to decide if the search should continue or be delayed for dawn.

Sitting at the table for this discussion caused a wave of unpleasant déjà vu for Morreign. Not long ago they held this conversation regarding Jacob, Tina, and Griff.

Boris Walker started, "We can go in groups and take torches, that'll give Rich and Errol something to see in the dark and should keep away anything we don't want comin' around."

Leo sighed, "I don't know, we need to find them, but there's the bear roaming out there with her cub. We stumble across her, startle her in the dark, that'll be a problem."

Boris added, "Sure, but only Sam's seen any sign of the bears. Pretty far off, too. And as long as we keep calling out and keep the torches burning, I don't think the bear'll be a problem."

A pause before Ram Bosh reluctantly said, "What about that fire last night? I'm worried there's two-legged threats out there as well. That would be more dangerous than any bear, and the torches will be beacons for them."

Last night, right after dusk, Sam spotted a light across the river. He gathered others and they all stood behind the trees on the bank to stare at the oddity. They talked at length, working to convince themselves they were seeing some sort of natural trick of the light. Eventually, the strange vision disappeared, and they went back up to the Lodge without deciding on what they had seen, wilfully ignoring the most likely explanation.

Now that Ram had burst the self-induced delusion, Morreign admitted to herself that she knew what she saw. A significant campfire. Strangers nearby. Maybe many of them.

Leo, in his soft tone, said, "We don't know what we saw. Even if it was a campfire, it was on the far side of the river, and there's been no sign of anything else."

Morreign, wishing she listened more to her instincts and told everyone about her dream, broke in, "Hasn't there been? Two young, smart and healthy men are missing."

Silence. For the decade since they fled she knew karmic luck allowed only peaceful people to find Malden. However, it would be fully naive to think all survivors would have cooperation and friendliness in their hearts. Regardless of this obvious potential threat, an unsaid rule developed over the years that the possible problem of being attacked by people would not be openly discussed, mainly because they realized there was little they could do if isolation alone failed. Now she felt painfully idiotic for putting her head in the sand rather than attempting to deal with the issue, especially given the prophetic dream apparently sent by her subconscious to warn her.

Before they could truly break the unwritten rule and begin discussing this horrific scenario, the Lodge door swept open. Morreign turned in her chair, her stiff hip aching at the unwelcomed twisting, to see Richard and Errol step inside.

Sounds of relief filled the room, even a few claps and cheers were given. However, the minor celebration cut off when others followed the two of them inside. In the dim light, Morreign glimpsed, among three road-weary strangers, a shock of red hair. Without thought, she yelled out, "Griffin. It's Griff."

A clatter of falling chairs as people hurried to their feet and rushed the doorway. With her ruined hip, she was slow to get up and the crush of bodies made it impossible for her to see what she desperately wanted to see, but she was sure Jacob had to be with him.

•   •   •

Tired and annoyed, Harrison asked, "I'm here. What's so important?"

The Viking stood up off the berm where he had been waiting. The thug didn't answer, only walked towards the river, expecting Harrison to follow. The remaining Viking had sent his scouting partner back to the main group to give Harrison the message that he needed to come up immediately. Greatly disliking being summoned but trusting that the Viking would not waste a word on something unimportant, Harrison promptly marched the half mile.

On the gravel-covered bank, the Viking stopped and pointed across the river, just above the treeline and downstream. "There."

Harrison looked but saw nothing. Not wanting to admit he could not see whatever was so important, he stared longer. There. A hint of whiteness, maybe a wisp of smoke.

He asked, "Smoke?"

The Viking nodded, pointing again, this time lower and further down, right at the far bank. Again, Harrison did not think he saw anything but branches and grass. He focused. Maybe a right angle behind some reeds indicating a man-made object.

He pointed one more time, even further downriver. An old tree, twisted and leaning out over the water. The Viking said, "We past that a while back but I did not notice. The other one. The redhead. In Thule. He said something about a crooked tree."

Shocked by the brutish man's memory, Harrison nodded and said, "He did indeed."

"Your rabbit, stopped right here. Stood, staring, muttering, before he shuffled on."

Harrison looked back across the river. Jacob stopped and then kept going. JR had come back, saying the kid wanted to rest and he could not get him to continue marching without being too suspicious. But then the kid kept going anyway. Harrison had hoped, the kid was nearing his home and realized he needed to rid himself of JR before he got there. However, if the Viking was right, it seemed he walked right past the settlement. Maybe JR slipped up, let Jacob know he was not merely some innocent hunter.

The pieces clanked together, it all made sense, if Jacob knew he was being followed by the Bankers he would also know he could not lead them to his home so he would keep going, pull the threat away, a mother hen running about to lead the fox from her nestlings. For an instant, Harrison deeply respected the battered teenager for his cunning and his toughness.

He looked over at the Viking and merely said, "Don't be seen."

The Viking more declared than asked, "I get first and second pick, and a third for my dead brother, if I want it?"

Harrison could not argue with this demand, and he nodded.

The huge man calmly handed over his rifle and slipped out of his filthy clothes. The massive, muscular body strode into the river and, in a matter of minutes, had swum the width and was climbing out on the other side. The remnants of Harrison's sense of humour wondered what the isolate villagers would think if they saw that naked, scowling monstrosity marching towards them.

•   •   •

For days Kinma mirrored Harrison's group as it marched on the other side of the river. The army was able to move quicker than Milo anticipated, faster than before. The foursome had hurried, rushing to get ahead of the men but the terrain on their side was more difficult to travel so they could not make up much ground on Harrison.

Griff had begun recognizing landmarks with his memories becoming more frequent the closer they got to Malden. Once he stopped at a poplar tree. It looked like all the other trees, except this one Griff recognized where he and Jacob treed a porcupine with their slingshots when they were nine-year-olds.

While the idea of sleeping indoors and having a real meal were extremely appealing, Kinma found their closeness to Malden daunting. The first thing she would need to tell these strangers was that a powerful, enraged force was about to be on their doorstep. Not a pleasant conversation, especially since a plan to help them did not exist.

Near dusk, they spied the two boys walking a trap line. Watching the baffled fear on their faces at the sight of Milo and Taco turn to confused but purely innocent glee when they saw their lost friend bolstered Kinma's resolve to save this pleasant group. And now, after moving past all the tidy cabins, stepping from the night air into the warmth of the long building, with everyone rushing to their lost son, that resolve redoubled.

Griff said, "Ok, ok, alright. Let me breathe."

The crush of people backed off slightly, and he continued, "I need to –."

A curly haired man interrupted, "Jacob and Tina? Are they with you?"

Kinma's heart hurt. Griff endured so much pain and hardship, finally made it home and only got an instant to enjoy the triumph of returning before being confronted with the awfulness he deeply dreaded. Suddenly looking very young, the boy's head hung, and his thin shoulders slumped. No one in the crowded space spoke but, after a moment, the people parted slightly, and a middle-aged woman limped through.

She looked tired to Kinma, tired but strong. Her eyes silently took in Griff who continued to look at the floor. The woman moved to him, Griff a head taller and half again as wide as the petite woman but, as she wrapped her arms about him, he melted against her, letting her wiry frame take his worn-out weight.

Griff mumbled, "I'm sorry Morreign, I'm so sorry."

The woman responded, "Its ok Griff, its ok. You're back, and that's wonderful. Truly wonderful."

Sounding like a stunned, hurt child, Griff tried to explain, "We... we, were together in this place, in this building. Back at Thule. They beat us, me and Jake. The man, this evil man, he was going to burn Tina, to get her to talk, talk about Malden, but she jumped. We were up really high and she jumped through glass. She died."

There were gasps and sobs from the crowd, but Griff continued, "I haven't seen Jacob since back then."

With tears now covering her cheeks, the woman looked even more tired as she said, "Ok, ok. You're safe now, you can tell us everything in due time. Rest now and, later, we'll all grieve Tina and Jacob toge-."

Griff pulled back and said, "No, Jake, he's not dead. He's out there."

•　　•　　•

Louisa tried to read the sounds of commotion coming up from the main room. She knew Richard and Errol were missing, and she figured, with great relief, it was them returning. However, the celebration seemed to end too abruptly. Normally, such an oddity occurring would lead to a great deal of excited talk regardless of the hour, but she could not hear any voices.

Hoping nothing else horrible happened, Louisa hurried to the stairs. Peering down through the weak glow, it took her a moment to comprehend before she let out an unconscious squeal and scurried down.

People moved out of her way as she jumped at him. Griff reacted in time to catch her as she threw arms around him. "Griff! How? I mean, you're here, you're really here?"

In the voice she did not know she missed until she heard it again, he said, "Yeah, yeah, I'm here."

She hugged him tightly, thrilled by the simple fact that her lost friend suddenly returned and, for a moment, she reveled in pure glee. Then, like a dagger stabbing her mind, she realized she saw strangers, but she did not see Jacob.

She was lowered to her feet, and Griff looked sadly down at her. Hoping against hope, she asked, "Where? Where is he? Is he dead?"

"No, he's not dead. He's still out there. Coming here, at least we think so."

Relief poured in and around her but then guilt smashed it away. Tina. Tina was missing, and she had not even noticed. She asked, "Tina? What about Tina?"

Griff merely looked at her and sadly shook his head. He continued to talk, but Louisa did not hear what he said. She knew she should be thinking about Tina, feeling grief, feeling sympathy for her distraught mother who was all alone but all that matter to her at that moment was Jacob coming back.

Then a woman coughed uneasily and said, "Um, hello? I'm sorry, very sorry to interrupt but, well, I'm Kinma, and this here is Milo and Taco and, unfortunately, there's something we need to discuss, and I think we best discuss it right away."

•   •   •

Success took luck. Harrison knew that, but he disliked relying on the Fates. The Viking being the one following Jacob when the kid stopped was luck, as any of the other fools would have taken the stoppage as nothing but an opportunity to rest. That wisp of smoke hanging in the calm air was luck as any breeze would have erased it from the sky. The redhead muttering about a crooked tree for the Viking to hear was luck. Too much good fortune, Harrison now needed to take control, make his own luck.

The Viking had come back across the water with good news. Without risking getting too close, he had surveyed the settlement. A long lodge, a number of cabins, some other outbuildings. They finally found what they had come for.

Harrison gathered the main group and told them their journey was nearing an end, the prize was in their grasp. Their eagerness was palpable, and Harrison was certain they would all rush across the river to do battle in a heartbeat, but he did not want to push his luck any further, so he laid out his more patient plan.

They would march two miles upriver through the woods, under cover of darkness to ensure no one from the village saw them. Then they would spend the next day laying low, resting. Come darkness they would cross the river, spread out around the settlement and attack from multiple fronts in the middle of the night while the sheep slept.

With the prize in sight, Harrison threw out his strict rationing rules and let the men eat whatever was left in their packs before commencing the short night time walk. As they moved through the trees Harrison allowed himself to feel a sense of relief and pride, his plan of following the kid had worked. All that was left now was the fight, and he had all the fighters, no matter what the outcome, he had done all anyone could have. He chewed a hearty mouthful of venison jerky and contentedly listened to the jovial talk of his men as he marched towards his resurrection.

•   •   •

Leo was explaining how they could possibly build a picket barricade with logs and fight off the attackers from there. All of this was too bizarre for Morreign to comprehend, it sounded like children making up a game. Realizing she needed to intervene or this foolishness would get out of control, Morreign turned to the woman named Kinma who seemed to be taking all this in with the same lack of surety.

Harshly interrupting the talk of useless fences, Morreign asked Kinma, "You lived with these men for years?"

Everyone stopped and looked at the two women as Kinma, appearing only slightly self-conscious, said, "Yes."

Griff had left to be with his family in their cabin, but, while eating, Kinma and the two men had given a quick overview of how they made it to Malden. Morreign could not help but be impressed by the strong woman, especially since she could have gone anywhere but chose to put herself back in the eye of evil.

Morreign asked, "Tell me about them, what're they like?"

Without hesitation, Kinma responded, "Worst of the worst. They call themselves the Bank, a remnant of a sick joke from years ago when they murdered some rich survivors, well I guess, to be fair, *we* called ourselves the Bank. Anyway, most of them have learned to act only to satisfy primal urges. Some might be decent enough on their own, but when thrown into the mob they are all degraded to a common denominator of demented animals. At Thule, they used women like toys and brutally fought anyone deemed weaker than them. This is all made even more awful by the fact that they're led by an extremely intelligent, extremely ambitious sociopath."

The two men, Milo and Taco, nodded their agreement as Morreign prodded the woman, "What do you know about this sociopath?"

"Far too much, yet, I suppose not all that much. His name is Harrison. He's a former businessman who was conscripted into the military. My husband, he probably knew him best and he talked of how Harrison was cold and harsh but, early on, right after the Bombs, he was brilliantly calculating and decisive when it came to improving their position which allowed them to survive the first terrible winters. However, over time he grew even harsher and colder, driven more by a need to maintain his control than to improve everyone's lot.

"In the last years, when you spoke with Harrison, it felt like you were talking to a poorly designed robot. He stares with these unfeeling eyes and you know the brain behind them is heartlessly dissecting every angle. But you have to acknowledge his fortitude and cunning, for a decade he's led a band of violent thugs and, not once, has his leadership been truly threatened."

Motherly worry soaked into Morreign. Her son was still out there, under the watch of a madman and his hoard of beasts. "And he's following Jacob?"

Nodding somberly, Kinma said, "Yes, Harrison did everything he could to get Jacob and Griff to tell him where their home was, but they somehow managed to remain strong and refuse. Then, Harrison let Jacob escape, and we were too foolish to see his plan. Jacob, of course, came straight for here, the meanest members of the Bank easily following every step of the way. We passed Harrison a day ago. They won't be far behind."

Morreign needed to remind herself that at least Jacob was alive when she had essentially presumed her son dead. This mental exercise did nothing to truly comfort her. She foolishly ignored her instincts, the same instincts that caused her to prepare to flee Thule way back before the Longest Night. Regardless, she forced herself to focus on the dire problem at hand: these monsters were coming for them, not in some hazy dream but in crystal clear reality.

The one called Milo interjected into the silence, "On top of all that, I've been out on patrol with Harrison, he's a great and patient tactician. He won't get tricked up on defences like hastily set up trenches or fences. Unpredictable aggression by us is probably the best option, use the fact that he doesn't know you're expecting him."

Ram Bosh snarled about being ready for the heathens. Others joined in, saying they would fight to the last man to ensure that no harm came to Malden. It sounded to Morreign like the blather spewed before a football game and, without thought, she slammed her bony hand against the table. "Enough. We need a serious plan, lives are at stake. All of our lives."

The pep talk stopped as they all stared at her. She ignored the hurt looks of bruised egos and calmly turned again to Kinma, asking, "These men have been traveling for over a month now?"

"Yes, but you should not think that'll make them weaker. They survived all this time since the Bombs by pillaging and scavenging. Thirty days out on a patrol is a long time, but they'll not be too put out by living rough. They'll be tired and hungry, but they've come here for food and women so they'll be very motivated."

Louisa had been standing, forgotten, in the corner. She stepped forward and softly said, "I have an idea."

Strange for a teenager take part in a meeting like this, but Morreign had learned Louisa was not to be underestimated. She nodded and said, "Good, I'm glad someone does. Tell us."

As Louisa spoke, Morreign first thought it was too fraught with risk, but then she realized they needed something risky given the odds they faced and the threads of Louisa's idea began twisting together in Morreign's mind, forming into a plausible plan. In an instant she started taking inventory of the supplies they could use while envisioning the method for implementing them. When Louisa finished, Morreign looked over at Kinma, Milo and the silent man they called Taco. They all nodded. Morreign said, "I like it. It might give us the chance we need."

Everyone leaned forward as she began to divvy out the necessary actions.

• • •

Kinma listened intently to the idea. They would be giving up their location and element of surprise, but it might work. Harrison was smart though, very smart. He might see through it. Regardless, Kinma decided it was worth taking the shot since, it seemed, it was the only shot they had to take. The others, including Milo and Taco, seemed to be similarly intrigued and they easily agreed with implementing the plan.

A lengthy discussion played out as a carefully orchestrated timeline was determined before Morreign doled out assignments and the meeting broke up. Kinma, not sure what to do, stood to follow Milo and Taco out of the lodge to help set up.

Morreign touched her arm, coaxing her back as the others left and said, "Sorry, I know I've only met you, but I appreciate what you did, coming back here and it seems you probably have the clearest sense of all of this. Do you think this'll work? Am I making a mistake by not settling in for a straight on fight when they get here? "

Looking into her tired face, Kinma did not think the woman was seeking approval or fake reassurance, but she genuinely wanted advice. Kinma immediately liked her, she had command of all these men but was humble enough to listen to a stranger. She answered, "In all honesty, I don't think a fight is winnable. Everyone here seems very proud and decent but, even if they had weeks to build up defences, Harrison would still win. Basically, I picture the Bankers streaming in here at night with their rifles and killing anything that moves before we can properly react. Or, if we have time to hunker down, they'll merely wait us out or burn us out. These are not the type of men to merely give up and go away."

Strangely, this got a chuckle from Morreign. "Yeah, the men here are hardworking and strong, but they're not killers, more likely to try and shake these assholes' hands than put an arrow in them."

Kinma could not help but laugh herself. "That's not a bad thing, trust me, I've lived amongst very able killers for far too long."

"You're right, and I shouldn't laugh, but right now I'd trade a few kind souls for one cold-hearted sharpshooter with a decent rifle."

Kinma said, "Yeah, but all we got is the kindly type, and we have to play that hand."

"Well, we also have Sam."

"Right Griff mentioned him. When can I meet him?"

"He was here, the one back in the corner with no beard."

Furrowing her brow, Kinma said, "I don't recall seeing him."

That got a sly smile from Morreign, "That's sort of his thing. Like in all other things at Malden, I imagine Sam will be key to us getting out of this mess."

"He's our cold-hearted sharpshooter?"

"No. Well, kind of, I suppose. He's hard to explain, but he handles things better than most. Anyway, what about Louisa's scheme? You think it can make enough of a difference?"

Having heard all about Louisa from Jacob, Kinma was not surprised the witty girl he so deeply loved was the one to come up with the most viable plan. She answered, "In all honesty, I'm not sure. It's pretty ingenious and way better than facing them straight on, that much I'm sure of. She's a smart girl."

Morreign leaned back and said, "She is, I'm learning it more every day. But, you know these beasts, tell me any flaws in the idea that you see."

Again appreciating that the woman was willing to have her plan criticized by an outsider, Kinma said, "Harrison might be able to sniff it out. He's not driven by emotion or even physical needs so he'll not be easily tricked. If it looks at all like a trap, he'll see it as a trap."

They discussed how to better camouflage the rouge before Morreign said, "Alright, we at least have a plan. If nothing else, that makes me feel better. We best get at it."

Turning to leave, Kinma noticed a sign on the wall with faded green letters, "Sychar Lodge and Resort." Before she could catch herself, she let out a soft laugh.

Morreign asked, "Something actually funny?"

"Oh, sorry, I noticed the sign. Interesting to see it here."

Turning awkwardly in her chair, Morreign looked at the simple sign. "Really? The kids found that under the porch years ago, we think it was an old owner's name."

While not raised religious, Kinma found a Bible in the first motel room her and her mother had stayed in when they moved north, and the rhythmic stories appealed to her teenaged self so she carried it with her in those early years to keep her company when she felt alone. Kinma said, "Sychar is a place in the bible. A man builds a well there, and Jesus comes along and sees a woman who he asks for a drink of water. This was strange back then, I guess men didn't talk to women alone in the olden days. But Jesus does and then he ends up teaching her about faith and hope."

Morreign turned back to the sign for a second before looking back to Kinma. "Interesting. Wonder if the owner's of this place knew that."

Kinma shrugged and said, "Don't know about the old owners, but the reason I laughed is because the man who built the well in the Bible, his name was Jacob. Sychar is the place of Jacob's well, the place where a poor woman learned about faith and hope."

For a moment, Morreign looked at the sign as tears broke from her eyes. She stiffly moved to Kinma and hugged her as Kinma felt her own tears rise up at the simple gesture of humanity. Morreign said, "I forgot to say thank you, you did not need to come here and risk everything. Thank you. No matter what happens, you gave us a chance. You gave me hope."

CHAPTER THIRTY-FOUR

AUGUST 4, 2046

DAY THREE THOUSAND EIGHT HUNDRED AND FOURTEEN

Despite being unable to see anything, Jacob thought his eyes were open, but he tried to open them again anyway. Only a sheet of unbroken grey. Dead, he was obviously dead. Before he could truly contemplate that circumstance, a tiny sharp pain hit him out of the abyss.

His ankle. A pain in his ankle. Without thought, he kicked, but something stabbed into his other leg. Pain in his calf. He kicked away at whatever was tormenting him and turned his face out of the dirt, blinking his eyes until his blurred vision finally cleared enough to see.

Coyotes. Their muzzles low to the ground as they circled him, darting in and then backing off. Far from bold but, if Jacob didn't move, they would get braver. All he wanted was to close his eyes, stay off his ruined feet and let his sick body sleep. His mouth felt like it was full of bitter slime, his head screamed with waves of throbbing agony, and the fever made his skin send chilling shivers throughout all his muscles. But he forced himself to move.

Sitting up hurt immensely and dizziness nearly overwhelmed him, but the motion caused the scrawny dogs to scurry back into the underbrush. Not long ago, being surrounded by snapping coyotes might be frightening; now, after enduring the true terrors this world had to offer, he barely noticed them.

Ignoring pain and vertigo, Jacob got to his swollen feet, and the skinny coyotes skittered away, chirping their displeasure at their meal not being dead. Silently thanking them for waking him from what might have been his last sleep, Jacob took one tortured-filled step, followed by another, and another, moving very slowly away from home, leading the danger away.

* * *

Fatigue pulled at Morreign, her hip angry at all the unusual activity and lack of rest. She took a deep drink of water, hoping it would refresh her. It didn't, but she moved to the front of the Lodge's main room regardless.

Everyone, dressed in heavy clothes, nervously awaiting the trip, stared up at her. While many seemed to have steeled themselves, a cloud of worry filled the space, and she knew they were intensely scared because she was intensely scared.

She forced her voice to fill the room, "I felt like this ten years ago, frightened, very frightened and unsure. We fled then, but I am calming myself with the knowledge that this is different, this is immensely different. Back then we fled through the Longest Night, knowing only vaguely if the life raft of Malden even existed and knowing we would never get to go back to our homes. Tonight, we flee again, but this time we will come back to our home, all of us and soon. Yet, I am frightened because we are facing a difficult threat but, as always, we will work together and protect one another and come back home together."

With that, she grabbed her pack, turned and strode out of the Lodge, trying to hide her limp and her reluctance at having to leave as she fought the urge to look behind her to make sure they were following. Thankfully, before long, others moved past her into the Clearing.

Paul walked up beside her. "Good speech."

She asked, "You think?"

"It was short and everyone followed you, so I guess it was good enough."

"I'll take that. How're you making out?"

He shrugged. "Feeling too old and tired for fleeing, for enduring another Longest Night but managing. You?"

"Same. Let's not make this a ten-year tradition."

He took a few silent steps and then asked, "You think this'll work?"

"I don't know Paul, I really don't, but when you've only got one option, you take it. What do you think?"

Without slowing, he reached over and took her hand, saying, "I like it, it is a sound plan, brilliant actually. Frankly, Mo, I think you've probably saved us again."

She squeezed his hand and replied, "It was Louisa's idea, I only fleshed it out. I think it'll be ok, the world can't be that cruel, I mean, it can't bring Jacob to our doorstep, have him go through all he went through only to have everything destroyed around us. The world wouldn't do that to him, do that to us, would it?"

Apparently deciding to avoid the question, Paul said, "Remember when we drove here how Jacob was fascinated with the winch on the truck, how he liked to flip the switch? That was all he cared about all that night while the rest of us were terrified. The whole time he was curious about how it worked."

She nodded, realizing Paul's instinct to avoid the scary reality was correct this time as worrying about Jacob could not help, it would only further complicate a complex situation. She forced unfelt cheer into her tone as she said, "Yeah, he almost winched your arm off."

Paul said, "Yeah, Mo, he does not give in to fear like other people. He'll be ok, he's smart and tough and will not give up on finding a way through all of this. I think we'll see him again."

Listening to her instincts, Morreign realized she agreed, and she felt slightly better as she softly said, "I think so too."

They walked in silence, Morreign focussing on each step instead of thinking of what would soon be occurring behind them. When they got to the creek, she said to Paul, "You need to circle back."

He stopped, and they looked at each other. "Take care of yourself."

"You too. I mean it, Paul, take care of yourself. I cannot lose you."

Paul nodded with a seriousness that looked odd on him before he jogged off, displaying that a hint of his juvenile, peppy gait was still present after all these hard years.

•   •   •

Harrison only sent out three scouts to get the lay of the land, and he ordered them to keep their distance from the settlement. Normally, he could trust his men to be smart enough not to be seen and ruin the element of surprise but, after thirty days in the woods, he was worried they might try to sneak in on their own to get a better look or even to steal a taste ahead of the others. Plus, he had done his own surveillance and what he saw made him even more confident as there appeared to be no guards, dogs or defenses. Not much scouting was needed, it would be a simple, multiple-front storm and conquer attack.

Set up a mile from the settlement, well hidden by the thick pine trees, the men were trying to stay quiet as they cleaned rifles, sharpened blades and use charcoal to blacken their skin. Would be normal to expect some nervous energy but the Bankers were all blood-tested, so Harrison only sensed excitement at obtaining the prize with no worry over the battle. As he watched them calmly joke with each other, Harrison realized this was the reason for all the cruelty and violence, for the intensity of his leadership.

Because his group was so hardened they would be able to easily conquer these much softer survivors and take what they deserved as the apex of the remnants of mankind. Having proven they were the fittest, they would then establish a society of strong people which would be able to flourish and grow outside the bounds of Thule. This was how natural selection was meant to work, this was how evolution was meant to work. And he would be at the head of it all.

Suddenly, Harrison's usual patience started to wane. He wanted to move now. He wanted to finish what he started ten years ago. He checked the sun. It hovered on the treetops. Waiting until the middle of the night was not needed. Two hours. He could wait two hours.

He stepped amongst the cluster of men and calmly said, "Two more hours. Two more hours and our ordeals of the last ten years will be completed and rewarded. We will take on our rightful role of the rebuilders of a better mankind."

•   •   •

Sam stepped out of the bushes. While Kinma had been told he could move silently in the woods, his sudden arrival shocked her. The group, ten men and six women, plus her, Milo and Taco, all gathered around as Paul asked Sam, "Anything?"

"They've crossed the river and are camped a mile to the east. Getting ready to attack."

Kinma asked, "Anyone see you?"

Sam merely looked at her with cold eyes, silence his only answer to the apparently foolish question.

Paul asked, "Jacob with them?"

Sam shook his head.

He then silently slipped back into the undergrowth, instantly disappearing. Paul, with too much nervousness in his voice, said, "Ok, well, we knew this was coming. At least it will be over and done with tonight."

The others nodded and returned to their uneasy waiting in the dim light. Feeling the tension, Kinma decided they might benefit from some distracting conversation so, in a low voice, she asked, "What's the deal with Sam?"

Paul scoffed slightly. "Yeah, you might say he lacks social skills, but he made this wilderness his home long before we got here. I can't even come close to being able to count the number of ways having him here allowed us to survive."

A hulking man who'd been introduced to her as Jacob's uncle, Leo, added quietly, "Taught us all how to fish the river and how to lay traps. Hell, we'd have nothing but skinny carrots to eat the last ten years without him showing us what to do."

She asked, "How'd he end up out here?"

Paul shook his head. "Not really sure. I've been out hunting and scavenging with him a thousand times, night after night with nothing but a campfire between us. I like to talk, my brother can attest to that."

Leo took his cue and said, "Came out chattering at birth according to mom."

"Right. At first, I tried merely asking Sam about himself but might as well be questioning a stone, a deaf and mute stone. After that, I tried being more subtle, poke around the corners, but that got me nothing. I'd tell him all about my past, hoping something would get him to speak up about himself but that was pointless, although I do like talking about myself. Eventually, though, I managed to hear part of his story."

At this, Leo, sounding surprised, asked, "Really? He talked about himself?"

Paul said, "Yeah, I decided, way back then, that I'd keep it to myself, you know out of respect for Sam as I didn't think he'd like me telling his secrets but, with what's happening now, I think it's ok to tell what he told me."

Everyone leaned in closer to hear as Paul continued, "We'd found this half-fallen down cabin. Sam said it was used by winter trappers, but it looked like no one had used it for decades. Anyway, the place was empty but, under a loose floorboard in the corner, we found someone's emergency supplies: a package of dried beans and a jar of what I guess you'd call moonshine."

One of the other men chirped in, "Don't remember you ever bringing any of that back home with ya?"

Paul shook his head with a smile. "Nah, we decided it was too fragile to make the trip so we made use of it where we were, hunkering down in the dark cabin, passing the jar back and forth. At first, there was only the usual quiet but, then, with the strong booze working, I began reminiscing about this time I went to watch hockey as a kid with my dad in Edmonton. Don't know why that struck me as important but that's what came to my half-drunk mind -"

Leo piped up, "Alright, alright, what did Sam say?"

"With his tongue apparently loosened by the drink, Sam said, honest to God, he said 'I used to like watching hockey'."

They all waited for him to continue, but Paul merely looked around, shrugged and said, "That's it, that's all he said."

They softly chided Paul for his stupid sense of humor, but the silliness served the purpose of relaxing them somewhat. As the sun sank and stars appeared in the night sky, more pleasant stories followed. Of birthday parties. Of storms weathered. Of pranks played.

Kinma served as their main audience and listened, occasionally prodding lightly. At first, the stories made her worried. She knew each of Harrison's beasts out there, and she knew they were not cheerfully reminiscing in preparation for battle, they were eagerly anticipating their cruelty and depravity. Morreign and Louisa's plan should give them an advantage but they would still need to fight and, while she deeply respected all of these nice people, she did not like their chances in a fight.

Then, as pleasant tales kept unfolding, Kinma's worry morphed into jealousy. These scared people knew only caring families and friends working together and had never even glimpsed the depths of depravity humans unhinged from society could engage in. Hardships existed for those in Malden, but there had been no inkling of the evil she saw daily for the last ten years.

They were actually talking about raspberry pie when she heard someone unseen say, "They're moving."

Everyone startled slightly before realizing it was Sam in the shadows. Fearful tension coursed back in as they all stood, happy storytelling forgotten. Kinma slid the handmade bow. Leo gave her onto a shoulder and checked her quiver.

As the others milled around, the very embodiment of nervousness, Milo sidled up next to her and whispered, "These guys aren't anywhere close to ready. Someone's gotta say something, at least make sure they're all pointed in the same direction and won't run at the first hint of aggression."

Taco looked her in the eyes and nodded in stoic agreement.

The idea of a speech did not appeal to her, but she realized they were right. Sam seemed to be the most rigid, the most cold-hearted, perhaps if he acted properly, the others would follow him. She moved next to Sam and, trying to sound surer than she felt, said, "I don't know you, and you don't know me but, before we head off together into this night, I'd like to say I've seen your home and heard your stories. The place you've built, the community you've created is clearly worthy of protecting.

"Where I came from, the place created by the madman roaming around out there in the dark should have been burned to the ground long, long ago. But it was not, it festered and grew and then rotted more and more, a place run and filled by inhumane monsters. And now that place has come here in force.

"These evil men and their leader will not hesitate to shoot, stab or beat everyone here to death if that means them getting half a step closer to sex, one tiny scrap of food or half a cup of cool water. If we hesitate, if we flinch, these animals will win, and they will utterly destroy everything you've built and replace it with their rot."

For a brief second, she met Sam's gaze in the growing silver moonlight, but it was impossible to tell what he was thinking or feeling. He merely gave a curt nod, before turning to stride into the pines, silently indicating for her to follow.

•　•　•

They only brought scant supplies, leaving everything else behind to make it look like they fled on short warning. So, despite it being summer, the damp chill of the night soaked into Louisa. Blankets would have been nice, but even more, she wanted a roaring fire, as much for warmth as for the comfort of having light to push back against the dark, brooding woods which seemed full of evil. However, no one would even discuss the possibility of lighting a fire tonight.

Louisa had tried to convince Morreign that she should go with the others and help in the fight rather than fleeing and hiding. Her request was politely denied, Morreign saying she would be good at keeping the children calm and quiet. Louisa expected the real reason was how the could not predict how she might react if Jacob was with the attackers. She could not come up with a decent argument to refute this unsaid point, so she followed Morreign's order and fled with the others.

Wrapping her coat tighter around her shoulders, she listened intently to the breeze like Sam taught her. No one was speaking, all conversation having dried up when the sun set. She did not know if they were scared of being heard or if they also were straining to hear distant gunshots like her, probably both. Regardless, she heard nothing but the chirping of two frogs nearby.

Griff slipped across the space to sit down beside her. He was fiddling with the short, yellow axe, the one him, Jacob and Tina always used to play the game Louisa was too bad at to join in on. After the trio disappeared, someone had stuck it in a poplar tree beside the river to serve as an informal memorial of sorts so now the yellow paint was faded and the metal was rusty. Louisa pressed her shoulder against him to steal some warmth and comfort as she softly said, "I wish all of this would hurry up."

"Really?"

The reason she wanted the night to hurry up was so she could see Jacob. She knew she should be afraid, afraid for herself and for all the others. But her main emotion was anticipatory excitement. Jacob was close, she could feel it. All she wanted was for him to be here with her and she no longer cared if this was a selfish want.

"I don't know, I guess I hate the waiting and not knowing."

"I'm pretty happy to sit and rest and wait, frankly. I'd wait forever actually. Although, I do feel like a useless twit, this is my fault, I should be out there with them, helping."

Louisa could understand why Morreign wanted Griff to stay behind. He looked painfully thin and tired and weathered. In no shape to fight if it came to that. Plus, when she looked in his eyes, they seemed strangely vacant and he sounded oddly distant when he spoke, his usual mocking tone completely gone. It was unnerving seeing her friend so changed.

Wanting to reassure him, she said, "None of this is your fault, it's all only horrible luck, and I think you've been through enough horrors that you can skip out on this one. There'll be lots to do after this is over and, if the plan doesn't work perfectly, we'll need your help to get us and the children out of here."

"Kinma, Taco, and Milo traveled all the way here too, and they went with the others to fight."

He had not yet told her everything about what they endured and she doubted he ever would be able to, but he had said enough for Louisa to realize it was beyond terrible. "Yeah, but they'd not gone through what you did before that. And they know these attackers, so I think Morreign wanted'em up there to provide their insight."

Griff, who used to love debate, gave up on the argument too easily as he merely said, "Sure, I suppose."

She opened her mouth to reassure him further, but she felt his breathing going slow and steady. Not sure if he actually fell asleep but he was definitely done talking. Pressing against him to steal some warmth and share some comfort, she sighed, forcing herself not to think of the pain her friend must have endured in order for him to have changed so completely. Staring into the blackness, she hoped time would heal him, bring back the coarsely funny and difficult boy she never thought she could want back so desperately.

CHAPTER THIRTY-FIVE

AUGUST 4, 2046

DAY THREE THOUSAND EIGHT HUNDRED AND FOURTEEN

Silence hung over the clearing. No light in the windows. No movement. Harrison knew the men wanted to rush in, but he figured caution was warranted as odd situations required caution. He made a crisp chirping noise three times, the sound carrying easily across the empty space, signaling the others to stay put.

He stood, clicked the safety off his rifle, enjoying the once familiar sensation of being properly armed, and slipped out of the trees. Sending in someone else to survey was an option, but he wanted to see things with his own eyes. Plus, taking on the risky assignments himself always garnered respect from the men.

Moving in behind a nearby cabin, Harrison peered inside the window. The room was gloomy but he could see the orange glow of embers in the wood stove. The dim light cast over the cramped space showed no people in the bed and dirty dishes on the table, a chair toppled over and a chess set scattered on the floor.

He hurried to the main building, moving in a crouch to a low window. Remnants of a recent fire in a stone fireplace and, through the shadows, he could make out a long table with dishes, but he saw no people. It was not late, unbelievable a whole village would be asleep already with things left in such disarray.

Carefully, he went to the porch and crept up the steps. No lock on the wide door so he opened it less than a crack and waited, holding his breath, expecting the barrage of an ambush but there was none. Leading with his rifle muzzle, he stepped into the lodge.

He quickly became sure the building was empty and a familiar wave of anger rolled over him. The fireplace still warm. Food, lots of food, prepared to be eaten in short order and all of it abandoned haphazardly. These people fled recently, very recently. They had been close, within reach, and they had all got away. One of his clumsy-footed scouts must have been seen.

His first instinct was to gather his men and track these cowards down, kill anyone able to fight back and harshly enslave the others. However, after a month of marching, the men would not take kindly to leaving warm buildings full of food to go floundering about in the dark woods. Also, there was a good chance he could be leading them straight in an arrow-filled ambush.

Harrison walked around the barely lit room one more time and decided it would have to be enough of a reward for tonight. He stepped out onto the porch and let out a crow's double caw to signal the eagerly waiting men that they could advance.

•   •   •

Lying on the hard ground, the cold dug into her hip like a knife. Morreign forced herself to her feet and then forced herself to take a handful of steps. She knew, if she did not walk about for a while, before long she would not be able to move at all and tonight would be extremely bad timing to come up completely lame.

Around her, a handful of people lay or sat, wrapped in their coats. No one but the children slept as everyone waited anxiously and uncertainly. In the dark night, people were unidentifiable lumps of shadow but, as she moved among them, she realized she could correctly name each of the human lumps as she recognized the sound of their breathing.

As she limped painfully past the shadows she knew to be Louisa and Griff huddled side by side, Louisa whispered out, "Morreign?"

Morreign did not really want company at that moment, but the girl stood up and began moving slowly around the makeshift campsite with her.

Louisa asked, "Can't sleep?"

"Trying to loosen up this damn hip. Don't think anyone's sleeping tonight anyhow."

"Griff might be but no one else is getting much rest."

The strikingly hollow look in Griff's eyes had concerned Morreign. She always figured his constant joking and ridiculing hid a deeper sensitivity and, with his defence mechanism of humor beaten away, she became worried Griff would be unable to deal with all he had been through. At least, for now, the boy was so exhausted Morreign doubted he was thinking about much of anything. If they had a future, she would have to look out for his emotional wellbeing.

"Stay close to him. Make sure he's alright, make sure he doesn't do anything foolish."

Sounding somewhat confused, Louisa said, "Sure. I will, but I don't think he's up for doing much of anything, foolish or otherwise. I'm sure once Jacob is back and things return to normal, he'll be ok."

Morreign only hesitated slightly before saying, "Alright, but keep an eye on him anyway. Things might not go easy, things generally don't these days."

•　　•　　•

Clearly, he could not stop them, best to let it play out. Harrison moved aside to supervise as the men tore through the heaps of supplies in the main building.

Shortly after calling them in, the well-trained men rapidly scoured the area and found nothing to kill or rape. Even in the darkness, they easily found the clear tracks of a mass of people recently fleeing away, moving away from the river, further into the trees. Talk of chasing the cowards down, mainly to take women, ended when Harrison raised the likelihood of them being ambushed in the blackness. Their easily distracted attention then shifted to the copious amounts of food. Tonight they would gorge and, at first light, they would chase down their prey.

There were only some brief squabbles over the best of the fare but, with more than enough for everyone, the minor arguments did not escalate far. Harrison usually followed the dictum that leaders ate last when on patrol but, given all the excess, he filled a plate and took a spot in the middle of the table as those nearby clapped him on the back. Harrison decided he deserved to, for once, greedily eat his fill and, when he was done, he would take his leave from the gorging brutes and relieve a guard outside.

•　　•　　•

Sam led the way, deftly stepping over roots and ducking under branches Kinma could not even see. Despite having spent much of her life in the woods, she felt painfully awkward as she tried to keep up and, when he abruptly stopped, she nearly crashed into his back.

Crawling the last ten feet through dewy grass, they reached the edge of the clearing beside the lodge. The windows were filled with light and people moved about inside. The predators were inside, not hunting through the woods. This was good news.

Sam pointed to one corner, and she saw a faintly visible shadow moving outside. As she wondered how Sam picked him out, the man crossed near a window allowing her to recognize him as Young Eddie carrying a rifle as he patrolled.

She whispered, "How many guards?"

Sam did not answer. Time seemed to stretch on forever as she focussed on keeping her breathing regular and quiet. Eventually, Young Eddie passed the window again.

Only one guard. It seemed wrong Harrison would be so lax. She opened her mouth to say this, but Sam pointed at the roof of a nearby cabin. Kinma strained to see and, eventually, the hint of the shape of a man crouched on the roof could be made out. A second guard in an elevated, hidden position, this was more like Harrison.

Sam whispered, "Only two. Rest inside. You watch, I'll get the others."

He slipped back into the trees to pass along the information. Kinma remained, laying on her belly, watching and listening. Her heart pounded in her chest, and a deep worry clutched at her. Despite being surrounded by violence and violent men for many years, she never actually took part in the killing until her last days at Thule. Tonight, intense bloodshed would come, and it would come because of her involvement as, without her warning, Morreign and the others might have surrendered. Likely Harrison would have done great damage to them regardless but, if this plan goes wrong, he would utterly and painfully destroy them for their defiance.

As she laid in the grass, fighting back fear, keeping watch and waiting for the eruption of fighting, she saw light spill out into the clearing. The door of the lodge opening. The sounds of loud men filled the night air for an instant before the light and sound faded with the door closing.

Two shadows came around the corner and met with the shadow of Young Eddie. Apparently, relieved of duty, the skinny man scurried off to feast with the others. In the blackness, she felt more than saw the man on the roof quickly slipping to the ground to hurry inside as one of the newcomers slowly climbed up to take his place.

When the new guard on the ground moved by the window, Kinma's breath caught. Only a glimpse in weak light but she was completely certain as, even without a clear view of the face, the haughty gait and rigid posture made it obvious it was Harrison.

Seeing the bastard striding through the dark, caused her to recall all the horror he caused, including the murdering of Hale. She now knew this course of action, coming after him, having Malden fight against him, was completely correct. Letting Harrison survive could not be tolerated, despite the risk, they needed to try to rid this world of him.

She carefully crawled backward into the trees. The others needed to know Harrison was out in the open and, perhaps, they could cut off the head before the body even knew they were there.

· · ·

Harrison knew it a sign of weakness, but he had to admit he felt better with a full stomach. He took in deep breaths of the fresh, summer night air. The pleasant smell of grass and dew filled his lungs. While not what he planned, perhaps a night of rest and reward was for the best. Tomorrow the men would be happy, and he was confident they would be able to easily track down the sheep in the light of day.

Keeping an eye on the night filled woods, he slowly paced out a lap of his new realm. Even in the starlight, the cabins seemed well maintained and stout. He did not like the idea of giving people separate accommodations, harder for him to know everything that was occurring so he would need to give some careful thought to setting the sleeping arrangements.

Piles of dry and split firewood filled the spaces under every eave. He plucked up a piece and was surprised to feel rough saw marks, somewhere these gardeners had a working saw. He set the stick back on the pile, pleased by the idea of no longer having to worry about keeping sufficient fuel supplies as getting men to chop and stack wood was a persistent problem at Thule. Having surveyed the food stores, Harrison knew there must be a decent garden. Even so, when he came across the wide swath of tilled soil full of carefully tended plants, a grin crossed his lips. The pending harvest meant they would be able to put away more than enough potatoes, carrots, and corn to easily last them through winter. He made a mental note to find out, when they tracked the sheep down, who among them knew how best to tend the crops and ensure they lived long enough to teach him the tricks.

The pleasant surprises continued as he toured further. Following his nose, tucked in behind a couple of cabins, he found a smokehouse with six grouses hanging amongst larger cuts of meat. They had been hearing the yips and howls of numerous coyotes for days so he figured that there must be game around, but he figured rabbits and squirrels, not sizable game like this. Ample meat would keep the men content while hunting would keep them entertained.

Moving back to the main building, Harrison revelled in his luck. They found a paradise. His reign would surely continue unabated.

He turned the corner in time to hear wet, angry splashing noises coming from the nearby cabin's rooftop. Harrison had placed Oliver up there as he was growing more and more lame from arthritis every day which made him eager to show any remnants of usefulness to avoid being excluded entirely. Before Harrison could scold the old twit for giving away his position, more retching was followed by a curse and the sounds of Oliver tumbling ungraciously off the roof. Without thought, Harrison leveled his rifle at the darkness, looking for the invisible attackers as he moved towards the fallen guard.

He leaned down to check the fallen man for injury and a sharp, stabbing pain struck Harrison's stomach. It forced him to double over, but the source of the agony was clearly internal rather than external as he felt his bowels go to water and vomit threatened to burst from his face. The food, the cowardly sheep poisoned the food.

CHAPTER THIRTY-SIX

AUGUST 5, 2046

DAY THREE THOUSAND EIGHT HUNDRED AND FIFTEEN

"We should move now. If we take out Harrison, everything else will be easier, much easier."

Kinma had hurried back to the group, eager to take advantage of being able to remove the Bank's leader. She tried to sound calm as she whispered, worried that showing too much emotion would make them disregard her as an overwrought woman, however, ire seeped into her tone regardless.

Taco nodded as Milo joined in to say, "She's right. Take him out, the rest will be a mess, probably end up fighting each over who's in charge."

They all looked to Paul, he shrugged and then whispered, "I understand and agree it would be good to remove the leader, but he is only one man. What do we do if he manages to call out an alarm? Fight all the rest out in the open? I say we keep steady on the plan, let it play out before we make our move."

It was not given as an order, more as a discussion point, but the others did not dispute the idea. Kinma was not surprised, she could practically taste the fear in the air. Maybe even more than fear for their own safety, a hesitation to kill hung over the group. These people seemed like they would choose to defer fighting forever, hoping old age would take care of their enemies.

Milo merely gave her a look shaking his head in minor disgust. Sam caught her eye and nodded but then, without a word, he stepped back into the trees. The rest settled back down, overly content to remain unbloodied. Kinma squatted down beside Paul, and whispered, "We can't wait all night. These are strong men, even with the plan in place they'll recover fast."

Kinma held herself back from adding that even if Harrison's group was greatly weakened by the poison, they would still make a worthy match for this frightened, untrained group. Keeping an agreeable tone, Paul responded, "Ok, we'll move soon but I want to make sure we take full advantage of the situation, we want them as weakened as possible."

They should have marched faster, having an extra day to get to know these people and let them get to know her might have given her enough insight to be able to explain to them the threat they were facing, might have given her enough sway to get them to listen to her. Not wanting to upset the uneasy group, Kinma decided to take her chances with Jacob's father. She pulled Paul further aside and whispered, "The plan is a good one, and it appears to be working but, at some point, metal is going to need to meet meat. Everyone here defers to you, I think you'll need to strike the first blow, and you will need to be decisive when you do."

Kinma felt the man nod next to her, but even that slight move felt hesitant. She sighed, all of this might end up being for naught.

•　•　•

Realizing the trap, Harrison tried to call out an alarm to his men, but his guts were being twisted in a vice and the intended yell came out as a gasp followed by a watery burst of vomit. He began to crawl, forcing himself to move despite the intense agony.

After stopping to heave and retch more, he laid back on the cool grass to catch his breath and listen. No more laughter or talking seemed to be coming from inside. Harrison feared he was entirely right, it was not simply a few pieces of badly preserved venison but a powerful poison lacing everything.

Rising on his knees to resume his desperate crawl, a crushing weight instantly landed on his back, pushing all the breath from his chest as he was compressed against the grassy earth. A hand covered his mouth as powerful blows cracked repeatedly into the base of his skull. He tried to struggle, tried to get the strong body off his back but the dizziness from the punches made the powerful nausea even worse, and he could not muster the needed strength.

Another blow to the back of his skull. He had to fight back. This could not be his death. After all he endured, his sad end could not be at the hands of a coward who poisoned him and attacked him from behind. Using all of his limited energy, he pushed up off the ground, not a strong move but enough to slightly dislodge the man for a second, allowing Harrison to turn over.

His attacker was short and wiry with shadow-filled eyes and no beard. Harrison could see no weapon, but the man now gripped his wrists tightly, using his knee to press down on his throat. Immediately realizing his weight was too far forward, Harrison managed to buck up, throwing the lighter man up and over his head. This broke the iron grip, but the bastard did not miss a step, springing around and twisting to land a powerful kick to the side of Harrison's ribs.

Despite the solid strike, Harrison managed to stumble away, gaining some valuable distance and he reacted just in time to catch the man's boot as he tried to kick him again. Using the leverage of his attacker trying to pull his foot back, Harrison let him yank him forward to fire out a wild right-hand swing.

Surprisingly, the blind, desperate punch hit, creating the satisfying crunch of knuckles connecting solidly with cheekbone. Apparently, the man was not used to brawling and did not anticipate the obvious counter-attack. Expecting the shot to temporarily incapacitate the smaller man, Harrison pulled him in closer, hoping to land a knockout uppercut, however, the attacker was not stunned and he immediately leaned into the move, smothering the punch as he grabbed Harrison in a bear hug and drove him back into the ground.

His poisoned insides revolted violently as the air rushed from his lungs and, before he could react, the assailant was back on top of him, his fists repeatedly striking his face and neck. Harrison stopped fighting back. This would be it.

The finality of death always intrigued Harrison as he could never figure why people cared so much about what happened in the world once they were gone. If you never knew what happened, how could you care that it had happened? As far as he was concerned, the earth would become dust once he died, everything ending with him. Resolved to his death and only waiting for consciousness to leave, he felt confused when the shadow stopped punching and a rag was crammed into his throat before being lashed in place.

Harrison wanted to react to this oddness but his stomach clenched in pain and his head swam mightily so he could do nothing as he was roughly rolled back onto his front. With a knee on his neck pressing his face into the earth, his arms were pulled behind his back and lashed together at the elbows, straining his shoulders to the point of popping. Then the victor silently lifted his trussed up prize to his feet.

Facing his attacker, Harrison looked into eyes with blurred vision. He realized the mad was annoyingly calm and unafraid, the type of soldier he always sought out. He simply put a finger to his lips in the universal signal of silence before turning him and pushing him towards the tree line.

Regardless of the painful bondage, the searing agony in his head from the beating and the torment raging in his stomach, a glimmer of hope found its way to Harrison's muddled thinking. The poison was a clever trick, but tricks were never enough. Only dedicated toughness and strong actions worked completely. This fool could have killed him, should have killed him and his mercy gave him hope.

●　　　　　●

Kinma had given up trying to rally Paul and the others into taking immediate action. The group was sitting in sullen silence waiting for whatever sign they were waiting for when Sam appeared out of nowhere and calmly said, "The guard on the roof fell off. Sick, not moving. I got the other guard on the ground."

This shocked Kinma. She asked, "Harrison? You killed Harrison?"

"Tied him to a tree."

"You left him alive?"

The man merely stared at her.

Kinma's concern over their kindness-fuelled reluctance was coming to fruition if the hardest of the men could not end the worst of their attackers, what would the others do? She said, "But he's come here to kill everyone."

The silent man merely looked back at her, annoyingly ignoring Kinma's statement.

Paul asked, "He's secure?"

A nod.

"It's time?"

Another nod.

Paul got to his feet, and the others shuffled up as well, immediately drawing knives, readying bows and picking up axes. Paul stood in the middle of the group, looking from person to person as he calmly said, "Think of every sweltering day spent chopping wood with blistered hands. Think of every black night far away from home checking traps in the snow with frozen legs. Think of all the endless trips hauling water from the river to the garden with aching backs. All that work, all that struggle and, if we falter now, if we flee or freeze or falter, if we don't do everything in our power right now to protect what is rightfully ours, we will be throwing all of our work away. Instead of leaving it to our children and their children, we'll be giving it to these bastards who have lived their lazy lives robbing and killing and destroying what others have built. Time to go to work."

With that, he stoically headed into the trees with everyone briskly following. As she hurried through the brush, struggling to keep up with the group, Kinma suddenly felt naïve and foolish, she had completely underestimated the resolve of these people.

When they reached the clearing, they spread out and broke into a fast jog as planned. This space was their home so, even in the moonlight, they knew every dip, root, and hole while Kinma found herself floundering in the dark, falling behind. They beat her to the lodge, and she watched as they did not hesitate before ripping open the door and darted inside. Biting back intense fear, Kinma gripped her knife and followed up the steps after them.

A body lay near the porch. Looking down at the filthy face with a tortured, purple hue, Kinma recognized Oliver, a rude, old man with a boorish laugh and arthritic knees. As she stepped over him to get inside a pungent, overwhelming smell filled her face. Vomit and shit. The odor of powerful sickness.

A gunshot cracked out and then another, and another. She could not tell where they were coming from, but those from Malden moved boldly forward regardless. Another gunshot. Then another.

As the mass made it through the doorway and spread out inside she could observe the chaos in the lantern light. Bodies covered the plank floor, a few men on their knees, trying to stand but most were curled up, clutching at their stomachs. The villagers moved about, rapidly firing arrows and swinging weapons at the incapacitated Bankers.

Walter, a stout man with a propensity for crude jokes, sat propped up in the far corner, a rifle held loosely across his lap. He was firing, but he seemed to lack the wherewithal to aim, his shots hitting harmlessly into the ceiling. Near the window, Young Eddie appeared less ill as he had managed reach his feet but, as he turned to face them, numerous arrows impaled him from various angles, and he dropped to the floor.

With no one fighting back, the Malden people paused to survey the scene, but only for an instant before Paul, followed by Leo and then the others, strode among the writhing men, slipping slightly on the slimy wooden planks as they ended their miserable lives. Paul moved to Walter, slumped in the corner, the only attacker maintaining any meaningful level of consciousness. Paul knock his gun away and leveled a hunting knife at the man's throat.

"Where's Jacob?"

Whites filled the ill man's eyes as he looked up at Paul. He opened his mouth, apparently to answer but instead of words, a greenish sludge gurgled out on to his tangled beard. Paul grabbed a handful of his dirty hair and shook the huge head, asking more forcefully, "Jacob. You were following him here. Where is Jacob?"

His face tilted back, a gruesome grin crossed Walter's face, and he said, "The kid? Dumb kid wandered off downriver, bastard thought he'd tricked us..."

"Wandered off? Trick you?"

Walter spat out a string of yellow bile. "Sick. Could barely move, birds probably eating his eyes by now so screw you and your friends..."

Kinma saw the big man's glassy eyes glance to the side. Following his look, she glimpsed blonde hair behind overturned chairs. The Viking. A terrible mistake. She should've warned Paul, should've made sure they dealt with the most dangerous man first. Before she could call out an alarm, the chairs flew into the air with incredible speed. The Viking, apparently having been playing possum, jumped to his feet, grabbed up his rifle and started firing.

An intense, piercing pain exploded in Kinma's arm, twisting her about as she tumbled back through the door and fell backward down the steps all the way to the grass. Before she could comprehend what was happening, a heavy boot stomped on her as the Viking ran over her, fleeing into the night.

Sam, reacting quicker than the others, stepped in the massive man's path but the beast easily and brutally knocked him aside with the butt of his rifle, barely breaking his staggering strides as the minor obstacle fell away. Kinma tried to stand, tried to follow him, but the searing pain ripping through her arm overwhelmed her as her body failed to listen to her mind's commands. She could only watch the brutal savage disappear across the clearing and into the darkness beyond.

CHAPTER THIRTY-SEVEN

AUGUST 5, 2046

DAY THREE THOUSAND EIGHT HUNDRED AND FIFTEEN

The sun did not stay down too in August, and a hint of grey light could already be seen to the east. Dawn. Morreign feared it might be the last dawn she would ever see. Hours ago, they heard distant gunshots. Not many shots and the sound was faint, so there could have been more they did not hear.

While she tried to keep everyone calm, she thought those sent to fight would have come to get them by now if they had won. When the impending daylight came, the Bankers would likely hunt through the woods, eagerly looking for the children and women who fled.

In the growing light, she surveyed the remnants of the residents of Malden. Weary women, a handful of scared children and a battered Griff. The women tried to placate the hungry children with the scraps of food they had brought while scanning the woods like deer catching a strange scent on the wind. Many eyes landed on her face, but they apparently saw her worry and uncertainty because they all quickly diverted their gazes.

Perhaps, if they marched back to Malden, they could surrender to the invaders and receive mercy but, remembering Kinma's description of those waiting for them, Morreign easily discarded this idea. Fleeing deeper into the woods seemed like the logical choice even if this group could not move fast or far. She had started getting everyone on their feet when there was a sound. Branches breaking, something large moving in the brush.

The sad group instantly huddled together around the children, clutching their pathetic tools turned to ad-hoc weapons. If she was not so afraid,

Morreign would have laughed at the futile sight but, instead, she drew her own kitchen knife and joined the trembling mass.

Breathing the only sound as everyone strained to hear without making a noise. They all jumped when one of the children, boisterous Adam, loudly barked out, "Marco!"

Before they could react, Morreign heard deep laughter from the woods before a man called back, "Pollo!"

Leo. He always played the silly game with the kids. Apparently, Adam's young ears were more honed than those of the frightened adults, and he recognized Leo's deep voice in the trees.

Leo and Errol stepped through the shadow-filled pines. They looked worn out, and their clothes were bloodstained, but they both carried rifles which must have been taken off the attackers. Met with a barrage of eager questions, Leo lifted his hands above his head and, with his massive grin, bellowed, "Woa, woa, it's ok. A few people got hurt, but I think everyone will be alright. Louisa's trickery, those mushrooms, worked brilliantly. We took care of 'em but we all need to go back right now 'cause one of them, a huge guy, managed to get away and he's got a gun. We've been looking for him, but he keeps eluding us -"

Louisa blurted out, "And Jacob? Jake is with them?"

Leo shook his head slightly. "No, he was not with them but-"

An impossibly loud crack startled Morreign, freezing her as it took a second to recognize the immense sound of a nearby gunshot. Leo gasped out a curse before he crumpled to the grass as everyone else dove to the ground. A mountain of a man stumbled hurriedly out of the trees, a light-colored beard covering his face and long blonde hair falling over his shoulders. Errol managed to fire back but missed as the intruder calmly took aim and fired back, shooting the young man in the shoulder and dropping him before barking out, "You all stay on the damn ground."

Leveling the barrel at Morreign, as she was the only person still on her feet because her hip would not allow her to dive down, he ordered, "Throw them rifles over here. Try anything stupid, and I put holes in all your skulls."

Her mind racing, Morreign realized the monstrous man must be the one Leo said escaped, must have followed him and Errol. With no choice, she picked up Errol and Leo's rifles and awkwardly flung them into the grass.

The glaring beast moved forward, she could see vomit in his beard and glassiness in his eyes but, despite his shambling walk, pallor tone, and vacant eyes, he seemed to be ignoring the poisoning as he carefully surveyed the group, a predator sizing up prey as he circled. Finally, glowering down at Samantha as she cowered over her daughter, Paulina, he growled to himself, "This'll work. This'll work."

•　　•　　•

At the impossibly loud banging, Louisa had instinctively fell to the ground. Even though she did not know exactly what was occurring, she knew it was far from good. She risked a glance up and managed to see a towering man's face as he spun his rifle and slammed the butt into Samantha's ribs before forcing her off her child with the thrust of a heavy boot.

Eight-year-old Paulina screamed and kicked, but she may as well have been an insect complaining about a thunderstorm as the beast plucked her up and tucked the struggling child under his arm like a loaf of bread. Samantha managed to get up on her feet. "Wait, wait. Leave her be. I'll go, it'll be easier with me."

Holding the rifle on the group with one hand, the bear of a man looked Samantha up and down with a penetrating gaze that made Louisa's stomach clench. Eventually, he tossed Paulina to the trampled dirt and waved the weapon at Samantha, snarling out, "Clothes off and no sounds or you die, die an ugly death before I switch my attentions back to the girl."

Samantha began to awkwardly undress at gunpoint, but before she could get her pants unbuttoned, Louisa watched the massive man throw her aside with a huge arm as he casually fired the rifle one-handed.

Louisa spun back to see that Griff had gotten up from the grass, his short-handled yellow axe held over his head. The beast had apparently seen this too as he expertly fired one round into the middle of the thin chest of her friend. A grimace of pain filled Griff's face, but he still managed to rear back and spin the axe from his hands. It flew fast, rotating exactly two times before burying itself where the gunman's shoulder met his neck, making a sickening, wet thud.

The rifle muzzle flew up as their attacker grabbed at his neck where blood now poured around the metal wedge buried in his flesh. Worried he would shoot aimlessly into the group, Louisa lifted and started to move at him, but before she could reach him, Morreign dove across the grass, throwing herself at the man's knees. Morreign let out a pained screamed and seemed to bounce off him as if he were a stone wall, but his leg did bend causing the beast to stumble over as he fired rounds harmlessly into the air before he toppled.

Instinctively knowing that hesitation could be fatal, Louisa scrambled over Morreign, plucking up her knife as she crashed down on the fallen man. The small blade seemed feeble but, when she used all her might to bury it in his huge chest, it slid in shockingly easily, finding its way between bone and his movement stopped completely.

Freed from the threatening gunman, the others scurried to their feet, rushing to help the wounded. Louisa managed to roll Griff on to his back, pleading with him to speak. He stared up at her with unblinking, cold eyes. Frantic, she tore open his coat and shirt, abruptly stopping when she saw the perfect hole right in the middle of his narrow chest. No one could survive such an injury, Griff was gone.

• • •

Kinma's arm throbbed horribly, but she did not think the damage would be permanent. The bullet went cleanly through her forearm, and a young woman named Emmanuelle did an excellent job of cleaning and bandaging the wound. Lucky. Luck seemed to have been on their side all night.

Two other villagers, Ram and Hurley, were also hit, one in the calf and one was grazed in the thigh, but they were able to staunch the bleeding and both would survive so long as infection could be avoided. Sam received the nastiest injury, the Viking's rifle butt to the head leaving him with the symptoms of a severe concussion. Still, only four injured, she would not have even dared to wish for a more lopsided victory.

The Viking, however, remained on the loose. While she cursed herself for not considering his existence in their planning, Kinma figured he likely cut his losses and was headed for the hills, never to be seen again.

Before he left with most of the men to hunt down the Viking, Paul ordered everyone else to remove the corpses from the lodge so none of the others would need to see the carnage left from the bloody night. Now, sitting on one of the cabin porches, under medical orders to rest, Kinma watched as the massive heap of Bankers' bodies they had piled in the middle of the clearing was put to the torch. She supposed she should feel some revulsion or at least a hint of sadness at her former companions meeting such a gruesome end but instead she merely felt a peaceful numbness.

As putrid, greasy, black smoke billowed from the heap of corpses, Paul reappeared through the trees and came over. "How's the arm?"

"Hurts but I'll live. No luck finding the Viking?"

"Nah. If Sam was on his feet, we might have had a chance, but with no moonlight, his tracks disappeared."

Paul looked around, becoming concerned as he asked, "Leo and Errol aren't back with Morreign and the others yet?"

"No. Not yet"

Paul pondered this for a moment before saying, "Guess it's for the best, they're still finishing the cleanup. And we have one other matter to deal with."

"Right."

"I could use your help since you know him. Are you strong enough to come with me?"

Her arm ached but the thought of getting to interrogate a beaten and tied Harrison was impossible to resist so Kinma nodded, and they hurried off the porch.

•　　•　　•

Someone roughly grabbed the gag from Harrison's mouth. His head throbbed, and his stomach continued to cramp as intense chills and retching racked his body. His arms were numb from having his shoulders harshly wrapped around a tree trunk, ropes holding him tight.

He forced his eyes open. His tormentors stood above him, but his bindings would not allow him to look up enough to see anything but shins and boots. An unseen someone asked, "Where's Jacob?"

Confusion filled Harrison's rattled mind. His mouth tasted foul, slimy with bile and coppery with his own blood but he managed to whisper, "Who?"

"My son. Jacob. You were following him."

The kid. They were asking about the damn kid. He was a two-days-walk downriver by now, thinking he was leading the danger away. Or his illness did him in. Either way, he decided the unpleasant topic was not something he should discuss at this point in time, so Harrison stayed silent.

A woman squatted down before him, her face right in front of his. Kinma. Goddamn Kinma. What the hell was she doing here? That idiot Clarence let her go. Her presence explained the poison. The sheep knew they were coming and set their trap perfectly.

"Good to see you again, Harrison, especially under these circumstances."

Her haughty voice made fury rush in through his agony but Harrison forced it down, knowing escape required him to be calm and collected. He said, "Hello Kinma."

She merely said, "Tell us where Jacob is, and you can go free."

Despite the pain, he let out a tiny scoff as he knew this was an obvious ploy, they would not be letting him go any time soon.

She continued, "Your asshole followers are all dead, you have no one left to lead. We can let you go, you're too pathetic now to be a threat to anyone. Frankly, the idea of you wandering around in the woods all alone, waiting to be killed by weather or hunger or a bear, appeals to me."

He did not doubt that the Bankers were all dead. They ate and drank even more of what he ate and drank. The sheep's cowardly trick worked and now, seeing Kinma, he understood how they knew they were coming. That fool Clarence could not keep Kinma even for a minute, and she rushed out here like Paul Revere. However, he knew her and knew she was not entirely evil. Maybe she was telling the truth. If they did let him go, he could possibly survive. Harrison said, "Jacob is out there."

A man's voice eagerly asked from above, "Where? Where did you last see him?"

Enjoying the desperation-filled tone, Harrison shook his head and calmly said, "First I need water. Call it a sign of goodwill."

Kinma and the men untied him from the tree and marched him back to the clearing on his numb legs. He could not look away from the smoldering heap, the remains of his invasion force, the remains of his command. He knew he should feel remorse and regret, but now he was only concerned with saving his future.

They walked him toward the main building and, off to the side, he saw Milo and Taco watching the flames licking up through the greasy smoke. Noticing him, they both gave a smile followed by a mocking salute. Another indignity added to his growing rage which he struggled to keep pushed down as they took him up the steps.

The smell of vomit and blood and gunpowder filled the air. Boots, coats, belts, blades and other items once cherished by his men were piled in one corner while the red stains covering most of the floorboards declared their violent ends. His well-trained, overpowering force made too weak to even make it outside and put up a fight. Remnants of the tainted food remained on the table. He cursed internally, unable to believe they were so easily fooled once they came so far and got so close.

After a whispered conversation, Harrison could not hear, they pushed him into a narrow side room. No window. A narrow shelf along one wall. An old wood stove in the corner. The men pressed him into the corner, sat him on the floor and handed him a plastic bottle of water. His arms trembled under the minor weight as he lifted it with weak hands. He drank. His tortured guts clenched for a moment, wanting to expel even water but he managed to keep it down and drank again. A couple of deep breaths and his head cleared slightly. One more drink and he looked up at his captors.

The leader looked haggard with a scruffy beard and curly hair, the arms of his coat stained brownish red with the blood of Harrison's former army. Strong family resemblance to the kid, likely his father. Kinma was thinner than when he last saw her, having endured the same difficult trip from Thule as him and a thick bandage covered her forearm, but her intense glare seemed formidable all the same.

Seeing no reason to lie, Harrison spoke, "We left Jacob downriver, about a half day's hike. I think he realized we were behind him and he wanted to lead us away, but we spotted the village anyway because he stopped to take one last look and my scout saw smoke above the trees. My guess is he's still stumbling along, thinking we're following behind him."

The father merely nodded and said, "Ok."

Kinma leaned in and said, "You best not be lying."

Harrison grinned and answered, "Scout's honor."

When they picked up a rusty chain, clearly intending to bind him to the wood stove, Harrison asked, "I thought you said I could go?"

The father muttered, "Not yet."

After carefully chaining his leg to the stove with a hearty padlock and retying his hands with a cord, they hurried out of the room. Sitting there, sick, beaten and alone, most men would have wasted their energy despairing about their situation and bemoaning their bad fortunes. Harrison, however, knew being alive meant he had a chance.

The soft fools had tied his hands in front of him, not seeing the battered man as much of a threat. He began searching his makeshift cell for anything useful, telling himself to remain confident he would find a way out in fairly short order.

•　　　•　　　•

With her hand on his wide chest, Morreign, her ruined hip screaming in pain after slamming into the gunman's knees, could feel Leo's heartbeat weakening as she looked down into the once strong man's eyes which were slowly closing, then flashing open for an instant before slowly closing again. A gurgling, rattling noise came from his slightly opened mouth, and tears rushed forward when Morreign realized where she recognized the strange sound from, in the last minutes of his life, little Huck made a softer version of that distinct noise.

With a trembling voice, Morreign said, "We're ok now, Leo. Griff and Louisa got the guy. We're ok. We'll get you back, everything'll be fine."

She stopped talking as the rattle stopped and she figured it was over, her brother-in-law gone but then he gave a weak cough as his eyes fluttered open again. He whispered, "Errol? Errol ok?"

She glanced over. Errol had been hit in the shoulder, he was conscious and talking. Impossible to tell but it did not seem fatal.

Morreign said, "He's ok. Flesh wound."

Letting his eyes close again, Leo nodded as he mumbled, "Good. Good. We screwed up coming here. Should've have known the prick could've circled back on us like that, probably walked right on our damn tracks and followed us straight to you. I'm glad Errol'll make it at least."

"You'll make it too, Leo. Rest easy, we'll get you back to the Lodge and get you fixed up."

A tiny grin lifted the corner of his lips as another rattle came out. When it passed, he whispered, "Sure, Morreign, sure, sure..."

Morreign realized that before the Longest Night, before they fled, Leo, like most friends, always called her Mo but soon after they arrived at Malden he only called her Morreign, actually only Paul ever called her Mo anymore. An odd thought to cross her mind as she watched one of her oldest friend's life slip away. She said, "Listen to me, I'm always right, you know that. Magical instincts and all that."

"'Fraid not this time. Tell my girls I love 'em, and I'm proud of 'em, ok?"

Choking back a sob, Morreign tried to sound strong as she said, "No, you'll tell them yourself."

With the hint of humor completely gone, he whispered, "Tell them for me."

Giving up the pointless ruse, she let the tears come and said, "Ok, I will."

With that, the awful rattle came back for an awful minute before the soft heartbeat stopped and Leo went entirely silent.

•　　•　　•

Jacob tripped. He did not know what he tripped over, it could have been nothing given how tired and wobbly his legs felt. Forget taking in water or food, all night his burning, swollen throat made it hard to even breathe in air.

His falling seemed slow, like a dry leaf drifting to the ground on a calm day. However, Jacob knew he was going to hit hard, and he knew there was nothing he could do about it, his arms to numb to move to stop his fall.

Crashing into the rocky ground pushed the last ounce of breath and energy from his ruined body. Standing back up might as well have been flying to the moon.

As sleep poured in at him and his eyes closed, he could only hope he led them far enough away. Then it dawned on his fever-wracked mind: he could not stay here. Harrison would find his body lying on the bank and stop marching, set up camp here where they could easily stumble across someone from Malden. Jacob needed to use the last ounce of his life to hide. Hide so Harrison could not be sure he stopped and would continue on, looking for his escaped rabbit.

With great effort, he got to his knees and, with great deliberation, he crawled up the gravelly bank towards the trees, trying vainly to hide his tracks as delirium threatened to overtake his thinking.

•   •   •

"What do you think? He lying?"

Kinma pondered Paul's question. Harrison did not do things without a reason. She shrugged. "Don't think so, the story is sensible and, I mean, why would he lie now?"

She saw renewed hope alright on Paul's painfully tired face, and she wished she had not raised expectations. Louder, to the group assembled in the lodge, he said, "Right. Ok, I know everyone is worn out, but we need to go look, need to go now before Jacob can get any farther away."

Not surprising, the weary people immediately rallied and eagerly formed into search parties before seeking out supplies and gear. Kinma wanted to go, find Jacob and bring him home but fatigue soaked through her and pain radiated unpleasantly up her wounded arm. When she offered to go, Paul probably sensed hesitation in her tone and kindly explained she should stay behind, keep an eye on Harrison and heal up. Kinma did not fight this decision.

Within fifteen minutes, she stood on the porch of the lodge to watch men and women of Malden marching, in boots still covered in the blood of their attackers, towards the river and silently wished them luck, deeply wanting them to get Jacob back to where he belonged.

CHAPTER THIRTY-EIGHT

AUGUST 10, 2046
DAY THREE THOUSAND EIGHT HUNDRED AND TWENTY

Intense discussions were going on in the Lodge, but Morreign felt too crushed, too wretched and too tired to join in. The continual conversations over the last few days were bizarre mixtures of muted relief at having survived the attack, worrying about the wounded, grieving over their losses, all mixed among angry debates over what to do with the captive Harrison. Now that was all joined by wonderings over how the search parties, which returned empty-handed this afternoon, had failed to find Jacob.

Morreign had needed to flee all the noise so, feeling slightly guilty, she had claimed she needed to rest her extra ruined hip, and she was hiding out in her cabin when she heard a soft knock. She wanted to ignore it but figured they would only come in to check on her anyway, so he opened the door and was surprised to find Kinma.

With deep empathy in her eyes, Kinma said, "Sorry, I hate to bother you, but I was hoping we could talk."

Feeling relief it was Kinma and not a Malden resident who wanted to pontificate about what they thought everyone should do, Morreign said, "Of course, come in."

She poured dandelion tea into a cup for Kinma, and the two sat at the table. Kinma asked, "You ok?"

"Yeah, yeah, the hip's sore but not nearly as bad as my head, listening to all that chatter. After what we've all been through, you'd think we could take a moment and simply reflect and recuperate instead of blathering on."

Kinma nodded and said, "Well, thanks to those poison mushrooms, there's a lot less recuperating than I figured we would need – suppose people are filling that void with talk. The poison truly was a stroke of brilliance."

Three years ago, Jacob and Griff had come across a massive patch of orange topped mushrooms by the Creek. Sam identified them as a type of fly mushroom, declaring them to be highly poisonous. Morreign, thinking of the children running free, had the immediate instinct to bury them but a plague of mice had been menacing Malden for months, and Boris suggested they carefully pick the mushrooms, dry them out and sprinkle some bait with the dust. Morreign remained uneasy about the poison being nearby, but she could not argue with how well it eradicated troublesome rodents.

When Louisa, whose parents attempted to mercy poison her as a child, interrupted

their meeting with the sad idea of somehow doing the same to the attackers, Morreign's mind turned to the metal canister on the top shelf where it had been silently waiting for the mice daring to return. She wasn't sure if the dried mushrooms kept enough potency to be effective, but she figured, at least the poison might make them slightly ill, slow them somewhat. When she heard of the terrible damage the mushrooms inflicted on the Bankers, ridiculously, Morreign's instant, unconscious reaction was to refresh and redouble her worries about having such a dangerous item sitting about.

"More Louisa's idea than mine, I wanted to throw those damn mushrooms out a long time ago."

Kinma took a sip of tea and then said, "I understand you're tired of the talk but, I'm sorry, I think there's one thing we truly do need to discuss."

Guessing what Kinma was thinking because she was thinking the same thing, Morreign said, "Harrison?"

"People are talking about locking him up or exiling him."

"As you can see, we do like to talk here."

Kinma, apparently taking this comment as indecision, leaned back and said, "Look, I know this man and I know what he's capable of. People made the mistake, back at the beginning, of following him, of giving him control because everyone was scared and hungry and he handled all of it much better than anyone else thought they could. Once he was ensconced it proved immensely difficult to oust him, impossible may-"

Morreign lifted her hand to cut her off. "I know, don't worry, I know. We need a definitive solution."

A relieved sigh. "Ok, I'm glad we are of one mind on this. At the Bank, this sort of matter was handled in draconian fashion by Harrison, I was not sure if the people here would act in the same way. You know the people here, how do we go about doing it without causing too much damage or upheaval? Maybe some sort of trial, a jury."

Morreign wanted to laugh. Kinma was worried she lacked the resolve to execute Harrison. In reality, the only reason Harrison continued to draw breath was because Morreign did not know if death was sufficient. Ever since the attack, she found herself reveling in a hazy dream of doing harm to the leader who caused so much grief, the man who hurt her child and ensured he could not return home. Torture was the wrong word, although that idea had crossed her mind in moments of weakness. Now, what she wanted was to humiliate him and make him endure at least a sliver of the emotional suffering she felt.

Sitting across from Kinma, Morreign realized she also did not want to close the chapter. Harrison was a link to Jacob. A weak one, but a link nonetheless. The last person to see her son.

Foolish. All of it. Jacob was gone, and the evil man in the Lodge was not going to change that. Harrison was a threat to Malden and threats to Malden needed to be eliminated. At least, in this case, the threat deserved his punishment. Boris' words rang in her mind, "Will doing or not doing something risk what's here?"

She sighed and asked, "Do you know what we do when someone peaceful stumbles across this place and then wants to leave?"

Kinma only cocked her head and looked quizzically at Morreign so she continued, "Most everyone here thinks we let them go but, actually, I walk them out of the Clearing, to an old plank bridge over the Creek, pretending to be pleasantly escorting them on their way, and then another member from the Committee puts an arrow in their back."

Morreign forced her ruined hip to stand up.

• • •

Kinma got up and followed the woman out of her cabin as she limped straight towards the lodge without another word.

Kinma knew how Morreign was going to handle Harrison, and she found herself respecting the decision. Malden embracing brutality seemed wrong as it destroyed her image of a tranquil paradise, but she knew the horrible man deserved to fall from a tall tree with a short rope around his neck. They needed to put an end to the evil bastard who terrorized and ruined people without thought or regret. The evil monster who marched for thirty days to destroy this place of kindness. The evil charmer who could get people to follow him against their better thoughts. The evil demon who ultimately killed Hale for wanting something better for everyone.

People inside the lodge were continuing to talk in small groups, and they turned to look at them as they came through the door. A few called out questions of Morreign which the woman did not appear to hear as she moved through the crowded room and, without slowing, plucked a carving knife off the long table.

Murmurs followed them as the others began to realize where she was heading and what she was planning. Paul stood up first and hurried after them, saying, "Morreign, I get, I do but you can't simply-"

Paul had been one of the people arguing for keeping Harrison locked up. Kinma, gently placed a hand on his chest, stopping him with a minute shake of her head as Morreign opened the door to the storage room.

•　　•　　•

Harrison, with bloodied and wrecked fingernails, had managed to pry loose a nail from a floorboard in the storage room. For days now, he had obsessively filed away at the chain holding him to the stove. He could not tell how much damage he would need to before the link would break, but he figured he might be close and this perceived closeness prompted his tired, ruined hand to scrape the nail faster against the metal.

The door opened, interrupting his work. Not time yet for them to bring him food, this was something different. He instinctively palmed the nail in his bloody hand while he stumbled to his feet, sweeping the weakened chain behind him. He managed to fortify his stance and fix his glare as a middle-aged woman limped in.

Harrison saw her before, the second day he was locked up, she had merely stepped inside the room, stared at him for a moment and then left without a word. While the others here had seemed hesitant and unsure, the look on this woman's face was different. Now, on her return, only the dirty knife clutched in her hand held his attention.

He said, "Wait now, we can talk about options. I was promised that I would be allowed to leave once I provided the requested information and I did that, over five days ago. So, now, I will simply go, never to be seen again."

She stopped a few feet in front of him and calmly shook her head.

Panic raced through Harrison, filling him with adrenaline. He reared back and kicked the leg held by the compromised chain with his all his might. The metal bit into his flesh when the slack ran out, holding tight despite his efforts. He strained further, thinking he could feel some give, surely it would break and surely the world would at least let him fight back.

The woman seemed unfazed by his struggle as she stepped closer. Harrison grabbed at her with his bound hands. The woman quietly said, "Stop."

Harrison ignored the order and bent to pull at the chain with his worn hands as he stated, "I can help you, I know things. I can work-"

A finger on his chin, lifting up his face, interrupted his one-sided negotiations. The woman looked at him, nothing but coldness on her face. He opened his mouth to try and convince her, but sudden, tight, enormous pain seared into the base of his neck. Then another intense pain. Then nothing. Then blackness.

•   •   •

Morreign left the knife in the base of Harrison's skull, letting it fall with him as the dead man tumbled heavily to his side.

When she turned, she was not surprised to see a number of people crammed in the doorway, staring with opened mouths. All she wanted to do was go back to her cabin, sit at her table, sip tea, look out the window and recall happy memories of her children. But, looking at all the faces, she knew she needed to say something, needed to let them know this would not be a place of unabashed brutality but that threats could not be ignored and that Malden could not be a place where evil would be allowed to fester and grow.

"Ten years ago, we were forced to come here, forced from our homes and lives because narcissists, greedy for power and attention, destroyed our civilization, a civilization built by millenniums of generations. They killed pure innocents who wanted nothing but to exist, killed them as if they were ants scurrying about their feet, simply to feed their egos and increase their control. I refuse to let those demons rise back up in this new world, in our world."

•   •   •

A cold spitting rain fell on Jacob. He didn't know if he could call it waking as Jacob merely became conscious at some point, pulled back into himself from the far-off place where he could not think, where nothing existed. He thought he had heard laughter. Or voices. Voices. Close by, saying his name, yelling his name through his deep sleep. His lips would not listen when he ordered them to move, ordered them to call back. The voices, which were probably only in his mind, moved on. But he thought a smell drifted through the damp, the smell of the coarse soap they made at Malden. Only a hint of tallow on the wet air but he knew the odor completely as it hung over everything and everyone back home.

He figured the voices and smell to simply be illusions, exhausted confusion making his wants worm their way into his muddled reality. He tried to shake it off, reminding himself he was in the middle of nowhere, hiding in a musty hole under moldy logs, waiting for death to take him. But hints of the smell persisted.

What if it was real? What if, somehow, someone from home was actually here? The simple idea made him warm with happiness, through all the hurt and pain and sorrow, it made him glad. Even though he knew any thoughts of home would make him more miserable later, when he learned it was all imagined foolishness, Jacob decided to let himself wallow in the idea, knowing he may not have a later to be worried about.

But, the end did not come and, eventually, his eyes drifted open of their own accord. Sunlight through a crack in the branches. Worry instantly struck at him: he had been there too long. Harrison must be close. Then, through the confusion, he recalled. He was no longer marching, he was hiding, hiding in a self-made tomb. He was to stay here forever so morning, noon or night made no difference.

An uncertain number of days ago, after falling on the gravel, certain he could go no further, he had crawled up off the river bank where he found some moss-covered deadfall under a massive pine, making a musty cave barely big enough to squeeze into. Unsure if this would do enough to hide his corpse from Harrison, he managed to break a few branches to cover the shadowed entrance to complete the grave before giving into sickness-soaked exhaustion.

Now, Jacob's head was splitting, and his body ached, but he could think again. He tried to figure how many days had he been curled up in the musty hole, wondering how he remained alive. Three days? Four? More. Then he realized something important, he was not being tormented by powerful chills. The fever was gone. He swallowed. Minor pain in his throat but not the scorching fire of before.

Extreme dehydration and vertigo made moving incredibly difficult, but he managed to climb out of his shelter. He could not stand, but stretching his sore limbs on the forest floor felt good, and Jacob was shocked as he could not recall the last time something felt good. He took in a deep breath of pine-scented air before his powerful thirst pulled him to crawl down to the river to drink.

.   .   .

Her bedroom felt painfully small. Louisa knew she should go out, get out of the tight space and take in some fresh air, do something useful but she couldn't. It was now clear and final, Jacob was not coming back. She needed to say goodbye.

Sitting crossed legged on the hard bed, she forced herself to let her best friend, the only person she could remember ever loving, leave her. With the hope of his return evaporated and all the thoughts of what their reunion would be like gone, a powerful emptiness filled her, and she knew it would remain for a long time. But, eventually, she would sleep and, eventually, she would wake up and, eventually, she would go help with chores and, eventually, she would feel partially alive again. Eventually. Hopefully.

CHAPTER THIRTY-NINE

AUGUST 14, 2046
DAY THREE THOUSAND EIGHT HUNDRED AND TWENTY FOUR

Walking up to the Lodge, Morreign wondered yet again if this might be a terrible mistake. Holding a funeral for Leo, Tina and Griff made sense, they knew they were dead. She was less sure about memorializing Jacob. However, Louisa said she wanted for them to have a memorial for Jacob at the same time as the others and Morreign she figured, with all that happened, it made sense to have the community mark it all on one day, give them a solely terrible, definitive event from which to move on from.

Before she limped inside, she turned to look at the sun rising over the Clearing. Tradition dictated for funerals to be held at first light. Morreign started that custom nearly a decade ago for no other reason than, back then, there was always so much to do she did not like people wallowing in misery all day as they waited for the ceremony, best to get it over with as soon as possible so people could get on with living. Apparently, she had forgotten that lesson, maybe she needed to apply it to herself, maybe this event did make sense.

Paul opened the door and silently put his arm around her waist as she stepped into the Lodge so they could say goodbye to their last child.

·   ·   ·

He could not move quickly, but he could move, and that was enough for Jacob. He did not know what happened while he recovered in his foliage cavern and he did not know how long he was in there, but he figured Harrison's hoard should have passed by, continuing to look for Malden in the wrong direction.

Regardless, the beasts surely remained out here somewhere, searching and hunting as Harrison did not seem like the type to give up. Jacob knew he needed to get back, get back and warn them all about the danger he had foolishly led to their doorstep.

Finally, as he stumbled around a bend, the crooked tree came into view. He expected to feel relief and joy at seeing the marker for Malden, but he still felt intensely weak while the river appeared deep and strong. With no choice, he stripped out of his rags and avoided looking down at his emaciated body as he waded into the frigid current.

•   •   •

Feeling like an uninvited guest, Kinma slipped down from the room she had been given upstairs and took a spot along the back wall of the Lodge's common room, standing next to Milo and Taco who both looked as out of place as she felt. She watched people solemnly file inside, realizing not only that she was a stranger here, but she was also entirely unfamiliar with the nature of the ceremony. There was a fleeting, uncertain, childhood memory of a great-uncle's funeral before the Bombs but other than that she could not recall any memorials. There were many deaths at Thule, but they were not civilized enough to hold formal services.

As the room filled, she knew she was supposed to be thinking about the poor girl she never met who jumped to her death. And the scared, hurt boy who told her all those wonderful stories to pass the dreadful time in their cell. And the damaged young redhead who walked all the way back here despite his injuries to warn his family. And the larger-than-life man she only briefly met who seemed to mean so much to this place. However, her mind kept drifting to Hale.

While Kinma knew life at Thule was immensely difficult she did not truly appreciate how unfair and miserable that existence was until she saw Malden. With that appreciation came a deeper understanding of how amazing Hale and his ability to love her in that horrible situation had been. Thinking back, seeing the ruined women working sadly in the kitchens or dancing sadly on the tables for the perverted men, she knew, without his caring and sacrifice, she would not have survived, or at least not survived with any sense of humanity remaining within her.

Once everyone settled, and the room grew quiet, Paul stood and began to softly sing. Within three notes, the others joined in, their combined voice immediately filling the space. Listening to the bitterly sweet song, she said a final thank you to Hale for caring long enough so fate could bring her to this place. Then she made a silent pledge that she would go back to Thule and get those trapped there against their will. She would bring them back here where they could live in safety, she would care long enough so she could return the favor paid to her by Hale.

•   •   •

Tears poured from Louisa, and she did not care that everyone around her could see. She let them pour as her shoulders shook.

As the others sang the soft song, she recalled when they were children, sitting crossed legged in the Clearing and she taught Jacob a lullaby her mother sang to her. Jacob was an awful singer, and his feeble attempts made her laugh. Instead of getting upset or stopping, Jacob continued to muddle through, partly because he was not one to give up but mainly because it made her happy, made her laugh.

When the song was done, people took turns slowly walking to the front of the room to tell stories of those they lost. Tales about Griff came first, mainly people talking about all the pranks and jokes he pulled but there were also some heartfelt stories about him as a child or how he eagerly helped Leo on his projects, always striving to learn. These brought a smile to Louisa's face despite the battering grief coursing through her. His sister, Emmanuelle, got up last and told of how, despite his cynical nature and constant joking, he truly cared for everyone. She was not at all surprised he forced his ruined body to march all the way home and was not at all surprised that he ultimately gave his life to protect others.

Tina's mother, Fiona, said she did not want people telling stories, deciding it would be too difficult for her to hear. Instead, Samantha recited a poem about the perseverance of tested souls, and they sang Tina's favorite song, the one by the Beetles that Walter could play on the guitar about holding hands. Fiona only made it through the first verse before she had to walk out of the Lodge.

Next were stories about Leo. People listed his long line of accomplishments and skills which allowed Malden to thrive and grow. Others talked of how he made up games for all the children to play. Paul talked of them growing up together before the Bombs, barely able to hold back the sobbing as he recounted the memories. This made Louisa forget about her pain over Jacob for a moment in order to feel compassion for his father who had lost his brother and his son.

Finally, Leo's daughters, Emma and Josie got up together. They tearfully spoke of how miserable they were after their mother passed. They knew their father was suffering from an utterly broken heart as Ainsley was his sunshine, but he choked down his grief in silence so his daughters would not see it. How he calmly consoled them night after night until he figured he could start gently cheering them up with jokes and games. The whole time he never faltered, never allowed an inkling of self-pity to show, never let himself truly grieve near them. They expressed their unending gratitude for all their Papa did for them.

Louisa's stomach clenched horribly not only at having to watch her close friend Emma's pain and at the heartfelt sorrow over the loss of Leo but because she knew it was now time for remembering Jacob. Some storytellers made people laugh. Many storytellers talked of Jacob's unending generous acts and extreme politeness. Most storytellers became overcome by grief. Surprisingly, listening to everyone, Louisa was sad but not tortured, she enjoyed remembering Jacob and took this as a hopeful sign that she may be able to find happiness at some point again.

At the end of the lengthy service, Morreign stood up. Louisa could actually feel the surprised confusion in the room. No one expected Morreign to speak as everyone knew how his disappearance crushed in on her, but when she opened her mouth to speak, she sounded as strong and clear as ever.

• • •

"The war destroyed the world of laws and rules, destroyed the world where you could call the police or an ambulance to come and take care of you if you were afraid or hurt. The world where lights and heat came at the press of a button, food arrived at your door in cardboard boxes while hot water flowed eagerly from taps. Jacob was a child in that lost world, but he became a man in this new world.

"I'd like to take sole possession of the pride for having raised such a great person in such trying circumstances, but I cannot claim it alone. His family, Paul, Leo, Ainsley and his cousins along with his little brother Huck, closer than any family I ever saw, showed him the importance of caring for one another. Griff, with his goofy ways, got him to relax and enjoy the good times, I've never seen two closer friends. Sam taught him, like he's taught all of us, how to live off the land and how actions speak louder than words that voicing discomforts and talking for the sake of talking was wasteful when tasks needed to be done."

A few people chuckled softly at this, everyone enjoying the running joke that Sam never spoke as Morreign continued, "We all, everyone here, worked to mold the man he became and the leader he would certainly have become."

Morreign, surprised by how easily the words were coming to her, turned her gaze to Louisa, holding the girl's eyes, as she continued, "And, perhaps most importantly, Louisa arrived. Never have any of us seen such a perfect and wonderful love as the one they shared. She brought intense joy to my son every day, and for that, I will be forever grateful."

Looking down at the girl, Morreign noticed Louisa's once bright, yellow hair now appeared pale, and her rosy face seemed drawn and grey. She resolved to help her, to treat her as the daughter she had become over all these harsh weeks. A new child. Her third child.

Returning her attention to the whole room, "It seems foolish in retrospect but, when we arrived here, a strange concern I had, amongst that pile of strange concerns all mothers of small children have, was that my boys would not have enough friends to become social and would not have enough to do to fill their days. There would be no more play dates, no more crowded classrooms, and no more afterschool activities. That worry disappeared as the children here showed us that, left to their own devices, they would happily play at whatever and with whoever was at hand. All of the children, including Jacob, then taught all of us adults not to fret about the things we did not have but to enjoy what we did have.

"When I think back, as I often will, I'll recall the giddy, energetic boy he was and the hardworking, generous, joyful and strong man he became. I will miss him deeply every day but I will remind myself I was lucky to have such an amazing person in my life and we all can take pride in who he was as all of us in this community created him. I thank all of you for that, and I vow to use my best to try and always uphold those qualities."

While her grief remained, as she slowly moved to sit back down, Morreign did feel slightly better and confident this improvement, while it would not be easy, could continue if she let it. When she came here this morning, she did not intend to speak but seeing all those familiar people saying such great things about their lost friends inspired her. Now, she knew she could refocus on improving Malden, creating a future for the others and that would give her more than enough reason to get out of bed every morning.

Samantha stood to start the last song, but Sam stepped forward and quietly asked, "Can I say something?"

Never in the last ten years could Morreign recall Sam addressing a group, even in an informal setting, but now he moved to the front, his normal stoic confidence replaced by a strange nervousness as he said, "I won't say much, but I wanted to let you all know that I think I learned far more from Jacob than I ever taught -"

Sam suddenly stopped speaking, turned his attention to the back of the room and, confused, asked, "Jacob?"

•   •   •

Crossing the river was not easy. The current continually threatened to pull him away, but Jacob kept an eye on the crooked tree as he forced his exhausted arms to stroke and his wobbly legs to kick. Eventually, he reached the far bank where he allowed himself to rest, lying on his back on the familiar gravel, enjoying the sensation of having made it to the place he never thought he would see again. Before long he pushed himself back up, desperately eager to see home, desperately needing to warn them.

When Jacob stumbled into the Clearing, having not seen or heard any people, he worried his trick had not worked, and he would only find the burned-out buildings and rotting corpses left by Harrison's ravaging army. Instead, he saw everything the same as he left it but with no people.

Perhaps the attack eradicated everyone and Harrison had already moved on. Hurrying as best he could on weak legs, over the intimately familiar green space, filled with panic, he became further confused by the muffled, brief sound of what he thought was laughter on the breeze.

Jacob stumbled up the three steps to the Lodge, his bare feet slapping the worn wood. He did not know what he may find inside, so he cracked the heavy door carefully and quietly.

No army of hulking brutes, his friends and family filled the entire space. Relief poured over him, and he could do nothing but stand in the doorway, overcome by the flood of bliss. He listened for a moment as his mother talked, with tears in her eyes, about how someone was created by Malden. He could see people were crying. He had seen an event like this before and decided it must be a funeral.

Oddly, Sam got up next, looking strangely uneasy. Before Jacob could move inside, his old friend with the keen, black eyes saw him in the cracked open doorway. As their eyes met, it fully dawned on Jacob's exhausted mind. They were there. They were all there. They were all there, and they were safe. Harrison must still be scouting. He had done it, he had deceived the evil bastard and beat his army to Malden. Somehow he had made it back in time.

Sam said his name. Everyone turned to look at him. A sea of wonderfully familiar faces, however, they all looked stunned, staring, unmoving. In the awkward silence, everyone in his world pondering his wet and disheveled form, an ingrained politeness made him feel awkward for interrupting, and Jacob did not know what to do so he merely said, "Sorry."

•   •   •

Louisa did not know how or when she got to her feet, but she was suddenly running. Jacob said something, but she did not hear it. Everyone else hesitated, apparently shocked by the arrival of a ghost. Louisa could tell it was truly him, and she crashed into Jacob as everybody else realized what they were seeing and the room erupted in laughter-laden cheers.

•   •   •

Jacob collapsed back onto the floor, her on top of him, laying on his chest, eye to eye. Jacob whispered, "Are you real?"

Tears wetting her face, she nodded, her blonde hair gently brushing his cheeks.

He whispered again, "I think you are real."

She nodded again, a grin breaking across her face, "Yes, yes, I'm real."

"I missed you."

Unrelenting, uncomplicated happiness filled Louisa, and a perfectly pure smile broke across her tear-soaked face.

Holding Louisa could have lasted for the rest of Jacob's life, but he recalled the potential doom moving about the wilderness and panic pierced through his joy. "Wait, wait. Attackers. Attackers with rifles. Lots of them."

Someone gently helped him to his feet as someone draped a blanket over his shoulders. He recognized the tattered blue yarn from his childhood. A blanket his aunt Ainsley had knitted years ago. Tears threatened as emotions flooded through him, but he composed himself enough to say, "They're coming, we need to prepare, we need to get ready to fight or run or something."

His father and mother slipped through the crowd, and Paul said, "Its ok, Jacob, it's ok. They came before you, days ago. Your friends warned us, and we won, it's over, we're safe, you're safe."

He looked at his mother, and she merely nodded with a powerful smile on her face. "Welcome home Jacob."

THE END

NOTE FROM THE AUTHOR

Word-of-mouth is crucial for any author to succeed. If you enjoyed the book, please leave a review online—anywhere you are able. Even if it's just a sentence or two. It would make all the difference and would be very much appreciated.

Thanks!
Eric

ABOUT THE AUTHOR

Eric Keller is a lawyer in Calgary, Alberta. In his free time, he reads slowly, golfs badly, skis cautiously and cheers enthusiastically for a middling NFL team.

Thank you so much for reading one of our **Sci-Fi** novels.

If you enjoyed our book, please check out our recommended title for your next great read!

People of Metal by Robert Snyder

The well-intentioned leaders of China and the U.S. form a grand partnership to create human robots for every human vocation in every country in the world. The human robots proliferate, economic output soars, and the entire world prospers. It's a new Golden Age. But there are unintended consequences—consequences that will place biological humanity on a road to extinction. Ultimately, it will fall to the human robots themselves to rescue biological humanity and restore its civilization.

View other Black Rose Writing titles at www.blackrosewriting.com/books and use promo code **PRINT** to receive a **20% discount** when purchasing.